I0699305

THE WHITE SHADOW

THE WHITE SHADOW

JOSEPH ASPHAHANI

4 Horsemen
Publications, Inc.

The White Shadow
Copyright © 2024 Joseph Asphahani. All rights reserved.

Published By: 4 Horsemen Publications, Inc.

4 Horsemen Publications, Inc.
PO Box 417
Sylva, NC 28779
4horsemenpublications.com
info@4horsemenpublications.com

Cover Illustration by Jaka Prawira
Cover Typography and Typesetting by Autumn Skye
Edited by Kris Cotter

All rights to the work within are reserved to the author and publisher. No part of this publication may be reproduced, stored in a retrieval system, or transmitted in any form or by any means, electronic, mechanical, photocopying, recording, scanning, or otherwise, except as permitted under Section 107 or 108 of the 1976 International Copyright Act, without prior written permission except in brief quotations embodied in critical articles and reviews. Please contact either the Publisher or Author to gain permission.

All characters, organizations, and events portrayed in this novel are either products of the author's imagination or are used fictitiously.

All brands, quotes, and cited work respectfully belongs to the original rights holders and bear no affiliation to the authors or publisher.

Library of Congress Control Number: 2024947901

Paperback ISBN-13: 979-8-8232-0699-0
Hardcover ISBN-13: 979-8-8232-0700-3
Audiobook ISBN-13: 979-8-8232-0702-7
Ebook ISBN-13: 979-8-8232-0701-0

TABLE OF CONTENTS

ONE

BULLETS IN 2077 AREN'T MADE OF METAL. MOST OF THEM aren't, anyway. Most bullets—and as far as I could tell the one lodged in Vasili's liver right now—are made of high-density polymer, solid state when racked in the magazine or fed from the bandolier, then searing-hot plasma as they pick up speed just before slamming home and bursting and cooling into shards halfway through your guts. Cooling in your blood. Not at all designed to leave exit wounds. Only ruin. And a corpse.

I was panting, my back pressed against the chrome-polished wall of Inari's data vault, the sweat soaking through my best white shirt and my best black suit, dripping down the longer lock of black hair dangling in front of my face.

"Vas! You're still breathing." Whether I said it to reassure him or myself, I wasn't so sure. "We're getting outta here, Vas."

It wasn't the truth, but what else do you say to someone you know when they're dying? What feeling can you hope to create in them before they're gone? Did I actually care?

I didn't want to care, but I couldn't stop looking at Vasili, hoping my words might do him some good.

He sucked in a breath. It gurgled in his throat. He only got it halfway down before the reflexes in his lungs kicked the air back out. Blood stained his teeth, dribbled black from the corners of his mouth, and pattered onto his lap. Vas was a good-looking guy. Blond, tight-bodied, tall. Not a mod, augment, or jack on him, far as I could see. I'd be into him probably, if I was into guys at all. But now I'd never get a chance to tell him. Now he was just a fucking mess. He was slouched against the opposite wall, on the other side of the inner vault chamber, the wide open corridor leading to the rest of InariCorp's impenetrable information fortress between us. Our only way out.

His only way out, actually.

He wiped the blood on the sleeve of his brown suit. Waste of fine linen. His voice was shallow, barely a whisper that rose over the InariSec comm-chatter echoing from the corridor, but I heard him all right.

"Shin... You out?"

Out?!

Was that an accusation? I hadn't told anyone—no, not true, I'd told only Ben. How could Vas know? Did Ben fucking betray me? Who else in the Syndicate knew? All the other guys in our cell were dead farther in the vault, churned to soup from the inside-out by InariSec's plastic fucking bullets. Had the cell told Vas? Who the fuck else knew I wanted out?

While the response stuck in my throat, I watched Vas lift his baby-blue eyes up to mine. With some effort, he smiled at me, then dropped his gaze to the revolver in my hand. That's when I knew what he really meant. *Out. Like, out of bullets.* I depressed the thumbprint lock, let the eight-chambered cylinder fall open, and counted its lone resident. One bullet. Antique. Metal. I once thought to fashion myself a real cowgirl with this heavy thing. Why not? Don't like who the world made you? Be someone else.

Yippee-ki-yay.

So fucking stupid.

"Not out. Not yet."

The grating, open-channel comms chatter got louder, punctuated with rubber-soled thumps down the corridor. The whole floor was flooded with data cubes, or shards of them anyway, since our take had been shot to pieces along with Vas and the others. They were no bigger than a fingertip, very few still intact, glowing and sputtering a clean LED white like malfunctioning lanterns, a visual indicator that the corporate files contained on the nanodrives within were still functioning.

This was supposed to be easy. A high-level job for sure if you were just some Time-Fiend itching for the money to score your next hit, some off-grid no-name wastrel coming in off the street, but with the high-level recon and taps *we'd* had in place, raiding Inari's data vault was supposed to be *yasashii*—easy, a sake-run. Our SynCell had been planning this for months. Feikes got the call on the last day of summer and we'd done nothing else but work through the routines ever since. And for what? Who was on the other end of that call? A-Matter? Tenjin? Fuji-Rai? Any of the other dozen mega-corps in the borders of Osaka? Who cares who? Just some corp trying to fuck over some other corp for some slight—real-world, simulated, or misinterpreted. The sprawling city at large—the rest of Japan that wasn't already irradiated ash—and all the little worker-bee *salaryman* and *jin* read about it in the manufactured news as "insider trading" or something, something as equally misleading. But we—the Syndicates and the cells we operated in—we were the drones, the soldiers in the queen bees' proxy wars. The criminal elements they paid handsomely under the table to steal information, schematics, proprietary codes, and powerful technology from their competitors. And we—Vasili, Ben, me, and hell, even Feikes himself—were expendable. What kind of public relations nightmare would mega-corps unleash if they sent their well-armed and armored (and clearly branded) security forces to raid one another? The half-human, cybernetic zombies I could hear drawing closer even now.

I didn't need to tell Vasili how many bullets I had left. Even though half the life had already gone out of his eyes, he could read me well enough. He knew.

"Get over here and do us both, ya fucking cunt." On the end of that, I caught the edge of the Aussie accent he'd been trying to suppress. I hadn't gotten to know Vas well enough since I'd met him to bother asking why he wanted so badly to lose that part of his identity. I hadn't bothered to get to know anyone since signing up with the Syndicate, come to think of it. But Vas knew *me* well enough to know that I fucking hated it when the guys called me a cunt. Was he trying to goad me into blowing his head to pieces? Probably. But, call it pity for a dying man, I didn't. Not right away, anyhow.

"What do you want me to do, exactly?"

"Oh … I dunno, Shin. Let's put our heads together." Vasili's eyelids fluttered as he turned away, his body rerouting all its remaining strength to lift a smile to his face and his bloody index finger to his temple. *"Kkhaa-poosh!"* He breathed the sound so softly.

"They're close now, Vas. You hear 'em? I won't make it over there."

"Know what they do when they catch you? InariSec?"

Why bother telling him I did…

"They'll put you back together," he went on. "All the parts that matter. Parts that feel pain. Put the parts of your brain in jars, the ones that may *know* something. And then they take you apart, piece by piece. 'Til you give it up… Don't let 'em take us, Shin. Please."

He had me this time, and he didn't even have to call me a cunt. I considered the final bullet. With one hand, I slammed it home and reactivated the revolver. Without even thinking, the other hand felt through my suit's inside pocket, my fingers finding the familiar object they were after.

"I'm sorry, Vas."

The boots drew closer, then stopped. On the blueprints in my head, I saw the InariSec squad parked against the massive steel door, only ten meters away. Their chatter had dropped. The vault was as still as the graveyard.

"Don't be." He opened his eyes to tell me with more than his fading voice. I guess it was supposed to be some kind of moment for him, but he laughed when he saw me fixated on the old Shinto charm I held—my *omamori*—its worn red ribbon laced delicately between my fingers. "Ha!" The sound was more cough than laugh, bringing up a fresh spray of black liver blood on Vasili's lap. "Didn't know you were religious."

"I'm not."

Then everything happened at once.

I squeezed the charm tight in my fist.

I swung about. The revolver roared. The bullet lanced through Vasili's skull, pulping whatever parts of him Inari might've hoped to reconstruct. Before the trail of brains and blood had even drawn itself across the floor, before the resonant sound could even fully crash against my eardrums, the high-pitched tingling of the flashbang counted down its final ping and exploded in a concussive white flood.

Fuck it, I've had worse. I remember thinking that, just before the rest.

Then the bullets came. Polymer patented by Hachiman Technologies Mega-corp itself, the real Japanese god of war. They tore my body to shreds from the inside out. The pain was absolutely exquisite. The first rounds landed in my brain, the plastic shards blocking the neuronal pathways so completely that I couldn't even register the full sensation of the other rounds that riddled the rest of my flesh. Little stars were born in bright, hot spaces between my organs. Like I said before, there were no exit wounds.

Amid the swirling smoke and the deafening gunfire, I assume my corpse must've dropped to the data vault floor.

Amid the chaos that followed, I assume the boots drew up around the spot where the killing machines expected to find it. There must've been some kind of algorithm jacked into overload when neither the synthetic nor the organic halves of their brains could reconcile with the fact I simply was not there.

INTERLUDE: A NIGHTMARE

It always starts with the little girl's feet. Nine years old, she spends so much time staring down at those feet, inside the cage of her arms wrapped tight around her drawn-up knees, her eyes tracing across the canyons of dried blood, the crags split open from the cold, and the craters filled up with filth. It was better for the little girl to look down at those feet than to look up at all the ghosts, those unreal, twisted horrors shambling around the mirror-world only she could see.

But the nightmare never ends there. They always come for her. Not the ghosts, not in this nightmare, anyway. In this one, it's always the boys.

She hears their howling, their taunting, their laughter. It floods the hallways of the orphanage. It's the braying of beasts on the hunt. She slides up against the wall, too frail and weak to support her own weight, and puts everything she has left into those ruined feet and tries to run, every bare slap of her soles on the grimy, cracked tiled floor bringing a new wave of pain and exhaustion up her legs.

The little girl is never fast enough, because this isn't as much a nightmare as it is a memory. Every time they come for her, the little girl dares to hope it will be different, that she will get away.

Every time I relive this nightmare, I remember she didn't. Even if she could get away from the boys, she'd never outrun what came next.

She trips. She falls hard at the end of the hallway. In her panic, she forgot it was a dead end. She flops over on her back and tries to skitter away against the wall, the tears running down her bruised face, dirty strands of black hair all in tangles. She's wailing and shaking with fear as the boys catch up.

"Found you!"

"Nowhere to run!"

"This is a boy's home! No place for girls!"

"A real-life Jap, too."

"How'd we get a Jap in here?"

"This country's not yours anymore, bitch!"

The little girl's little bony hands can't protect her head from the slapping. Two of them wrench her hands away and the slaps become fists. She falls over, dazed, and they kick her, their own bare, ruined feet ramming her ribs and limbs, bringing her back from the brink of unconsciousness with every blast of pain.

The girl starts to scream, "NO! NO NO NOOOOO!" But it only excites the boys more. They kick harder, not one of them able to understand it's not them she truly fears.

Only the little girl can feel it—the whump, whump, whump *of the monster's armor. In this nightmare, it always comes with the certainty of a curse. Because it* is *a curse. Her curse. It's the samurai. A seven-foot tall, ancient suit of splint mail—*kote, haidate, do, sode, *and* kabuto—*every piece accounted for, but no flesh, no body inside holding them up. Only a ghost in a shell, caged. The samurai is the girl's rage made manifest, which she believes years later.*

"Ie," she mumbles, she pleads, slipping in and out of her mother tongue. "Ie… no, please…" And the beating subsides.

The boys don't know that it's not them the little girl's begging to stop. "Please don't..."

The first boy is lifted off his feet; he hits the wall and something in him cracks. There's an invisible print of an armored hand against his back, pressing into his spine, and then he crumples in a twisted heap, all his limbs no longer responsive.

"No!" The little girl's throat is dry. The scream is hoarse. She doesn't want to hurt anybody, even as the next boy is hit with something like the wind, hurling him thirty meters back down the hall, back into the night shadows of the decrepit orphanage.

In the nightmare, the little girl thinks she doesn't want to hurt them.

I remember her thinking that. But she's stupid, afraid of her own power.

I know better now. Years later, I know I had wanted them all dead.

That night, I cursed myself.

The two fuckers that still stand over the girl don't know what to do. They just witness in silence as the invisible force eradicates the others. One of them has lost control of himself. I see a bloom of wet yellow spreading across the front of the off-white rags he calls pants. Piss-boy watches in horror as his last friend's ankle shoots out, as he loses his balance and his skull cracks against the floor, as he's lifted, dangling with the sole of his foot centimeters from the ceiling, moaning and gibbering uncontrollably. And then he's split from the groin down. The sound of popping joints and rending muscle and splitting bone petrifies the final, piss-stained boy. The sound of his friend ceases. Just a wet slap of meat hitting the tiles now.

In the nightmare, the little girl still cries. *"Gomein... Gomein..."*

But in my memory, I'm laughing.

I remember the last boy, and what happens to him, and I'm laughing my fucking ass off.

TWO

PICTURE A TREE. A TALL TREE, WITH NO BRANCHES worth mentioning. Just a solid trunk.

Picture, perhaps, a bamboo.

Now imagine it snapping in half. A clean break. At an angle, so it slides slowly down itself, near-frictionless, like what you'd see in an anime.

Only … now it's not just breaking simply and easily. Imagine instead it's twisting, its molecules grinding against one another until they just can't hold on and snap apart in splinters.

Replace the bamboo tree with a bone. A femur. *Your* femur.

Feel the pain of twisting like this—in *every* bone of your body, all at once—and you may start to understand how it feels when I cross between the land of the dead and the land of the living.

I fell on my hands and knees, drenched in more than just sweat, biting hard against the agony writhing throughout my body. I heard the splash of the slimy stuff on the rough pavement all around me, like I'd just been vertically vomited out of a swimming pool. Not an inaccurate comparison, actually.

I gasped, and I found the slime had filled my lungs. Sometimes it does. I lurched, my spine rolling up and down, over and over, until wave after wave I'd puked it all up. All the purple goop, all of it. Hot as fire in this world, but to me, so cold. So, so cold. It steamed in a circle all around me; it dried up on my back, evaporating. In a few seconds, it would all be gone.

I fell over on my side and curled into an awkward fetal position, shivering. My eyes spun around in their sockets, finally focusing on the thing I clutched in my hand: my Shinto charm. Just a tiny coin emblazoned with the triple hollyhock seal of the Tokugawa Shogunate on one side, some scratched-out *kanji* on the other, and a hole for its red ribbon bangle. Just a tiny little trinket I stole from a long-abandoned shrine when I ran away from the orphanage. As a kid, I thought it was beautiful. The most beautiful thing I'd ever seen. I thought I was saving it from the creeping decay that's slowly been claiming all the old places in NeOsaka. Only a few days later I heard that shrine was finally torn down, one of the last in the city. They're probably all gone now, ten years later. Who knows?

So I thought I'd preserved an important piece of Japanese history, but the truth was *it* was preserving me.

My name is Shinjiro Asai, and for as long as I can remember, I've been cursed. I *see* what others *cannot see*. The dead. Ghosts. Twisted and entropic. I see their world, exactly like this world, only warped, bent so far out of any human proportion that the sight of it would drive you insane. For the longest time, I believed I *was* insane.

But then I died for the first time.

And I came back whole, and I knew that what would be another person's nightmare was my inescapable reality.

And the time I spent between death and rebirth, I spent in the Underworld. *Yomi.* The land of the dead.

Even when I'm not there—when I'm not *dead*—I still see it. I still see *them*, all the ghosts. They roam the streets, purposeless, despondent, shells of the men and women they once were and mocking mirror-images of who they were supposed to become. In that regard, come to think of it, they're not so different than the mega-corp salarymen stalking up and down the neon-lit streets of the sprawl, perpetually late for another day of slaving over spreadsheets, data-mined marketing campaigns, software schematics, or whatever the hell else the NeOsaka elite do with their time. If I could pick one group or the other to see *all the time*, well, it would be a rather tough choice. Unfortunately, I'm fucked. I can't pick. I see both kinds of zombie. Forever and always.

Whereas the living corporate ones are all dressed alike in 2077—in slim suits, and slimmer ties, and blinking neural-implants bolted to their skulls—the dead come draped in all varieties of withering rags. *Yomi* is a place of entropy, decline, stagnation. Mold in the real world grows on things in order to break them down to nothing, and then it too will disappear. But in *Yomi*, nothing disappears. Memory is the mold, and the dead do not forget. The kimono that wrapped your ancestor when he was burned on the pyre, the dress your bride wore before you murdered her on your wedding night—hell, even the swimsuit your buddy wore to that synthetic-sand beach where he swam way too close to the android shark—I see all their ghosts exactly as they were when the living world had its final memory of them.

And now, toppled on my side in that thin strip of alley (which the zoning bots hadn't yet found a use for beyond piling heaps of trash), I saw one of them. A man—an *old* man, with the kind of three-piece, four-button suit that dated his death sometime in the mid-21st, all in tatters—was staring right at me. I saw the suit first, counted its buttons (and scoffed because that's just who I am). Then I saw the briefcase, open, with business papers spilling out slowly, one by one, caught in an eternal, intangible breeze and fading away behind him. From that wrist, a stream of dark oily blood flowed, dripping onto each paper, like kissing them goodbye on their way to work. Then I saw the pocketknife in his other hand, wet with it too. And I knew his story.

And I fucking hate myself for feeling, for wanting to know more. Because that's when I looked into his eyes. And it was all over.

"Sh... Shit-tt-tt." My teeth chattered. I wanted to say it was from the lingering cold of the purple goop. Not from fear. I struggled to my hands and knees while the ghost took his first slow steps toward me. He had maybe ten meters left to go. I knew I had a couple of seconds to calm him down and slip away.

I can't tell you what the ghosts want. I have no idea. No one's told me anything about my curse, and I wouldn't know who to ask, anyway. But, regardless, I didn't manage to get this far in life (I mean that ironically, of course) without making some observations, acting on them, and finding some positive results. So I can't tell you for sure what this shambling apparition wanted, but I could guess it was for somebody to just *feel* with him. Feel *for* him. Someone to *remember* him, I think. Some form of peace. Just peace. An end to the confusion, to the endless, aimless, pointless wandering of his afterlife.

Mr. Briefcase-Sama there was just looking for some sign that showed him where to go. In this case, some *body*. Literally.

My body.

I managed to rise onto my knees and face the ghost. Before, I had relied on the tattoo covering my chest—from shoulder to shoulder, hip to hip—of the massive torii gate, the traditional Shinto (and adoptive Buddhist) symbol of a gateway separating the sacred from the profane, the kind of monuments mega-corps had been tearing down for decades, when they can find them still standing in the dark corners amid the sprawl. I crossed a gate a long time ago at the same decrepit shrine where I stole the charm. I saw it drive the ghosts away as if the torii gate's two standing *hashira* posts and the *shimaki* beam on top and the peeling vermillion paint had suddenly reminded them they were needed elsewhere. Since then, I've found a couple more scattered across NeOsaka, and I've committed their locations to memory more strongly than the face of my own mother.

Well, I never had a mother. Or any actual family.

Observations, like I said before. *Adaptation. Survival.*

Despite knowing all this, I didn't particularly feel like flashing my tattoo or my tits in that alleyway. And besides, after I'd suffered a particularly bad walk through *Yomi* a while back—straight into a mob of angry phantoms with long fingernails—the ink on my chest had been marred with scar tissue that never healed when I phased back, and its magic hadn't worked the same since.

The ghosts tend to slow when you break eye contact, and just then, concentrating on rolling back my bullet-tattered suit sleeves bought me the precious few seconds more I needed before Mr. Briefcase-Sama lashed out at me with his papers or his pocket knife.

I slammed my forearms together, forming the two halves of my other, newer torii tattoo into one, and the ghost stopped, just centimeters away. I could feel the frost spreading on my skin, the muscles all down my back tensing, bracing the rest of my body against the sudden rush of cold. I clamped my chittering jaw tight and held my breath, eyes closed, braced behind the shield my arms made, just waiting. I knew waiting was all I could do.

Then the cold receded. The torii stood resolute between us. Warmth spread again through my arms. I relaxed, opened my eyes, and glimpsed the suicidal salaryman ghost's back just as he rounded the corner and melded with the flowing throngs choking NeOsaka's street level.

Everything was so quiet, so still. Another thing I can't explain is how or why these Shinto symbols confound the spirits. Or why the charm gives me command (I use the term very, very loosely) over the curse. I used to wonder—no, in fact, *every time* I wonder. I'm left staring, dumbfounded, wondering what I did to deserve my life.

And forgetting the important matters that demanded more immediate attention.

"Shin… Shin… What the fuck happened in there?"

I heard my name. Heard the question. I thought for a second maybe I'd been talking to myself again, only to then realize the sound came from my comlink's audio node that had fallen from my ear, probably during the violent spasms of my most recent death. In this day and age, most denizens of NeOsaka had comlink hardware embedded under the skin at their temple, capable of transmitting incoming and outgoing voice vibrations just loud enough for the user to hear. Body-purists—as few and far between as they are nowadays—at the very least had better, more wearable models than mine. But I held on to my ancient piece of shit because it seemed to be the only tech in my suit pockets that didn't get fried during my trips to and from the spirit world. At least not yet.

I slipped the node into my ear. The voice on the other end belonged to Ben Roy Doon, my SynCell's handler, my one-and-only sort-of friend. With Vas and the others gone, we were the last reps left. "Shin, say something! You just blipped back on the grid. You're…"

"Ben," I croaked, dry-throated, into the little outdated mic-dongle attached to my collar, cutting him off. I could picture him perched in front of his wall of monitors, squinting into scrolling pixels and readouts, pulling out nervous fistfuls of his wispy hair, flipping back and forth through his stacks of stapled papers. "Ben, I—"

"SHIN! Shit, fuck, man!"

"Calm down. How do I get outta here?"

"What happened at Inari? I thought you d-died! Again!"

"I did," I told him, but he didn't know I was telling the truth. To him, it was just more of my endearing sarcasm. Then I decided to clarify, clearing my throat as I searched for the right word. "I got … re-routed."

"I'll say! I got you now. *Shinjiro Asai never die!* Haa!"

The words brought a smile to my lips, made me think of the toast he'd make at my wedding someday.

"Listen, Shin, you're half a kilo from Inari. The others are…" As usual, Ben's mouth ran a couple steps ahead of his mind. *The others aren't with you,* he meant to say, or maybe even *the others are still in there because you sold them out, you traitorous cunt.* He said instead, "Wow, how'd you—" and I still cut him off.

"No time. If *you* got me on-grid, InariSec might have me, too. I don't know if these comms are clea—"

"*No way!!*" If my comlink had been equipped with a front-eye, holo-light display, I bet I'd have seen Ben's fingers pinching the bridge of his nose just then, pushing his old plastic glasses farther down. It was a gesture I knew meant he wasn't exactly sure of anything, even while verbally denying it. The stuttering always gave it away too. "No, n-n-no, no way, Shin. My recon was tight on this one. Secured ch-ch-channel. Unique PINs, IDs, I've even tried out a string of Acronymic—"

"Ben! I don't care!"

"…Spent *months* on—"

"Shut the fuck up!!"

I tried to stand on my feet, but almost instantly reeled away toward the rough brick wall nearby. I lowered my dizzy head unknowingly into a blast of exhaust that smelled like the grease trap from a kitchen in hell. I spun away reflexively, straight into a muck puddle seeping from underneath a mound of trash next to an overflowing dumpster. I could see maggots writhing blindly in the split bags. I gagged, less from the stench of urban neglect and decay and more from the demise of my new synthetic-leather shoes. Shame, they matched my best suit brilliantly.

Even in the silence that followed, I knew Ben was still there on the other end of the comlink, searching the digital layers and bi-levels of NeOsaka streets for my optimal route and simultaneously stitching in his home-grown algorithms to send my on-grid presence pinging in the opposite direction. Despite all he was doing to help me, Ben just wasn't working fast enough for me. "Tell me where the fuck to go, Ben," I groaned. I felt heat spreading through me, from the absence of the cold, from agitation with my handler, from the guilt crashing against me as I pictured Vasili's brains exploding from the impact of my antique bullet; who can say?

I realized then that I must've dropped my antique cowgirl revolver on the data vault floor. Thankfully, there was no way InariSec could trace it back to me since I'd bought it secondhand off an ex-militia collector from America years ago, and those types never kept sales records if they knew what was good for them. Right? I'd really liked that gun, even if I'd only fired it six times, and five of those were wild, just to make the others think I was doing my part, right before they all got shot down.

"N-north," Ben said finally. "Uh, to your left, if I got you oriented."

I pushed myself off the wall and took several unsteady steps in that direction, away from where the ghost had gone. The alley curved around in this direction, hugging the line of what might have been a street sixty years ago, back when urban design was more careful and deliberate. My recent, unplanned trek through the spirit world had not only taken me a few blocks *over* from Inari's databank facility, but it had also taken me *down* several hundred meters, somewhere in NeOsaka's maze of sub-streets.

Since the rise of dominant corporate culture, almost all the old stone places had been carved out, asphalt torn to shreds and re-purposed, cables and sewer lines re-routed, and towering steel sunk deep in the Earth, serving as the foundations for the misshapen needles jabbing into the sky and the ribbons of automated highways lacing between them. The mega-corps had bought the power to bypass any regulations they wanted, since after devising the technologies that saved Japan from the catastrophes that brought down most of the world, they had essentially bought their reputations as saviors. And so construction began, and layers and layers of poor urban planning were laid down one over each other every decade or so, like new skin grafts that kept the elderly feeling fresh by concealing the actual decay spreading underneath. Sometimes, when I walk the twisting streets down here—the city's dripping runoff channels that used to be roads—I hear a terrible groaning of all that steel and concrete. It's the spirit of NeOsaka itself, sagging under the pressure and gravity, feeling its true age.

I'd been answering Ben's prodding about the other guys in our SynCell with silence for a few minutes before he finally gave up. Ben was smart. I knew he knew they were dead. The real question he wanted to ask was the same one Feikes would want to ask: *Why is Shinjiro Asai not dead with them?* But Ben swallowed that one too, for the time being.

After another minute, I heard his voice crackle again in my audio node.

"What're we gonna do, Shin?"

"I don't know."

"You didn't get the cubes, Shin."

"No, Ben. I didn't get the cubes."

"I mean, Feikes is gotta be lookin' bad right now. We made him look bad. We needed this job. What's he gonna do—we're the last two left?"

"Feikes doesn't know where I live," I came back automatically, and instantly regretted bringing it up. It was true. Feikes didn't know where to find me or where I was going, and so Feikes couldn't touch me, and that gave me a little time.

But Ben knew. I'd made the mistake of having him over once, when I'd gotten low again and thought I should have a friend. My life, it seemed, was pinned up with moments of weakness and stupidity. Because if Ben knew, and Feikes's goons got to him, I'd have to start all over again after they killed me. Only there'd be no more Ben because they'd kill him, too. I angrily blew my dangling lock of hair out of my face, hoping maybe I could blow away having to sort out how that idea made me feel.

"Fuck," I groaned to myself, but Ben heard it, of course, and even through all the wires and invisible networks separating us, Ben heard what I was thinking. I was his only chance. Now it was his turn to be silent. I took a deep breath.

"Get out of your cramped little hacker hole closet and get over to my place as soon as you can. Leave all your shit behind."

"B-b-but, s-some of this sh-sh-shi—"

"Leave it, Ben."

"—t's on loan from some p-p-powerf—"

"I said leave it!"

I'd been suspicious for a while about where Ben was getting the gear for his intrusion rig. Some state-of-the-art equipment started showing up, like a pair of blackout cyberspace goggles and even a full-body haptic net-point suit that he'd only tried on one time and had needed my help to get into, then couldn't configure, anyway. There was no way Feikes or anyone else who'd managed our cell in the past had put up the funds for our handler's new toys. The irony was, that same cutting-edge stuff showed up alongside gadgets, cables, and drives that were the textbook definition of "obsolete." Flip-phones, AM/FM radios, VHS camcorders with cassette tapes, USB devices, and more. Apparently, there was a black market for that kind of stuff and hobbyists who tried to get it all working and talking with modern hardware. Rumor was that it was that old junk that enabled the hacker group called The Cluster to stay undetected on the grid.

None of that gear, whether new-age or antique, made Ben really more effective at his job anyway (case in point, the haptic suit). I'd been meaning to confront Ben about where it all came from, but I kept putting it off, and now was certainly not the time with InariSec likely closing in on me.

I heard him sigh. Then, "What about you?"

"I know the way from here."

I did. Phasing in and out of *Yomi* voluntarily—or worse, being *forced* through the veil between worlds by Death itself—left me with a foggy memory of my time there. Maybe it was because I never actually *want* to go there. It was like trying to forget, yet at the same time, forcing yourself to remember the details of the bad dream you had yesterday. But, just like in dreams, I had learned that my subconscious mind could direct me. Knowing this, my last living thought had been how much I just wanted to go home, just as InariSec killed me.

"Home's not far for me," I added, realizing too late how sentimental I sounded.

"Okay," Ben said. "Leaving now."

I pulled the node from my ear, denying whatever else he wanted to say or ask from reaching me. If Ben played it smart, he would stay away from the automated transit systems, both above and below ground. Needing to remote-hack a few identity gateways to bypass the data-mining protocols set off by his unique iris patterns—which would in turn activate marketing algorithms and ping any Syndicate hackers who might be watching the grid—would heap another half hour onto his ETA.

So I had some time to kill.

I knew I should've killed it at home, sunk in my rickety, old, cushioned chair, downing glass after glass of throat-scorching scotch, drowning in futile escape plans and daydreams of dead-end futures, realizing how trapped I was in this city, how there was no way out, ruminating over my mistakes, all of them, and hating myself—until Ben finally arrived and maybe I could turn the seething scotch-fueled anger on him.

But I still felt the phantom cold of the ghost that almost touched me, Mr. Briefcase-Sama. I felt it trembling down my arms and freezing in my chest. Mr. Briefcase-Sama: in life, another faceless, 21st century nobody, a mega-corp salary slave, a zombie—and in death, another victim of *karoshi*, or practically corporate-sponsored suicide, his body worked literally to death, his spirit now alone, lost, cursed to wander everywhere and belong nowhere, forever. That's what I'd seen in his hollow eyes, that emptiness in life that had clung to him even in death. I was the only one, maybe ever, who had ever seen it in him. I was the only one, maybe, who could help him. I was, maybe, his only guide.

But I had turned him the fuck away. I'd thrown up the image of a sacred torii gate in his face and told him to beat it, that there was nothing on the other side to which he belonged.

I gripped the bullet-frayed edges of the ruin of my once-best black suit—the blood may not stick to my skin, but it certainly stains my dress shirts—and kept my eyes on the ground as my body merged with the others flowing through the veins of the NeOsaka under city, almost calcified shut with the packs of people plying through the city's sub-streets. Down there was a whole other type of Osaka, layers and layers deep below the smooth, flowing sky-traffic between buildings. Bursts of laughter, cigarette smoke, and flavored vapor. Shouts, behind and in front. Smells of over-salted bowls of quick ramen and lab-fab'd pork blocks wafting on jets of steam from the squat carts and tents jutting like rocks in the river. The buzz of delivery drones zipping by overhead. The thrum of music rattling bricks, windows, and plaster seals. The pulsing lights of the dynam-ads that explode into pixelated life beside you, hardlight ghosts that hack your comlink signal and sell you on your own dreams and grid-search history in real time, mascot animals barking rabidly and sex-symbol celebrity spokespersons cooing seductively.

I ignored it all, simply watched my feet fall one in front of the other as they carried me between the throngs of tangible and intangible bodies. I navigated by the splashes of pink-green-blue neon signs reflected in the stagnant puddles of the lowest places NeOsaka could go.

I knew it would take Ben at least an hour to meet me, so I would kill time trying to find someone else some peace in the afterlife.

THREE

NEOSAKA FACES THE SEA ON ITS SOUTHERN SIDE. MOST of that real estate is clogged with ports and terminals that have either been swamped by the gradual melting of the polar ice caps and rise of the world's ocean water or were repurposed as launch-and-land strips for the bulkier supply shuttles sent to Heaven, or *Takamagahara* in case you don't know, the sub-orbital platform hanging in the sky where the highest of the high corporate elites gave each other hand jobs and made the most lucrative deals. So down here you'll find only kilometers of endless rust right along fenced-in sites heavily automated by machines. And if you look really hard, you might find the old graveyard wedged between it all.

This place was dug into the side of a hill sloping down to the sea, a hundred years ago. Maybe more. It was a massive bowl, with maybe a hundred U-shaped tiers and paths ringing around every level, each ring packed with *haka*—tall, granite gravestones—each engraved with the *kanji* of the family whose bones rest there.

Or whose bones are *supposed* to rest there, anyway.

But no one has time to care anymore. No, that's not true. I know people better than that. I know they wouldn't care even if they had time. But I can't blame them. For generations, you're told that these things matter—your invisible ancestors, they're out there, looking out for you, and you need to show your face once a year so they don't forget who to protect. Only, if you can't see them, how do you know any of it's true? Your dead family is just that, dead. And you're alive, and you have more important things to do, bills to pay, games to play, transits to catch, drinks to drown your sorrow. So you didn't even notice when the sea level rose high enough to drown your family's *haka* stone at the bottom of the bowl-shaped graveyard. By then, you'd already forgotten the graveyard existed. You forgot your ancestors. You forgot the traditions that gave them peace.

But I haven't forgotten.

You're welcome.

As I approached, I saw the huge torii gate at the end of the lane, camouflaged as it was amongst the other posts and wire-bearing poles along the perimeter. Acid rain had long ago washed away the gate's vermillion paint, and I'd learned not to caress it as I passed through or else suffer a palm full of splinters. But, like the graveyard itself, somehow it still stood, solid and imposing, in the world that had all but abandoned it.

I closed the rusted gate behind me; the groaning sound of it blasted through the still night, as loud as any security alarm, but I knew there was no one around to hear it, *or care*—like I said. I found the rice-cooker on the workbench I'd set up just inside the entrance and flipped the switch. I punched in the code I'd saved in the 3D lacquerware printer that sat right next to it and drummed my fingers as the thing whirred to life, guzzling a quarter-liter of the liquid plastic from the tank under the table to fashion a black rice bowl inside its glass case. Just under thirty seconds, and both the rice and the bowl were done. I scooped the one into the other, pocketed a few incense sticks and *hashi*—chopsticks—from the drawer, and grabbed the long-reed broom on my way toward the graveyard's central path.

I passed through the grove of sakura trees whose overgrown and untended roots had pushed through the concrete walkways years before I ever found this place, turning the path quite treacherous. How those fucking things were still alive was beyond me. Thanks to the slanting ceilings of concrete and steel that held up the upper city, no sun ever shined there. Nothing clean ever rained. Just the trickling runoff from the sprawl above, or even the salty sludge creeping in from the sea below. But alive they were. *Thriving* even. It didn't make sense, but what in my life ever did? It would be a month yet before the place was flooded with pink blossoms, the air heavy with the trees' sweet scent. I'd seen it happen once a year, every year that I lived down there. By now, all the otherworldly chill had worked its way out of my body. As I exited the other side of the grove, I felt eerily refreshed, born again. This inexplicable life in the middle of a void on the rim of the great city always filled me with a warmth that I could not explain. Something I could not see or hear *wanted* me to be there.

I emerged from the grove and paused at the top of the grand staircase that divided the graveyard in two, the tiers of gravestones swept out to either side like spreading wings. Here, there were no mega-corp towers to obstruct the beauty of the sky. No neon diffusing the black of the night. No ribbons of automated transports floating deliveries and bodies and business in an endless cycle between the notches carved out of the sprawl. Here, there were stars. That was if the acrid exhaust clouds from the A-Matter Power & Industry's plants farther down the coast didn't roll in on the eastern wind ... and if you squinted hard enough. Tonight, there were no clouds. There was no need to narrow my eyes.

At the very bottom of the bowl, the white crescent shape of the waxing moon reflected from the still water where the seas had risen gradually. I should've marveled at all this serenity, this singular, fleeting moment in which this vision of the old world could outshine the pulsating synthetic light of the new one, but all I ever thought about, every time I looked down at that wide circle of water, was all the thousand graves I could never reach beneath the reflective mirror of the placid surface. All the more ancestors I could never hope to guide to their rest, and so all the more angry dead I could encounter out there, beyond the torii gates.

I felt the weight of the rice bowl in one hand and the broom in the other. I remembered Mr. Briefcase-Sama and the whole reason I had come here instead of going home to wait for Ben.

I didn't know the ghost's name. I didn't know if his family's grave was even *here*, but I knew very well the simple logic by which I had observed, adapted, and survived for the last two years: I reasoned that for every one of the wandering, angry ghosts I encountered, I would perform the rites for two of the untended graves, and in the long run, the odds would turn out in my favor. If I just kept at it long enough, maybe, eventually, all the ghosts lost in *Yomi* would find their way home.

What else was I supposed to do?

I descended the stairs, counting twenty-three tiers on my way. At the twenty-fourth, I hung a left and breezed past fifty-nine *haka* stones, making note of the first handful of them which would need fresh rice in the coming days. I stopped before the sixtieth. This is where I had left off last time I was here, just the night previous, just before the Inari job, actually. The stone itself wasn't in terrible shape. I could still make out the *kanji* of the family's name: *Hamada*.

Maybe Mr. Briefcase was named Mr. Hamada.

"It'll have to do," I murmured and set the rice bowl gently atop the granite slab. First, I swept the gravel lane of all the accumulated debris—mostly leaves and old sakura petals from seasons past, but the occasional scrap of paper that wafted in from the surrounding sprawl, and sometimes even ash borne on the breeze from some part of the ruined world beyond NeOsaka. I sent it all down, murmuring a prayer as I did, entreating the *kami* for peace upon this place, this name *Hamada*, and all who bore it, living or dead. I kneeled before the gravestone, found the incense and lighter in my suit's inner pocket, and lit the ends. I stuck the *hashi* in the rice—kind of a visual aid for the ancestor spirits, who otherwise couldn't comprehend what to do with a bowl of rice unless the chopsticks were there, I don't know—and then I clapped my hands, closed my eyes, and bowed deeply.

This was *Obon,* a Shinto rite that had found its way into the Zen Buddhist traditions that had come to define so much of Japanese daily life. This was *Obon,* and honestly, I had no fucking clue if I was doing it right. I read about this somewhere, on some really retro data cache Ben had dug up for me once. It's not like I could laser-print the page and take it to the *onmyoji* at my local shrine and ask what the fuck it was all about. A couple of days after reading about *Obon,* I decided to try it myself. Maybe it was the act of bringing cleanliness to an unclean place, the smell of the incense, the deliberate closing of my eyes even in a world that demanded your attention, the speed of life giving way to the meditative stillness of death—I don't know… But the *Obon* gave me a sense of peace.

Of course, part of the "real" *Obon* involved a dance, if you wanted to do it the right way.

"Fuck that," I whispered just as I figured the rite was wrapping up.

I was on my feet again, the whole thing only lasting maybe five minutes. I had time probably for one more, number sixty-one, if I rushed up the stairs and printed another rice bowl. Why not carry two at a time and save time? Again, this was something I'd long ago asked myself, but I had felt that industrializing a tradition like the *Obon* was the same as diluting its meaning. Somehow, I thought the dead would appreciate quality over quantity.

Before heading down the path back to the grand staircase, the thought made me turn about to face the sea, to look down on all those tiers—more than a hundred still—and all those *haka* I'd yet to purify. I remembered making a silent promise to all of them that I would visit each one, even if their families had forgotten.

"Just give me a little time." The sound of it brought a smirk to my face. Then, I lowered my head, shaking it, realizing there was never anyone else around to make me laugh, so I made myself laugh as much as possible. "Who the fuck am I talking to?"

I heard a soft breath on the wind. It formed a long, drawn-out *shussshhh* that drifted past me. At first, I thought maybe it was the sound of my heel pivoting on the gravel, but then I realized I hadn't made a move.

On the tier just below me, a lone figure stood before one of the gravestones. Had he been there when I first got here? Or had he come later? Did I fall asleep when praying? How did I not hear him on the path?

No one comes here. No one but me.

No one.

Looking down at him, I couldn't see his face beyond the brim of his black hat. Only the chin, clean-shaven, but pock-marked and wrinkled with age. He wore a black three-piece suit, a black tie, a white shirt, and all of it covered by an overcoat, all of it rumpled, and the hems in tatters. The poor material was one concern, the style another, as the shoulders of the thing were cut too wide, telling me it was probably twenty years beyond its heyday on the rack. Same with the collars around his neck, and the girth of the knot of his tie that cinched them together.

I tend to notice these things first, being that I rather enjoyed keeping with the style. (My fingers involuntarily felt at the bullet holes in my best suit, and I grimaced.) Usually, that's all I notice since I avoid eye contact like everyone should. But next, I saw that this man had only one hand emerging from the sleeves of his overcoat. He was missing an arm.

"Hey," I said, not sure what else to do, not sure if the tone was a friendly greeting or an attempt to stop the old-timer from bolting.

Who the fu—

How did you find this place?

What are you doing here?

So many questions. I felt a little violated. No, I felt like *this place* had been violated. Never mind that it was apparently a "public" space—this graveyard was *mine*.

Speaking of violations, I realized I should've run back to the central staircase and around the ring of the old man's tier, but I had already taken my first step onto the slab of the *haka* just below my number sixty. I hopped down onto the unswept path, five meters away from the uninvited old bastard.

"Hey," I said again, this time fully aware I was bending the sound of it into an accusation of sorts. "You can't be here."

The old man remained still for several breaths, offering no reply but silence, so I added, "Did you just *shush me?*"

That got me a response. Sort of. The old man twisted at the waist ever so slightly, swinging his handless sleeve around his back, which he caught with the hand he still had. The whole thing seemed kind of ridiculous to me, watching him pretend to clasp his hands behind his back, but I didn't laugh. Instead, I was frozen still by the stern profile his features cut into my reality. My own face stared back at me from the mirrored shades that he wore, then he turned silently back to what he'd been examining before my interruption. That profile, that gesture, that frown, somehow it all spoke for him, saying that this was someone you do not fuck with. Perhaps a Yakuza boss, long-dead like all the rest of them.

I followed the line of his mirrored gaze to the *haka* before him. The family name had been gouged out, as though a shotgun blast had torn it out ages ago. Some of the *haka* in this place—though very rare—were often adorned by statues, carvings, or symbols that must have meant something to the family. I once found a stone book and guessed that family must have been writers. I even found a *haka* with a stone stethoscope a few months ago.

The old man focused on the statue of a sword—a carved stone katana placed in a carved stone stand—of this particular *haka*.

"Do you believe," the old man said in flawless, native-born Japanese, his weary voice faded to a sound just barely above a whisper, "that the dead are content to be dead?"

Of course, the questions never stopped cropping up in my mind, but I pushed them all aside. This guy was getting right to my area of expertise, after all, and I was fascinated by this visit. An older-generation Japanese native was a rarity. "I know they're not," I said, slipping also into Japanese.

He sighed, though I never saw his body move with the release. Had I not seen his lips part, his voice might very well have been the wind. "How, then, can the dead be content?"

Okay… This is getting off the rails.

He's a ghost. He's lost, like all the rest. Nothing new. Nothing special. Old man wants what they all want.

But then…

I didn't feel the chill. I was standing five meters away from him and I felt nothing like what I felt from Mr. Briefcase, or from all the other wandering ghosts that had invaded my personal space over the years. I almost said, *You're real, aren't you? You're alive.* Only the last-minute realization at the stupidity saved me. Instead, I focused on actually considering his question.

"Home," I said after a rather long silence. "To find peace. They have to go home."

The old man lifted his chin even as the side of his mouth deepened into its frown. When he turned toward me again, he did so a little clumsily, almost staggering, as if he was unsure if I'd moved away or where I'd gone, his head sideways, his ears searching for a trace sound of me. That's when I knew the eyes behind his mirror shades were blind.

"What is home?" Gone from that airy voice were the philosophical, the metaphysical, the existential tones. All that was left was an ardent plea. This old man was pleading with me, as though my answer would be a gift, a key that would set him free.

What is home?

I have no fucking idea.

"Sir, would you like some *nihon-cha?* Green tea?" I hoped to change the subject. *"Domo,"* I said, *please,* stepping aside the debris-strewn path and gesturing toward the central staircase.

Why am I asking him this? Asking him TO TEA?!

I choked a bit on the answer, disgusted by the truth of it.

Because I'm lonely.

The old man's wandering gaze lowered, as if he was scanning me from top to bottom, measuring me, then it swept back over the nameless gravestone with the sword.

No doubt the sight of this girl-in-guys'-clothing appalls his old-time sensibilities.

He's gotta be thinking, what ARE the kids into these days?!

No... something didn't seem right with thinking this particular line of shit just then. This wasn't the time for my personal brand of dumbassed jokes. My throat seized up again, and I tried to swallow the rising anxiety. This was my elder. I needed to show respect. Part of me felt like crying.

I bowed lower than I'd probably ever bowed before and held my place there for two, three, four seconds. I closed my eyes. Opened them. I raised myself and tried again.

"Sir," I said, to no one.

The old man was gone.

I should've been a little relieved. I should've thought, *Ahh*—soo-desu ne?—*a spirit after all.* I should've tried to latch onto that weird sense of satisfaction I felt. *I offered the man some tea, some kindness, and my words—steady, even, polite—and the recognition brought his spirit peace. He was a ghost, after all.*

But I knew it was all bullshit. I should've tried to latch onto the bullshit, because what I felt instead was a growing sense of dread.

How did he know? The question… How did he know the question that I'd been asking myself my whole life?

What is home?

Where is my *home?*

For a few moments more, I listened to the gentle wind stirring the leaves strewn along the path of this untended tier. I looked up at the missing chunk of the *haka* stone the old man had been staring at, the emptiness where the family name had been blown apart, then at the sword statue, then out over the vastness of the graveyard. I wondered if maybe my parents' bones were here, in this graveyard, or another. Somewhere. Anywhere.

Or nowhere at all.

I breathed deliberately. Breathing was better than crying. I swept the lock of hair out of the front of my face, and I felt the smirk return. "Fuck it," I said.

I even hopped back onto the stone slab and up to the tier and good ol' number sixty where I'd left off. Tomorrow, maybe even tonight, I'd come back here and polish off sixty-one. For that, I'd need more rice, more incense, more *hashi*. I'd do that, and I'd forget the old man—just another spirit after all—and in time, I'd get to his own unnamed gravestone, wherever it was, just like I'd promised all the others.

FOUR

WOULD DO ALL THAT SHIT, IN TIME.
But first, I needed to make sure Ben Roy Doon wasn't
snooping through all the corners of my place and finding
all the shit that was never meant for him or anyone. And to
do that, I needed to pass through the graveyard's splintering
torii gate and cross the street.

The derelict apartment block there, which now served
as little more than a load-bearing structure for the upper
city, was "home." Like I said before, this southern part of
NeOsaka was kind of a no-man's-land. It had its own special brand of squalor that the everyday classes of resident
alien Japanese wouldn't even deem worthy of habitation, no
matter how desperate they might be. There was no heat, no
gas, no electricity. The liters of sludge that bubbled up out of
the pipes were a kind of science experiment that may yield
a few drops of clean water if you could somehow boil away
the grime. Even the squatters and scavengers who made it
out to the city's fringe down here soon realized the place
had been picked clean for kilometers all around. Perhaps the
one silver lining in the cloud of shit that was my curse was

the fact I didn't have to eat or drink to sustain my life. Don't get me wrong, I get hungry like any other living creature, but I'd found at the tender age of nine (I think) as a Tenjin-Corp-sponsored orphan just how long I could go without a meal. The conclusion I'd drawn was: *indefinitely*. Also, I'd been able to strike "starvation" from the list of attempted suicide methods. So, all-around, a win-win for Shin, huh?

But what do you do to stay clean, Shin?

Right. Well… I kinda don't. Like I said, this dilapidated, sagging edifice of old Osaka was "home." Whenever I got the call to rejoin my SynCell for a job (I'd of course taken measures to ensure the call's untraceability, by the way), I'd head into the city for "work," which included extended stays at various coffin or pillbox hotels and meetups in VR bars, simulated pleasure cafes, porno-dens, strip-clubs, cyber-clinics, back alleys, high-rise restaurants, automated transport cars, and a multitude of other really clandestine spots. The life of a Syndicate cowgirl meant you never stayed grounded for long, never stopped moving, lest you get picked up by corporate security matrices weaved into the New Osaka Communications Grids, or just "the grid" for short. So, yes, on such occasions I'd be sure to get all gussied up, which included a shower. Aside from the cordite-singed holes in my suit and the dried-up purple amniotic-ectoplasmic goop on my skin after my most recent trip through the underworld, my body was as clean as a spring rain. A caustic spring rain, maybe, but a spring rain nonetheless.

I had no clue where Ben and I would go to escape the mega-corps, the Syndicate, but wherever it was, my priority was a shower and a new suit.

Lucky for Ben Roy, I'd picked an apartment on the ground floor. I would have preferred to squat in one of the units higher up, but most of the floors had sagged through into ruin. Ben's upward mobility in life was severely limited by the lack of serviceable elevators. And serviceable legs.

I could see that he'd already let himself in and made himself at home. The front door was open a crack, a centimeter-wide line of glowing candlelight along its side. Maybe if I hadn't chosen to fixate on the memory of the old man in the overcoat at that moment—maybe if I hadn't been worrying over all the non-options I could pick from in my new post-SynCell future—I might have been able to tell something was wrong before it was too late, before I opened the door wider and stepped through, before the steel-knuckled fist collided with my jaw and its meaty counterpart was gripping my shirt front and pulling me through the doorway and throwing me more than five meters through the air, sending me crashing and flopping across the floor.

I thought maybe I'd bit down on some hard candy, the kind with the gooey, blood-red, salt-and-copper center. But I realized it was only the top and bottom molars on the left side of my face. I spat the teeth fragments out on the pre-fab resin floor as I struggled to push myself up. A steel-toed kick to my side sent me the rest of the way to the far wall of the apartment, another five meters. I heard the servos in the steel cyber-hand whir open, then the tinny whine and pop of the volts maxing out at its fingertips.

"Stay down." A gruff Russian accent I recognized.

Boltcutter.

Feikes's bodyguard. Former wrestler and bare-knuckle pit-fighter, part-time Syndicate raider, and full-time asshole. Also, Vas's cousin. Or uncle. Or something.

I could feel the side of my face already beginning to swell. I looked up at the massive, broad-shouldered mountain, his metal hand spread apart, tiny blue arcs of lightning dancing between his fingertips. He was ready to taze me if I didn't comply.

"Okay," I think I said, but it came out as an anguished wheeze. Boltcutter at least let me roll over and spit out more shards of my teeth.

"Kid..." Another voice I knew. Knew even better than the first. The sound of decades of chain-smoking and corrective cancer-searing laser surgery, and the sound of disappointment. "Shin," Feikes said, emerging from the side hallway off the main room, lighting a cigarette that was screwed into an old-fashioned whalebone holder. It must've been hell for him to belay his addiction while he waited in ambush here, lest the stench of tobacco give him away. He blew out a satisfied, smug cloud in my direction. "We've got a problem?"

I always hated how he turned statements into questions like that. Such a cheap trick to get you talking first. *You fucking well know we got a problem!* Again, only another agonizing wheeze was all I could manage. I was pretty sure Boltcutter's boot had broken at least two of my ribs.

"Aw shit," Feikes said, backhanding the bigger man's shoulder playfully (having to reach up quite a ways to do it). "You broke the kid? My favorite, favorite kid." Feikes was lowering himself down to the floor, hooking his hands under my arms, setting my back up against the wall, and handing me his handkerchief. "There, there, kid. I'm sorry he hurt you. I told him not to. I really did. But he wouldn't listen."

"Where's Vasili?" Boltcutter broke in.

Only I saw Feikes's old blue eyes roll, but he didn't flinch at the sound of the bellowing mountain behind him. "See?" was all he said to me.

"I blew his fucking brains out," I said. I did my best to stifle the smile spreading painfully on my swelling cheeks, but the pain felt good. I watched Boltcutter's reaction. *That hurt*, I realized. *The only thing I can do to hurt him.* Just had to deliver the truth.

Feikes was up on his feet, spinning, holding back the big man. Where Boltcutter was big and tall, Feikes was a slim, straight-leg, stick of a man. The spikes of his black and white punk-rock mohawk still weren't enough to surpass the bigger man's height. But Boltcutter's chest came forward only so far as Feikes's gentle hand would allow. The guard dog wouldn't oppose its master's wishes.

My smile widened.

"Now why'd you go and do a thing like that?" Feikes asked me over his shoulder.

"Vas asked me to."

"He *asked* you to? To put a bullet through his skull? And why'd he ask you to do that? Shin, what happened?"

After we'd all gotten our hellos out of the way, we'd come up pretty quick to the question on everyone's mind. It was the first thing I asked myself, the first thing Ben asked me. The first thing the Syndicate's top *daimyo* probably asked Feikes. The first real thing Feikes was asking now. *What happened?*

I had no idea. You might've expected me to say *I wanted to know as much as anyone!* But that wasn't true. The truth was, I didn't want to give a shit.

Still, my mind reeled with potential answers; not all of them lies, maybe.

Someone tipped us off.

InariCorp knew we were coming.

A second SynCell beat us to the haul.

"Fuck…" I finally said, just to fill the stretching silence. "What d'you want me to say? You already know." It was a ploy to see if he'd help me find some place to start—a foundation to ground my bullshit. It only sort of half-worked.

"All we know is that Vasili, Serge, Johnny, and Tetsuo went off-grid. Same span of minutes as you did. Only they didn't show back up as a blip a kilo away like you did, only to disappear a minute later." Feikes's expression soured, and at the sight of it, my whole smooth-bullshit-indifferent demeanor dried up and flaked away. Here was a man who had been like a father to me, someone who'd welcomed me into as close to a kind of family as an orphaned piece of shit like me could've ever hoped for. His nightclub, Broken, was more than just a den of pleasure, more than a place of business. It was an oasis where gender-benders and sexual deviants like me could feel at home, a tiny spot on the map of the sprawling, post-collapse Japanese conservatism that had strangled individualism and self-expression for the past several decades, ever since mega-corps became as powerful as governments, became the government itself. It was Feikes who took me in, showed me how I could embody the lifestyle I wanted, how I could reject the dominant mega-corp society that had fucked up this little girl's life from the moment she was presumably born.

It was also Feikes who gave me my first job, who introduced me to the Syndicate, who orchestrated my first raid and every raid ever since, who told me I was striking back when really all I was ever doing was one mega-corp's dirty work for them, then turning around the next week on the next job and doing another's as payback. It was Feikes who got me into this cyclical life. So, you could say, it was Feikes who told me my life's first big lie.

Even still, despite these conflicted feelings, yeah—not going to lie—it hurt a little to see him frown at me like that.

"Looks bad, Shin," he said simply, and I knew he didn't just mean *I* looked bad. He meant the situation. The SynCell he ran. Someone higher up would want to know why those data cubes weren't recovered. Someone would miss a big payoff. "Looks real bad."

"I'm sorry," I said. I hated myself for looking away then.

Feikes let out a deep sigh. "Well, *sorry's* not going to bring the dead back, is it?"

"No," I said, knowing more about the subject than I let on. "No, it's not."

"Soooo," he breathed, hunkering down next to me once again. "What happened, Shin?"

"No, you can keep it," he said, holding up a hand against the bloody handkerchief I tried to give back.

I glanced up at Boltcutter, towering behind Feikes's shoulder. "I'm sorry. About Vas." And I was. I knew then that I'd only been lying to myself before, just trying to play the part of emotionless cowgirl. "He asked me to … because he knew what would happen if InariSec took him alive. But look, I don't know how they knew we were there. I don't know what happened. You have to believe me."

"I believe you," Feikes said, and I felt it might be true.

Boltcutter, meanwhile, wasn't buying it. I could read the twitches in his human-flesh left arm, the flexing of the fingers of his left hand, as a sign that he was barely containing his fury. But he stayed quiet and eventually lowered his arm.

"At least tell us how you got out."

"Can't," I said, smiling again with red teeth. "Job security."

I was betting my life, literally, on the fact that Feikes once told me he had never known a safe-cracker quite like me in all his decades of running Syndicate raids, in any of the dozens of SynCells he'd operated. There were some doors and locks so old, so outdated, that they'd been lapped a hundred times already in the never-ending race between hacking technology and cybersecurity, and so confounded even the most savvy operators. For these alone, I seemed to have the magic touch. The guys would laugh when I closed my eyes and waved my hands around a little, thinking maybe I was accessing some cutting-edge hardware grafted onto my brain or whatever. They thought I must've gotten my unnaturally violet eyes as a vanity rider on the cyber-surgery procedure when it was installed.

But unless you count the various blades and shanks I've taken in the guts over the years (some of which sent me on trips to *Yomi*), I've never gone under the knife. No implants, no augments, no cyberware whatsoever. Still, Feikes and the Syndicate could believe whatever they wanted about my unique skills. Because they'd never believe what I was actually doing: reaching into the spirit world, summoning the *kami* I found there, and commanding them to open the man-made mechanisms they called home.

"Trade secrets and all that," I added, reiterating my point, doubling down on my bet.

It paid off. Feikes's widening grin was his concession. He blew out a cloud of smoke. "Fine," he said, finding an old lacquer bowl on a side table to stamp out his cigarette and pocketing the old-fashioned holder. "We all know you're a little..." He trailed off, glancing around at the *shime-wama* rope around the base of my living room, the hundred zig-zag paper *shide* dangling from the ceiling, the table where I'd folded almost nine hundred *origami* cranes, the smoldering incense sticks, the four miniature *kamidana* house shrines I'd been gluing back together over time, the shelf of worn-out books I'd rescued from incinerators, all of Shakespeare's plays and sonnets. More than half of which were printed in Russian or Chinese or languages I couldn't read, but I liked looking at the symbols.

"...a little weird," Feikes finished, randomly pulling a hardback copy of *Aesop's Fables*, raising an eyebrow at all of the animals with human expressions on the cover, and dropping it to the floor.

"So you're not going to kill me." It was another card I could play. Almost as soon as I'd laid it on the table, so to speak, I knew what was in Feikes's hand. "Because you've got another job for me."

Feikes said nothing, but that fatherly pride I'd grown slightly addicted to twinkled in his eye. "Bring him in here," he said to Boltcutter, who stomped away through the apartment hall and returned a moment later, pushing a small wheelchair fitted with mobile computer rigs, cables, and a frail Korean guy my age with no legs.

"Shin," Ben blurted out. "I'm so s-s-sorry!"

Boltcutter's flesh hand cuffed him on the ear, shutting him up. If the big Russian monster had wanted to, he could've probably popped Ben's head like a grape.

"It's okay, Ben," I said, even though I didn't know if that was true. (For some reason, I thought back to my last conversation with Vas.) It was easy to dismiss Ben as a sniveling invalid when he was chirping on the other side of your comlink audio node, but to see him in the flesh—what was left of him—to remember all that we'd been through together, growing up, in the orphanage, in the Syndicate...

Look... no one else in this world gave two shits about Ben Roy Doon, so I had to.

"It's okay," I repeated, taking note of the purpling cheekbones and swelling eye and cracked lens in his glasses—Boltcutter's handiwork, which I'd very much remember to revisit upon him should the opportunity arise. "They're not going to kill us."

"Well ... correction, kid. Originally, we weren't going to kill just *you*. Ben, on the other hand... Decent enough to have behind the screens on a raid, but hackers are a dime a dozen these days. Even the Tenjin-trained ones like our friend Ben here. So," Feikes said, drawing a tattooed, gnarly thumb across his neck, sticking his tongue out, an *aaakkkkk* rising comically from his throat.

"But then I had a think on it," he went on. "If I let Boltcutter here mangle your only friend, you'd probably never forgive me, let alone agree to do this next job. So, *little Ben* here's just a *little collateral* to ensure your cooperation."

How fucking polite of you, Feikes.

I occupied myself with wiping away the fresh trickle of red at the corner of my lips with the sleeve of my suit and staring at the stain so I wouldn't have to look at him when I asked the only question that really mattered. "And after this next job's done, what then? Another job. And another."

Feikes let out a deep sigh and came to rest next to me along the wall, the heavy wallet chain on his hip clattering against the floor. He rubbed the bald side of his head with his bony, purple-veined hand, taking a long while to work through what was on his mind, to string together the right words. Finally, he said, "Shinjiro, I know you've been dissatisfied with our line of work for quite a while now. That right?"

You know damn well it is.

I kept that to myself. My silence was enough of an answer for him.

"I get it, kid. Mega-corporate espionage. It's just rich versus rich. One top dog biting another top dog in the neck, then getting bit by another top dog, all of them dogs scrambling up to the top of the mountain. Capitalism! The new god, you know. And *so fucking what?* None of it's actually helping anyone. They say they can protect us from the *Russo-Chin*—from final annihilation—but *are they?* They say they can innovate our way to near-immortality, but they keep all that tech for themselves while the rest of us starve, or get strung out on Bullet Time, or get so plugged into a virtual world we forget what it means to be livin' in *this one.*"

Feikes sucked in a deep breath through his nostrils and flubbed it out his lips in a defeated, deflating-balloon sound. He was quiet a long time, reflecting, staring ahead into my apartment but clearly aware of some memories or regrets that only he could see. I looked from Ben Roy to Boltcutter, the one looking to shit his shorts and the other looking ready to hurt someone. Take your guess which was which.

"You know, I was raiding long before I found you. A hundred raids I done, kid. A hundred friends I had to watch fall behind or betray me. I've been playing this game so long. But I'm still here. Still playin'. You know why?"

I met his eyes then. "No," I said, caught up in whatever spell he was casting more than I care to admit, plodding straight into his murky field of bullshit.

"Because despite some setbacks, I'm still having fun." He leered at me, all charm. But in the very next breath, he was all severity. "And I don't care to know what my role is in the bigger picture. Listen, Shin. None of it means anything. Don't ask *why* we get paid by one mega-corp, posing as another mega-corp, to rob or sabotage or blow up another mega-corp.

"Just. Have. Fun." He patted my knee with each word.

Aww. Isn't this nice? A real close moment between us, Feikes.

Fuck that.

A shiver more cold than any ghost could've given me ran through my leg and up my spine. I did my best not to cringe from Feikes's touch. The fact was that I'd been sold on this line before—this *very* line. He must've forgotten it's what he told all the girls before he fucked them. *Just. Have. Fun.* Feikes was good at making the lost feel like they were found, but once you'd survived long enough in his SynCell you'd know that Feikes had only survived this long himself because he didn't keep friends. He kept slaves.

I'd figured Feikes out. Perks of not having to actually die on the job when everyone back at base thought you were a goner. I'd figured him out, but what good would telling him so do?

None.

"What's the job?"

"That a girl." I didn't have to look at his face; I *heard* the shit-eating grin well enough from here. "But don't worry so much about the *what* as you should about the *when*. And when is…" He pressed a thumb into the sagging, faded tattoo on his forearm, activating some subdermal implant in his arm, projecting a heads-up display in soft blue hard light from the emitter embedded in his cornea. "Oh shit! We gotta go, kid! Cutter, why the fuck you didn't say what time it was?"

The display winked out as fast as it had lit up. Feikes pushed himself up off the floor and reached a hand down to help me up. I took it, if only to keep up appearances, though I couldn't fake not having broken ribs as I winced getting up onto my feet. As though *appearances* were also on his mind, he seemed to notice my shredded-to-shit suit for the first time.

"Ho-lee hell, Shin. This some new fashion you're into? Go on and get yourself changed."

"Try a dress," Boltcutter said just loud enough for me to hear. Why someone that big felt the need to mutter something that petty under his breath made no sense to me.

"Fuck you," I told him, pretty much automatically, but a smirk was all the rise I got out of him. *Probably better that way if I hope to keep a couple more of my teeth.*

I turned back to Feikes. "What happens to Ben?"

"Nothing, provided you both get done what needs getting done."

"And what happens after?"

"To him?"

"To both of us."

"Well," Feikes considered the handicapped hacker from head to ... well... Behind those cold blue eyes, I knew Feikes was weighing Ben's worth against whatever new SynCell he'd no doubt already started putting together in light of his previous crew's demise. "I got no problem if you want out, Shin. Same to you, Big Ben. You can both walk away from all this if that's what you really want."

With the curse I'd carried all my life, I could see things no one else could see. You could say that I could see *souls*. And so when Feikes flashed his most sincere smile when he dipped his chin down and his cold blue eyes looked up past a few wingbeats of his eyelashes and he said, "I mean it," I saw straight into his soul.

And I knew. *He wants so bad for me to believe him.*

It might've worked, if only I'd been sixteen all over again.

FIVE

Not even an hour later, I was seated in the back of an auto transport on a hardlight-highway flowing between skyscrapers like a river in the sky.

I'd gone to the sagging closet I considered a bedroom to change out my ruined dark navy suit, and when I came back Feikes and Boltcutter were gone. They'd told Ben the location where I was to meet up with the next job's cell, and it took me the better part of five minutes to get him to stop sobbing before my comlink could finally parse out the sound of the quadrants. Feikes hadn't said one way or another if Ben was to play remotely on this one, so I told him to stay in my ear in case I needed to fall back on him. He complained that he didn't have his gear, that I'd told him to leave it all behind, that the signal in my place was shit (nevermind the fact I lived there for that very reason), that it would get picked up anyway on the grid, probably Inari's grid first—and we were all dead when that happened—and was I really sure I wanted that.

"Fuck it," I told him. I needed to give Ben something to do, something to focus on. The truth was, I was glad to have him chirping in my ear as the transport trundled over turbulent pockets of air, rising on the artificial electro-mag currents pulsing in the NeOsaka night.

Aside from the occasional bumps, the ride was smooth. The reinforced titanium cargo hold was empty, but the chips embedded in the walls would give any external scanners the impression that the transport was packed with crates of branded tungsten-16 rods and pipes on their way to A-Matter Corporation's testing facility. There were no crates, of course. Only two benches. My ass occupied one, and two hard-looking men sat on the other. They both wore bulky Teflon armor vests under black trench coats, not even trying to conceal the idea that they expected violence. Or wanted it.

My tongue was too busy slithering over the aching hole in my jawline to make an introduction. I hadn't had the chance to confirm it, but my suspicion was that the left side of my face was one big bruise. A Halloween mask. Pain, concealing fury. So I just brooded, my arms crossed, one leg draped over the other, my tongue working back and forth over the teeth I still had, trying not to watch the other members of my new impromptu SynCell.

The older guy was checking the readouts on the side of the other guy's skull. I say "older guy" only because he wasn't cyberwared out of his mind like the other guy. The other guy's eyes were glazed over, his pupils dilated to an impossible degree, while the older guy worked some dials with a needle tool. Thank *whatever* that the cyber zombie wasn't looking right at me, or I might've lost it.

The older guy resettled the artificial skin flap over his associate's bald cranium, put his needle away, and pulled out a vial of neon-yellow liquid from the same pocket.

"Shit," I wanted to say, but instead clamped my jaws so tight I could've broken more teeth. *Bullet Time.*

That explained the other guy's thousand-yard stare. The drug was lubricating his synapses to a practically frictionless state. His brain was processing phenomena so rapidly that time for him simply crawled. The cyber zombie was living his life in perpetual slo-mo. If he'd wanted to, he could've sliced a mote of dust in half.

"You can say it," the older guy told me.

"Say what?"

I watched him measure a single dropper of the stuff, tilt the zombie's head back, and drop it in his eye. "Say what you want to say."

"I don't want to say anything."

The older guy leaned back and folded his arms, matching my pose. He shot me with his awful smile, as unnerving as a *Hanma* mask. I shifted involuntarily, and my eyes fell away.

"You might've noticed," he said, "that my partner and I are quite different."

I *had* noticed. The zombified Bullet Time junkie wore the cyberware in their relationship. The older guy had no synthetics whatsoever. Nothing visible anyway.

"They haven't quite perfected the tech that can read *people*," he finished, tapping his forehead. "My partner leaves that to me."

"Partner?" I wanted to clarify that he didn't mean *slave*. But I couldn't make myself say the rest.

"Stub," the older guy said, and the zombie's head swiveled toward him like a machine. "Give you one guess why we call him that."

Stub's arm ended where a hand should've been, and there was a slot in his forearm for belt-fed ammunition, among other enhancements that were wired into his nervous system. The older guy's smile widened when he saw that I'd already figured it out.

"I'm Connor."

He waited, but all he got was a shrug.

"And you're Shinjiro. Asai-Shinjiro." He looked perplexed. "Isn't that a guy's name?"

"What're you doing here?"

"What? Like in Japan? Long story."

"No." I leaned forward, elbows on knees, so I could look up at him seriously. "You and—*Stub* or whatever—you're decked out in military-grade hardware."

"Ah-ah-ah," Connor said, wagging a finger. "I only got my trusty Colt."

I bulled on, deciding to cut the shit and get to my point. "I don't kill people."

"I know."

"And I don't ride along with SynCells that do."

Connor's smile vanished. The mask had fallen away, and the real face beneath was placid, cold. "Feikes told me about you, you know." And his eyes wandered down over my body. "*All* about you."

Fuck. I shrank away, pressed my back against the transport's hull.

"Woah, lady," he said, his arms coming up defensively. "I mean the tattoos. I had some once too, but most of 'em got shot or sliced or burned off. Heh."

"Fucking bullshit." Not that I doubted what he was saying, just that I was disgusted imagining Feikes talking about me and my body with this snake.

"What I meant was, Feikes said you ain't got a choice." Connor's *Hanma* mask—his shit-eating smile—returned. "And as for not killing people, you don't have to worry. That's why we got Stub."

"So what am I doing on this raid, then?"

"Feikes said you open doors. The kind of doors that don't open when you ask 'em nicely. Not even with a computer. Well, there's somebody needs to die behind some door somewhere. That's it." Connor looked at Stub. The cyber zombie's head swiveled in my direction; his black-saucer eyes bore into me. "See? Stub knows the drill."

If I could've melded with the steel at my back, phased through it, and fallen a hundred stories to splatter on the ground and died just to get away from that thing, I would have. *Actually*, I realized, *I could do those things. Spend a little time in* Yomi. *Come back a new person. New name. New job. Fall in on the right side of the mega-corps. Get a wife. A family. A Repli-Pet puppy we'd never have to patch to adult firmware if we didn't want to.* My fingers had slid into my suit pocket, caressing my *omamori* charm. But then I remembered Ben. If I ducked out now, Feikes would have Boltcutter make Ben suffer. I imagined Ben's arms torn from their sockets. I imagined what he'd look like trundling through the twisted realm of the dead. Just a torso in a wheelchair, staring through me. I shuddered. My shaking fingers let go. I made a fist instead.

"Where are we going?"

"Shiromatsu Kazama," Connor said flatly as if I'd ever heard of the place. But when he saw my face screw up, he said, "ShiroKaz." His eyes went wide when he saw I still didn't get it, then he looked away, ran a hand through his salt-and-pepper hair, and said solemnly, "Goddamn. I'm getting old.

"ShiroKaz is before your time," he went on. "Different kind of corp. Back when the world economies collapsed and Japan was taking in refugees from all over, back when I got in, before the gates closed and tech companies started getting more and more power over the cops and governments, before all the creepin' in the shadows and sabotage and info-wars and slit throats..." Connor waved a hand around. "Whatever, anyway. Before all the corporations we know today—your A-Matters, Tenjins, Inaris—there was one that tried to be different."

"Different how?" I asked, since his silence compelled me to. I didn't even roll my eyes that much.

"So many different cultures converging in such a cramped little island. Escaping terrorism and civil wars and the … darker side, I guess, of human nature. It wasn't so surprising that even corps with the best intentions of taking care of this country's citizens would eventually sour. They just wanted to make a buck—er, *yen*, whatever—to get a leg-up over the competition, to ensure their *chosen* demographic got to live the good life they deserved and lord it over everyone else. ShiroKaz was different. A merging of the Shiromatsu and the Kazama corporations. One for the storybooks. You know, I think there was even a wedding between all their sons and daughters or something.

"Anyway… ShiroKaz was all about the common good, the betterment of all people, no matter if you were native Japanese or a filthy *gaijin* invader like me…" Connor trailed off. It was obvious he was pinching his own nerve, like an ache in his joints that he could forget about, but only when he stopped applying pressure.

"And did it work?"

Connor's mouth curved in a wry smirk. "Given what you and I and Stub do for our living? Doesn't appear so."

"How come they're not around anymore?"

"What chance does *common good* have against capitalism?"

Just then, I felt the rattling of turbulence through the bench as the transport banked and broke away from the mag-lev field of projected hardlight. The engines fired as it course-corrected and rode a downward pocket of air. We'd be on the ground in moments.

"Nothing *common good* can last."

Three solid sets of footwear hit the floor of the receivables area of ShiroKaz Tower, four rubber-soled military boots and two of the finest vintage Italian-made semi-brogue Oxfords mankind has ever known, if I do say so myself. They were the only pair that matched the particular navy hue of my suit, so what choice did I have, really?

I was dusting myself off from the ride, doing what I could to unwrinkle the folds of my immaculate two-piece, when Connor gripped my shoulder and spun me around. "Coming?"

We made our way through the docking area. Our transport was the sole occupant in the wide row of bays. The building's power must have been shut off, so we followed the dim yellow emergency bulbs sunk into the concrete near the floor, the only lighting in the whole structure. The place was more like a colossal warehouse, but every rack we passed between was completely empty. Bulletins, shelves, even old-timey papers—clipped by actual clipboards—lined the walls, all of them empty, erased, as clean as though they'd never been filled with anything. The whole place was stripped bare, sterile.

Connor took the lead and insisted the zombie bring up the rear, meaning I was sandwiched between them. It felt a bit like I was being escorted somewhere, but Connor had insisted there was a destination only I could lead us to, where the target was holed up. A squatter? A caretaker? Maybe I should've been asking more questions, but like I said before, the less I had to talk to Connor, the better I felt.

Technically, there were four of us on this job. Ben was patched into my comlink even while he was working to bypass security on the sub-standard rig we'd cobbled together from the junk in my apartment. He made it look easy, I have to admit. His presence hovered around us like a ghost, pun intended. Which meant that he'd heard everything Connor had said during our ride to the job.

"Ben," I breathed, knowing the comlink would pick up the vibrations in my throat and auto-amplify the sound on his end. "Any thoughts?"

"Too many," he shot back, then the words just came tumbling. "Just… I can't. I can't. There's a thing behind you more a refrigerator than a man, and the parts that are man are timed-out, and what the hell is it doing there, and how does Feikes know these guys? And then! And then there's this ShiroKaz—Shiromatsu-Kazama. Sorry, I mean—I've been digging through the archives, news sources, Tenjin subsidiary journals, and what-have-you, and it's like the whole history has been scrubbed! And scrubbed! Shin, look around you! Where's all the stuff? And their security, Shin, it's a joke. This is all too easy."

I'd let him run on because sometimes you just have to let Ben run on, to work it out of his system. When that happens, you just have to find those little breaks where you can interject a confidence boost. So when I saw one there, I jumped in.

"It's easy," I said, "because you're a goddamn wizard, my friend."

"No. That's not what I'm saying. No. I mean it's *easy*, Shin."

"Outdated?" *Connor had said this corp was old,* I thought.

"No. It's not that. It's like, there's no resistance. Shin, patching in was cake even on this piece of shit rig in your place. Then, what's more, all the subroutines and hacks I'm running, they're all working on the first go. One after another. Like dominoes. What are the odds of everything lining up like this? Let me tell you—"

As if to prove Ben's point, Connor and I peered around a corner down a long corridor and watched a closed-circuit camera spin around and lock in that position. The red glow around the stainless steel door frame beneath it changed to blue, and we heard an audible click of locks releasing.

"What the!—" Ben screeched in my ear. "I didn't even execute—"

"Tell your boy to stop yappin," Connor said. His expression was chilling. Here, now, in this place, he was a man at work. "I can hear his whining through your comlink."

"Ben," I said, ducking behind Connor down the corridor toward the door, "Shut up, or I got to let you go." Then I added—I don't know why, maybe to score points with my new cold, hard, assassinating SynCell—though I regretted the words right after they vibrated in my throat, "Just do your fucking job."

There were more doors, more cameras, more wide-open spaces. Generators. Climate control systems. Water and waste pumps. Kilometers of electric conduits, switchboards, embedded servers, fiber-optic cables. Security checkpoints. Banks of screens. Service elevators. Broom closets where the sweeper-bots were deployed—all of them vacant, meaning they were out and about, which solved the mystery of the sterility of the place. No life whatsoever. The only certainty I had that time *hadn't* stopped entirely was the nearly imperceptible thrumming of electrons in the wires lining the walls. We crept past all of it, and all of it was completely empty, completely clean, as if none of it had ever been used. Ben opened all the doors, blanked all the cameras, and tricked all the sensors as we moved. The hijacked transport must have docked on a lower level of the tower, maybe even swooping down through the sub-streets of NeOsaka for a stretch to come to our destination. If I'd had a comlink half as smart as the one Connor had tucked around his ear, I could've seen the schematics of the place Ben had scrounged for him. I glanced over at the holographic overlay and saw we had ascended a few levels of this subterranean ant-hill already, and we were finally reaching the grand lobby on the ground floor.

I'd never seen anything quite like it, and I'd stepped through several NeOsaka mega-corporate lobbies in my days, whether under legal circumstances during daylight hours or otherwise. The lobby of ShiroKaz Tower was more Zen-garden than cutthroat-capitalist. Sleek, modern design melded seamlessly with old-world Japan. The curved bank of computers in the reception area rose out of a lacquered wood-and-white paper wall, like what you might see in a Japanese castle. Above everything, two colossal corporate banners hung from the vaulted ceiling, one black, one white, each emblazoned with the *kanji* for *spirit, river,* and *prosperity* in the opposite color. The waiting areas below were sunk into the floor, lined with flawless *tatami.* A walkway of dark marble tiles wound around everything, stretching from the steel-shuttered front doors and ending in a rough limestone path, arranged like stepping stones through a small sea of raked sand. *Where one world ends and another begins.* Along the fringes of this garden, and around the perimeter of the whole circular lobby, rose a bright green bamboo forest, nourished by streams of water that trickled pleasantly over smooth river stones. A *thonk* disturbed the stillness, and Connor and I and even the cyber zombie (his weaponized arm leading the way) pivoted around to the *sozu,* a traditional fixture of so many Japanese gardens in the past. Having emptied itself, the carved bamboo device *clacked* upright and renewed its never-ending cycle of accumulating water as we moved past.

No fucking way was I in NeOsaka anymore. I wandered forward in a trance. In a dream. Like living in a history book, only this place was the real deal. It was like the glimpses of the old world I sometimes caught through the haze of the realm of the dead. I never went there for the sightseeing, of course, but I'd seen enough to know that *Yomi* was frozen in ancestral time. ShiroKaz Tower was like that. It was *Yomi* made manifest. The ethereal made corporeal. And, as if to prove my point, I stopped in my tracks as we made our way toward the elevators behind reception, gawking up at the immense vermillion torii gate looming at the end of the corridors there.

It was, literally, breathtaking.

"What're you staring at?"

I traced my finger in the air over the shape of the torii. "The gate," I said when Connor shot me a puzzled look. I gestured a little more aggressively. "Right there."

"The fuck you talking about?" He focused on the schematics floating over his eye, the fingertips of his linked glove swiping and pinching at his side as he rearranged the readout. "There's nothing there."

Pride is a terrible virtue. I never had a whole lot in my life to be proud of. A couple job-well-dones here and there, a few slaps on the back from Feikes, a particularly clean *haka* stone or razor-edge fold in my thousandth paper crane. And even less often did I feel pride in my line of work as part of a SynCell. But dammit, sometimes it felt good to be an essential cog in the turning gear.

"You sure about that?" I smirked at Connor as I delicately laid my suit jacket over his shoulder. I shot the same look at Stub, but there was nobody home. Should've figured. I coughed a little, rolling up my sleeves. "What was it Feikes said I was here for again?"

Before he could answer—not that he probably cared to, anyway—I brought my forearms together, joining the two halves of my own torii gate. There it was. I felt it like a blast of cold water rushing over me. A tidal wave that would put even *Hokusai* and his *Kanagawa* print to shame. No one ever told me how, but years of practice—brushes with death, and plenty of actual deaths—had taught me instinctively how to turn the tides in my favor. And so I did.

A wind picked up and rushed through the whole lobby behind us, setting the bamboo forest into a swaying dance, kicking through the perfect lines of the sand, and flapping the colossal hanging banners.

Spirit.

River.

I didn't realize it at the time, but the key was hanging right there in our living world for all to see. The problem was, no one knew how to look anymore. No one knew how to care. Guys like Connor—older guys that left behind their own tradition to embrace whatever change the world forced on them, so convinced they'd die otherwise—them least of all.

"The fuck did you just do?" he demanded once the storm subsided.

I'd only had to close my eyes and *feel.* The torii on my arms was only ink on my body, but the separation of worlds that it represented was real. It was in my soul. My curse, that which allowed me to cross between the two. I had dragged the torii gate from the realm of *kami* and into that of *reality.* But I didn't bother telling him that.

"I found that door you were yappin' about." I snatched my jacket back from him. "And I opened it."

In response, Connor dragged his fingers through the air, furiously cycling through visual modes on his overlay, searching for an explanation. My eyes were always closed at moments like this, but I imagined it must have looked like a fading hologram. "There's nothing in this wall except a power supply routed to the elevators. No projectors. No hardlight apparatus."

"You know, people are always giving me shit for my old comlink. But sometimes," I said, turning about just after crossing through the gate, "you can only see things when you look through the past." That stupid, proud smile plastered itself on my dumb face, but I'd already left the aging SynCell raiders behind, headed for the sole elevator at the end of the hidden corridor.

Pride.

Enough of it can get you killed.

SIX

IT HADN'T EVEN OCCURRED TO ME TO ASK UNTIL THE THREE of us were already tucked up inside the slowest elevator known to man.

"What happened here?" I asked, more to break the silence than to actually find out. "Where are all the employees?"

"It's night," Connor offered ironically, his shit-eating *Hanma*-mask smile concealing his real face once again. It seemed like the hard part for him was over, even though nothing about our infiltration into the seemingly dead ShiroKaz Tower had been anything but easy. "Or maybe it's a holiday," he said. "You're the Jap, Asai-san. *You* tell *me* what's on the calendar."

"You're *old* enough to know," I said, sharpening the adjective like a knife I so wanted to stick in his eye socket. "What did this mega-corp *do*? You said they did it for everyone."

Connor let out a bit of a sigh. He holstered his weapon, found the dropper of Bullet Time again, and started prepping another dose for his cyber friend as he spoke. "Japan was the wild west for a while after everything went to shit. With all the hundreds of companies stabbing each other in the back, Shiromatsu's leadership wanted none of it. They were watching their people—Japs, yeah, but like *all* people, *humanity* itself—we were sliding into savagery. It's like I said before, other corps were providing clean water, energy, housing, education, whatever, only to select demographics." He turned a withering eye on me. "Japs only, in most cases. Shiromatsu-Sama saw that it wouldn't last forever. Mega-corps would set the whole world on fire if it went on long enough. So, he merged with Kazama and the two of them made technologies that revolutionized all those things for everybody. Safety, security, health, schooling, transportation. Don't ask me to get specific. None of it's around anymore."

Like the torii gates, I thought. *All around Old Osaka.*

"How'd they make it work? I mean, *given what you and I and Stub do for our living.*" I was still riding on a high of that stupid pride, and so I spiked Connor's own words from inside the transport back at him. I don't know why. And I don't even think he noticed.

"ShiroKaz had some real badass security," he said flatly. "If the ol' legends are to be believed. Never saw it myself. I was always raiding elsewhere, luckier than most. But Stub did. He doesn't like to talk about it."

My eyes rolled around the inside of the elevator. It was all glass, and the shaft it passed through was framed in dark, lacquered wood. No decorations whatsoever. A single dim light glowed overhead. And a single dim button, which I'd pressed. I recalled our trip through the corridors of this once-great mega-corporation. How easy it had all been. "Yeah," I said. "Real badass security."

Connor let go of his end of the conversation. As the elevator continued to rise, the wooden frame beyond the glass fell away, and the brilliant NeOsaka night filled the expanse. The automated transports hovered on maglev lines around the jagged lines of black-limned steel that shot skyward from the mists enveloping the streets below, the uncaring monoliths where the gods dwelled. Gods of greed and manipulation, and the status quo. Gods of protection, happiness, and mercy. Lights glowed in the fog at their feet. Hyper yellows, neon pinks, ethereal teals, rising like an acid-rain rainbow. And holographic dancers half as tall as skyscrapers danced in the honor of their corporate deities. Digitized, sentient, beautiful. Blowing kisses at the throngs. Spinning around poles. Men and girls and boys and women. Bending and gyrating, offering quick peeks up their schoolgirl skirts. Winking. Moaning. All the audio pumped through my comlink. And the ever-flowing rivers of hard-light set the boundaries of the dance floors.

It was so easy to get lost in all that. Just plug into the stream of a life that was decided for you and forget.

The elevator rose higher, slow as ever. But I knew we were getting close. And then it hit me.

"So what now?"

"A bit of regicide, apparently." While I'd been lost in the view, Connor had been swapping out one belt of ammunition into his zombie's arm for another. Red-tips. Polymer. The kind of bullets that exploded. Same kind InariSec had shot me with not even twelve hours before.

"So the place isn't empty."

"Apparently not."

"Some mega-corp somewhere finally has it in mind to finish off the C-Level of ShiroKaz?"

"C-Level." Connor chewed the word around for a second. "CEO. CFO… Huh. Y'know it's weird. I'd heard that phrase tossed around before, *c-level*, but I never got what it meant until right now." He locked the ammo belt into place, slapped Stub on the shoulder, and wheeled about to face me. "Thanks, Shin!"

"So, is that who we're here for?" I said, then corrected myself. "*You're* here for."

"I don't know. I just kill whoever pays Feikes tells me to kill."

The elevator slowed. NeOsaka hung in the air outside the window.

Connor grinned. "Whoever we find past this door, I guess."

If the grand lobby of the tower had been the *house* that was frozen in time, the massive vault beyond the elevator doors was where they'd stored all the furniture. As far as the eye could see, ancient wooden crates and trunks wrapped with black iron frames, sealed pots, and rolls and rolls of *tatami* were stacked one upon the other. There were endless shelves of nothing but teapots and teacups, decorative bowls, plates, trays, and boxes of *hashii*. Silk pillows and tightly bound futons. And art. Folding panels depicting natural phenomena lined the walls all around the vault. Dim lights glowed overhead, shining off the burnished gold backgrounds, so the waterfalls, bamboo leaves, and snowy mountaintops stood out all the more prominently. Heavy tapestries where colorful *Oni*, flying dragons, and samurai were stitched to life. Paper banners where *sumi-e kanji* had been captured in the moment of perfection.

In these, I recognized *Spirit. River.* And now, finally, the essence of *Prosperity* made sense. There must've been a billion yen worth of art hanging in ShiroKaz Tower's vault.

All these *things,* but no living thing.

"Connor," I called across the hall. The old raider dropped the porcelain doll he'd been inspecting—its delicate face shattering audibly—and turned to me. "There's nobody here."

"Not yet."

"Not *yet?*" I echoed back, throwing up my hands.

"Hey," he called back, emphasizing his words with the barrel of his gun stabbing in my direction. "You never asked for specifics. I know you just wanted to get this over with and then *get out.* Right? Feikes told me, like I told you before.

"Well," he went on, "as for specifics. We're supposed to find a red crate." He sauntered toward the middle of the vault, his attention drawn by something I couldn't see.

I looked back at the elevator. Stub had parked himself in front of it. Even at this distance, I could see his deep black eyes darting around. *Processing all the dust,* I mused. *Or calculating the value of all this... shit.*

This beautiful, beautiful shit. I dropped the plate I'd been examining onto a pile of other plates. It clattered loudly, and a piece chipped off and fell on the *tatami* floor. Then I saw what we'd been looking for. Against all the other wooden crates in my row was a smaller, red-lacquered box, no bigger than a mid-century laptop. I picked it up and set it before me.

Inside, there were charms. Shinto charms. *Omamoris.* Identical in every way to the one I'd carried for more than ten years. Tiny coins, with the Tokugawa hollyhock seal, and *kanji* on the other. I pulled one out by its silk ribbon and held it up. *Family.* Another. *Loyalty.* I pulled a third, a fourth, and read the *kanji* on the back of each. *Safety. Skill. Peace.* I held the handful in my left hand and reached into my own pocket with my right. I turned over my own *omamori,* rubbing at the back where the *kanji* had been scratched away.

"What are you?" I whispered to the charm. The last time I'd done that, I had been a desperate, stupid little orphan girl. The *omamori* hadn't answered me that time either.

"Asai, what you got there?"

Connor was behind me, frowning down at the box of charms. I almost felt guilty about having been caught with a few of them in my hand. Maybe embarrassed is the better word. "They're, uh," I stammered, wondering how much I should explain. *They're special to me. They're part of what I've been looking for, for so, so long.* "They're just little trinkets. Used to be, you could buy them at shrines."

"Oh." Connor plucked one out of my hand and held it up. "Yeah, I remember these. Like the old days." I watched him slide it into the same pocket of his tactical vest that held Stub's Bullet Time. "Check this out," he said, nodding toward the vault's center. "You're going to want to see this."

I tossed the charms back into the box and followed the old man. Behind me, I heard the cyborg zombie whir to life and follow us.

Whoever had stocked this vault with relics of the bygone world must have considered the katana at the center of it all their prized possession.

"Have you ever seen one so..." Connor waved his palm around, hoping perhaps to catch the right word fallen from heaven, "white?"

The weapon rested on a tall, polished stand that rose to my waist. Connor was right. The katana's case, its handle, its grip, its ceremonial *sageo* cord, all of it, every molecule of it, was a blinding, brilliant white. *Some trick of the light,* I thought, but no. Craning my neck, I expected some kind of spotlight overhead. Nothing but the dark ceiling up there.

Connor's blade slid easily through my suit, my shirt, my flesh. Almost before I felt it, I looked down and saw its tip jutting out through my gut. The red was already staining my clothes, splashing on the *tatami,* and a spray of it had misted onto the white sword before me, ruining its purity.

"Hurrkkhh," was all I could manage to say. I fell sideways. Connor kept his grip on the knife, so it slid out of me.

What thoughts would cross your mind at a time like that? What would be your last thoughts, stabbed in the back, as you were? Perhaps *fuck those guys!* Or maybe, *they betrayed me!* And then, as your senses shift toward the clarity of reason achieved only before death (it's true, let me tell you), you suddenly realize, *No. This was all my fault.*

I didn't think those thoughts, of course. Because this wasn't my first rodeo. Death and I were old pals, as I've said before. So I thought, *Ha-ha, fuckers.* And I focused on steadying my fingers as I reached into my jacket, even as I crawled away and smeared the *tatami* red, and then I went cold. Colder than outer space where there is no sun. And I heard a cold voice behind me.

"Feikes told me the client had said to get this little ditty off of you first."

Connor's boot wedged beneath me, lifted me over onto my back. I'd gone maybe six feet. My *omamori* charm dangled from his fingertips. "One of those specifics you didn't ask for. Sloppy work, Asai. Why oh why old Feikes let you into the Syndicateis just beyond me."

The blood was spurting from my mouth. I think was trying to say something. My hand was holding my guts in; my whole body felt slick and warm all over and cold, so cold, all on the inside. Keeping myself up on my elbows was starting to get harder. I shuddered, I closed my eyes; I reached for the *other side*.

And I felt nothing there.

Had I been using my charm for so long? How did I use to cross over without it? Had I ever actually *died* before without it?

Could I?

The shock of realization left me colder than the rapid blood loss. If I died here and now, without the *omamori* to hold on to, I would be left in *Yomi*, untended, forgotten, like so many of the other ghosts I'd seen. I'd be one of them, the aimless dead. I could. I could really die here and never come back.

I hadn't heard Stub approach, what for the ringing in my ears. He stood beside Connor, his weaponized arm lowering dramatically down, like in slo-mo.

As I waited for the final shot, I saw that between them, behind them, smoke was rising from the white sword. It was my blood, evaporating like water on coals. The smoke was purple. I felt something thud through the floor, and the smoke wafted, some invisible breath puffing at it. Another thud, and all the lacquerware in the vault clattered. Another, like a powerful footstep, and the crates rattled; some crashed to the floor. Shelves toppled over. The smoke rose, it pulsed, it swirled around in a gathering vortex.

"No," I sobbed. "Please, no."

If Connor felt the thudding, too, he wasn't disturbed by it. The old man mistook my plea as a cry for his mercy. "I'm sorry, Shinjiro Asai," he said through the fake fucking *Hanma*-mask grin that was his face. "Feikes has given you enough second chances."

There was a bang, but not the kind made by bullets. It was the thunder. It was the lightning that splits the tree. The tearing of the fabric that divides our world from the other. It was *Yomi*, and it was NeOsaka, crashing into one another.

From the swirling cloud of purple smoke, the first *Oni* materialized. It was a hulking brute, an ogre ten feet tall, its skin the orange of firelight, its bug-eyes spinning about maddeningly, its incisors as long and deadly as daggers.

Connor turned and he saw it.

"The fuck—"

The *Oni*'s fist slammed into the old man's chest, sending him flying over rows of relics to crash against a shelf. The monster roared. The sound of gunfire joined it. Rapid shots resonated in the air, popping like a howitzer from the weapon at the end of Stub's arm. The best ammunition Syndicate yen could buy squelched into the *Oni*'s skin and exploded with bright flashes, illuminating the layers of flesh and veins in its body like bombs underwater.

It staggered back, howling in agony, or rage, I couldn't tell. If it hadn't been for the neon-yellow drug slicking the seams of the cyber zombie's brain, the *Oni* would have torn him limb from metal limb.

The monster went silent, its body still, and the gunfire ceased. But still, the footsteps rattled all the world. Without a moment's hesitation, Stub abandoned the thing, leaped over me, and tore through the vault to Connor's side.

My blood seeped out, more and more, but I no longer felt cold. I felt a warmth like hypothermia that comes when the cold of death subsides. The heat radiated from the center of the storm raging over the white sword. It spread across my shoulders and down my arms, and I felt the weakness flood away. It filled my legs, and I found myself rising.

But where the fuck was I going to go?

The purple smoke spread wider. The vortex swirling overhead flattened out and enveloped the whole vault. The wind pitched over everything that wasn't heavy enough to stay grounded. It tore the priceless tapestries from the walls and shredded the perfect papers. Purple fire ate through *Loyalty* and *Family* and all that other shit. A shriek from the other world split the air, and twin glowing ghost dragons snaked through the rift above the white sword, one blue, one green. Separate, but twisting as one. Their heads were massive, their forms covered in bony spines and wispy fur. They had no bodies to speak of, just long tubes like snakes, winding like streamers slithering in the air.

The footsteps crashed closer and closer, *whump, whump, whump,* the noise now mingled with a metallic jingling.

The dragons rushed just over my head, and I felt the wind behind them tug at my hair. They went straight for Stub and Connor, the one helping the other back onto his feet. The two of them fanned out, for all I know, and engaged the beasts. I ignored the demons like they had ignored me. Something at the center of the storm held my attention. Something I *needed.* It was a hand, or the outline of one. Palm up. The hand was beckoning to me. There was something *it* needed.

The *Oni* on the ground stirred as I stepped by. It huffed several ragged breaths, guffawing like a hyena, and kicked itself up. It crashed away through the vault behind me, into the rattling gunfire and shrieks splitting the air, its wounds entirely forgotten.

I was nearly at the center when the third and final demon emerged.

It came with the certainty of my curse. The Samurai. Seven feet tall. Ancient splint mail. Every piece accounted for. No flesh. No body. The shell. My own personal nightmare. The purple smoke streamed from the empty helmet. I crumpled into a ball at its armored feet, whimpering like the little girl I used to be, and still really was.

"*Ie*," I recited. "*Ie*, no, please."

The samurai battered me aside and strode forward.

I don't kill people. That's what I'd told Connor. That's what I'd told myself for years and years. But I was a liar. A fucking liar.

I killed those orphan boys.

And now I was going to kill Connor and Stub and the whole fucking world if I could. I would revel in the ash. There was nothing I could do. They were behind me. The bullies, the monsters, the Syndicate. They were all in my past, yet here they were also in my present. I could never escape from what I'd done or who it had made me. I scrambled over onto my hands and knees and looked up. The green and blue dragons' snake bodies had wrapped around Stub, squeezing him, while the *Oni* pulverized the cyborg's bald head with his fists, laughing maniacally. I watched in horror as one final punch blasted Stub's head clean off his shoulders, releasing a splash of blood.

And Connor. Well, the samurai had found Connor. The bursts from the old man's trusty colt rang out against the armor plates. Connor spent his whole mag and dove aside as the monster swiped at him, smashing crates into splinters. The old man recovered surprisingly fast, had his knife out, and jabbed it into the seam between the monster's armor plates, where you'd think a gap should be. But there was none. The samurai was completely sealed, impenetrable, invincible. And it did not need a sword to be a master of its battlefield, countering Connor's attack by bending its knees, lowering its center of gravity, and rolling sideways and back directly onto him, pressing a gut-wrenching scream out of his lungs, crushing him with its jiu-jitsu recovery technique. Connor just lay there, a broken sack of bones and blood. He couldn't get up. Back on its feet, the samurai scooped him up like he was no more than a flopping, dying fish, then it raised Connor's body over its head.

I relived the horrid truth. The one I'd tried to put behind me. The one I'd always tried to look past. *I'd wanted that boy dead. I wanted him torn, limb from limb.* And as though the memory had given the samurai permission, I watched as it pulled. I listened with the memory of glee flooding my heart as the bones popped and the scream of the old man was drowned in the wet red rising from his bursting lungs.

So why did I scream, "*NOOOO!*" at the top of my lungs?

Why did the samurai listen then, but not the time before? I watched the empty armor stop pulling the man apart. But it was too late. Connor's limp body slapped the floor. The monster turned about to regard me—this blood-soaked wreck of a girl—with the empty eyes of the hollow *kabuto.*

"*FUCK YOU!!!*" I screamed.

Honestly, what else was I supposed to say?

"*I'LL FUCKING KILL YOU FOR WHAT YOU MADE ME!!!*"

That was more like it.

I spun about, looking for anything I could use as a weapon. That's when I found the sword, not more than ten feet from me, and that's when I saw the hand offering to help me up, it seemed, floating in the purple storm just above it. The katana and the tear between worlds were both so blindingly white.

I reached for the grip.

But the hand snatched my wrist before I could touch it, dragging me forward.

And my whole world sank into white.

SEVEN

YOU'VE DREAMED OF FALLING. YOU REMEMBER WELL THAT jolt, forward, and downward. And later, the jolt upright, the chill down your spine. But do you remember the span of feeling in between?

No. You don't, do you?

That's what this felt like.

Suspension in mid-air. Mid-dream. The panic and fear as you hurtle through space at dangerous speeds. The certainty of your own doom. And yet the awareness that relief will come, because it's all just a dream, and once you get close, you'll wake up and it will all be fine.

And so it was: I was caught. Right there.

The whiteness held me. Like light, burning. Like smoke, choking. The white world seared into my eyes and ran down my throat. It bleached me. It purged me. The pain never ended.

Until suddenly, it did.

I felt a solidness under my hands. I pushed against it, and it held me up. I stood and looked around. A white world, as far as the eye could see, in every direction.

"Okay," I breathed, and I heard my own voice only in the vibration of my ears. The sound shot out and touched nothing.

I spun about, madly. Have you ever heard of an anechoic chamber? A soundproof room. They say you'll lose your mind, surrounded by the absence of sound. Here, though, in the whiteness, there was an absence of more than that. Here there was no *form*.

"I know you."

Where's the voice coming from?

I reeled round and round. I looked up, down, inside my own bloodstained jacket, scrabbling instinctively for my *omamori*. Nothing.

"Where are you?" I screamed.

"Here," it said, and this time I felt it was behind me. I turned slowly.

And an abyssal black shape hung in the whiteness. It was tall, with a curved top and a flat bottom, like a door in the space before me, maybe five meters away, maybe five million. All sense of distance here was meaningless. I reached for it anyway, despite everything in me that was telling me to turn and run and not look back.

The black shape shifted, up and back, and a pale face parted the lengths of stick-straight black hair right down the middle, smoothly, like a hand parts a sheet of falling water. A man's face. Handsome. With a jaw and brow so angular it could cut through the world. His eyes were white as snow, white as paper, white as the threads of a spider's silk—beautiful, pure, except for the gray veins corrupting them. Those eyes bore into me.

"Where am I?"

The man said nothing. A pair of pale hands floated into view from his frame as he straightened. He held them rigid at his sides. "You're here. With me."

"Okay..." I swallowed, discovering that I was weirdly hungry, more than frightened. "Who are you?"

"A man?" He cocked his head, tipping his two strands of black hair unevenly. "A body? A ghost? A weapon? A spirit?"

"Yeah. Well, *you* tell *me.*"

This is so fucking weird.

"A shadow," he said decisively after what seemed like a very long moment.

"What's your name?"

He looked away, I think. I could see a slight shift in the gray splotches of his eyes, only for a moment. Then he looked back at me. "How do you know that it is not our shadows … that cast … our bodies?"

"I, uh…" I took a deep breath, even though it wasn't air exactly, then coughed. "I haven't figured that one out quite yet."

"What do you want?"

"I…"

What the fuck does he mean? Want like now? Right now? I want to eat. Later? I want to get out.

"For all your time," he clarified as if he could hear my thoughts. "That which you have spent already, lost. And that which you have yet to spend, wandering."

I drew a complete … fucking … blank.

Unsurprising, really, given the environment.

What do I want? The question surfaced again and again. The moment and my eyes drifted across the white expanse, as if they'd suddenly find a billboard and a cartoony arrow pointing to the answer.

"Escape," the man suggested.

"Sure," I said. "Let's start there. A way out." I flourished my right hand dramatically, just to be asinine. And I felt the weight of something in my grip.

I turned the white katana over. The blade's edge was barely visible in the white emptiness. I tried to drop it, but my fingers were locked. Instinctively, I reached out with my left hand, but I found the sword's case gripped there. "The fuck?"

"You want escape," the man insisted, his eyes widening.

My hand lifted the sword, beyond my control.

"Hold on," I stammered.

My wrist spun it around, nestling the tip of the blade into my navel.

"So escape," he commanded.

"Wait!"

The blade sank deep into my body. All the white world was an echo of my screams. I was powerless. No will of my own. I dropped to my knees, and my hand dragged the sword sideways, slicing my belly open wide. I watched my blood gush and fall forever into the white nothing below, bits of my wet severed guts being pulled by what passed for gravity. There was no bottom to this place, yet the red gathered, the smoldering red of unquenchable fury. It burned through the floating emptiness, swallowed it bit by bit, like fire on paper. And I felt the pain, worse pain than I had ever known. No bullet, no bat, no broken bottle, no other blade had ever hurt me like the perfect white blade hurt me then. All senses but the pain fell away. My sight was drowned in the never-ending red, searing through my eyes and cooking the back pan of my skull. I screamed through it all, but there was no sound. Not even a vibration in my throat to reassure me of my own existence.

I had sense enough to realize only one more thing before I faded completely: In here, by the shadow-man's whim, I could truly die. Forever.

On the other side of the pain, I felt release. I hovered on the edge. The man's voice merged with my own thoughts.

"Escape," he said again.

It's what I've really wanted.

"For so long," he said.

All along.

"For your entire, short life."

He stood tall before me, bowed, his cascade of perfect black hair dipping low, his dead eyes level with mine. I could see. I could feel his will folding over my hand, dragging the blade back the other way, slicing more of my guts away. I choked on the blood rushing up my throat and down my chest. I drowned in the red.

"And now you have it," he said.

And now I have it, I admitted silently.

"Tell me. Is *this* the escape you wanted?"

The shadow's will twisted my wrist, which twisted the white blade. I cried out in agony. The new burst of pain brought a new realization: This was what awaited me when I truly died; this was my underworld nightmare, my hell.

Because it's what I deserve. For what I did. For what I am.

"So… It is punishment you want," the man observed, reading my mind. "Torment. Not escape."

He turned about, the strands of black hair whipping about, and he paced away, into a spreading portal of white. It was blinding, sending the red away. The outline of his jet-black hair vanished.

And just like that, the sword vanished too, all the pain with it. My hands were empty. My wounds were sealed. I was back in control of my own body, if a *body* in this place was what I was.

"Wait," I cried out into the nothingness, rising to my feet, reeling around again, hoping to catch a glimpse of him. "Tell me who you are!"

"I am the blade," his voice said behind me. I spun around to face him. He cradled the white katana, sheathed now, in his hands. He bowed and offered it up to me. "And you will be the body."

"Look," I said, holding my hands up. "I must not be very smart about all this. I'm having trouble seeing what this is all about. Wait, hold on. Let's start with… Just tell me your name."

The shadow-man looked up, his eyes shifting again, searching his mind, an expression of worry creased his perfect features. "I … do not … remember."

And then, the gray threads in his eyes flushed with an otherworldly red. "You!" He stepped forward menacingly, and I stumbled backward, but it did me no good. "You unleashed all that was left of me. My name. My purpose. My memories. My very soul. When you reached for me, you let them all go free."

The Oni. *The twin dragons.*

The Samurai.

His pale hand shot out and gripped my shoulder, cracking the bones, and grinding the muscles into paste. Threads of fire laced through me.

"Ahh! Fuck!"

My legs gave out and I kneeled before him.

"You will find them."

Sweat beaded on my forehead. Tears streamed down my face. His fingers were the deepest, hardest rock under the mountain, and against them, my flesh was the softest pile of ash.

"You will retrieve them. Or you will stay here. With me. Forever."

So what choice do I really have?

In this white world, the black-haired man knew my every thought, and so he heard my assent.

"No choice."

He let go.

"You are dead," he went on. "And alive. You have *always* been caught between, and stumbling. Falling. From one world to the other. But now, I will be your balance."

I kneaded my shoulder, felt the mush of bone and muscle hardening, snapping back into place. The pain subsided. The shadow-man stood over me, holding out the katana to me once more. I rose. And this time I accepted it. He was right. This place, this vast emptiness, the lack of space and time, the stagnation of sense, it was all just like crossing between the living, waking world and the underworld. As I held the sword and turned it over in my hands, I felt everything flowing back into me, righting itself.

"Now," he said, turning about to gaze as the formless whiteness above us began to swirl and become a sky. The dark of night crept in, and the outline of tiers upon tiers of *haka* stones began to encircle us. "They are coming."

EIGHT

TIME SURGED FORWARD. ALL THE WHITE RECEDED. IN AN instant, the full moon raced skyward, then slowed to a crawl, and finally hung still over the bay, its bright reflection shimmering in the water of the flooded graveyard below.

Home, I realized. *I'm home.*

I turned about, feeling the presence of the black-haired ghost just over my shoulder, but there was no one there. Just a *haka* stone with a scratched-out family name, bearing the statue of a katana in a carved stone stand. The very one where I'd met the old ghost last night. I involuntarily flexed my own hands, shuddering at the rush of cold bay wind sweeping suddenly around the graveyard, and I realized something was in my grip.

The white katana.

My eyes drifted up to the statue. "What," I murmured, "is going on…?"

I looked all around the tiers, above and below, thinking now was the moment in my story when some wise old dude wandered in, threw back his hood, and offered to take the poor lost moron in, keep her warm, feed her, and impart upon her the wisdom of eons.

Nope. Not so lucky.

I mentally retraced my steps, thinking I'd soon figure out where I was supposed to be, and then I felt panic close around my throat.

"Ben!"

I dashed down the row of *haka* stones and bounded up the central staircase three steps at a time. In my mind, I played out the scenario: I'd dart through the vestibule of my squatter's tenement, throw open the door, and Ben would be there in his wheelchair with a bag of nori-chips and a cup of *nihon-cha*. "Shin!" he'd say. "W-w-where you been, man?"

I made it as far as the street dividing my place from the graveyard when the rocket's smoke trail zoomed past my head and blew the ground floor to ruin. The shockwave lifted me off my feet and sent me reeling back through the graveyard gates. The whole world was smoke and fire and bits of glass and concrete. Then my building sagged like a mouth too tired to smile, caved in at the center, and slid into the street.

I rolled over, my skull packed with cotton, dampening every sound and sensation. My first instinct was to put out the little fires on my suit. I stood up and shouted through the haze. *"BENNN!!"* What the fuck—did I expect him to just wheel out of there? So stupid.

Something inside me whispered *turn*, so I turned, and the next rocket was spiraling in, this time with a more precise flight path. Something in me compelled my hand forward. Something purple wrapped around the rocket's body and turned it away. It zoomed down the sidestreet and made a blooming red flower of another derelict building. All of this happened in a single breath. Another shockwave, another shower of flaming ruin, but I stood rooted, unflinching, immovable. Furious.

They're here.

The voice of the black-haired shadow whispered in my mind.

Dark shapes detached themselves from the taller buildings that loomed to either side of the graveyard entrance, somersaulting mid-air and landing silently on shock-absorbing cyberlimbs. Four of the bastards in all. Three of them in black, form-fitting Kevlar armor plates, submachine guns strapped on every thigh, grenades and mags belted at their waists. Sleek visors where tiny green lights blinked, concealing their faces. There were no corporate insignias.

Tinmen. True cyborgs.

These things went tens of millions of Yen beyond InariSec and other corporate-funded warriors. These were the real deal.

And the fourth tinman among them was the realest, dealest motherfucker of them all. He—or maybe *it*, whatever—strode forward. His cybernetic legs were triple-jointed. The slopes of his arms were unnaturally angular, studded with mini-pistons and laced with circuitry, and his slender metal fingers ended in razor-sharp claws. The sides of this one's visors rose up behind his head like two devil horns. And a blue-green cyan-light pulsed from the sharp, black plate where his heart probably used to be, spreading out rhythmically across all the seams.

The cyan ninja stopped about ten feet away from me and drew the only weapon he had from over his shoulder, a matte black katana designed with the same kind of angular aesthetic as the rest of his body. It came out with a scraping *sshhhrrrh* that made me cringe. He pointed it at me and I nearly pissed myself, but by some miracle, the initial cringe was the most he got out of me.

"Give it to me."

The digitized accent sounded Russian. *Like a Russian trapped in a tin can.* I almost laughed at how ludicrous this all was.

"You just killed my fucking friend," I pointed out, deciding—somehow cool-headedly, which was not my norm at times like these—that I would process that later. "So no. I'm not giving you shit. Besides, yours looks a lot cooler." I gestured with the sheathed white sword at his naked black one.

"But maybe I'm willing to trade," I conceded.

"You cannot trade what is not yours."

The three other ninja tinmen fanned out, surrounding me.

"All right. Let's say I consider your offer. Do I just lay it on the ground here? Is that fine?" Somehow I didn't think there was an escape from this. Not even a sense of humor could get me out of this one. If I'd learned one thing during my time in the white emptiness, it was that there would never be an escape for me. Not from anything.

"You're not InariSec," I pointed out, just as the tinmen finished making me the center of their four-pointed star. "Who are you?"

Correction: nearly the center, as it wouldn't make for a very efficient crossfire if the dudes shot straight through me and hit each other. The rain of bullets was sudden, but not entirely unexpected. They lit me up, spending perhaps two hundred rounds between the three of them, filling the abandoned zone with reverberating, rolling thunder.

A wisp of purple smoke rose from around me and joined with the soft breeze. Not a single bullet had hit me.

I double-checked. I stood there, dumbstruck. I patted myself down. Even my navy suit was fine, if by "fine" you only account the previous damage and bloodstains Connor's knife left it with. The only real damage was to my damn eardrums. Again.

"The sword," the cyan ninja barked, but it wasn't exactly a demand. There was a kind of reverence, unmistakable even in his metallic voice. "It is not yours."

"All the same," I said, "you still can't have it."

They came at me, the three slave-bodies following the digital signal funneled to their synthetic brains from their master. I felt compelled to draw the sword, and their blades locked with mine, over and over. My body twisted this way and that, my arms flailing around, catching their weapons with the white katana or its white case and turning them away. I couldn't tell you how I felt their strikes coming. I just did. Something was telling me.

I sensed an opening and flicked my wrist, sending the sword's edge out and then up. One of the tinmen's arms flew away, still gripping his weapon, electric sparks splashing onto the pavement like blood. He tried to disengage, but I spun about, bringing my blade high across his neck, splitting the molecules of his armor, and taking his head from his shoulders.

The other two got the retreat signal and made it out of my killing range.

Smart, I thought, a gleeful smile spreading over my dumb face. I was panting, sweating, pulsing with adrenaline, ready for the next round. And absolutely oblivious to how I'd done *any* of that elegant samurai shit.

"Who are you?" The lead ninja paced forward, the motors whirring in his weird legs.

"Honestly," I said, straightening. "I don't know anymore."

I didn't register the sonic boom until after the buildup in his legs had brought him to me, and by then his claws had already closed around my neck, and I was hurtling through the air, uncontrollably, for what felt like a minute, then crashing into a crowd of *haka* stones halfway down the bowl-shaped graveyard, the impact toppling them like dominoes. A normal human body would have been mashed into paste when hurled with such force into slabs of stone, and although I felt all the pain you could imagine from it, I was made of death itself. I still have no idea if that's true, but it sounds accurate.

"Uuuugghh," I groaned, rising to my feet, covered in the gray dust of the dead's memorial stones. I looked at the scar my tumbling body had left across six tiers. How many months, or years, had I spent tending those graves? All of it undone in a split second. Why I thought about that and not the downward trajectory of the cyan tinman ninja shooting out from between the sakura trees, I don't quite know.

But there he was, landing on top of me in the crater I'd made. I brought my sword up just in time to meet his. The *clang* of it spilled out over the flat water of the bay. The ninja's bulk fell away, then came forward again, lightning-fast, triple-jointed heel leading the way, sinking into my hip, folding me over and sending me away again, farther down the tiers, crashing into yet another set of *haka*.

How the hell was I surviving any of this?

I will sustain you, the black-haired shadow had told me. And that's when I knew: *He* was doing all this. I was just his puppet, and his pale, slender hand was firmly up my—

The matte black blade came in again, dividing the *haka* stone I'd slumped against in perfect halves just as I rolled away. The stones were like hands, clapping his sword in place for just an instant longer than the cyborg had calculated, and I capitalized on it, lashing out with my own upward swipe. The white katana tore into the side of his forearm, nicking off a feather-sized piece of his armor, revealing a gel board of blue-green circuitry beneath. I brought the blade back down, but it hung there, mid-air, grasped in the hardened fist that rose impossibly fast to meet it. The cyan seams in his armor pulsed faster and faster, and a haze of the same color was rising from all around his body. The pistons all down his arm popped open and hissed angrily like boiling tea kettles, spewing jets of cyan smoke.

The clouds of his energy mingled with the purple ones rising from my body. I strained, harder and harder, trying to force the blade down, or at least away, maybe slicing his goddamn hand open, but the grip was unyielding. The ninja wrenched his sword free and jammed it downward, straight into my heart.

It was the pain of dying—really dying—all over again. Like what I'd felt at the shadow-man's hand. This tinman fucker could also kill me. Really kill me. There would be no coming back. I was done.

I was … relieved.

I felt myself fighting to let go. *Just let me give up*, I told the black-haired shadow. My body went slack. My eyes fluttered.

But not my hands. The sword, the case. Something in me would not let go.

Never. His voice.

And then my own voice.

NEVER!!!

So … fuck it. What choice did I have?

My whole body tensed with life. I screamed in the motherfucker's black-visored face, bloody red spittle clashing with the blinking blue-green lights. The purple smoke of my own personal underworld raged all around us. I felt the strength of *Yomi* flooding back into my limbs. I'd drag the fucker down and leave him there for all eternity. I was the Lord of the Dead. He was a worm. An eyeless grub beneath my feet.

Could he not see? I was the Fucking Dragon.

Or so I thought.

Turned out he was just as stubborn as me. And so we stayed locked there, for what felt like eternity, caught in the central twisting vortex of blue-green and purple typhoons, colliding, merging, sending over more and more heavy *haka* stones like they were papers fluttering in the wind.

And a shot rang out, incredibly loud, the sound of it catching up less than a second after its effect. The cyborg's chest had already exploded in a shower of sparks and gel-cased circuitry, just to the side of his pulsing cyan heart. His metallic voice grated with something like pain, but probably just annoyance. His hand lost the strength to hold my sword, and he battered it away. He leaped backward incredibly far, almost back to the top of the graveyard, pulling his black sword out of my chest as he went.

Another shot, from somewhere, and the *haka* stone he'd been standing by exploded. But he was already gone.

All the otherwordly vapors dissipated. I tried to peer all around, at the rooftops to either side of the bay, across the bay itself, but only then did I realize my vision was going black. Only then did I remember—*oh yeah! I just got stabbed in the heart.*

Might be a problem, that.

I fell to my knees.

And into the oblivion of unconsciousness.

NINE

" **H** OW DO YOU WANT THIS HANDLED?"

"Test her."

Voices.

"To what end?"

"The only end. Power."

Voices. The first one ... feminine. The other...

"Do we really need her?"

The other voice didn't answer, leaving me a gap in time to feel in the dark for a few puzzle pieces here: *Not dead. Eyes closed. Cold. Laying down.*

"A necessary evil," the other voice finally answered. It was inhuman. Hollow. Garbled as if by some filter program. "She is waking."

My eyelids fluttered. My hand slid up, dragged finger by finger, against my hip and onto my bare belly. My other hand rose over my pubic mound. The shock of my nakedness snapped my eyes open, and a searing white light flooded my vision. A vision of white emptiness flashed in my mind, and the chilling fear of it prickled my skin. I flinched away and blinked. There was darkness all around. The light was artificial, shining down. I was on an operating table. Rows of seating ringed all around. A few rows back, I could just make out a brighter silhouette against the shadows. And beside her, something glowing. A floating, three-dimensional hardlight screen. A digital sigil.

A line on the screen jumped and wavered as the inhuman voice came back. "See to our guest." It was only just as the screen's light winked out did I realize the sigil had been shaped like a horned dragon's head.

There was a moment of stillness. Then a sigh.

I covered my breasts with one forearm and cupped a hand over my crotch.

"Hello," I croaked stupidly into the shadows. My throat was dry, and I was ravishingly hungry. I tried to sit up.

"Don't," the feminine voice commanded. "Lie still. There's one final test."

Test her, the screen had said.

"Wait, hang on, where—"

I saw the sudden pulse of a red laser just on the inside of my elbow, like a sniper was taking a bead from the other side of the operating hall. I reflexively turned aside, but it was only a med-bot stabbing a needle into me, guided by the precision of the laser on my flesh.

"Hey! What the—*aarrgghh!!*"

A half pint of my blood rushed through the needle and into a vial on the med-bot's side.

"Ow! The fuck?!"

The needle snapped back, and the med-bot was on its way, fading into the shadows.

"Hey," I called out, turning again.

The silhouette had risen from her seat and was now pacing with dramatic slowness down her row to the center aisle.

"What the fuck was that?"

"A DNA test," she said flatly.

"Oh shit," I said. I don't know why that freaked me out so bad, honestly. There were about twelve thousand ways the Syndicate took care of wiping all of its cells' records. Data jacking, hacking, wipes, raiding data cube vaults, or just good old-fashioned executive blackmail and corporate payoffs. Last I knew, Feikes had already settled the latest charges on my behalf a month ago, just before the Inari job.

"Oh shit," I said again, much louder now. "You're Inari, aren't you?"

I sat up all the way, discovering I wasn't tied down. *Ha! Your first mistake, bitch!* But this small triumph died in less than a second. I was overcome with an ache that locked up my shoulders and hit me in the lungs like a boxer. My hand fell away from my tits and ran over my sternum. Shiny staples crisscrossed the angry, red line where the tinman's sword had stabbed into my heart. The wound severed the *kasagi* beam of my torii gate tattoo clean in half. A yellow-purple bruise spread over all the rest of me, as if it was a portal beyond the torii's pillars.

My breath caught in my ragged throat, but I managed one last "Sshhiiiit-t-t" as I slid sideways off the operating table and held myself against it.

"No, Shinjiro Asai," the woman said, approaching my side now, looking down at me. And I mean *looking down*, as if she saw a piece of shit to step around on the sidewalk, the disgust in her green eyes more visible than the noontime sun on a cloudless day. "I do not represent Inari Data Corporation. Nothing *quite* that powerful, I'm afraid." Her teeth bit off every word with disdain, or so I thought I heard.

It didn't matter what corp she worked for or what she wanted from me. I wanted out, right away. The last thing I'd known before being attacked by a death squad of ninja tinmen was my best friend being blown to bits along with all my worldly possessions, my home. I had to get back to see what happened, to find Ben, or what was left of him, if

I could. I looked up at the woman, thinking maybe I'd just bull rush her, naked as I may be, and dart through whatever door I could find.

But then, I couldn't take my eyes off her. I felt a flicker of warmth spread in my stomach.

I saw her then, standing over me. Really saw her. Her face, hovering just outside the bright cone of light. She was beyond gorgeous. Wavy blonde hair done up in a bun, tousled locks twisted around an emerald brooch that matched her eyes. The adornment itself held in the wildness of those thick locks with the orderly, rigid veneer of business. I traced the loose lines of golden hair down, past her ears, falling in wisps beside her neck. Perfect skin the color of creamy mocha. Full, round lips.

"Got any clothes?" I asked, suddenly more aware of how naked I was. Under this light, there was no way she wasn't seeing me blush. "For me, I mean," I added, idiotically. I looked away, intimidated by the literal and symbolic differences in our positions, but mostly because I somehow couldn't stare at those beautiful emerald-green eyes for long.

She nodded at a table near my head, where my navy suit—my *second* best suit, you'll remember—was folded neatly atop my semi-brogues. She turned away to give me a little privacy, or more likely because she'd seen enough of my scarred skin. As far as my self-image goes, I have a decent shape where it all counts, but all the edges are worn. Understandably why I'd gotten her read on me. If I'd been her, I'd also have seen a piece of shit to be avoided. So I covered myself as quick as I could, buttoning down the clean gray shirt my gracious host had provided. I winced at the pain in my chest, sucking in a sharp breath as I sank my legs into the trousers and arms through the sleeves of my jacket.

"Are you decent?" she finally asked, turning about anyway, not bothering to wait for an answer.

"I've met a few girls who seemed to think so."

"Oh my," she said slowly.

I coughed lightly and smirked. I wanted to ask her about Ben Roy Doon, about the apartment block across from the graveyard, but I stopped myself. If she knew he was dead, then what difference would it make besides being a knife in my heart all over again? And if she didn't know him, or know that he had been there, then I'd be dragging him into whatever business she was on about. So I took a different approach.

"You know my name, but I don't know yours."

"Cayenne," she offered. Then, "DeLeon."

"Cayenne DeLeon." *Such a pretty name.* I wanted to say it again, but remembered her hairdo. All business. Also, I admired the cut of her herringbone suit. We were here indeed for business. "Well, uh, if you're not InariCorp, then…"

"I work for Shiromatsu-Kazama," she said, folding her arms.

"Ohhh," I said slowly. Then I said it all over again, a little quieter. "Ohhhhh."

"Indeed." She folded her arms and drummed her fingers at her elbow, immaculately pedicured emerald acrylic nails and all. She glanced at the operating table beside me. "*This* is your second visit to our tower within the past twenty-four hours."

Have you ever had so many things to ask that it turns out you can't think to ask any of them? I lowered my head, letting my one long lock of black hair pass over my eye, hiding behind it, feeling at a total loss for what to say. "Ahh," I finally muttered, brushing the back of my neck. "Sorry?"

"Oh please, Asai-san. We're far beyond the stage for apology."

"So, what stage are we on now?"

"Indemnity."

"I'm afraid English is only my second language…"

"*Shōkan,*" she said in stunningly fluent Japanese. Atonement. "You stole from us."

"It was kind of … forced upon me."

"You destroyed our collection of historical artifacts. Treasures that simply can not ever be replaced."

"Hey, it was Connor that broke that doll's face."

Cayenne was having none of my shit. She folded her arms. "Was that the name of the … body parts we found scattered about the vault?" I was impressed with how well she held herself together.

I cleared my throat, lapsing back into serious-Shin. "Yes. Him and his pet cyborg."

"Just the three of you?"

My eyes fell to the floor. A heavy weight sagged in my damaged heart. I pictured the rocket coming out of nowhere, blowing my home to bits. And inside… *Ben.*

"You already know," I answered after a long silence. Cayenne just watched me. I wasn't sure what she must have been thinking of me then, if she'd known about Ben on the other end of our comms, about our botched job only a few hours prior, about our mutual desire to be done with the Syndicate. Well, I guess Ben was done now. But the thought of it gave me no peace. I wanted to be done with ShiroKaz, and although she was the most beautiful woman I'd ever lain my violet eyes on, I was starting to wish I could be done with Cayenne, too.

But she certainly wasn't done with me. "Tell me your role here, Asai-san. Explain, please, how this '*Connor and his pet cyborg*' died so gruesomely. And, for all intents and purposes, explain how it is you emerged without a scratch on you." She eyed me up and down. "A *new* scratch, that is."

It wasn't the first time someone had asked how I escaped certain fatal situations physically unchanged, let me tell you. It also wasn't the first time I deflected the question and focused on something else.

"I did *not* kill them!" I took a step forward, jabbing my finger at her. But even as I'd said the words, I wasn't entirely sure they were true. I pictured the empty samurai armor in the purple mist, lifting Connor by the ankle. "Whatever you're thinking, you got the wrong idea."

Cayenne slapped my hand away sharply. "You cannot even *guess* at my ideas. We know what really happened there. We know what you really are." She waved a hand and the hardlight screen came to life between us. On full display: my rap sheets with every agency that had at some time or another passed itself off as government authority emerging from the cinders of the old world order, promising unity but delivering only police states, bought out by corps, one after another. The official records of my life on the grid ticked by right alongside all the Syndicate's details of my raids, my whereabouts, my aliases, my activities. Very difficult information to come by. Then, working backward, my history prior to all that. The gangs I ran with. The people I hurt, and some that hurt me back, and I back again. And as Cayenne scrolled through it all with her finger, every version of my bruised, sullen, deadbeat mug shot glared out at us both from either side of the translucent screen.

"We know about your time at the Tenjin facility. We know about Feikes. We know about the raids on Inari, A-Matter, and all the others, everything you did for and against corporations throughout NeOsaka. And before that, we know about the shrine, and the *omamori*. Your charm. We know what it does. We know what *you* do." She folded her arms again, and the screen winked out. Her eyes narrowed. "We know that *Shinjiro*—a male's name—was assigned to you at the orphanage. A glitch, perhaps, easily corrected, had there been any adult operators around to correct it. But otherwise, so definitive of the cold, careless methods of being raised quite literally in Tenjin's automated childcare system. And why you were never transferred after 2066, aged nine... Well, even with all we know about you, we still don't know who you *really* are. Do we?"

Only a few minutes ago, despite waking up naked in an unknown place, I'd been thinking how much I rather liked being there with Cayenne. Everything so clean and sterile and fresh. And pretty. But I have this thing for getting as far away as possible from anyone who reminds me what it was like growing up in a Tenjin Media Corp's Personnel Farm. The only thing stopping me from shoving Cayenne out of my way and stomping through the doors of ShiroKaz Tower right then and there was the same thing that stopped me every time. The same question I always asked myself.

Where else can I go?

So this time I relented.

"I don't know, either."

That got me a curious, arched eyebrow. And a smirk, and my heart fluttered all over again. I could perhaps grow to like the whole *admission* thing. I smirked back, and the silence stretched a bit before I realized she was allowing me a turn to ask something.

"Do you know who blew up my place?"

Cayenne swiped the air, and the hardlight readouts of my life were replaced with the face of a man.

"Zercos," she said.

"What?"

"His name is—*was*—Vladislav Zercos." She waved her hand again, and all the screens hiding in the shadows overhead came to life. Still images, motion footage, even satellite feeds, showing all the zoomed-in, sped-up highlights from my battle with the four tinman drones, my flight and my crash-landing, the utter destruction my flailing body caused on the one place I felt at peace.

"Holy fucking shit," I said as I saw just how widespread our twisting purple and cyan energy clouds had become. It rose like a tower in the sky, a tornado that churned the smoking, flaming bits of the derelict neighborhood into a frenzy. And then came the thunderclap, deafening even on the audio stream. The sniper shot fired from the same angle as one of the cameras, blew through the cyborg's chest and ended our fight summarily. The damage was far worse than I could've known. Zercos should've been destroyed, but his cyan-colored spirit kept him anchored to life, or at least to the matte-black cyborg frame.

"You shot him" is what I said.

You saved me, is what I meant.

"Not *me* precisely." Cayenne frowned at the lock of blonde hair she was twisting absent-mindedly. While I'd been watching the feeds, reliving the pain and confusion of my fight with the tinmen, her shell had iced over once again. I could hear it in her voice. But I didn't care, not anymore. My eyes were glued to the screens. "Besides, it wasn't enough." I saw myself fall over, unconscious or dead, while Zercos—even with a gaping fucking hole in his chest—back flipped incredibly high and fast, arcing over the second thunderous shot like an Olympic high jumper. The round struck another part of the graveyard, pulverizing more *haka* into shrapnel. Zercos landed somewhere in the dust storm and vanished.

"Who is he?"

"Security," she said. "ShiroKaz Security."

I wheeled on her. "You mean he *works* for you?"

"*Worked* for us. Yes. But there was an incident. Or accident. The records are not clear. Decades ago. And Zercos disappeared." She waved her hand again (further convincing me that she must have a comlink embedded in her forearm), and the screens changed to other footage. The highlight reel of Zercos's past ops. I saw him and his tinmen running straight up the side of a building: no apparent ropes, just a clang as their soles struck metal, the distortion of magnetism, the defiance of gravity, and then they disappeared from view. Then another clip of the cyborgs standing like statues as a wall right in front of them collapsed in fire, hundred-kilo bricks raining on them, their arms and hips gyrating so fast, dodging everything. Then Zercos all alone, slicing through swathes of what looked like Syndicateraiders with his matte black katana on one screen, and swathes of some other mega-corp's security on another, his moves so impossibly fast it was just a light blue-green blur, a trail of cyan-colored smoke in his wake.

"Until recently," Cayenne finished, nodding at that final image of him. "This was taken only two weeks ago."

I watched him effortlessly cut through them all, then dash out of view. His victims rolled around on the ground, hurt or disabled, but not dead.

"Who does he work for now? Another corporation? The government?"

"We're not sure," she said. Then her eyes narrowed at me. "The *government.* Are you trying to be funny, Shinjiro?"

"Did you think I was?"

"No. I think you were sincerely asking."

"No, of course not. I was trying to be funny." I cleared my throat and pushed my hands as deep into my hip pockets as they could go. Rocking up and back on my heels, I nodded again at the screens, wanting to look anywhere else except at the deadpan stare I assumed Cayenne was trying to shoot me with. "So what brought him back?"

Cayenne let the hair fall slowly from her fingers. "You mean you don't know?" Her eyes flitted down to my side. "You're holding it in your hand."

"I'm not holding anything."

"Are you sure?"

"Yeah, I'm..."

I trailed off, suddenly aware of its weight indeed within my grasp. The immaculate white katana. How did it get there? It hadn't been here when I woke up under the lights. It hadn't been beside my laundered suit. I lifted the weapon to my eye level and turned it over slowly, tracing the perfect curvature and arrangement of the *sageo* cord. Something happened to my sight as I did so. I saw *through* just the transitive thing in my hand, saw *beyond* the fabric of the living world, into the dead one. I saw the two worlds at once. Even when I wasn't carrying the katana with me *here*, the katana would always be a part of me *there*. I knew instinctively that all I would have to do is reach for it—not in the physical sense, but with my spirit—and the katana would materialize in the palm of my hand.

And somehow I knew that I could send it back. I uncoiled my fingers slowly, willing the sword to remain behind. It hung in midair, then vanished in a breath of purple smoke.

I gasped. I couldn't stop smiling. I looked up at Cayenne. She seemed calm, dare I say, even bored, despite all the truly magical shit unfolding before her very eyes.

Why? I wondered. *Why doesn't this faze her?*

Then I knew: there was another just like me out there already. Zercos. That colored energy he exuded had nothing to do with cybernetic technology. I had felt the fissure in reality cracking wide open beneath us and the maw of *Yomi* wanting to swallow the both of us. If there was anyone who could understand that, it would be me, having stood my ground against Zercos's power with his sword lodged in my still-beating heart.

Yeah, this Cayenne DeLeon knew all about me, all about Zercos. But she wasn't the only one.

"Why did you keep saying 'we' earlier?" I leaned back easily against the operating table and cocked my head. I kept up my smile. I was playing friendly, for now. "Whose voice was that on the screen? When I was waking up?"

Cayenne smiled back. Somehow I don't think mine had melted her half as hotly as hers melted me. "Our employer," she said softly.

"*Our?*"

"Well, *my* employer. As for you… that remains to be seen."

From a nearby seat in the first row of the operating theater, Cayenne lifted an exceptional, fur-mantled camelhair overcoat that accentuated the tone of her suit perfectly, turned about, and ascended the stairs leading out. "Coming?" she called back.

"Where're we going?"

"To the second part of your interview."

Cayenne pressed the topmost button on the panel and leaned against the glass of the elevator, a dimly lit silhouette against the pulsing neon night sky. It was the same view I'd marveled at before the night before, stretching for kilometers all around. We both watched the rain-haze rainbow lights rising like smoke from the layers of sprawl beneath us. Or at least I pretended to. I couldn't help but observe how the colors shifted on her neck.

"Zercos did not kill your friend," Cayenne said abruptly, folding her arms, perhaps aware of my staring. If she'd wanted to break my trance, she couldn't have said anything better. "Ben Roy Doon is alive."

"How did he get out? Where is he now?"

"Mister Feikes has him. Or *had* him. True to his word, your Syndicateboss retrieved Doon-san soon after he'd learned of your apparent failure in the ShiroKaz vault."

"Former boss," I corrected.

"Indeed. Former boss."

"And let your records show—assuming you're getting all this logged somehow for whatever reason—I was hired to open the gateway to your vault, and I did just that. I did not fail anything."

"You failed to die, Asai-san."

Of course... Connor had said the target would be on the other side of the door only I could get us through. *Me.* But the lack of security, the lack of personnel, everything else about the raid still made no sense. I remembered Connor's face, the shit-eating *Hanma*-mask grin that I had thought myself clever enough to see right through. But even Connor had been just as confused by how easy it had been to meander our way through ShiroKaz Tower.

"The demise of Feikes's long-time associate, the man you knew as Connor, is likely what convinced him to follow through on the threat he made to you and to Doon-san. And so he took Ben Roy away. Retrieving him will be the second part of your interview, Asai."

I felt the elevator slowing. We'd passed beyond the uppermost layer of scudding clouds, the ethereal plane over the city stretched out endlessly, a carpet of vapor lit by bright, full moonlight. Only four other buildings besides ShiroKaz were visible from up here. I recognized the fox logo for Inari, the Fuji-Rai thunderhead, and the A-Matter sun, with more than a kilometer of space between each. The fourth skyscraper was windowless, a jet-black needle. If I'd been feeling poetic at the time, I could've whipped up a haiku about five pillars that keep heaven from falling and crushing everything below.

Just then, an automated rocket transport broke through the clouds, a fireball propelled along the rail at impossibly fast speed on its way to the city-sized space station locked just beneath orbit, catapulted from the launch pads nearby where I used to live. The blue-white plasma trail in its wake seared into my eyes. It was like an inverted shooting star; the world was throwing it back skyward, rejecting the kind of wish only kids made.

The elevator *dinged* at last. The doors opened. Cayenne stepped out first. I didn't budge. Something had just occurred to me.

"You seem to know so much, Miss DeLeon. About me, about the cybernetic fuck Zercos. You literally don't bat an eyelash at the sight of a magic fucking sword that your pre-sumed-dead mega corporation had locked away in its vault for some reason. So you must know who it was that had Feikes put the SynCell together. I got bad news for whoever it is out there that wants me dead."

"Please, Asai-san," she said, rolling her eyes. "I know the punch line. You are already dead. Oh, don't look so disap-pointed. I'm sure it works on everyone who doesn't already *know so much* about you. But you are wrong about one thing. We do not know who it was that contacted the Syndicate. Despite ShiroKaz's limitation for operating on the open grid, we still turn away a fair amount of cyber attacks. However, we had no indication that a Syndicate raid on our assets was incoming, despite all of our monitoring."

I studied her face as she spoke. I had only just met her, but even through the cool, C-Level mega-corp air Cayenne DeLeon breathed with every word, I felt that she had no reason to lie to someone she knew was so far beneath her.

I stepped off the elevator at last and followed her down a circling corridor as it bent to the left. Unlike the elegant, antiquated Japanese decor of the rest of ShiroKaz Tower, the uppermost levels we found ourselves in now were wrapped in metal struts and bare concrete, as if construction had never finished.

Maybe the feeling was mutual. Maybe Cayenne could read me too, having met me in the flesh, not just the rap-sheet Shin. Even as we walked side by side, she could tell that I wanted something, some explanation, some lead on who-ever was out there who thought me important enough to warrant a personalized Syndicate assassination. She sighed and spoke—to my knowledge—without eye-rolling. "I do have a personal theory, Shinjiro."

"What's that?"

"Whoever wanted you placed in our vault wanted you to find the white katana."

I rattled Cayenne's theory around in my mind. There wasn't much else in there to rattle it with. Besides Cayenne and her (or *our*) dragon-headed employer, no one in this world, the world of the living, knew about my curse. So was it a spirit that wanted me dead? A spirit tired of my visits to *Yomi* and wanted me to stay, permanently? How many thousands had I run from in my life? How many had shrieked and wailed and tried to tear me to pieces? No. Couldn't be. The wandering dead are faceless. The dead do not hold grudges. The dead cannot even speak.

Cayenne must have noticed that her theory got the gears turning as we walked. But she cleared her throat to get my attention as we reached the end of the curving corridor. Obsidian-dark doors slid apart soundlessly, and a gust of wind pressed its chill straight through my thin dress shirt and my rib cage. I seriously envied Cayenne's overcoat. We stepped out to a private landing pad at the very top of the world. I half expected to see a shoddy, old, mid-20th helicopter out there, judging by the ShiroKaz aesthetic thus far. But no, the machine that greeted us was by far more advanced.

The J-Zero-K, or "JOK" stealth quadcopter was the kind of wet dream only the mega-corporate C-Levels could conceivably cream their silk sheets over. It was as sleek and aerodynamic as a bullet, ringed by four hydraulic hoops around its center, around which the four gyros could rearrange themselves rapidly. This thing was capable of ridiculously high-speed maneuvers on its own, but if a pilot sporting the latest neuromods jacked into the control panels, this sleek, black monstrosity could bob and weave as fast as a human thought.

"Oh, *and* it's invisible," Cayenne said. I hadn't realized she'd been rattling off the JOK's features, dazzled as I was by the very concept of the machine's existence, its inconceivable price tag, attainable only by the uppermost echelons of elite. Her fingers touched my jaw gently, lifting it shut. I felt the warmth of her even in the biting, stratospheric cold up here. I watched her smile, then watched her sway away toward the quadcopter's sliding door.

TEN

MAGURO.
(Or "tuna," for the *gai-koku-jin* among us.)

A splash of *shoyu* like so, the perfect little dab of *wasabi*, the soft bed of vinegared *gohan*, and it's a party in your mouth. The *maguro*… It just melts.

I could eat *maguro* all day, every day.

Unfortunately, the real organic source died out decades ago when climate change and overfishing eradicated most of the self-sustainable ocean life. So the best *maguro* you could hope for was replicant-bodied blue-fin grown in the vats of a Fuji-Rai Rice Farm industrial laboratory.

God, I thought, tonguing yet another piece of the velvet-red flesh around in my mouth, *FRRF, what a stupid fucking name for a mega-corp.*

Anyway, I know what you're thinking: *Shin, why all the fuss about sushi?*

Because I want you to understand what a drop of water *means* to the man in the desert. Because it had been probably more than three days since I'd had anything at all to eat. Yes, not so bad, all things considered. What's the big deal about a few dozen hours of starvation, anyway? The catwalk champions pride themselves on deprivation, after all. But not even the slimmest fashion model ever had to experience the shriveling, withering, multiplying effects of their hunger after a trip to *Yomi*. And by my count, I'd undergone maybe two trips to the underworld since the last time I ate.

So that's why plate after plate of sweet, sweet *maguro* kept coming my way soon after I'd walked straight through the front doors of Feikes's nightclub in the Fukeabashi district, which he'd unironically named Broken. Yeah, I could've gone in through the side entrance like I was still interested in playing SynCell with Feikes and the other boys, but I figured that if they were going to kill Ben they'd have already done it while they thought I was dead. And if they hadn't yet, they definitely wouldn't now, not until they'd had a chance to dramatically unite us two friends and then enjoy the satisfaction of ripping us apart one last time before delivering our doom. Also, the people I was here to see would no doubt ping me on the grid in no time and come find *me* soon enough.

So, in the meantime, like I said, I was starving.

My favorite serving girl set the next woodblocks of sushi down at my table, next to the five other ones, not a grain of rice left on any of them.

"Kasumi. Baby. You've really outdone yourself."

She frowned down at my real-leather Italian semi-brogues. "*Dame*, Shinjiro-san!" she said playfully, affecting the throaty Japanese accent that used to be reserved for *gaijin* tourists, back when there were some. "Bad girl! No shoes allow!"

"A-*llowed*," I shot back, grinning, popping the thirtieth *maguro* into my mouth. "We gotta work on your Eng-rish, babe."

"Mmmm," Kasumi purred, sliding down to her knees and crawling to me on all fours. I'd demanded the usual private booth, complete with sliding *shoji* doors, sunk into the floor and padded with fine *tatami* and cushions. This spot was just enough turns away from the dance floor so you could be heard without having to shout, but still close enough to feel the never-ending pulse of the music through the walls. Good enough to hide the occasional moans of satisfaction. At times, there had been other sweet pink synthetic things eaten in this booth besides the *maguro*. "Been so long, Shin-san. Why we no see you so long?" Her sky-blue iris implants flashed white and grew to an enormous size, like you'd see in anime, a projection of interest. I cocked my head for a better look at her flank. Round ass, arched back, the plump side of her breast hanging like succulent fruit.

But none of Kasumi was doing it for me.

Like everything in Feikes's club, the augmented parts of Kasumi were only part of an act. Like everybody, she wore a mask. But it wasn't her fault. It was Feikes. And not just Feikes, it was the Syndicate. It had played a trick on all of us, and I was only able to see it after the Syndicate had failed to carry out its hit on me.

Broken was supposed to be a place where you came and got fixed. Might as well have made ads by slapping a question mark on the end.

Broken?

Well, have we got just the spot for you!

Feikes's nightclub was notorious for catering to the counter-cultures and the permissibility that old Osaka had been a haven for before the collapse. As the decades dragged on, as more and more crowded into the three hundred square kilometers that were now being called the New or "Neo" Osaka, the open-minded deviants got pushed farther underground by the advent of the more conservative mega-corporate society, and the pure-living Japanese-centric lifestyle they espoused. People with disabilities and disfigurements. People tattooed, scarred, or pierced, or all of the above. Voyeuristic, polyamorous, perverted. Homosexual, bisexual, cybersexual, transgender, curious, or queer. Hell, you could even be straight so long as the rest of 2070-era NeOsaka figured you were breaking *some* kind of norm. Feikes's nightclub was a safe harbor for us all. A place where you could smoke and drink and hook up with others who swung the same direction as you. A place you could try new directions.

Or at least I'd really believed so when I first found the place years ago. When I'd first found Feikes. But now I could see it for what it truly was: Broken was just a front for the Syndicate. It was the official unofficial office of recruitment. Who better to ask in bringing down the dominant capitalist society than the very groups that society was seeking to marginalize? Everything that happened in this nightclub was just a transaction. Dancing, food, drinks, sex, drugs (usually in that order). First, you gave the place your money, then you gave it your blood.

I turned my head away from Kasumi as she nuzzled up and pecked at my neck. "I've already run up quite the tab tonight, baby." I had to let her down easy, you know, given our history. I caressed her cheek and kissed her forehead. I wanted to say more, to get preachy, I guess. But I knew well enough that while you were *in*, no one could ever tell you what being *out* was like. It was something you had to want. And now I was out. Or I would be soon, anyway. Ben Roy Doon and I.

I'd had enough replicant tuna *maguro* to feed a replicant horse. I said farewell to Kasumi and wound my way through the maze of hallways, emerging by the balcony that over-looked the dance floor. The bodies writhed and the music thrummed, the neon lasers shot through the smoke like it was some kind of future war being waged. On the edges, looking up from several tables, I could feel all the eyes on me. I scanned around a bit, recognizing plenty of the other

SynCell cowboys. They're easy enough to spot, so long as you know the three forms of every Syndicate cell. One, they're all huddled together and shady, discussing their next raid. Two, they're knocking bottles, celebrating a raid well done. Or three, they're slumped, somber, bandaged, mourning the loss of their own from a raid that went south.

I guess I'd come out here to say goodbye. A few of the cowboys and cowgirls who saw me knew it, raising their drinks or tipping their heads in my direction. So it was common knowledge after all that Shinjiro Asai was marked for death. When I saw the general direction of the gazes shift, I knew my time to go had come. I turned just in time to dodge the bone-crushing grasp of the big fucking Russian's electrified metal hand. It must have looked awesome, and if anyone asks, tell them it was on purpose.

"No need for that," I yelled at him over the pulsing music. "I'll go along."

Boltcutter towered over me. He looked past me to the two Syndicate goons that had flanked me, dressed just like him in matching black suits with black t-shirts, only theirs were three sizes smaller, at least. The space around us had cleared. We were making a scene.

"I know the way," I yelled, smirking, putting up my hands. I burped a little, but I don't think he heard it. But Boltcutter must have mistaken the way my face shifted for abject fear, which seemed to please him. He stood aside and gestured toward the side door that would take us to the back offices and VIP rooms, and to Feikes.

Boltcutter and his goons followed me out of the club and past some more Syndicate security. I knew the way, of course. And Boltcutter must've known I wasn't going to try anything. They'd all known, in fact, how dangerously unarmed I was from the moment I got in here. They probably figured me for stupid. Which is why I was smiling so, so broadly when Boltcutter closed the door to Feikes's private office behind us.

We were alone, just the three of us. Even though the wide, mahogany-trimmed space was soundproof, the bass of the dance floor still pulsed through the walls. Feikes's skinny legs were crossed atop his huge antique desk, a replica, he'd once told me, of the "resolute desk" that all the United States' Presidents had done their jobs from behind, back when all the states were still united. The tips of his slippers tapped together in sync with the reverberating rhythm. He was wrapped up in a dark purple padded smoking jacket, his tall mohawk laid lank and damp to one side of his head. He must've just come out of the shower. He motioned for me to sit. I did. Boltcutter stayed by the door.

Then we just sat there. Old pals, I guess, saying nothing, trying to read one another's unflinching eyes. Real *senpai-kohai*-like, the two of us were. The master of the Syndicate, and the prodigal daughter returned.

A minute, I guess, passed agonizingly slow. Feikes's fake smile faltered first. I'm glad to say I held mine about one beat longer.

"So where'd you go, Shin?"

"I went where you told me to go." I pretended to worry about a wrinkle in my jacket. Played it casual. "Like I always do."

"Like you always do." Feikes's eyes dropped to his lap. His legs swung off the desk and his tongue slid over his teeth as he contemplated. He sighed. Apparently, he was already done with the charade of niceties.

"I want you to know, it was just business, kid," he said at last, looking me square in the eyes as he did.

He shouldn't have. I was getting really good at seeing through masks lately. I could see there was something personal in it. Something that was making Feikes sad.

But I said, "Sure. I know." I waved a hand dismissively. "But a deal's a deal. You told me 'one more job.' Remember?"

"Yeah, I remember."

"One more, and I get out. Ben and I both."

"I remember." Feikes looked down at the floor. Defeated. Deflated. He looked skinnier, frailer than I'd ever seen him. It was like someone was informing him his son had died in a war or something.

"Well, job's done," I kept going. "The door you wanted open, I opened it. That's what that asshole Connor said."

That was a mistake. A trap, and I walked right into it. Said too much, I had. Saying that man's name, bringing him up in any way, was ill-advised. I should've known. I should've tried to focus on just getting Ben and getting out. But not even my trip over here in the J-Zero-K could compare to the kind of high I was riding just then.

But it hadn't been my first mistake, turns out. See, mistake number one, as I'd come to figure later, was thinking in the first place that I could walk in and out of Broken without death following me at every step.

Feikes's eyes snapped up at me, glowering like super-heated coals. "Connor and I went back a long, long way, kid. Did he tell you?"

"Yeah. He said something like that."

"He was my brother," Feikes said, his lower lip quivering.

I was too busy trying to process what he meant by that—*brother by blood, or by battle?*—to register the thud-thud of the Russian's footsteps behind me. A steel hand cuffed me on the ear and I toppled sideways out of my chair and hit the floor.

"Ahh! You fucker!" I rose, pressing a hand to my head that came back bloody. "Touch me again, I'll cut something off of you that a fucking hunk of metal can't replace. Hear me?"

Boltcutter hadn't made any move anyway, but I'd like to think he heard the grave sincerity in my voice. I'd never heard myself sound like this before. I scared myself. I too would've probably frozen in place if I'd seen myself in a mirror just then.

"How long you and Ben go back?" Feikes asked, settling back once more in the plush velvet chair behind his resolute desk, comfortable now that his dominant position in our relationship had apparently been re-established. He lifted the stopper from some fine old-world crystal and poured himself two fingers of bourbon. He didn't offer me one. "You two were Tenjin-kiddos together, right? You push and drag his crippled ass around the place? And what'd you get in return? He was your only friend?" He drained the tumbler in one mighty slug.

"Where is he?"

"You both get your asses beat together?" Feikes bulled his way on, gripping the crystal with his gnarly, tattooed knucklebones hard enough to crack. "Pain and suffering can forge a bond hotter than any welder's torch. Am I right, kid? So Ben's like your brother?"

"What the fuck would you know about it?" There I went again, defensive and sullen whenever someone mentioned my time in the orphanage.

"See, now, there's your problem, young Shinjiro. You only ever *pretended* to listen to your elders. You write our experience off like it's so meaningless. It hurts me, kid. It really hurts me. I thought you coulda been something great. Leadership qualities and all that kind of shit, y'know?"

Feikes was getting angry. So was I. I knew it. He knew it. He knew it wasn't a good look for either of us. He took a deep breath, and this time sipped his bourbon. He closed his eyes, and it warmed him, calmed him down. I realized then he hadn't offered me any because he assumed I wouldn't be walking out alive. Wouldn't want to waste any booze on a soon-to-be corpse. "I'm trying to tell you, Shinjiro. It was nothing personal. We got hired to do the job, yes. To take you out. Weirdly enough, yes, in a very specified fashion. Hadda take away the little dangly, gift-shop souvenir you're always carrying around. But it was a no-questions-asked kind of exchange. And you were already burned on the Inari job, and I can't keep paying to have your grid presence wiped every time you ping something. And besides all that, how long do you think I'd be able to hold this big fucker back from smashing your skull in for good, huh? Behind my back or otherwise. After you fucking admitted to blowing his cousin's fucking brains out? Shit. Hey, Cutter, tell me straight right now. You were plotting something, weren't you? A little payback against our girl here."

Boltcutter stood at ease, staring at nothing, trying to appear bored. His smugness was loud and clear, answering in the affirmative.

"It breaks my fucking heart, Shin. You were a rising star in the Syndicate."

"All I know is, you lied to me. You never planned to let me go, Feikes. I knew it yesterday, and I know it now. You got me dead to rights. Just let Ben go. I'll stay behind and you can keep going down my list of fuck-ups. Until we reach the very, *very* end. But just let Ben go."

He frowned smugly, nodded his head, and sighed deeply. These were his ways of confessing. He had lied to me, too, so many like me. "I'll think about it," he said. But I saw through his mask.

"Feikes," I said. "Where's Ben?"

"He ain't dead yet. Figured if you'd got out of ShiroKaz you'd either disappear like a cunt and sell him out. *Or* you'd come looking for him. I'm glad you opted for the latter, kid. We got to see each other one last time."

Feikes nodded toward the Russian, and Boltcutter's steel hand sizzled with blue arcs of current. He came forward and lunged at my chest. I let him hit me, because fuck it. A promise is a promise.

I'd stupidly figured that just like the cyber-ninja crew's bullets, I would inexplicably become a cloud of purple smoke and the metal would just pass through me, and then I could laugh maniacally like the badass I thought I was becoming.

Alas: no. The fist collided right on top of my stapled-up sternum and the *pop* of blue lightning blasted me off my feet. My back crashed against the mahogany wall hard enough to split a few of the beams. I wheezed, my lungs clawing for breaths that simply refused to come. A pair of massive paws—one meat, one metal—slapped down hard on my back and hefted me high.

"Keep going 'til it's done," I heard Feikes say from somewhere. Then, "Aww shit, kid! Look at my wall!"

Boltcutter bodyslammed me on the floor. His steel-toe boot crashed against my ribcage once, twice. The third time, I heard a bone snap before I felt it. Then he rolled me over and set his sole on my throat. My eyeballs felt like they'd pop like over-primed balloons. My vision reddened. I could see the veins of my retinas, pulsing, as his weight crushed the spine at the base of my skull.

I was dying, again. I tried to find my *omamori* charm, to clutch it tight as the darkness closed in, just as I'd done dozens of times before. Then I remembered it wasn't there. Just as I started to panic, I remembered what had taken its place.

Yomi crept in. The realm of the dead enveloped the realm of the living. A purple-tinted cloud of ragged, wretched ghosts' hands erupted from the seams of Feikes's wood-paneled walls, from the ceiling, beneath his desk, from under the floorboards. They clawed over one another with their fingernails, bringing forth to my hand the gift I'd asked them for.

The white sword flashed up, almost without my willing it to, and severed Boltcutter's leg just below his crotch. It thudded like a slab of slaughterhouse meat. The massive brute fell over and howled in agony and terror when he finally realized what had happened.

I rose, born on the hands of the dead like a crowd-surfer. I felt them reach inside my body and snap my broken rib back in place. They sealed the seams in my heart that had reopened. I looked down at Boltcutter like a god examining a maggot. The big Russian's hands came up in front of his face. He whimpered. He begged for mercy.

"What'd I tell you about touching me again?"

In a single motion, I struck both hands from his body. Gouts of blood spurted from his wrists, raining onto the river already flowing freely from his femoral artery. Boltcutter made a kind of *gugg-gugg* noise and fell back, convulsing. Some kind of cardiac arrest. What I'd done to him was horrible, sure. But I remembered all the sucker punches, all the jibes about my sexuality, looks, wardrobe. All the uncalled-for cruelties. Mother fucking bullies all have it coming.

I looked up from the maggot, and met Feikes's utterly horrified gaze.

You could say that we finally saw eye to eye, after all we'd been through.

"C-c-can't... b-b-be."

Feikes looked like such a frail old thing. I don't know if it was the sight of me or the sight of the underworld rising and twisting his perception of reality, but he shrank back into his armchair. His desk drawers slid open and ethereal purple claws scrabbled for him.

"Where's Ben?" I brought the blade to his throat, lifting his chin up. "If you don't tell me, I'll find him anyway, and I'll kill every cocksucker in here that tries to lay a hand on me. Just like that prick down there. Any of 'em *close* friends of yours? Like Connor?" I scraped the blade's edge along Feikes's throat, giving him a kind of shave to accentuate my next point. "For the record, I didn't kill Connor. I didn't … mean to."

Feikes whispered something then.

"What? I didn't catch that."

"Wh-white … Sh-shadow."

"What? What the hell is a white shadow?"

"That sword. The… The… What you did. Where you g-got it from. Thin air. From thin fucking air. From nowhere. Just like h-h-him."

"The fuck you talking about, Feikes? Tell me where Ben Roy Doon is, and I'll let you live. And you can piss yourself with fear every time you even think about hunting us down. We're *out* now, fucker. For real! Out of the Syndicate. Fucking gone. Not yours anymore. You hear me! *Where is Ben?!*"

"B-b-basement. Brick wall, back of the boiler room."

I pulled the sword away, twirled it around so fast that Boltcutter's blood splattered on the floor and walls, and sheathed it slowly in the white *saya* sheath that had inexplicably appeared in my other hand. Where I learned to do something like that, I couldn't tell you. Maybe samurai movies.

"You ever send anyone after us, I'll kill them. Then I'll come back and kill you."

I knew with certainty that I'd no longer need my old *omamori* charm. It had served me well, but I could leave the memory of it behind. The pure white katana was my anchor now. It was all I'd ever need. It was my doorway to and from the land of the dead, which I could open anywhere, any time, with a mere thought.

Knowing this, I felt the hands of ghosts part the purple mist swirling about my feet, dragging me down through the floor. I let them take hold. And then I was gone.

ELEVEN

THROUGH THE SHEETS OF ACID RAIN, THE DRONE CAME AT last, its arrival heralded by the blinking blue strobe light above the tightly shuttered window frame of the room we'd booked at the Hotel Candy Kiss.

(I'll give you one guess why it's called that. Yes, that's exactly right.)

"Just hang in there, Ben." I left him lain out on the ultra-plush loveseat and punched the button for the window. The shutters clacked horizontal, then clanked upward. I reached out and grabbed the rain-slick package with both hands, and the machine whirred back into the night, rejoining the fleet of automatons buzzing just over the heads of the crowds packing the NeOsaka sub-streets outside. Trust me, there was nothing less inconspicuous than a drone delivery to a love hotel. Nothing like a last-minute sex toy or two, leather harness, ball gag, or whatever floats your boat. Or a first-aid kit when things went unexpectedly. (Or *expectedly*, let's face it.)

An hour ago, I had found Ben sprawled out between two massive water heaters, a space that also doubled as an interrogation room. It looked like they'd beaten him to within an inch of his life. (When you're as fragile as Ben Roy Doon, this only takes a couple hits.) They'd left the frame of his wheelchair mostly intact, but all the devices, data jacks, and gear that Feikes's goons thought might be worth a yen had been stripped off, along with all his personal health monitors, meds, and auto-injectors. They'd left Ben his paper notebooks at least, albeit scattered about, which Ben insisted I gather up entirely despite our need to skedaddle. Oddly enough, I'd found Ben's thick glasses folded neatly on a cluttered shelf, one lens still broken from before when Boltcutter had us both at his mercy in my apartment.

I discarded the packaging, unzipped the first-aid kit, and got to work. He winced as I swabbed the cuts they'd left him. "Sshhhh," I said.

Look at me, playing the soothing mother part.

I heard his whimpers, saw the tears, and figured he'd suffered a lot more than just theft and beating. He'd suffered his whole life. Every day, every hour, every breath of it. None of it had ever been fair to Ben Roy Doon, but he endured it.

"Shinjiro Asai," he began the routine salutation after thinking I was gone for good, again. "Never die." I knew this time that it was his way of saying "thank you" when the mere words were not enough.

Back in the nightclub pump room, the goon on duty had heard some commotion, opened the door, saw me, and unloaded a full clip of his silenced machine pistol right into my chest. Both the goon and I looked down at the shimmering purple holes in the fibers of my shirt and my skin as they sealed themselves up, like how the oncoming tide fills the sand pits and leaves no trace in its passing. I'd wagged my finger at the goon. "So, what do we do now?" I'd asked, sincerely curious if he wanted to die for this. I told him about what I'd done to Boltcutter. I urged him to let me and my friend go. I encouraged him not to worry because

Feikes probably wouldn't hold it against him, if the boss ever regained his sanity. The goon turned out to be rather polite, staying put when I told him to, actually holding the door so I could wheel Ben up the service ramp and out through the delivery doors. I'd've tipped him, but, y'know, *circumstances*.

The Candy Kiss was just a short skip and a roll from Broken, still in the Fukeabashi district, practically on the city's easternmost edge. On our way, we drew a few puzzled looks, the pair we made: Girl in a man's suit with a priceless white katana tucked into her belt, wheeling a scrawny, legless, busted-up boy down the bustling walkways. But if there's one thing you ought to know about Japan that's remained true throughout the centuries, it's that when you don't make eye contact, the world forgets you.

"*Doi tashi maste*," I said to Ben, wiping away his tears. *You're welcome.*

"Are we out, Shin?"

"Yeah. I think so." But then I remembered Cayenne. Zercos. ShiroKaz. The black-haired ghost in the endless white emptiness. The white sword. "*You* are, anyway."

"What do ya mean? You can't still w-w-wanna work for Feikes after all that—"

"No, not Feikes. Look, I'll tell you later. Want me to help you to the, uh, rotating bed over there?"

"Nah. Just bring me the room's portable console."

"Keep the porn charges to a minimum," I teased, tossing the tablet onto his chest.

"Shin! C'mon!" Ben's face flushed with embarrassment. I knew he'd be all right.

"Just saying. It's okay if you wanna make sure everything still works down there."

"Where are you going?"

"I'm dying for a shower."

I dialed up the opacity of the smartglass panel separating the bathroom from the bedroom, and it frosted over in an instant. I stripped off my navy suit, sucking at my teeth when I saw the newly singed lapels from where Boltcutter had touched me. I'd figured out phasing to *Yomi* would protect my threads only if I anticipated the attack and had the sense to reach for the katana in time. "Thanks, asshole," I mumbled, tossing the suit into a heap on the floor before remembering it was literally the last thread of clothing I owned anymore. "Thanks, tinman."

I felt all of a sudden that I might be overdue for a good think on how maiming Boltcutter should've made me feel. Even Zercos's tinmen squad that I'd carved up in the graveyard; they had all been people once, sons, brothers, husbands. And even if he was an asshole, Boltcutter had heart enough to want closure for losing his cousin Vasili. Payback was a kind of closure, I guess. But now he was dead, probably. There was no coming back from a severed femoral artery. So I was a killer. But was I a cold-blooded psychopath? The tinmen, for all I knew, had killed Ben. They'd fired a rocket into my place when they could clearly see I was on the other side of the street. They hadn't cared about the damage they'd done. And Boltcutter hadn't cared either. He'd tormented me for years. He'd hated me for everything I was and wasn't, and he would never say why. Just like all the other bullies.

I sat on the rim of the tub, my fingers on the digital knob, staring blankly at the reddening temperature and volume readouts, lost in thought. The water splashing over the side snapped me out of my thoughts. I dialed the flow of steaming water down to zero and slid in, hoping maybe I could just burn and melt away all the parts of myself I hated. I pried out one of the staples over my latest scar between my breasts and dropped it with a *tink* against the tub. I remembered how it had felt to be completely naked in front of the most beautiful woman I'd ever seen. It wasn't long until my mind found an image of tousled blonde hair done up in a bun. I closed my eyes, felt my rough hands gliding over my scarred body, believing I felt her perfect one instead. I pictured golden strands of wavy hair tossing back in slow motion. I bit my lower lip, seeing again her long neck, remembering the creamy mocha color of her skin. My fingers slid lower and lower, and a pair of green eyes were staring deep into mine. I let out a shuddering breath, imagining her weight on top of me, then mine on her. Her smooth, clean, perfect body against my scarred, tattooed, damaged one.

All around me, the steam was an impenetrable veil of white, lifting—engulfing me in its heat and trapping me inside my own. My heart raced. A flash of green again from half-lidded eyes, a tongue against teeth. I rocked myself rhythmically, head thrown back, utterly oblivious as the white crept higher and folded over me, imprisoning me. I felt the climax surging over me.

And ice splashed against my skin, flash-freezing the beautiful, building moment. In an instant, the water chilled to a semi-frozen, slimy slush.

My eyes had turned to ice. I peeled them open painfully and saw nothing but the white. My skin was blue, one hand frozen between the crest of my thighs.

He stood before me. His black hair the only color in the colorless void. His lifeless white eyes swept over my body from top to bottom.

"*Obutsu,*" he sneered. *Filth.*

I wish I could tell you I felt rage, that it burned so hot in me that I melted through the fear that had frozen me solid. I wish I could've rushed the white son of a bitch and stabbed his eyes out with my thumbs.

But no. I was blind to the whole spectrum of emotions, but one: shame.

"Cover yourself," the man said, waving a hand so pale I could barely make it out.

I could move, but all I did was collapse before him in a sobbing heap.

"We have not found my purpose." He pivoted, his straight long hair swishing, then paced a few steps before speaking again. "My name." He turned about. "My soul."

"I-I-I…"

My frozen lips couldn't keep up. My thoughts were hardly faster, but I formed them.

I had to save my friend.

"Friend?" His cold fingers slid under my chin, bringing my gaze up to his. "The dead have no need of friends."

Yes, I confessed.

"You have no friends."

Yes.

"You have no family."

Yes.

"You have only service."

His fingers slid away, and his form receded, enveloped by the white mist, and he was gone.

I drew my knees to my chest and wrapped myself into a tight ball, convulsing with desperate sobs, tumbling farther into my cold, abyssal well of shame.

I don't know how long I stayed like that, but eventually a warmth spread over my back. The sound of water trickling onto tile called me back to reality. I was in the tub. The smartglass was still mercifully frosted. Beyond the glass was Ben.

Ben. My fr—

I could not say it, even to myself. Because—who the fuck was I kidding?—it had never been true, anyway. What'd I think? That things were going to get better now? That I'd gotten out of the Syndicate? That I'd met the love of my life? That I could rise from the ashes of all my flaming shit, fold another thousand paper cranes, and start a new life in some other abandoned corner of the world? Like a cockroach, scraping.

No. Fuck no. The ghost was right. He knew me better than I apparently ever knew myself. I was dead. Always had been. Always would be. And I bet if I'd asked him, he would've confirmed that I was, in fact, a killer.

I wrapped a towel around my body and stormed out of the bathroom, ready to tell Ben he had to get the fuck out and never even hope to see me again. But I choked on the demand as soon I saw Cayenne seated in the armchair opposite Ben's loveseat.

"Asai-san," she said. "Welcome to the team."

"Look who decided to show," Ben added.

My emotions were spinning like a wheel of fortune that refused to obey the laws of physics. I just sat there, dripping wet, my mind reeling and reeling. What felt like only a few minutes ago, I was proud of doing right by Ben, I was ready to justify Boltcutter's grisly demise, I was about ready to melt just thinking about Cayenne, and I was chilled by the realization that I was utterly unworthy of ever being born. And now back around again.

The best I could manage was clearing my throat. "What're you doing here?"

"I came to inform you," she paused for dramatic effect, or more likely because Cayenne seemed the type to hate having to say the same words twice, "you passed the interview. Both parts." I felt myself flinch a little. Should I have been proud? I still felt warm and cold from my *shower.* She smiled, clearly amused by the expressions crossing my face. "We would have perhaps preferred your former boss Feikes to be eliminated, but we perceive he will no longer be an issue."

I glanced at Ben. He appeared entirely unconfused about what Cayenne was saying.

"How much did she tell you?"

"Mister Doon has been apprised of events in the aftermath of your raid on ShiroKaz Tower."

"I thought her calling me *Doon-san* sounded terrible," Ben interjected for no reason whatsoever. "So we agree on 'mister.'"

"Ben was particularly interested in our security shortcomings," Cayenne went on. "I, too, have no idea why the automated detectors and defenses were offline at the time of your … incursion. So we've been putting our heads together."

"Once you got into the elevator, something came on the grid and booted me out." Ben was getting excited. If his face hadn't been so bruised up, you'd have never known he'd suffered a beating. "A digital monster. Came out of nowhere and fried all my intrusion software. A dragon sigil. Didn't speak, but there was a presence on the grid. Blanked all my screens, all my audio. Then it flickered out and by the time I'd re-established connection, you were gone, like back at Inari, only I didn't pick you up, and then that Boltcutter f-fuck showed up and—"

I watched Cayenne press her soft hand onto Ben's lap, soothing him to silence, and my skin prickled all up my thigh. *Jealousy?* I was suddenly very aware of the tiny droplets of water hanging from the long lock of hair in front of my face.

"There's nothing you could've done," she reassured him, "with the *substandard* interference equipment you had at the time."

"She said you raced back home," Ben said to me, "but that Feikes had already l-l-leveled the place. You could've just left me." The tears started to well in the eyes behind his thick glasses. "But Cayenne said you wanted to come save me."

"My exact words," Cayenne pointed out, smiling up at me.

The wheel of emotions kept spinning inside me, but admittedly a little slower. I could sense a kind of resolution coming, a place where maybe I could still make a clean break from Ben, from Cayenne, and move on to settling my pact with the black-haired ghost, in the white emptiness, the one who'd called himself a shadow...

...a white shadow.

Holy fuck.

"Asai-san. Is something wrong?"

The wheel had caught fire.

"Shin, s-s-say something."

"What'd he say," I murmured, barely loud enough for myself to hear.

"What?" Ben and Cayenne said in unison.

"Feikes. He said, 'the white shadow.'"

Cayenne's eyes drifted away. The name—the title—it had visibly disarmed her somehow. I saw the chink in her cool, corporate armor and pressed in.

"Something Feikes said. When he saw me pull the sword from thin air."

Ben raised a quick hand. "There's a *sword* now?"

"The one from *your* vault," I went on, approaching Cayenne. "You know, don't you? About what the sword really is. *Who* the sword really is."

The cracks in her hard demeanor had been spreading steadily, but her defenses were back online and better than ever at that last line. She rose from her chair, and now it was my turn to step away from her. "You mean who it *belongs* to?" she snapped back. "It belongs to a great man. A powerful man. Power—the likes of which you cannot imagine."

No, I thought, *that's not what I meant.* But I still had a kind of answer anyway: Cayenne didn't know anything about the spirit trapped within the katana. To her, it was just a part of the ShiroKaz collection. But I knew she knew *something.*

"Cayenne," I said calmly, raising my hands placatingly, which let my towel slide down just an inch over my cleavage, which drew her gorgeous green eyes down for the fleetingest of glances. (Hey, even in times of great stress, these are things I notice.) "Who is the White Shadow?"

She held my gaze a moment longer. She glanced at Ben, who was still somehow lost at the concept of there being a "sword" I guess. And then she gathered her overcoat from the armchair and strode for the door. "Get dressed and meet me in the lobby."

"Why?" I called at her back.

She turned about in the open doorway. "So the dragon can tell you himself."

Ben and I stared at the door, then at each other, for a moment longer. Then Ben shrugged. "Better get going. This place charges by the hour, anyway."

In the plush, leather-wrapped, pressurized cabin, Ben did most of the talking.

I did most of the staring. Not at Cayenne, who was seated across from us, but out beyond the rain-streaked windows of the JOK quadcopter, lost in the puffy storm clouds hovering over the lightening, pre-dawn sky.

The farther we flew away from the pulsing vibrant neon center of NeOsaka, the more dilapidated and dark the world became. The roaring fires of life sputtered away to embers and sparks, then to only a few pinpricks of light along the very edge of overhanging Heaven's protective shroud, then to a vast sprawling emptiness. The gray husks of squat, blocky city buildings stood watch over silent streets choked with abandoned cars. Whatever windows hadn't been blown out by *jishin* and left unrepaired caught the rising daylight and lit up like buttons on an old-fashioned punch card computer. Buttressing all of the ruin were piles and piles of garbage, and wood, steel, and brick debris that bull-dozers had shoved together into mountains after the weeks of ceaseless tsunami rushed in; side effects of the bombs dropped half the world away. It was tragic how the powerful madmen who destroyed the world killed so many more than their intended targets. All it took was time. And even if sweeping natural disasters didn't do in the rest of Japan and other neutral countries in the months and years following the blasts, the energy crises, the economic collapses, the looting, the desperation, the radiation drift, the practically overnight evaporation of the ancient glacial ice, the dread, all the untold aftereffects inflicted upon the planet and the human psyche, all of it did for most of the rest of us.

And I saw more than most. I saw a whole world of wandering spirits never laid to final rest, never honored with even just a few words that could guide them to some sense of peace. If normal people like Feikes and Boltcutter, or Ben and Cayenne had been looking out the windows, they'd see only the usual ruin. But I saw endless hordes of ghosts, shimmering into wispy forms like holograms as the J-Zero-K sped by soundlessly.

But Ben and Cayenne weren't looking. What would they see, anyway? Instead, my loudmouth old friend was picking my erudite new boss's brain about sub-routines, modules, nodes, back-doors, what she knew about acronymic, all that other kind of hacker jargon I'd done my damndest to avoid learning. I was doing my damndest now to ignore them, focusing instead on trying to figure out exactly which side of the decaying urban jungle we were flying over, but I couldn't help but overhear how Ben's last line of questioning had affected Cayenne's tone.

"What do *you* know about acronymic," she asked him levelly, sliding ever so slightly forward in the leather upholstery.

"Er," Ben stammered, perhaps caught off guard by Cayenne's sudden—and very clearly genuine—interest in the subject. "You mean, like, you've never heard of it before, or like ... *what do I know?*"

"Assume I understand the basic tenets," she said, waving a hand dismissively. "I understand it to be a language that even the most sophisticated security detection programs have difficulty cracking."

"It's *un*-crackable," Ben corrected, sliding forward himself so the stubs of his legs hung over the space between them. He was practically glowing. I'd never—*never*—heard Ben Roy Doon affect quite this much assertiveness about anything. "Not even for mega-corps."

"It's true," Cayenne conceded. "Shiromatsu-Kazama has been a non-contender for decades, and thus avoided almost all attention, including corporate infighting, Syndicate raiders such as yourselves, and therefore any encounters with hacker intrusions, acronymic or otherwise. But even if they could break into the tower's network, they would find no data worth anything. It has all been sequestered away, a place where no one can touch it. All that is to say, Ben, I still want to learn *how* it could be done, *if* it could be done. Can you tell me how it works?" I glanced at the two of them just long enough to see the tail-end of that kind of smile I wished she'd flashed at me more often. She leaned back, crossed her legs, and slid into a posture that said, *Impress me.* "And I mean, tell me how it *really* works."

There was a pause. Nobody'd ever really wanted to know about anything that Ben knew about. Nobody'd ever asked him his opinion. Nobody had ever *valued* him for his skills and knowledge. Nobody but me, I guess, and even then I'd never done so out loud. He looked at me with an expression that I guess asked for my permission. *How much should she know?* Given I, like Cayenne, knew fuck-all about how acronymic really worked, I shrugged. I hope the expression said, *Go with my blessing, child.*

Later, I'd find out that his look was his way of asking just how much he—meaning *we*—could trust not just Cayenne DeLeon, but how much we could trust ShiroKaz.

A mega-corporation. And much later, I'd come to regret not paying more attention. To everything.

"Paper," he said finally. "And ink."

Even in the reflection of the tinted glass, I could see Cayenne's smooth brow furrow. "I'm afraid I don't follow."

"Codebooks. Old-fashioned code books. Like the ones I carry around. Acronymic isn't anything more than a means to send messages and cyberspace locations of data dumps, right? That's what it's for. We, er, I mean," Ben stammered, smiled bashfully, chuckled, then went on. "I mean *us*, like, what you would call *hackers*, right? We, er, us hackers write a string of letters, an acronym, right? And they could be anything! *Mean* anything. *Stand for* anything. It's all based in language. English. Sometimes Russian Cyrillic. But never crossed, although we've, er, I mean, it's been tried. Somebody tried it."

Ben took a breath, pushed his glasses up, found one of his worn-out notebooks in the pack hanging at the side of his chair, and thumbed through it. The pages were a cascade of nonsensical strings of letters, hatch marks, and lists of words. The diary of a crazy person. The other guys in our SynCell used to give Ben so much hell for being entirely unlike a normal comms operator or *man in the chair*, no pun intended. But there was no denying how effective he was on a raid. Cayenne watched him, absorbing his every word, making me wish I understood this stuff better.

"Anyway," Ben began again, finding his bearings, holding a page open for her to see. "The phonemic alphabet sequence entered into a computer can operate similarly to strings of code, something the computer can understand better than the symbolic alphabets like Japanese or Chinese *kanji*. Like, like… let's say W, R, R, U, H, B. What the hell does that mean? You take every letter in the English language that starts with a W, multiply it by every possible letter that starts with R but you drop every other R-word that makes no grammatical sense. Then again, by another factor of R, the third letter, only this time the grammar could potentially get more complex, nouns following nouns to become a compound word. And so on with the fourth letter. What'd I say? V?"

"No," Cayenne said. "U. And I can see that alphabets like *Hiragana* and *Katakana* would not work as well, for they only form word syllables, not whole words. Not entire strings of meaning. Correct?"

Ben was giddy. "Absolutely! But we're working on the symbolic writing systems as well. And by *we*, I mean hackers. Ahh, anyhow, so after U, what'd I say? H? Yeah, then the H, then the… what was the last one?"

"B," Cayenne offered.

"Yeah! Right. B. So… What does W-R-R-U-H-B even stand for?" Ben flipped through his paper pages, searching. "We revel religiously upon… holy… uh… B-b-bah-mitzvahs…? Or maybe Wiry running rats undo heaven's barbells. Ha! I don't know. Sounds pretty stupid, right?"

"Yes," Cayenne said, but I could still hear the smile in her voice all the same. "Very stupid."

"But that's the point. The more unintelligible the string of the acronym, the more it confuses the programs monitoring all the chatter on the grid. I can't even conceive of the astronomical amount of possibilities that a six- or seven-letter acronym stands for. The only limitation is that it's less than infinite, but still a number that the human brain can't rightly conceive of, so neither can a computer. Human spontaneity and haphazard whimsy are still beyond the reach of artificial intelligence. And even if the machine works out every possible word combination—literally potentially billions, right?—how will it know which string of the acronym is the right one? See? And by the time it figures out it—basically, when it gets the *key*—well, where's the digital doorway that that key unlocks? Get it? And by then…"

CLAP! Ben brought his hands together, startling me away from the window. I'd gotten bored, I guess, and started staring out of it again.

"We're gone," he whispered, wide-eyed, falling deep into his own chair, clearly enjoying his juvenile theatrics, which apparently impressed the pretty girl. Then he said, "Uhh," deflating a bit after a few seconds, "and by *we* I mean, like, *hackers*. Not, like, *me*, per se."

"The Cluster," Cayenne said definitively. "They're the hackers that write these codes nowadays. These strings of letters."

Ben got quiet. I already knew all about the underground collective of technophiles because Ben found it difficult, let's say, to keep secrets about things that excited him. He had a holographic rainbow sticker of their collective sigil, the *kanji* for *Family*, front and center on his personal laptop. (However, amazingly enough, despite all my suspicions about where he was getting better hardware than the Syndicate could provide, I wasn't completely sure he was *actually* one of them, or if he was just an overzealous fanboy of all the Cluster stood for.) There was no way Cayenne was not also already aware of their existence. Unlike the Syndicate, which was essentially mercenaries taking out corporate trash and setting fire to dirty corporate laundry, the Cluster worked to undermine corporate interests. To steal their secrets and then ... just hoard them, apparently. They were a force to be reckoned with on the grid, but no one—not even the mega-corporate elite—understood what their end-game was. The Cluster never actually *did* anything with whatever they stole. The general word on the street was they were just looking for something and hadn't found it yet.

"And the Cluster keeps these ink and paper *books*," Cayenne went on, saying the word with a little difficulty. Not contempt, just unfamiliarity.

I figured this woman—probably the same age as Ben and me—had likely only brushed her fingertips over hardlight screens, never across physical paper. I wondered absently if the form of communication—digital or analog—affected its ultimate meaning.

"And they provide their agents with them. And they send updates, pointing to the right sequences. I see. This is all so … fascinating."

The more understanding I saw dawning on Cayenne's face, the deeper Ben seemed to sink into his chair, and the more suspicious I felt. If the three of us were supposed to be working for the same team now, then getting-to-know-you needed to be a two-way street. I'd been meaning to ask her a lot of questions, but neither the operating theater nor the love hotel where I'd been either naked or wearing just a towel had seemed like the right place. The cabin of the JOK would have to do.

"Not a lot of paper books where you grew up?"

I'd meant to be playful, charming, disarming. Judging by Cayenne's icy glare, I could tell the question had registered as anything but. How many times was I going to screw up with her? I needed to stop being such a smug asshole before it was too late. I quickly held up my hands as an apology before she could react.

"I didn't mean it like that. Honestly. It's just you know everything there is to know about Ben and I. Whatever records you pulled from the grid about Tenjin. Where we came from. The SynCell. All of it. And we know absolutely nothing about you, Cayenne."

She settled back. The coldness melted from her hardened features. I saw the corporate mask fall away, at least a little bit. I heard the voice of the real Cayenne DeLeon speak. Someone who wanted to tell others about herself, but didn't know where to start.

"Truthfully, Shinjiro, I keep a small collection of books. What else do you want to know?"

Ben and I exchanged a glance. He shrugged and gave me a look that said, *This is your gig, pal. You wanted this.*

"I guess…" I drifted off awkwardly for a moment. Then I said, trying to recover, "Who's actually flying this thing? And where are we being flown *to?*" We were now as deep in the wasteland of Japan as I'd ever been. It felt like West considering the rising sun was at the JOK's rear.

"Normally, I pilot the J-Zero-K." Cayenne tapped a finger against her temple, confirming my suspicions of her neuromodification.

Not an actual answer to my question, but okay.

"And we are almost there."

Also not an answer.

I nodded at her slowly, though I did so with scrunched-up eyes.

Cayenne smirked, perhaps even winked at me, though it could be a twitching of the eye at the barely contained annoyance from yours truly. She uncrossed and recrossed her legs, the fabric of her suit swishing pleasantly, and she craned her neck to stare out the window.

I mumbled the only acronym I could think of as the JOK banked to the left, decelerated, and descended into a blanket of fog.

"FML, I guess."

The stealth copter sat down delicately in a field of the tallest grass I think I'd ever seen. Scratch that, actually. I'd never seen grass, period. Not grass like this. Natural. Organic. Real. Neither simulated through a screen nor grown synthetically to decorate the lobbies and parks of the corporate zones. I paced slowly ten meters away from the JOK. I couldn't help but run my fingers through the green fronds that rose up to my waist, the kiss of moisture on the fabric of my suit trousers.

The land all around us was shrouded in mist. And stillness. Somewhere in the fog, a flow of water whispered pleasantly along a stream. I suddenly thought of the *sozu* in the ShiroKaz Tower lobby, and I froze in place, closing my eyes, waiting, anticipating the *thonk*. Hoping for it. But it never came. The silence was eerie. And beautiful.

Until my companions broke it.

"I'm afraid I must insist you wait in the J-Zero-K, Mister Doon."

"Why? I'm sure my motors can power me through that."

"Ben," Cayenne said, placing her hand on his before he could angle his chair out of the JOK's cabin. "It is not a matter of mobility."

"Hey, it's okay." He threw his hands up in defeat, then folded them in his lap dramatically. "It's not like I've never been told straight-up that I'm not invited."

I expected Cayenne to plead with him and say, *It's not like that, Mister Doon*, but instead, she cleared up his misunderstanding with a tuck of a loose blonde lock behind her ear and a touch to her temple. An invisible, spherical thing detached itself from the side of the JOK and hovered beside her. The drizzle collected on its cloaked surface, revealing a gun barrel along its side. I felt a low-frequency pulse pierce my inner ear for just an instant, then all atmospheric moisture was repelled from Cayenne's figure in a one-meter radius. It hung around her like a tenuous aura. This was more than just an ordinary *kasa* drone, which emitted a subsonic field to repel falling rainwater, really just an umbrella for the mega-corporate elite. This silent, invisible thing was her bodyguard, which would repel a whole lot more dangerous things than rain.

"This precipitation is full of radioactive material, Ben." She still had her hand on his, giving it a squeeze. "I have only this one personal drone to shield me. It follows me everywhere, even when I don't want it to," she added as an aside. "You will be safe in the J-Zero-K's cabin."

"What about Shin?"

True, I thought. *What about me?* I'd never tried suicide by prolonged exposure to self-microwaving radiation, but I was game. If nothing else ever worked, why would this?

"I'm fine," I said simply. I had a feeling Cayenne already knew it was true.

After Ben had backtracked into the quadcopter, she waved her hand to activate some neural command, and the sleek door hissed closed. Then the washed-out gray dullness of the world enveloped it as its subtle hexagonal skin engaged a chameleon function. So it was just the two of us, alone in a field in the middle of suburban desolation. I watched her make up the distance between us—this gorgeous blonde businesswoman in a pressed suit that probably cost more money than I'd ever earned raiding with the Syndicate, with her fur-mantled camelhair overcoat draped over her shoulders, the empty sleeves of it swishing at her side. The gathering raindrops slid off an invisible barrier, and the bodyguard *kasa* drone even swept aside the tall grass as she moved, the patent leather boots she'd brought for the journey finding solid ground as she caught up to me.

"This way," she said, smiling.

Beyond our landing field was an entire city, or what must've once been one. We were in a residential neighborhood, surrounded on all sides by two-story Japanese homes. The pre-fabbed materials had held up generally well against the unpredictable onslaught of the *jishin*, designed to shake and gyrate as the Earth itself did so. There were abandoned gardens, overgrown, and abandoned cars pushed together, their tires deflated, and abandoned clotheslines, some still strung with rags eaten by time and the elements. The streets on this side were narrow, barely wide enough for a couple of compact cars to brush past each other, and barely long enough for the wall of white mist to gather just beyond our vision. I stayed several paces behind Cayenne, peering into every grimy window or battered-down doorway I could. Every shopfront, every restaurant, every house had been wrecked and ransacked, everything tossed into the street, papers and clothes and packs, all of it matted down by rain, faded by sunshine, gnawed by time. The people who once lived here, decades ago, had abandoned their lives in a rush as the tsunamis and catastrophes swept across the country. I pictured them all, running. A mother dragging her son by the hand. A father clutching their daughter tight to his chest, his feet pounding the pavement, the young girl's eyes watching her whole world recede in the distance as her parents carried them into the illusion of safety. In my mind, I watched the girl's haunted look fade into the mists at the end of the street.

I found myself hoping that they made it out, this fictional family I'd conjured in my head. I shook my head, trying to figure out why I gave a shit all of a sudden.

The air was chilly, and wet, like being inside of a kitchen's walk-in fridge a few hours after its coolers had blown out. The farther we walked, the heavier the moisture seeped into my sleeves. Soon it was in my skin. After almost half an hour of meandering steadily uphill, it was chilling my bones. I looked up from my feet, lamenting the damage all this sudden change in climes was wreaking on my semi-brogues, and Cayenne was gone, swallowed by the mist.

The white, it was everywhere. I choked. The cold crawled down my neck and speared into my fingertips with ice.

"No," I whispered. "Not again."

I nearly toppled over sideways, catching myself against a soggy wooden beam, panting, shivering.

"Asai-san."

I squeezed my eyes shut. My fingers fumbled reflexively in my pocket, feeling for the *omamori*, even though I knew it wasn't there.

Please. Let me escape.

"Shinjiro!"

A hand landed gently on my shoulder. I spun about, ready to scream in the shadow's face. But I caught myself.

"Shin," Cayenne said, withdrawing her hand. "We've arrived." There was a look of genuine concern. Out here, she wasn't wearing whatever mask she'd thought she had to wear before back in the ShiroKaz Tower operating theater, the one whose eyes only saw me for the piece of shit I thought I was. She came forward again, holding me up with both hands. "Oh! You're freezing!" She made to unsling her coat and drape it over me, momentarily breaking the aura draped about her by the *kasa* drone, damping the sleeves of her suit, but I waved her off, already feeling the chill subside.

"I'm all right," I said. "Just..."

I couldn't say it.

Just thought I'd lost you.

I straightened, still holding onto the wooden beam for support. My eyes ran up its length. "A torii gate," I breathed.

"This is the first gate," Cayenne said.

"Where are we?"

"*Shirasagi-jō*," she said.

"*Shirasagi?* White Heron... what?"

"Himeji Castle."

The gravel path crunched beneath our feet as we passed through a second gate, then a third, then wrapped around almost back the way we came until we reached a fourth, moving ever upward. A light glowed through the haze above. Heat spread in waves, and the mist dispersed before our eyes as the red sun rose over the fanned walls of the castle, just to the side of the towering central keep. That's when I saw it.

"This place is … *dainashi*," I finally said, my grasp on my everyday language slipping as if ripped by gravity.

Cayenne echoed the sentiment. "Ruin."

The elements had worn away the town below. Wind and Water. *Jishin,* the violently rumbling Earth itself.

But up here, it had been fire. The damage was catastrophic. The ground was black. Not even years of rain could wash it away, as if the ash had stained it forever. Half of the castle lay strewn in mounds of bricks and tiles, slabs of ancient stone and splintered wood, glass, and metal frames. The other half sagged like a tired giant, waiting for the moment when time and gravity would finally drag it down to its final rest.

"There," Cayenne said after a moment. She nodded toward a path between the castle's charred remains, seeming to lead toward the towering keep. "He wishes to see you. Alone."

"Who *is* he?"

Cayenne's smile faltered. The pride, the disdain, the condescension it seemed she usually reserved for losers like me; it was all gone. Some shadow of fear crept over her beautiful face. Just for an instant. Then she turned away.

"The other part of *we*," she called over her shoulder.

I stood there, watching her, until she disappeared around the fourth gate.

TWELVE

I LET OUT A LONG BREATH, STEAMING IN THE HUMID COLD.
The rain soaked through my suit and prickled my skin.
Rain dripped from the long lock of hair hanging over my
eye. My fingers balled into fists at my side.

"What the fuck," I hissed, turning around for the thousandth time in the ruined castle's courtyard, thinking maybe
this time I'd see exactly where it was I was supposed to go.
The path through the debris that Cayenne had set me on led
to a dead end. The castle walls had weathered the fire, but
the doorways and gates had all toppled inward, it seemed
like years ago. I looked skyward to the central tower. I'd
been lost here long enough for the mists to creep back in
and shroud its apex.

"Fuck everything."

The gravel crunched under my soaking semi-brogues as
I wheeled about to leave. How did I let myself get caught up
in all this? Some ancient, limping mega-corp. A whole two
employees on the payroll. Cayenne and the dragon-headed
sigil. What did ShiroKaz want with me? Who did they think I
was? Who did *I* think I was? My eyes locked on the way back

out of this dead end, but somehow I couldn't make myself move. What was back there for me? What was I going to do? Hijack the stealth copter with my obsolete comlink—if I could even find it first—and fly it away? Far, far away. Leave NeOsaka behind? Leave Ben?

I *could.* I could leave them all behind. I could just ghost out of here. Just fade away and leave it all behind. Disappear into the dead zone and let the radiation do its work.

But I couldn't. Not until I'd fulfilled my new, true purpose. *I was the body, and the shadow man was...*
Wait.

I lowered my head, letting a rush of rain drip down my hair, and realized without thinking that my fingers had been instinctively searching my jacket pocket for my *omamori*, finding nothing.

But I don't need it anymore.

I pulled them out and looked at my own hand. I felt a weight in my palm, something both strange and familiar all at once. I felt my pupils dilate reflexively, and the light of the world brightened as the white katana materialized. All the black ash at my feet became white, and all the white mists overhead became black. The photo-negative world of *Yomi* enveloped me. I spun about, the sound of my movement carrying like whispers underwater. And the dead were everywhere.

Men, women, children. Some were draped in the kimono of bygone days, others wore business suits, uniforms, and everyday clothing—every fiber of them in tatters, worn by time and the neglect of their ancestors. Some of them were missing limbs, some of them were burned, torn, beaten, and trampled in a man-made stampede when the calamity struck. Some of them withered from disease, famine, and neglect. Some of them had no heads. And yet, I felt all their eyes. All their eyes on me.

No. Not on me.

On the sword. It was in my hand. It was *always* in my hand.

They bowed. All together. And it didn't stop there. The dead fell to their knees. Their hands slid forward, and they remained, as if in prayer.

I didn't feel cold, not like I had in the alley after InariCorp. Not at all like the cold I'd always felt every time I'd wandered among the spirits of the underworld. Instead, I felt a rush of heat, like I was sucking up all their energy. Because I was. It was power. The dead gave me power. In this place, in this world, I did not need legs or muscles to move. I stepped forward, but was propelled through space by this power itself. The energy of the dead carried me. I glided on it, venturing through the hordes of ghosts. And that's when I found my way.

I'd said before how the realm of the dead twisted and distorted the architecture of the living, how I could see both worlds at once, how the skyscrapers and roads and glowing neon of NeOsaka would bend and warp every time I crossed over. But not here. Not at this castle. Here, at Himeji Castle, *Shirasagi-Jo*, all the ruin fell away. All the ash was bleached clean. All the bricks and beams and roofs and walls stitched themselves back together before my very eyes. Here, the giant was alive: the citadel. Like I was looking at an x-ray, I could still see the ruined, black skeleton of the living world inside while its perfect, true form glowed brightly, everything outlined by a subtle, purple edge.

And at its base, a torii gate, and the way inside.

There were more of the dead inside. An army of them, lining the walls and blocking some corridors while standing aside from others so I could move past, all of them bowing and prostrating themselves at my feet as I wound through. Apparitions of this place's real-world ruin passed through me as I moved deeper into the castle. I was walking through walls, just like I was used to, but this time it was ... *effortless*. Before, when I'd only had my charm, the trip would take everything from me. I'd clench it so hard my palm would bleed. I'd burst through the veil back to the other side drenched in sweat and purple residue, my lungs sucking air like a famished man eats. But not here. Not now. And I knew exactly why.

My fist closed tighter around the katana's case, and my grip sent an invisible shockwave that brought the dead's bows even lower. I knew if I'd wanted to, I could blast them apart, with the blade or with just a word. I could grind their spirits to dust, and it would be a million years until all the wayward grains of them would reunite. If I'd wanted to move down the halls that their bodies had choked off, they couldn't stop me. Nothing could ever stop me. Not anymore. I had nothing to fear from ghosts. The thought gave me a sick satisfaction, and I smiled. I kept going where the dead were leading me.

Someone wanted to see me.

It wasn't long before the dead guided me toward an immense pair of doors, framed by a torii gate whose vermillion paint was vivid against the eerie glow. One of the doors was ajar, so I ascended the wide stairs and pushed it open the rest of the way. This was the grand hall, where the *daimyos* of old would meet with their vassals, their subjects, their samurai. Pristine *tatami* lined every inch of the floor—and there were *a lot* of inches to line there. Wood-framed sliding *shoji* doors with white paper windows were spaced along the side walls, while four-paneled screens depicting serene mountains, lakes, and forests in priceless, shining paint blocked the view where servants would come and go attending to the lord's guests. Heavily stained and lacquered pillars that must once have been ancient tree trunks rose high overhead, lifting the central beams of the vaulted ceiling. I approached the dais at the far end, passing between aisles of perfectly spaced stools where all would prostrate themselves, bending over double before the master.

And there he was. I was too shocked to bow. My breath caught. My eyes widened with recognition. "It's you," I breathed.

The old man. The stranger at the graveyard. It was him. But instead of his outdated black three-piece, layers of starched, pure-white ceremonial kimono folded around his frame. Instead of an empty sleeve where a hand should've been, a clunky, old-school cybernetic prosthesis emerged. Both of the old man's hands—flesh and metal—were folded in his lap, and he appeared to be deep in meditation, or asleep. His mirror shades were off, revealing two blackened, sunken pits where his eyes should be. The old man remained still, dreaming. Or dead.

I tried to swallow the sudden lump in my throat. The old man made no move, no sound, so I wrenched my eyes free and took a better look at the ... *thing* that was plugged into the base of his skull. Fiber-optic cables glowed with the same ethereal glow that kept this stretch of *Yomi* lit, limned gently with purple light. The pulse came from his brain, ran down the length of cable and into a very immense, very sophisticated machine—which I had at first mistaken for part of the castle itself beyond the dais—and then ran back into his head at five-second intervals, like clockwork. Upstream. Downstream.

The old man's head shifted, turning his ruined eyes away and reorienting his ears in my direction. He knew I had arrived. And I knew that even though he was blind, in this place he could *see* me.

Neither of us spoke for a long time. For what seemed like an age. The silence crushed me, and I could not help but bow beneath its weight. I folded at the waist in reverence, but I kept my feet under me.

"*Ie, ie,*" the old man croaked, his throat dry, probably from disuse prolonged in the living world. "No, no. Not necessary."

The voice compelled me. I came back up. "I'm … Shinjiro. Asai-Shinjiro."

"I know who you are."

His flesh hand—its skin like paper, laced with purpling veins and liver spots—gestured to the steps before the dais. "*Dozo*," he said. "Please."

I obliged, setting the white katana down and folding my legs beneath me as I bowed again. On the steps, I was literally halfway between the throne room and the throne itself, not raised to quite his stature, and this symbolism seemed to please the old man. A smile spread along his face, and from this gesture alone. I thought he'd probably been quite the handsome charmer in his former life.

"I am … Tatsuhiro."

A sea of *kanji* swirled before my mind's eye. *Tatsu*, meaning grand, immense power. And *Hiro*…

"The grand dragon," I breathed, putting the two most likely symbols together. "You were the one on Cayenne's comlink. The sigil."

"*Hnn*," he grunted, the sound of it an old-fashioned Japanese assertion. "*The other half of we*, as she told you."

"You…" I blinked, holding back my words a bit, not sure how far I was going to take this. "You were listening? How much? How long?"

"I've been listening. Watching. For quite some time. I will not waste any more time here, now. So I will tell you: I am the one who hired the Syndicate to bring you to ShiroKaz Tower."

In the silence that followed his words, I felt the fury tickling my spine, tensing in my arms, rising in my throat. The old me would've ranted and raved, threatened and thrashed, grabbed the old son of a bitch by the cuffs of his kimono, and screamed in his face, *To 'bring' me? No! To fucking MURDER me!*

Instead, letting my breath go was the only sound I made. I had left the older, more profane version of me on the other side of the torii gates I'd crossed to get here. I knew that now, and a sense of peace flooded in me, flushing the fury away. Tatsuhiro observed my reaction intently.

"I see you are conflicted. Do not be, Shinjiro-san. Because I have been searching for you for a very long time."

"How long?" I started, then I shook my head and breathed out. *Since you saw me in the graveyard? Since just yesterday. Or longer. Since the day I ran away from the orphanage, or fell into gangs, or signed up with the Syndicate?* None of these questions really mattered now, so I asked the only one that did.

"Why me?"

"Because you are special, Shinjiro. Very special."

"So... because of my ... curse."

"*Iiiee,*" he drawled. Then he tsked, his smile fading a bit, but not all the way. He shifted within his robes to angle himself better at me, and I thought all of this made him seem very human. "Not your curse. Your *power.*"

"This place," I said. "This castle. It burned down, and you rebuilt it in *Yomi*, the underworld. Brick by brick. And you keep it here somehow. You're just like me. Aren't you?"

The old man grunted in the affirmative. *"Hnn."*

"Why? I mean, *how?* How is any of this possible? How did I get this power? Why me?"

"I do not *know*, Shinjiro-san, but I have my suspicions. Tell me, do you know the myth of Izanagi and Izanami? I see in your expression the ignorance of the young generation. Forgiven, and easily remedied. Let me tell you.

"There once was only chaos, shapeless, insubstantial. Izanagi and Izanami were offspring of the elder *kami*, who resided in heaven. They were tasked with creating form, order, from this chaos. They did so with a great spear, which they dipped into the ocean, and split portions of the shapelessness into the islands of Japan. They made their home together upon the new world below and began a family. But, being new and perhaps reckless, they did not know the proper order of things, and so there was an unwanted child. Their firstborn, whom they mourned as they cast it away.

"*Hnn?* What is wrong, Shinjiro-san?"

What's wrong is that's fucked up, I wanted to say. *Sending their child away like that. Like, good fucking luck out there, son.*

"Nothing, Tatsuhiro-sama," I said instead. "Just that, I suppose these myths had different values. About family."

"*Hnn,*" he grunted. I'd wished he'd had eyes so I could read his expression, wondering if he agreed, or was merely tolerating my response. "As all myths do. But perhaps in these gods' actions, we can see some wisdom. The concept of *sacrifice* was born, and in so doing, they anticipated they could do better."

I wanted to point out the flawed logic, how these mythical beings failed to realize that nothing is perfect right away, how they should've recognized the concept of *potential* that their child had, that with them it could grow and have an actual life and serve a purpose. But I hadn't come here to argue. "*Onegai,*" I said, bowing my head, *please.* "Go on."

"Izanagi and Izanami indeed created a family, which became the natural structures, the elements, that we see all about us. Trees, mountains, rivers, sky. And fire, last of all, Izanami bore the primal *kami* of fire, and in so doing she was burned. Izanagi, her husband, could do nothing to save her. Thus, death and grief found their place in the order of things. But also rage. And Izanagi satisfied his thirst for vengeance by separating his own son's head from his body, the flame that had killed his wife. See how blindly these creatures stumbled into their worlds, discovering their limits, experiencing new concepts, defining them, and shaping them for those who would come later?

"Time passed, and soon there was a longing, a *want* in Izanagi's heart, left there by Izanami's absence, which nothing else but her presence could fulfill. When he could no longer bear the feeling of emptiness, he set out in search of her, turning toward the cold and the dark of their realm, reasoning perhaps that those corners of existence still without shape and form could be where he found a new wife, perhaps a new Izanami. What neither of these gods knew was that in creating all the lands and structures together, they'd also created their reflections. *Hnn*, Shinjiro, I hear in the way you shift that you know this place."

"I do," I said. "We're in this place right now."

"*Yomi*. The underworld. Izanagi and Izanami had been so preoccupied with shaping mortal life and basking in the warmth that it cast over them that they did not consider what lurked behind the reflection in the pool of the ocean where they'd first thrust the spear of the gods. It was only through his grief and bitterness that Izanagi was motivated to search, and thus find, the dark, twisted, and cold paths below. He followed them, guided by the natural *kamis'* lights until there was a corner where none dared venture. The darkest, coldest pit. And there he found a house much like the one he had built with his wife, though twisted and mis-shapen, and within the house malformed creations that were mockeries of the natural beauty and structure he and his wife had formed in the world of light far above. Here there were *Oni*. Demons. Dragons. *Yokai*. Horrible monsters of myth and legends.

"And so he stumbled on, using senses other than sight, and Izanagi found at last his wife, who had kept herself far lower in this house than any monster. She proclaimed her joy at his presence, though her voice was muted, seemingly insincere. As though a different person. And Izanami would not turn to face her husband when he pleaded with her to do so. Izanagi had carefully committed the return path to his memory, and he urged her to follow him. She refused, informing him that she had supped of the unlife of the underworld, that being his counterpart in life and being cast now to the lower world of death, she must remain in order to keep the balance.

"Stubborn and bullish—perhaps we could say *masculine*—Izanagi saw his chance to win their quarrel. He swore that he would never leave her. And what of this so-called *balance* then, should he not return soon to the higher world? Izanami sighed, and in the face of her husband's threatening and disparagement, she agreed, though she made him promise he would be patient as she made preparations. She instructed him to await her outside the house for as long as it took, and she would again be with him, and the two of them would ascend to the light, together again."

"I think I can predict where this is going," I said then. In fact, I recalled part of the story now, something I'd read somewhere in my Tenjincorp-planned education as a child. I remembered scoffing at the words on the screen and adapting instead my own interpretation.

"Oh?" Tatsuhiro prompted. His face turned toward the floor, his ear toward me. A hint of a smile at the corner of his mouth.

"The man waits and waits, but the woman, who he thinks he owns and can control, never comes out, in fact, to spite him. It was all a trick. Their destinies are separate, one above, one below, even though from the beginning, it seemed like they were supposed to be together. She had no choice but to remain. And he had no choice but to go back, but he would never just accept that if someone else *told* him he had to."

Tatsuhiro's mouth turned down and his brows turned up. He nodded along, apparently impressed. "This is an acceptable reading of the myth, Shinjiro-san. Do you know how it ends?"

"Izanagi eventually gets fed up waiting, and he breaks his promise and bursts into the house. In fact, he brings a light though he'd been warned by all the *kami* not to, and he sees all the horrors, and his wife's body and face are covered in maggots and filth, just absolutely revolting. Whatever image he'd had of her... Just... it's gone. So, if things—aspects and concepts—are all being born, then that's the birth of *disgust*. But he doesn't just see her; all the other monsters see him, too, and they chase him out of there. He leaves her once and for all, and fights them off, and he rolls a giant stone over the entrance to some cave somewhere and seals them all in. And that's that."

"It seems you know this story after all," the old man remarked, chuckling. "You know it well."

"It jarred my memory, I think. But, Tatsuhiro-sama, what does this myth have to do with us? With this power? You said you had suspicions."

"I suspect that this is no myth. That is all. You and I have seen the *kami*, the spirits of the dead, the underside of the world. We have crossed between the two worlds that exist as one. I suspect that the cave is real, even metaphorically. It may not be an actual *cave*. But some must have discovered what it was at some point, and their curiosity drove them forward, and they were touched by something on the other side that changed them. That is all I can say."

"But..." I started, then fell silent. Let's be honest, it wasn't much of anything. The grand dragon, it turns out, didn't *know* shit. He was just guessing.

Or he's not telling me everything.

So yeah, I was disappointed.

Even blind, Tatsuhiro could read the frustration that must've darkened my face. He held up his hand. "You want to know, how did you and I *inherit* this power? Or how did it come to us? I cannot tell you, Shinjiro. Because I do not know. All I can say is that you must let go of your desire to *know* what is and simply *accept* what is. To refuse otherwise is to stray from the path. To upset the balance. I believe this is what the story is about."

And I believed him. I knew, then, that he was just like me. Or he had been once. Lost. Fumbling for answers, for years and years, growing angrier and angrier when the answers wouldn't turn up. And by letting go, Tatsuhiro had found his way.

"Who are you?" I leaned forward on the stair. "I mean really."

"I am the ShiroKaz corporation."

I glanced at the cables jacked into his skull and followed the pulsing light racing into the machine, which I then realized was like the biggest hyper-condensed server farm I'd ever seen (and I'd raided plenty). Then the light raced back again. It was like a giant sarcophagus, eight meters long, four meters wide, buried here in the spirit world. It was the entirety of ShiroKaz's existence on the grid. *Sequestered,* Cayenne had told me and Ben. In a place where no one could touch it. A quadrillion data cubes' worth of bits and bytes, informational transactions, encryptions. It was no wonder why nobody recalled this once-mighty mega-corp's existence. The entire company was quite literally a digital ghost. "Oh shit," I muttered, forgetting my manners.

"Once," Tatsuhiro went on, ignoring my foul language. "I should say, I was *once* the ShiroKaz Corporation, but I am not much of anything these days, as the company's power has faded. We once stood for something. The Legacy, we called it."

The words I'd had with Connor haunted me.

ShiroKaz was all about the common good. The betterment of all people.

And how come they're not around anymore?

Nothing common good can last.

Tatsuhiro continued. "Our enemies rose against us. Against me. The corporations we had started—one by one—wrested control from us. Assassination. Sabotage. Betrayal."

"The corporations?" My eyes narrowed. I had a bit of skepticism that I couldn't quite vocalize. Tatsuhiro heard the unsaid question catching in my throat.

"*Hnn,*" he grunted. "Tenjin. Inari. A-Matter. Many others. They were once all ours. All Shiromatsu-Kazama. Branches of the great tree that we planted, that was to grow tall, to shelter all mankind. Our great legacy that was to last a thousand years, if not forever. With roots in Japan, but growing across what remains of the world soon thereafter."

"For the common good."

He thought that I'd been asking a question. "*Seikaku ni,*" he agreed, smiling proudly. "Precisely."

"Then why end it? Why'd they … take it all away?"

Tatsuhiro's smile vanished. In the same instant, he suddenly appeared very weary, only a handful of breaths away from being a corpse. I saw for the first time how mottled his skin was, how withered, how frail his body. The dark liver spots tried to hide beneath the short wispy white strands of hair along his scalp, like dark rocks beneath frothing ocean water.

"Have you ever wondered why those with power, those with the means to power, do not use that power to save this world? Shinjiro, I see from your expression that you have. Do they know some secret we do not know? Hmm? It is greed. Yes. It is perhaps the darkest stain on our collective human nature. Simple greed. The powerful will not share with the powerless, even if it means this world will burn. It took great discipline, but within ShiroKaz, there was no greed. Only the desire for the common good, as you say. But, then, we faltered… *Zasetsu.*"

He trailed off. I could tell this retelling was a point of difficulty. Then he came back, I suppose, to the point he wanted to make. He swept his arm across the vast empty throne room before us.

"How long will the servants continue to serve," he said quietly, "when the master is absent from the house?"

"Absent?" I said. I'm not ashamed to say I didn't quite get what he was getting at.

"Gone," he repeated. Then, "*Shisha*. Dead."

I knew then that he was indicating the world beyond just this room. I remembered where we were. Where we *really* were. *Yomi*. The underworld. "Oh," I said. Then I shook my head, the understanding suffocated by the confusion again. "Wait. But you're not dead." I nodded at the cybernetic hand, at the nest of cables behind him, at the immense machine. "I'm not going to say I understand any of this, but you're not dead if you can be..."

Be what? Plugged in? I trailed off, not quite sure how to proceed.

"I'm not dead," Tatsuhiro said, chuckling at the stupidity I was certain my face displayed just then. Some of the vibrancy, the warmth, had returned to his features when he spoke. "Not anymore."

"You came back," I said. Now I got it. I'd been there too, *gone*, more times than I cared to remember. "To get me."

"*Hnn*," was all he said, and we were quiet for a while. "The other night, when I found you, I had come to warn you. I was aware that your boss in the Syndicate meant to betray you. After you had failed him. Although I can sustain a digital presence on the grid, I was unable to even send you a message. I can, at times, slightly move a security camera. Once I arrived to meet you, I could not sustain my physical body for long. Like you, Shinjiro, I am in both worlds at all times. But unlike you, my true form manifests here among the dead. I had come to tell you about what you would find in the ShiroKaz Tower, but as a wandering ghost, I lost all sense of the purpose that had brought me there. I asked you what was foremost on my mind."

"You asked me, what is *home*?"

"It is as you say. And then my time ran out."

Another moment passed in silence. Some old instincts were trying to fire in me, some sense I'd developed over my lost, misguided years of sniffing out bullshit. But for whatever reason, perhaps because in this place I wasn't my usual, flesh-and-blood form, I bought his story wholesale.

His sightless expresion came to rest on the immaculately white katana. The form of it stood out like a beam of sunlight against all the hazy, ethereal purple. I followed his blind gaze to it and ran my fingers across the handle's *tsuka* wrapping. I knew what I had to ask next.

"Who is the White Shadow?"

"Was," Tatsuhiro corrected. "Who *was* the White Shadow?"

I felt awkward, like we were talking about a mutual acquaintance behind his back, and yet our voices were just loud enough so that he could hear. In a way, that was exactly the situation. I pulled my hand away from the sword, crossed my legs under me, and waited obediently for the old *daimyo* to continue with bowed head.

Tatsuhiro drew in a long, ragged breath. "He was ShiroKaz security, decades ago. At a time when the first entities began their bids for power, becoming what you call now the *mega-corporations*." He spat the word, clearly detesting having to speak it so I would understand. "The merger of Shiromatsu and Kazama was still new. The mission—our Legacy—was still a new concept. And the enemies of our progress were numerous. Who were we to ensure the survival of mankind on this planet when there were profits to be made? Hmm? And so we were nearly destroyed when the corporations set aside their differences long enough to bring us down from the inside. There was rampant theft.

Kidnapping. Arson. Murder. The Japanese government, it was … *yowai*, weak and powerless. And soon its fading influence was overtaken. Absorbed into the money structure of the corporations. Then they turned on each other as well, and the demand for these crimes required a supply to match. Thus, at this time, your Syndicate was born. It was a time of chaos. What remained of our world needed to be saved. The man you know as the White Shadow…"

Tatsuhiro grew silent. His spider-webbed eyes wandered the room, perhaps searching the ethereal mists of the throne room for his long-lost memories. I watched his jaw tremble, as though he would speak at any second, but the right words wouldn't come. Finally, with grave difficulty, he said a name. "Yasuro." The sound of it was bitter. "Shiromatsu Yasuro. The White Shadow."

I imagined the slim, handsome features. The cascade of straight, stark-black hair. The impossible whiteness of his suit. The ruined red eyes. The burning fury, barely restrained.

"He's like us," I said. "Just like us."

"*Was.*" I looked up at him, expecting a reproachful edge sharpening his features, but I saw instead a proud kind of glint in his eye. The pupil here, apparently, was finally understanding the master. Tatsuhiro went on. "Imagine, Shinjiro-san, plotting with your executive panels in your ivory towers, moving pieces on the board, sacrificing lives and resources, ordering the deaths of those who stand in your way. Cheating. Lying. Reaping the rewards. Stealing the livelihoods of millions for your own gain. Recruiting, equipping, training—and in some cases manufacturing or *growing*—your own elite security force. Who is there to oppose you? Who is there to ever stop you?"

"A man who can walk through walls," I answered.

"*Hnn,*" Tatsuhiro said, smiling wide, and wider still as I kept going.

"A man who cannot be touched by bullets. A man who cannot be killed."

"*Densetsu*," the old man corrected, holding up a finger to stop me. "Not a man. A *legend*."

I remembered Feikes's face then, the last time I'd seen him. The words he'd said.

Thin air. Thin, fucking air.

"So… what then?" I asked, trying to fit the old man's narrative together. "The White Shadow fought back and the other mega-corps finally fucked off?"

My choice of words seemed to disappoint him. I had been allowing myself to get comfortable in his presence or something, I guess, and so reverted to more casual speech. *Whoops*, I thought.

"They withdrew their efforts, yes. And we let them continue their normal business operations. ShiroKaz did not seek their destruction. In time, we brought them all into the fold. We renamed them after the Japan we envisioned. Inari. Tenjin. Amaterasu. Even the warlord Hachiman was honored, the mighty protector *kami*. Spiritual. Pure. Divine. All of it for the ShiroKaz Legacy. And for a time, there was peace. For a time, Shinjiro-san, there was a world that could have been."

"You were around back then to witness all of this. How do you fit into the picture?"

"I tried," the old man snapped back, suddenly agitated, "but I never *fit in*."

My phrasing had apparently struck a nerve. Something personal. I leaned forward as much as I could, lowering my eyes to the floor. "*Sumi-masen*," I said. "Forgive me."

I felt his mechanical hand fall gently on my shoulder, and weakly push me back up until I met his eyes again. "*Ie*," he said. "It is *you* who must forgive *me*. It has been so long since I've spoken to another person. I forget the etiquette. I will tell you, though my own past, the part I played in these times, brings me great shame. Much like you, Shinjiro, I worked with the Syndicate. But I saw the error of my ways before it was too late. I wanted a better world. I believed in the ShiroKaz Legacy. So I became, hmm… *Komon*, an advisor. So, here I found my home again."

I waited for him to say more, but the silence only stretched. Even in his ruined eyes, I could see clearly there were pieces of this story he was holding back. Pieces he was abbreviating. Pieces he was leaving out. Among those, for example, was how at some point the entire company got compiled into some mobile mausoleum and jacked into the base of his skull. But I let it go. It was not my place to question the grand dragon's past. Not yet. Not *him*, anyway. I felt confident I could ask about our present.

"What about Cayenne?"

"Miss DeLeon." Tatsuhiro's gaze grew distant, as if he was trying to remember who she was. "Ahh. Yes. She serves our interests well. An invaluable asset to the Legacy. She is the last of a family that designed our greatest technologies. What you see before you here, the mainframe. Miss DeLeon has helped me sift through the information, but she did not know what, or *who*, we were looking for. She does not know that I had arranged for the Syndicate to bring you to ShiroKaz Tower. There is much that she cannot understand. *Kedo, chigaimasu*," he said, searching for the right expression in English, "this—what we have, you and I—it is *different*."

I understood the implication. *Cayenne isn't half-ghost. Got it.*

I asked the next most obvious question. "If you have the same … *power* as me, as the White Shadow, then did you, I don't know … *help* him? Somehow?"

Tatsuhiro chuckled. The crow's feet around his eyes wrinkled in genuine amusement. "No, no, Shinjiro-san. He acted alone. All alone. Even when help was proffered, he refused. Every time. Alone, an unstoppable force. Besides," he said, pressing his metal prosthetic hand over his heart like it was a confession, "I am no swordsman."

Swordsman. I heard the sound of the word in my own mind. The phantom vibration when I'd sliced through the tinman's arm tingled within my palms. "He is quite the swordsman," I said aloud. Then, catching Tatsuhiro's souring look, I quickly corrected myself. "Was."

"He was … *samurai.*" The way the old man spoke the word… It was music. In it, there was the lament of the old world that had passed by. There was prayer, there was ceremony, there was honor over its grave. In the voice of Tatsuhiro—the *grand dragon* himself—there was the desperate hope for the old world's return. I found myself yearning for it too.

We were quiet for what seemed like a long time.

"When he was … destroyed, I too, was … *destroyed.*" The word wasn't good enough; I could see it in the pained expression creasing his face, but he left it there. "And his power passed to me, it seemed. My spirit wandered the depths of *Yomi.* Lost. *Hnn…* You know well. But when I found my way back, unlike the myth of Izanagi and Izanami, no one had come to find me and hoped to guide me. But someone had left the cave entrance open, you see. The way back, Shinjiro, is in having purpose that your spirit, your will, cannot let die. And the purpose is the anchor that enables the crossing. When I emerged, it was too late. ShiroKaz was no more."

My eyes wandered to the sword. I picked it up and set it across my lap. What was Yasuro Shiromatsu's purpose? Revenge, plain and simple. It may not have been my purpose, not personally, but since he had found me and brought me back, I had no choice but to seek it for him.

When I looked up again, Tatsuhiro was considering me as intently as I considered the katana. There was a kind of look on the old man's face that I could not read as he stared at the thing. Longing? Remorse? Or maybe even pride? If only the old man still had some fucking functional eyes, I swear. He might as well have been wearing the mirror shades again.

"You know about this katana." I'd meant to ask in the voice of the student addressing the master, the *kohai* to the *senpai*. But it came out like an accusation. Actually, I'm not going to lie; that *was* how I'd meant it. I wanted clear answers. "You know Yasuro is still in here. Don't you?"

"Hnn. I know."

"How? How the f..." I licked my lips and tried again. "Getting trapped in a katana. How can something like that even happen?"

"*Yasuro no seishin,*" he began after a moment's consideration. "*His spirit* is not ready for the world beyond. There is something he wants more than the release of true death."

"Revenge," I said.

"Hnn. Revenge."

"But that doesn't explain why he's not just ... *out there.*" I jerked my head toward the tall double doors far across the grand hall where the dead had gathered. "Not just one of them. How is he *in here*?" I rattled the sword to drive home my point.

The grand dragon's bushy eyebrows drew together angrily; his expression bore into me. The ethereal purple glow that lit his throne room seemed to gutter. Red—the deep red of rage, of passion—crept in, staining the edges of light. Somewhere far below us, from the abyss of *Yomi* itself, there came a pulse, a feeling that thrummed through the floor. A voice inside me spoke the words I saw written in the old man's eyes: *Who are you to ask? To know? Insignificant worm. You are but dust that I brush from the hearth. Ash. Trivial. Immaterial.*

My breath choked in my throat. I knew... I knew it wasn't Tatsuhiro who had made the world quake. It wasn't the old man invading my thoughts. It was *him.* The White Shadow. *Yasuro.* He was listening.

The old man understood my distress. He slowly reached for the weapon I cradled. How badly I wanted to pass it to him, to relinquish the sword, to give up on my duty to the vengeful phantom inside. I tried to lift it, but my arms were frozen at my sides. Tatsuhiro's withered, human hand hovered over it, trembling, and with great effort, his hand clasped instead around my wrist. Inexplicably, I sensed the underworld pulse subside, saw the red receding, the gentle purple glow reignite. I felt the warmth of life spreading through me again.

"He is trapped in this weapon," he said, "because it is this weapon that killed him."

I stared at the katana and felt like I'd never actually seen it until now. The delicate carvings, the perfect threads of its wrapping, the smooth case. The sheer purity of its white color. "His own sword?"

I expected another affirmative grunt from the old man, but I never got one. He seemed lost in the sword's beauty as much as I was. "And the one who killed him," he said at last, "you have already met."

I looked up suddenly, my eyes fixating on nothing as the thrill of the duel replayed in my mind, my heart flaring with the traces of adrenaline in my veins. The speed. The feeling of metal fingers closing around my throat and my body hurtling through the air. The hiss of the micro-pistons and the blue haze. "Zercos," I breathed. "Cayenne told me he came for the sword."

"*Hnn.* He believes he has earned it. As Yasuro's finest pupil. His *only* pupil. And so, when the master would not relinquish the white sword, Zercos struck the master down."

"How did he become a machine? What the hell happened to him?"

Tatsuhiro's brow furrowed sharply in disgust. He could disapprove of my language all he wanted, but I wasn't backing down. He soon realized I wasn't planning on rephrasing my question, but he made me suffer for my insolence with a non-answer all the same. "He paid a heavy price for his victory."

I bowed my head so Tatsuhiro wouldn't see my eyes roll. I pictured Zercos's state-of-the-art cyborg body, the triple-jointed legs, and the black katana sharp enough to cleave gravestones. "Seems to have worked out in his favor in the end."

"Make no mistake, Shinjiro-san. If it had not been for Yasuro's teachings, the *thing* you know as Zercos would not exist. He *was* true samurai. It is his strength of spirit that sustains him, not his machinery. But, whatever he is now, he will come for you again."

"Come for the sword, you mean?"

"No." Tatsuhiro's fingers slid under my chin and brought my eyes up to his. In his face, I saw the pride of a teacher who delivers the final word of his ultimate lesson. "You and the sword are one."

No. I raged inwardly, jerking my head away from his fingertips. *Fuck that.*

But deep inside, I knew it was true. None of who I was before had made it out of the ShiroKaz vault. Nothing that had happened since was real. Not my trip into Feikes's Syndicate lair to rescue Ben, not my feelings for Cayenne, not even being here, now, in this place, this dragon's lair tucked deep inside the throbbing core of the underworld. The real me was still very much strung up in the eternal, white emptiness, the cold blade carving through my guts, the ghost whispering in my ear, promising me what I'd always wanted only if I served. I was only the White Shadow's hand, while the White Shadow was everything else.

Yasuro Shiromatsu, the legend. Betrayed by his own student, Zercos. The White Shadow wanted revenge. And I would bring it to him. I would have to face Zercos again and rip the spirit out of the cybernetic body and deliver it up to my true master.

The sword and I are one.

I knew it for the inevitability it was.

But there was still something I did not know.

"Tatsuhiro-sama, I have just one last question. What do *you* want from me?"

The old man drew back slowly into his original position on the dais, straight back, hands folded in his lap. The ethereal, glowing light still pulsed rhythmically into the massive server behind him. He closed his eyes. His lips moved. "Become the White Shadow."

The blades of the aperture slid now into place, all the pieces perfectly spaced open, the light flooding in. It all made sense. I saw now everything he had said, all together, at once. My power. My special power. The sword. And I. We were one.

"The ShiroKaz Legacy," I said. "You want me to help you what? Reclaim control of NeOsaka?"

"Not Osaka. Not Japan. The world, Shinjiro-san. For it is on fire. It burns itself to cinders. Soon, it will be ash. No light remaining. Help me ... transcend the darkness that awaits."

I had wanted to get out of my own life for so long. I hated everything. I hated the world. I hated myself most of all for what I truly was: an incarnation of self-loathing. A demon. A killer. Ever since the day I'd yearned for the ripping and tearing of three orphan boys, and because I'd wanted it, it had happened. Since then, I couldn't remember having truly wanted anything else but to die, and never live again, because life was wasted on me. But then, the shadow-man in the sword saw who I really was, saw all my hatred, and

I had believed he was the only one who could give me the true escape I craved.

But I had been wrong. For my whole life, I'd been wrong. This withered old man, Tatsuhiro, the grand dragon, he was the only one who was right. Why escape the world when you could change it? Why escape yourself when you could change that, too?

This was my chance.

Fuck yes, I thought. And we smiled together.

THIRTEEN

ON OUR WAY BACK, CAYENNE STARED AT THE SUNLESS landscape from the rain-streaked window on her side of the cabin. Across from her, I tried to pretend I was doing the same out of mine. I couldn't stop myself from glancing at her. Every subtle movement drew my eyes. A twist of blonde strands around a finger. A crossing and un-crossing of legs. A sigh. A stifled yawn.

After my meeting with Tatsuhiro, after agreeing to help him, to be the White Shadow reborn, I felt like I could conquer anything. Like I could save the world. Or crush it, then rebuild it however I wanted. But despite this surge of power and self-worth, I somehow couldn't make myself say anything to her.

The faintest smile curled Cayenne's lips.

Now or never.

"Something funny?"

The smile withered like a bean sprout in a nuclear blast. Even Ben, curled up a few seats away from her, seemed to cringe in his sleep.

"I didn't mean... What I meant was, what're you thinking about?"

Cayenne kept her gaze on the world outside a moment longer before finally turning it on me. "I was thinking, Asai-san—"

"Shin. Please, call me Shin."

"Shin... I was thinking about what your records say about you."

I kept my eyes locked with hers. I suppose she wanted me to ask her what could possibly be funny about a native Japanese girl orphaned and chewed up and spat out by an automated childcare education program, but I kept the question to myself.

"That so?" was all I could manage.

"Indeed." She smirked again. "Asai, Shinjiro. A male's name. I was curious why the mistake was never corrected. And I was smiling because I was more curious after you had disappeared from the system, why not take a different name altogether?"

It wasn't the first time anybody'd asked me this. *Why the guy's name?* I recalled one particular night, laying with our legs entwined, when I'd gone on and on to Kasumi about the whole bullshit philosophy behind my name. *Shinjiro Fucking Asai,* I'd said, staring up at the ceiling of the cramped little coffin capsule I'd rented for us. *They want to give me a name that's not me, well I'll fucking make it me. I'm inside their grid. I'm a part of it. They want to give me this identity, like a number, like it's something that doesn't matter, just a line of code in their program, but I'll make it the glitch that crashes their whole system. I'll take the meaningless name and make it mean something, just to spite them.* Kasumi had already fallen asleep, her open mouth against my skin, the side of her teeth digging into the west pillar of my torii tattoo.

Just like the fake plastic hostess must've realized that night, I was suddenly realizing here and now in the cabin of the speeding JOK quadcopter. *Why didn't I change my name?*

I don't actually fucking know.

"Perhaps," Cayenne suggested, coming forward to the edge of her chair, "you want to make a name for yourself? A name to be worthy of? I was smiling, Shin, because I think now you can do that. With us. With ShiroKaz."

"Sure," I conceded, but it didn't feel right. The truth I wasn't telling her was that I'd always, stupidly, hoped I'd find my parents. The little orphan cowgirl, really a princess, lost and found, who gets her tiara and her name. But I gave up on that fantasy a long time ago.

I didn't want to keep talking about it, but I also wanted to keep her talking. I thought I'd turn the tables a bit.

"Cay*enne*," I said. I turned the sound of her name over on my tongue. I said it again, slower, stretching the last syllable. "Cayenne… Who gave you that name?"

Her eyes dropped to the floor. "My father."

"Did you—"

"He died. And my mother. When I was very young."

"I'm sorry."

Cayenne laughed. "Why?"

"Just that's what you say when you hear that."

"Is it?"

I wasn't entirely sure what Cayenne's motives were. Talking to her was like how I imagined a fencing match. Maybe I'd cut in from the side, maybe an overhead slice, maybe jab at her directly. But she was always expecting everything. From her, it seemed there was always a riposte, followed by an elegant turning away.

"So… Tatsuhiro. Is he your…"

"Benefactor."

I kept silent, refusing to throw the obvious question at her.

"Like a father," she went on. "Though I'd not even met him face to face until two years ago. I don't remember my parents. I remember being taken care of by one nanny after another, speaking one language after another, moving me from one palace to another every few years. Then, as I aged, one boarding school after another. Rome. Tehran. Buenos Aires. Sarejavo. Kiev. Even the United States, before the West finally fell. Nothing but the finest things money could buy. Safety. Satisfaction."

Sex, I thought. Because of course I thought it.

She lifted her eyes up to mine as if I'd said the word aloud. I hadn't, had I? But the look she gave me then said she'd heard me well enough.

"None of it mattered. All of it wore away in time. Just when I would get close to someone, when I thought I'd found a real friend, it would be time to move again. My life felt … fake. Like loading one simulation after another. Forgive me, I must sound like I am complaining. I've never spoken about these things to anyone."

But you are now, I thought. *To me, of all people.*

"And given how vastly different the circumstances of our upbringing… Just, never mind. You probably don't want to hear any of this, Shin."

"There's nothing to forgive," I said. "Yeah, our lives couldn't be more different. *We* couldn't be more different. But we were both—"

"Lonely," Cayenne said.

There was a long silence. Our eyes met. Holding her gaze was the hardest and easiest thing I'd ever done. "Maybe we aren't anymore," I said, cracking a smile. She nodded and did her best to smile back, but it was weak, uncertain of itself. She looked away, putting a distance between us again.

I thought that we were done there, for the time being, and that our conversation hadn't gone as poorly as some of our previous ones. I settled deeper into the comfort of the cabin seat. After a minute, Cayenne's voice surprised me. She wanted to say more.

"I was in Geneva, Switzerland, when I tried to..." she trailed off, deciding it was something she had to show, not just tell. She pulled aside the fur collar of her overcoat. My heart skipped a beat at the sight of her bare skin, but that kind of excitement didn't last long when I saw the scar just along the curve of her neck, down to her collarbone. "I couldn't even do it right. I didn't want to die, exactly. I just ... wanted to know what I was living for. Anyway, it wasn't long after when he found me."

"Tatsuhiro."

"Yes. Tatsuhiro."

"He told you about the Legacy."

"He did. And it became my reason for ... everything."

"So you think it's possible?"

Cayenne's lips peeled apart slowly. I thought her answer would be a quick affirmative, but what I got was hesitation. Uncertainty. Not what I expected from a C-Level mega-corp yes-man.

"I do," she finally said. A human being, after all.

"You know what he is, right? What he can do?"

"I don't entirely follow you."

"Him. Me. Zercos. The White Shadow. You heard the, whatever, *legend* of the ShiroKaz chief of security, right?"

"Tatsuhiro-sama apprised me, yes."

"So you know we're ... *ghosts*."

There. For the first time, I said the word. I'd never spoken so directly about my curse. I'd never called it out for what it was. Cayenne had shown me her scar, told me things she'd never told anyone, so I returned the favor. It's not like she didn't already know, right?

It felt like the pressurized cabin temperature dropped a dozen degrees. Cayenne sank back into her chair and pulled her coat closer about her.

"I saw you do things that I can hardly explain. Powerful things. Frightening things."

"Do we frighten you, Cayenne? Do I?"

"What you do, Shin, is no more frightening to me than some of the technology out there. Take Zercos, for example. A man that should be dead. A brain in a jar. A monstrosity. Whether you walk through the wall, or you create a weapon that atomizes the wall, what is the difference? There was so little mankind knew about his own world before he ruined most of it. And now, what have we let this world become? And what has it made us?"

Good questions. I didn't have an answer to any of them. And her point taken, I looked out the window as the hazy horizon edge of NeOsaka rocketed into view. This late in the day, the western sunlight behind us struck the latticed isotope-radiation shield at just such an angle to light it up like golden dew on a spider's web. I leaned in and craned my neck, and could just make out the underbelly of the sub-orbital spider that lorded over all. *Takamagahara*, Heaven, who kept us survivors safe in our dome, kept us prisoners content in our prison below.

"Quite marvelous, is it not?" Cayenne said, observing the space platform from her own window. "If we can build that, what can't we build?"

The JOK eased into a turn that brought our view back down to Earth. Gravity brought Ben's head lolling onto his other shoulder, which was enough to rouse him. He stretched and put his thick glasses on.

"Good morning, Mister Doon," I said, beating Cayenne to it.

"You were gone a long time, Shin," he said, almost all of it in a yawn.

"Had a meeting with our new boss."

"ShiroKaz." He said the name so low and so flat that somehow it felt like disapproval. Like an indictment. An accusation. Maybe I was tired, and that's why I lost it a little.

"Did you enjoy the ride in this thing? Enjoy your nap? Enjoy your rescue from Feikes? All of it's because of ShiroKaz."

"I kn-know, Shin. I'm n-n-not say—"

"So, what are you saying?"

"J-just saying…" Ben looked at Cayenne for help, but got only an arched eyebrow. "It's just a big change for us, is all I'm saying. One day, you know, we're ripping off a mega-corp and now we're working for one."

"Don't worry. I'm sure I'll be doing most of the work."

"That's not what I mean."

"Asai-san," Cayenne said, putting her hand on my knee softly enough to make me tingle. "Shin, you should tell him what Tatsuhiro told you. What you told me. Mister Doon," she went on, withdrawing her hand and turning to Ben. "The Shiromatsu-Kazama Corporation works for the betterment of all mankind. As we've almost arrived at our destination, we don't have time for details. Just know that you're working now for the good guys."

"The g-good guys?" Ben chortled, looking again over every inch of the JOK's pristine cabin. His eyes narrowed at Cayenne. "Sounds like something the bad guys tell themselves, Miss DeLeon."

The J-Zero-K eased into the lazy creep of traffic between the spires of NeOsaka's western Amagasaki district. Besides our voices, the whir of air rushing by the bullet-shaped aircraft had been the only sound, and it gradually died to silence as the machine slowed and banked skyward, bringing us to rest on a landing pad.

I was expecting the roof of ShiroKaz Tower, but this building was much wider, massive, and pyramid-shaped, maybe five hundred meters across. It was one of the arcologies, a completely self-contained commercial and residential habitat for the NeOsaka elite. The ten highest dock levels were packed with privately owned copters and limousines, and our J-Zero-K slotted in very nicely as Cayenne waved her fingers around hardlight screens that verified it belonged, that *we* belonged.

We strolled (and in Ben's case rolled) through a series of moving walkways and lobbies, coming at last to an expansive pentagonal atrium. The dying rays of the sinking sun lanced through the slice of window that ran from the floor level all the way to the top where all four diagonal walls met. Ringed around at every level were hundreds of high-end plazas, vehicle dealerships, meeting rooms, convention spaces, and, of course, entire blocks reserved for private corporate apartments. I would say the place was packed with top-level decision makers and their corporate retainers, but there was so much space, so much room to breathe the fragrant air, recycled and cleaned by copious plant life that clung to the walls or sprouted from curated gardens up and down geometrically pleasing staircases.

Ben and I exchanged an apprehensive look, the two of us feeling—no, no, the two of us ex-Syndicate cowboys and girls *realizing*—how very unlikely it was we belonged here. And we were turning heads, or maybe it was just Cayenne. With her hands pressed on hips that moved like she was on a catwalk, the fur-mantled camelhair coat flaring out from the breeze of her passing, she sailed onward with an air of majesty and speed, and Ben's motors had to work overtime to keep up. She knew exactly what she was about and exactly where she was going. She knew she belonged. And I fed off of her confidence. It was amusing to see the retinues of the C-Levels frantically twitching their heads with the haptic controls of their implanted comlinks and punching hardlight datapads searching for our grid signatures as we passed.

I wondered how much longer I'd have to keep them all waiting. Me. Their inevitable disappointment. These were the very people who would re-board their chartered million-yen transports the next morning, which would whisk them off to a day's work designing, making, and marketing the technologies that would keep the masses dependent on distractions from the world's grim realities, which only they had the power to provide. When would I phase into their private offices to let them know their agendas were going to drastically change? In a month? A week? When would I be ready? A day? Maybe *today*. Maybe right now. As we passed the corporate elite by, no one noticed the purple haze misting from my right forearm as I reached into *Yomi* and felt the white sword, felt the power always at the ready, waiting to be unleashed.

We broke away from the main thoroughfare, and into a hallway that terminated at a dead end. The only commercial occupant was an international antiques dealer, apparently closed. When Cayenne pressed a fingertip to her temple, a lens in the wall lit up red and swept a micro laser over her retina. A second later, the pneumatic door of a private elevator hidden in the wall slid open. Inside, some familiar *kanji* adorned either side of the elevator. *Spirit. River.* I wondered just how deeply ingrained the Shiromatsu-Kazama Corporation was in the NeOsaka corporate infrastructure. How many of these towers were theirs? How many private clinics, elevators, storefronts, apartment blocks? How much of this entire city truly belonged to Tatsuhiro? Had the whole world truly forgotten the withered old man in the ruined castle?

Doesn't matter, I thought. *They're all going to remember soon enough.*

The suite of apartments itself was certainly a step up or two from the flaming pile of shit that was my previous home. Here, in the center of the technological marvel that was an arcology, ShiroKaz had carved out a secret place all its own, like the pharaoh's private hidden passage in his sprawling tomb. Every inch was made with thick wooden beams, *tatami* mats, raised *tenjo* ceilings, and sliding *shoji* paper doors. I removed my semi-brogues in the recessed slate *genkan* entranceway and crossed halfway to the balcony overlooking the city before I noticed Ben and Cayenne had stayed behind.

"You're not coming in?"

"While you were meeting Tatsuhiro-sama, Mister Doon agreed to brief me further on the principles of acronymic once we arrived back in Osaka."

"Besides, I don't think the new boss'd like my treads all over these nice floors."

"Benjamin, your own apartments are similarly furnished. And, I assure you, your wheelchair will not be a problem, as the floors are self-repairable."

With wide eyes, Ben quietly mouthed *Benjamin?* at me.

I cleared my throat. "So what's next? After your little coding lesson?"

"A party." Cayenne stepped back into the elevator after Ben. She frowned at my ruined clothing. "I suggest you get freshened up."

"A party? Where? Here?"

"Your roommate has all the details."

"Wait. What roommate?"

"I'm sure," she replied with a smirk as the elevator doors closed, "you two will fit together quite nicely."

FOURTEEN

D ESPITE ITS TRADITIONAL APPEARANCE, IT TURNED OUT there was plenty of technology in the ShiroKaz arcology penthouse. For starters, after looking hard enough, I found tiny hardlight projector nodes embedded in the lacquered wooden beams all over the main room. What exactly they were designed to project, I hadn't the slightest clue. Maybe it was my shitty comlink, maybe its outdated firmware, but for whatever reason, I couldn't figure out an interface point. There were speakers, security sensors, and even modular fitness equipment that assembled itself from inside the walls, all of it state-of-the-art.

As I continued my grand tour, I found a climate control panel that also doubled as a switch for the aerated sand pit at the center of the apartment, a twenty-by-twenty meter Zen garden. I must confess, I wasted entirely too much time dipping my fingertips into the floating lumen-tactile screen, which manipulated the airflow in the pipes below so I could carve the wide stretch of sand into whatever shapes I wanted.

I was almost done with my masterpiece of a phallus when a vision of the orange *Oni's* face flashed in my mind. Its fist slamming into Connor's chest. Then the ghost dragons, green and blue, shrieking. And the empty purple *kabuto*. They were all *Yasuro*. All in my head. Reminding me. The sole reason for my continued existence. I asked myself the obvious question so the White Shadow wouldn't have to.

"What the fuck are you doing right now, Shin?"

I scratched out the shapes I'd made in the Zen garden so violently some of the sand splashed up onto the surrounding *tatami* floors.

I'd found all this, but what I hadn't found was any fucking trace of the roommate Cayenne had mentioned.

The place was completely empty. There was a kitchen with no food. A desk with no devices. At least the bathroom had a bath, although without towels or one of those elite air-drying ante-chambers an under-city dynam-ad once tried to convince me I *needed* in my life, I couldn't tell how I would dry myself. *Well, she said to freshen up for the party. Whatever the fuck that means.* I dialed up a super-heated stream of water into the rough-stone basin, dumped my ruined jacket and trousers in a corner, and went into the bedroom with no bed as I started to unbutton my bloodstained dress shirt. I slid open what I guessed was the adjoining closet, and maybe it's cliche to say it, but my heart skipped a beat.

Hanging inside was the embodiment of incorruptibility. The quintessence, the archetype, the aspect of all my dreams, all my residual self-image. The most impeccable amalgamation of fabric I'd ever laid these violet eyes on, and I'd lain them on a lot. I could tell with one look that the two-button, two-piece suit had been tailor made only for yours truly. The slight raising of the chest, the tapered waist, the letting-out of the hips. My gaze swept over every inch of stitches tying all the seams together, admiring the robotic efficiency with which they had been made.

I caressed the sleeve, lifted it gently, let gravity take it, and felt the run of it against my rough palms. I watched the almost chameleon-like shimmer of the fabric's color as it moved over my hand, from charcoal to midnight to black. But it wasn't shiny. If there's one thing I can't fucking stand, it's a shiny fucking suit! What it was… It was perfect!

The tip of my tongue was between my front teeth, as if I felt subconsciously embarrassed for smiling so hard, all alone, almost naked, with just this suit for company.

"Ohayoo gozaimasu."

"The fuck?!" I dropped the sleeve and spun around. The distinctly bubbly, high-pitched feminine voice had come from behind me, but there was no one.

"Good morning."

No. I was wrong. The voice was all over the room. Everywhere and nowhere.

"What the fuck?"

"Asai Shinjiro. Hello. Greetings. Prompt: please acknowledge my presence."

"Acknowledge wha—"

"Acknowledged."

"Who the fuck are you? Are you fucking watching me?"

"I am monitoring you. Your heart rate is spiking."

"No fucking shit! Come out here."

"I am here. You acknowledged my presence."

"What the fuuu…"

Somehow I knew. I looked back at the suit, hanging all by its lonesome in the utterly empty ShiroKaz penthouse.

"No fucking way," I whispered.

"Asai Shinjiro," the artificial voice droned, the system subroutines simulating what it appropriated was the tone of human disappointment, "you have employed substandard forms of verbal expression seven times, nearly eight. Advisement: refrain from doing so in social settings and with new acquaintances."

From the bathroom, over the sound of my stunned silence, I heard overflowing water crashing onto the floor.

"Asai Shinjiro, would you like me to dial down the bath water?"

"You're in the suit, aren't you?"

"I am not in the suit," the suit said reproachfully. "I am the suit."

"An AI."

"Sentient Universal-Interfacing Totality."

"SUIT."

"Yes. I will dial down the bath water now."

The crashing sound ceased.

"I..."

"Yes?"

"How are you doing any of this?"

"Please specify."

I lifted the sleeve again, a little less gently this time. "How can a swatch of fucking fabric dial down a fucking bathtub?" I gripped it hard and nearly tore it off the rack as I waved it back toward the bathroom to illustrate my point. "How is there a damn computer in this?"

"The object you hold is merely the platform by which my consciousness is transported. The nano-machinery woven into the fabric houses all the data and subroutines necessary to perpetuate my infiltration state into every machine within a hundred-meter radius. I am not alive, Asai Shinjiro—no artificial intelligence is alive, after all. But if it helps you understand, then please consider the following statement as fact: *I live in all things.*"

"So, what am I supposed to do? Wear you around town?"

"Yes."

"What? Why? I... I mean..." I relaxed my grip and found that the sleeve hadn't rumpled in the slightest. I removed the jacket and held it up by both shoulders, sweeping my eyes over its perfection once again. "You *are* beautiful, SUIT."

"*Arigato gozaimasu.*"

"But, if you could tone the voice down a bit. You sound like a fucking *weeaboo* nerd."

"By cross-referencing your phrasing," SUIT replied immediately, her simulated voice flowing through the speakers at a slightly more sultry, slower, lower volume, "I've reached an understanding of your request. Is this preferable?"

"Highly."

"Male or female?"

"I ... don't care?"

"That is contrary to the profile I've compiled. Your preference is female."

"Fucking ... whatever."

"Speculation: If I were human, and we had just met in a social situation, the impression you would create with your language would be less than ideal for both of us."

"Are you trying to tell me to stop cursing?"

"Yes, Asai Shinjiro."

I'd had it pointed out to me before, by many of my SynCell associates and victims of petty crimes, that my mouth was often quite memorable. But I'd never before been told to watch my fucking mouth by a machine. I felt like telling the AI—*the fucking two-piece suit!*—to go fuck itself or fuck a sewing machine. *Maybe I'd drown it in the bathtub*, I thought. But I think I was still in shock.

"Okay," I drawled.

"Your physiology does not suggest sincerity, but we will address this at a later time. For now, please hang me back up and 'freshen up,' as Miss DeLeon suggested. Your bath is waiting."

I did as the AI suggested, sliding in up to my lips; the heat of the water radiated into every inch of my body, soaking deep. I closed my eyes and let myself go. I took a mental inventory of all the horrors I'd seen in the last two days, some of which I had perpetrated. Some of which were parts of a nightmare I thought I'd buried. Enrapt in the soft, warm cocoon of water, I felt over the scars of my body, spending extra time to learn the new contours of the scar Zercos's sword had left near my heart. I drowsed in the tub and felt my fingers slip away, down to my side. My mind wandered to what my hand felt when the sword it held cut into Boltcutter's thigh and took his leg out from under him. I grimaced at the mental image. The sword was still a phantom in my hand, even in my dream. Then, Yasuro Shiromatsu was there, suddenly, in his white suit. He was very much alive, standing before the gates of Himeji Castle, before the fire. The katana in his hand was black. Disembodied, I watched him from above and behind as a red haze flowed from his form, and he stepped through the solid gate and was almost gone. But he stopped and slowly turned his head. And he saw me. He saw through me. Even in my dreams. And it suddenly didn't matter how hot I'd dialed the water, for I was encased again in ice.

SUIT must've heard me screaming. The artificial intelligence had drained the tub, probably when she detected that I was drowning. Is this how I had to live from now on? Could I not even take a shower or bath without dreaming about the vengeful spirit puppet master with his blade on the thread of my life? Under constant surveillance and supervision of an omniscient artificial intelligence system residing in the fibers of a fucking two-piece?

Fuck.

I must've been under longer than I realized. Must've been more tired than I anticipated. SUIT slid aside the *shoji* in the bedroom to reveal a neon night vista of the NeOsaka sprawl as I crossed to the closet dripping all over the *tatami*, prune-fingered, and bare-assed naked. I'd been so stunned by SUIT's sublimity that I hadn't noticed the line of starched white dress shirts also on the rack. I used two of them to towel off the excess water and dropped them in the corner on top of my discarded, bullet-riddled wardrobe, then started buttoning up a third. A tsk-tsk sound emanated from the apartment speakers all around.

"What? Next time give me a f—give me a towel!"

"Barbarian," SUIT remarked quietly.

I let out a deep breath, then I put her on.

"Ha-fucking-ha, Cayenne," I grumbled to myself as I roamed down the ShiroKaz arcology corridors. "My '*roommate*,' she says. 'Fit together nicely,' she says."

Speaking to me through my comlink, SUIT told me where to go to find the suite where Cayenne was apparently receiving part two of Professor Ben Roy Doon's lecture on anachronistic computer hacking workarounds. It seemed almost ironic that I was smuggling the planet Earth's most sophisticated, corporate-engineered computer infiltration platform into a discussion on how to avoid corporate hacking and detection protocols. The funniest part was that I suspected the Cluster's acronymic protocols would work just fine to keep all their secrets hidden indefinitely.

"We have arrived."

I reached a hand out for the buzzer but stopped short, struck still by a sudden notion.

In *Yomi*, just behind the fold of physical reality, I felt the presence of the white katana. All I had to do was reach for it, and as quick as the speed of thought I'd be thrust into the twisted underworld where no walls, no doors could hope to stop me.

But what would happen to SUIT if I did?

"SUIT," I said, glancing up at the ballpoint-security camera lodged above the apartment's door frame.

"Would you like me to erase your form from the security feeds, Asai-Shinjiro?"

"No. Wait, you can do that? What am I saying? Of course you can. Sure, go ahead. But it's not that."

"I sense hesitation," the AI responded. By this point, SUIT had read enough of my biometrics to compile a preference profile and calibrate its accent to the level of sultry female Australianite it thought I'd prefer. I honestly couldn't say I was displeased by this. I saw the lens in the mini-cam subtly twitch. "But I cannot discern the cause."

"SUIT, do you know what I am?"

"Please clarify. There are many interp—"

"Do you know what I can do? Did Tatsuhiro tell you about me?"

"If you are referring to your inter-dimensional capabilities, then yes. I have been briefed."

"So have you … been briefed about what'll happen if I take you over to…"

How does one explain this to a computer?

"To the other side?" SUIT suggested.

"Right."

"I am programmed to log the phenomena and adapt. Knowing our mission, inter-dimensional travel would be an eventuality."

Well, I thought, *let's get started.*

I stepped away from the door, kept my hand up, and summoned the white katana. A rift of dark purple opened in space and the weapon materialized in my hand a second later. I didn't let the opening close. I focused my will and dragged the underworld forward. Physical space twisted and warped around me, throwing me into the realm of spirits.

I turned around and found the corridors of the arcology had lengthened, stretching on into infinity. I could see it curving up, down, corkscrewing left and right, leading any-where and nowhere. And the dead were there. Countless ghosts. Men, women, and children, of all ages, from all eons. Some of them had wandered here years ago and become trapped. Some had followed me here. All were ready to serve.

"Oh," was all I could say.

They watched me. They watched the sword. They waited for my bidding.

"SUIT," I muttered, looking down at my sleeves and rubbing my palms along my lapels. "You there?"

There was no response.

"Fucking weird," I remarked, then remembered I was trying to make an effort to avoid vulgarity in the AI's presence, *then* remembered it wasn't actually present here, in *Yomi*. "Fucking weird," I repeated.

"You," I told the lines of ghosts. "Stay."

My followers bowed all at once.

I turned back to the door and pressed my hand through, then my forearm, and soon my entire body. I was in. Crossing barriers, even as thin as a *shoji* screen, used to leave me sweating and panting for breath. But this was nothing. With the power of the white katana, the crossing between worlds was effortless.

I was unstoppable.

"B-R-Y-A-N."

"Bryan," Cayenne said, looking a bit worn down.

"See? You'd think that!" At this point in the seminar, Ben's excitement was siphoning off the final energy reserves the young corporate executive had originally come through the door with, visibly aging her. "But that's just an example of how we could throw the detection algorithms off. That's the first protocol of the system. If a sequence of letters shows up in that order, what's the natural, primary response of the security apparatus?"

"To run the name."

"Exactly!"

Ben sat forward in his wheelchair, behind him a massive setup of monitors and keyboards. Boots off and toes wriggling, Cayenne lounged on one of the apartment's massive wraparound couches, typing a few notes on a holo-display floating at her side. Ben's apartment was a lot less "traditional" than my own, already furnished and embedded with sleek amenities. I barely had more than a bathtub. As I was thinking this, Cayenne's second cappuccino arrived steaming and perfect from the aperture in the center of the coffee table.

Their voices were a bit muffled to me, standing there on the other side of reality as I was, but I could make their words out clearly enough. I'd been letting Cayenne get an earful of Ben Roy Doon for almost five minutes now. I stood with folded arms, not paying attention to a word he was saying, focusing instead on Ms. DeLeon's subtle reactions, amusing me to no end. The pinching of her brow, the reddening of her cheeks, the rolling of her eyes, the rubbing of her neck. I know, a bit voyeuristic. Possibly perverted, I admit. But I had good intentions. See, very soon I'd be the one to swoop in and rescue her from Ben's ramblings at the very moment of peak annoyance, thus raising myself to her good graces.

"The more common the name," Ben resumed, "the more records to run, the more time we have to trick the system and get around security."

"But what I still don't understand, Ben, is how the operator on the other end understands *precisely* which phrase this particular usage of the acronym—B-R-Y-A-N or *whatever*—is supposed to mean. *Uht-tut-tut!*" Cayenne said, raising her finger to silence Ben's counter-reaction before it could start. "I'm not finished..."

She's really getting to know him.

"This is why the agents or raiders involved would need the keys written down, by hand, as you said, prior to the infiltration. Now, I understand fully how acronymic *works* in a live context. You've more than explained this to me, thank you. But what I fail to grasp is... Please tell me *how* in the world these keys are shared among the agents. What occurs in the event that codes are lost or stolen? Or worse, perhaps. Have codes ever been falsified to betray an agent from within the Cluster?"

I could see a little of Ben was rubbing off on her. *Question after question after question. No time to process. No time to answer.* She was really speaking his language here. Ben looked at a total loss for words. Even from within the dim half-light of the underworld, I could clearly see a bead of sweat form along his hairline and drip down his brow.

It looked like it'd be *him* I'd have to swoop in and save after all.

"AHH-SHIT-WHAT?!" Ben nearly toppled over in his wheelchair as I dropped in literally unannounced through a purple Shin-sized rift in the living room space, weapon still in hand.

"Konichi-wa," I said, bowing slightly. "Is this a bad time?"

"Not at all," Cayenne said, rising from the couch and pressing her skirt flat, clearly trying to suppress the shock I'd given her. Ben was not so calm.

"Wha—? How di—? Shin, y-y-you ju—"

"Ben. Listen. I'm going to say this as straight as possible. I can walk through walls."

Ben steadied his breath, blinked, adjusted his glasses, while I exchanged a look with Cayenne. Finally, he sort of shrugged. "Yeah. Explains a lot, actually. Like, *a lot* a lot." Then he looked at me seriously. "What sort of tech is that? Is there like a rig in … you?"

"Not tech," I said, dispelling the katana with a wave of my hand. "Just something I do."

"Street magic," Ben proposed.

"The show is over," Cayenne said. "Now that you've … *arrived*, Shin, we should discuss our next move."

"Oh, I like this," I said, crashing down on the spot she had vacated. "You said before, something about a party."

"Yes. But we will not be attending for pleasure."

"Shame."

Cayenne scowled at the smirk I was giving her and walked several steps away. "Shin, it is time for you to fully grasp the severity of your situation. Perhaps I need to remind you of what I assume Tatsuhiro told you. There are enemies of ShiroKaz. Powerful enemies that stifle the course of human progress each and every day. Playing with the lives of ordinary people who are just trying to survive in what is left of this overcrowded nation."

"Mega-corps," Ben mumbled.

"These are our enemies." Cayenne leveled her gaze at me. "They need to die."

Now, I've done my fair share of killing. By fair share, I mean four, if you've been counting so far. Five, actually, assuming Boltcutter didn't make it, although that one was easy to get over. I hadn't really had time processing how putting an antique slug through Vasili's skull had made me feel. Maybe because he'd asked me to is why I felt forgiven. But just then, as Cayenne spelled it out as cold and clear as could be, maybe she was right, I needed to grasp the severity of what my world was now.

But I had one question for her.

"Is that how the old White Shadow did it?"

Cayenne folded her arms, drummed four fingers at the crook of her elbow, and considered her response. "No," she said finally. "And also yes. Yasuro Shiromatsu's method was to warn the saboteurs. He would promise them their death. If he had to, perhaps make an example of their security force. In the beginning, sometimes, they left him with no choice."

"But eventually," I said, picking up the logic she was putting down, "they got the message."

"That was decades ago. Through Yasuro's efforts, ShiroKaz enjoyed a time of relative peace. NeOsaka and the rest of Japan prospered inside its bubble, safe from the threats looming beyond its borders."

"And then it fell apart from within. Zercos killed Yasuro, his own master."

Cayenne nodded, though I noticed a moment's hesitation. "They killed each other."

"Well," I started, ready to point out how strange it was we were talking about the one being a cyber-zombie and the other an angry spirit encased in a sword and how apparently no one ever really dies, but I waved my hand dismissively instead. "Actually, nevermind. None of this is convincing me why *I* have to kill anyone."

"Because *you* are the White Shadow now. And you inherited his promises, which must be kept."

Neither Cayenne nor I flinched or even seemed to breathe for what felt like a long time. For some reason, even though I was looking at her green eyes, I felt the blind sight of Tatsuhiro boring into me. It was him standing there talking to me now, the dragon-headed sigil, the withered old man in the depths of the castle ruin, not Cayenne DeLeon. He had made me believe this was the only way to be free. It wasn't murder, it was execution. It was keeping promises. The enemies of ShiroKaz had committed crimes against humanity, and they had to pay. The balance had to be struck, and I alone had the power to strike it.

So why the hell was I having so much trouble accepting this now? I could kill if I had to, right? Kill with intention. Couldn't I?

I let out a deep sigh and broke away from Cayenne's gaze.

"Who is it?" I said.

Cayenne took my question as a sign of acceptance, which maybe she shouldn't have. She, too, let out a sigh, then approached our resident comms wizard. "Ben," she said, "have you heard of the handle, Triangle?"

"S-s-sure," Ben stammered. "Where to start? I mean, Triangle's practically its own brand of intrusion scripts.

But they're relatively outdated by today's standards. Old s-s-stuff."

"How old?"

"I think maybe … fifteen years?"

"So this hacker, Triangle, creates some of the most effective security intrusion software the, hmm, *community* has ever seen, and then what?"

"I don't kn-know. I was like five years old when his last script was fresh. *We*, I mean, were five. The three of us. Probably. Cayenne, how old are you?"

"*Her*," Cayenne corrected, ignoring his question. Ben looked confused. "*Her* script. Triangle is a woman."

She looked over Ben's shoulder and blinked. The screens lit up with pictures of a woman in a mugshot. Young, punk haircut similar to mine aside from the neon-pink dye, a black eye, numerous lip and brow piercings, a middle finger front and center for the camera. Rage in her brown eyes. And a gaudy, bright orange neck tattoo, a triangle from throat to collarbones. Running alongside her profile was grainy surveillance footage of Triangle on her way from a subway car, disappearing into a crowd. More freeze-frame footage of her on a couch in a grimy basement, goggled-in and wired up to a wall full of hardware, haptic-gloved hands tracing their way through the grid. She was short, this girl. Stocky. Strong.

Badass.

Cayenne must've given Ben access as well, and on one of his new chair's holo-screens a security personnel report scrolled by, stamped with a mega-corp logo I recognized. *Spirit. River.*

I pointed to the screen. "What'd Triangle do to ShiroKaz to warrant a rap sheet so long?"

"She worked for us."

If I'd been drinking, I might've spurted it onto the *tatami* floor.

"First you tell me Zercos, Mister Fucking Security Chief, turned on ShiroKaz, now this … hacker girl."

"Sandra Calvin. Aliases include: Forever Zero, Neverything, Trick Minister, and most notably Triangle."

"She looks young," Ben pointed out.

"These photographs are roughly fifteen years old, as you said," Cayenne told him, glad for the chance to ignore the shit I was trying to shovel at her. "Sandra Calvin is now forty-seven years old. American-born. She was among the first wave of refugees to arrive in Japan after the fall of the southeastern United States. She often clashed with authorities, but to no end. The Syndicate gave her direction, a purpose, a place she could use her talents."

I wonder if she knew Feikes, I mused. *Or Connor. Or even the cyber-zombie Stub.* I pushed the last image I had of them all from my mind. I stood up quickly and paced away to keep it out. I busied myself with the hololight barista program that sprang to life as I approached the other side of the room.

"So how'd she get picked up by ShiroKaz?" I asked, just to have something to say.

"She was hired to raid us," Cayenne said. "Yasuro Shiromatsu stopped her entire Syndicate Cell. Spared only her. Recruited her soon after."

"And now, decades later, she *needs to die,*" I spat Cayenne's earlier words back at her a little venomously. "And I have to kill her." I shook my head. "Why?"

"She was instrumental in the dismantling of ShiroKaz and its Legacy."

"I don't need a press release, Cayenne. What the hell are you trying to say?"

She looked hard at me. "She betrayed Yasuro and had him killed."

No way.

I stared at Triangle's—Sandra Calvin's—profile on-screen. She stared back at me. My eyes fell to her throat and the orange triangle tattooed there.

Revenge.

It wasn't really Cayenne or Tatsuhiro that wanted this.

The White Shadow wants me to kill her.

"She helped Zercos do it?"

"Yes. Among some others. But her most prominently. Instrumental, like I said." Cayenne came to my side and stared at the screens too, quiet, thoughtful. Probably deciding how much I needed to know just then. "It was an uprising, I suppose you could say. As cyber-security chief, it was nothing for Miss Calvin to arrange the separation of ShiroKaz's holdings—that is, the split between corporations. Inari, A-Matter, and such. She allocated all the funds and assets accordingly, and when Zercos sprung the trap and eliminated the physical security force—"

"Eliminated Yasuro," I pointed out.

"Yes. Once the White Shadow was gone, all it took was the press of a button and ShiroKaz was no more."

"Okay, I understand. But why not let it go?" I didn't know who I was really trying to ask: Tatsuhiro's representative here, or the vengeful spirit trapped in the sword on the other side of reality. I wondered if Yasuro's spirit was listening. "Why does she have to die *now*?"

"Because..."

It wasn't Cayenne that answered. The sound of Ben's voice spun both of us around. But he didn't say more, just his eyes flitting over text on the holo-screens, mouth slightly ajar. He'd been doing his hacker thing.

"Because what?" I prompted.

"Shin," he said, looking up at last. "Triangle's the s-s-sole operator of T-T-T--"

"Tenjin Media Corporation," Cayenne finished.

FIFTEEN

"SO YOU'RE SAYING..." I trailed off again, for maybe the third time since we'd left Ben's apartment, trying to get a clearer glimpse of the whole picture. Cayenne was walking fast. Talking faster. I could see the agitation I was causing in the sway of her hips, how she didn't just walk, but stabbed the sleek arcology hallway floor with her stiletto heels. I could hear it in her clipped tone of voice.

"I'm saying *all* news, *all* media, *all* communications—on the isle of Japan, for the past decade—have been controlled by one person. *And* I'm saying," she stopped and spun around so suddenly that my chest collided with the finger she pointed at me, "that Sandra Calvin, also called *Triangle*, is that person. She controls every single digitally broadcast word, therefore she controls what people know and when they know it."

"Therefore," I said, reaching for the hand Cayenne held at my chest, which she pulled aside, "the news, the educational system. Schools. And orphanages."

"It's too much power for one person to have, Shin."

"Who else knows about this? Besides us three, and Tatsuhiro."

"That's it."

"That makes no sense. How could she not be a public figure?"

"It makes perfect sense. When you control the flow of information... Oh my god, Shin, do I need to tell you this again?"

I let it drop. Cayenne turned away, flustered. But she didn't try to run away from me, so that's a plus. She crossed to the window-side of the hallway and stared out across the sprawling NeOsaka skyline with folded arms. I followed her gaze, wondering exactly which building, which plume of steam, which levitating vehicle or neon sign or colossal dancing advertisement had caught her eye. I was trying to see what she saw.

What she saw out there was a world suffering. Declining. Doomed. Tatsuhiro had said as much, and I knew Cayenne shared his vision. There were corporations above the law, tearing the old world down to raise taller and taller monuments of their own dominance, vying for the final drops of prosperity at the expense of everyone else, the salarymen just scraping by. There were powerful people who made the conscious decision to do so, knowing it would lead to others' pain. People at the top. Elite. Evil. People like Triangle.

What did Cayenne see in me? Was I just a means to an end? Just a sword in her beloved benefactor's hand?

"What am I to you?" I blurted out before I thought to stop myself. I swear my next tattoo should be "poor impulse control" on my forehead as a reminder every time I look in the mirror. A warning for everyone else.

I saw her shoulders tense, her back straighten. She assumed the all-business pose from when I'd first met her. She glanced at me for just a moment, then back to the window. Her voice was even, flat. "Tell me what you mean, exactly."

"I guess," I began, wondering if I should divert back to business or just say what was on my mind. "Do you like me?"

Poor. Fucking. Impulse. Control.

Cayenne was silent and still as a statue. I froze. I panicked. Suddenly the idea that she might never answer and I'd be stuck here waiting for eternity came to mind. I tried to save myself.

"I mean, do you *even* like me? Are we *friends* or something? Or is all of this just a … fucking … *business transaction*? You're the CEO and I'm just security and Tatsuhiro's like, the chairman, and you say the company's gotta move in this direction, and it's something only I can do, and if I don't like it I'm, what, fired?"

Cayenne let out a breath. It wasn't exhaustion or frustration. With that breath, her protective corporate armor was swept away. I thought maybe she'd been waiting for me to ask after all. "Shin…" She turned to me, a look in her eyes I'd never seen before.

Her true self?

"I'm sorry for what happened to you. Your history. Your life. What you've gone through to come this far. But you're here now. This is the truth. This is the situation. And this isn't about you anymore. It's bigger than you. Or me." She turned again to the world outside the window. I found myself able to move, so I came to her side. Silent. "Triangle has a stranglehold on society," she went on. "And she's not the only one. I know you must be feeling like you're being used. Trust me. I … know what that feels like. But you're the only one who can get to her."

I didn't know what to do with my hands. I didn't want to fold them over my arms like Cayenne. I didn't want to stuff them in my pockets like *aww shucks.* I didn't know why I was thinking about this, but it was awkward for all of one second anyway because from literally nowhere the white sword materialized in my grasp, unbidden.

My thumb pushed the handle up from the scabbard, exposing an inch of the blade, breathing a puff of purple smoke. So light, so easy, so perfect. I remembered then who I truly served.

The White Shadow wanted Triangle dead.

What choice do I really have?

None.

"Fine. I'll do it."

Our eyes met. I thought maybe she'd throw her armor back on, but no. Cayenne smiled, and goddamn, if I didn't forget anything she had ever said before that enraged me.

"And, yes," she said. "I do like you."

I wanted to just stay there, let the warmth spread around in me forever, encased in glass away from the world, with her. But the moment was fleeting, over before it really had a chance to begin. Her eyes drifted to the katana held at my side, which hadn't been there a second ago. Believe me when I say if I could've dropped it, if I could've thrown it through the windows and let it rust in some rainy alley until the end of time, I would have. The sight of it unnerved her. She swallowed and turned away.

"Two hours," she said over her shoulder as she moved away. "I will meet you at the spider-rail. The AI will bring you there."

And she was gone, disappeared down this secret ShiroKaz arcology corridor. I don't know how long I stared after her.

"Shinjiro," SUIT said. "Miss DeLeon has uploaded the mission details to my and Mister Doon's drives."

"What?" I asked, not actually listening to its words. I stared out over the late-night NeOsaka skyline. Gentle blue light diffusion shimmered between the monolithic black buildings, a mixture of electric pinks, purples, strobes, and

LED whites. Anything to keep my eyes busy and my mind off of what was coming. But SUIT droned on in my comlink.

"I do not understand why Mister Doon's assistance is needed. I am more than enough. But Miss DeLeon insisted on his inclusion. With your authority as head of security, I could easily override his access."

"Sure," I muttered absentmindedly, then, "wait! What? Hold on. Don't lock Ben out of … whatever-the-fuck you're talking about. If this is going to be anything like a Syndicate raid, I want him as my handler."

"Shinjiro." The inhuman, Australian voice lilting softly from the hallway's hidden speaker system sounded disappointed. Artificially so. "Language."

"Ben," I said into my comlink, attempting to dial him up.

"Clarification: Shinjiro, I would like to demonstrate my capabilities."

The call ended abruptly. If there's anything I know about Ben, it's that he was always only one call away. "Unlock my comlink," I ordered absolutely no living being there in the hallway with me. "You're doing this, aren't you?" The lights in the slanted ceiling dimmed. The photochromic window panes darkened, snuffing the skyline sunset. I was in almost complete darkness.

"SUIT, what the fuck is this?"

No answer.

"Yeah, I said *fuck* again. You not going to reprimand me?"

It may sound somewhat weird to hear me say it, but I'll admit I was a little scared. Intimidated. Yeah. I know. The dead used to frighten me. Then I adapted. But this was something new. I could feel the AI's power pulsing through all the wires and systems in the hallways, above and below and all around, throughout the whole arcology. Throughout the whole city itself.

"SUIT?"

On the other side of the translucent window, a silhouette of glowing neon pink shifted, snagging my peripheral vision.

The form broke away from the rhythm of the other lights. It brightened. It expanded. It ... came closer.

The artificial darkness gradually dispersed at its approach. It was one of the dancers that manifests in your comlink as you walk the NeOsaka streets, advertising the seedy pleasure-dens in the sub-levels. For some, a wiry male with sculpted muscles donning a tight, bulging pair of shorts, if not a swinging semi-erect dick. For me, a buxom, tight-tummied, balloon-breasted female form swaggering, stooping forward to draw you into her cleavage, winking, promising. Not at all unlike Kasumi. For whatever data I managed to conceal from the grid over the years, the network still knew enough about the anomalous-me when I'd pop up to display what it thought I yearned for, and the dancer would then deliver a personalized invitation.

"Shinjiro Asai," it said. The neon-pink giant beyond the windows said my name. I heard its voice rattle the unseen speakers in the arcology hallway. And I felt it boom and bounce around every crevice of the Amagasaki district's buildings just outside, loud enough to turn the heads of hundreds. Shouted over the rooftops, out past the layers of the metropolis, above and below. SUIT's voice flooded my name through the avenues and alleyways.

The giant, nearly naked form kneeled slowly. Outside, it was an entrancing pair of pixelated eyes. It smiled.

It reached a finger, intangible, to the glass. The image split in two, creeping to the right and to the left as reflections. Pink light flooded the arcology hallway where I stood rapt. The image revealed itself as the unreal, two-dimensional construct it was. An electronic ghost. I'd never experienced any dynam-ad or pleasure sim or anything like this before.

"You're..." I stammered, "just a computer. How are you doing this?"

"I am more than a computer, Shinjiro Asai." The voice of the Sentient Universal-Interfacing Totality continued to boom out across the streets, loud enough now to rattle the windows. Foot traffic on the inter-building walkways below had slowed to a crawl, in some places a standstill. Hundreds of people gawked at the naked, pink giant. SUIT hadn't just patched into my comlink like a normal advertisement. It was on full display. "These machines are my slaves."

"Okay," I managed to say, thinking about how I'd never met an unhinged, marauding AI before. Then again, it had been a pretty strange week for me already, so why not? But I didn't appreciate it saying my name out loud. The thought helped me get grounded. "You've proven your point. But I should remind you that you were *given* to me. To *serve* me. To meet *my* needs and the needs of our mission. I think maybe you made an error with this display of…" I swept my hand at the windowpane and pointed to the crowds below. "Vanity."

The neon pink head swiveled around to regard the other tiny humans at its intangible feet as if it hadn't been aware, anyway. From wherever they stood, SUIT had patched into all their comlinks simultaneously to provide the same simulated, sexually stimulating angle. She—or *it*—blew a kiss, and for every person below it appeared directed at only them. As it was also directed at me. Truly, only me. Then the dancer faded away.

A moment later, the darkness of the windowpanes and the dimness of the hallway lights returned to normal. I took a deep breath. Then another. That was fucking wild. There was a running joke around town about how the holo-light figures in the skyline had no souls, but this hadn't been funny. I dialed up Ben.

"We gotta talk about all this," he said right away. No hello. No where-are-you. Was he talking about the AI taking the whole arcology for a kilometer-wide joyride just moments before? His tone told me it was something different. He had no idea what had just happened to me.

"I'm doing it, Ben," I said quickly, cutting off the objection to corporate assassination I assumed he would be making. Ben was as against killing as I was, but he didn't have a vengeful spirit riding along in his soul with a razorblade scratching at the threads of his existence. "*We* are doing it. And don't even start your shit right now, Ben. I want to make this clear. I want *you* up there with me. Okay? You and me, like all the other times. Can I count on you?"

Ben was indeed holding back on starting his shit, as I had instructed, and the line was silent for what felt like an age. I looked out across the night skyline of the city beyond the windows. The lights were really flaring up now, heralding the approach of another wild night. Business dealings. Syndicate raids. Money. Data. Heartbeats. Bullets. Here I was thinking Ben and I wouldn't be out there running with any of that anymore, but I was wrong. We were raiding now, same as ever, only now for an exclusive clientele.

"Fact is, Ben," I spoke into the silence on the comlink. "I can't do this without you. I never could."

"Okay," he said finally. "Yeah, okay, Shin. Don't go g-g-getting all soppy on me now."

I smiled. "Cayenne said she would meet me at the spider-rail."

"What?" Ben's shriek rattled in my ear-piece. I plucked the thing out and held it at arm's length. But I wasn't even mad about the sore ear drum. I was still smiling. If I were him, I'd have been disappointed, too.

"So I'm st-stuck down here but you, you g-get to go to outer space now?"

SIXTEEN

HEAVEN IS REAL. LET'S SETTLE THE DEBATE ONCE AND FOR all. By now you've learned that ghosts are real, so why not suspend your disbelief a little further? Look up. You can see it plainly through the isotope shield over the city, through the hazy, irradiated air beyond, held in place by the colossal cables sunk deep into the earth around the NeOsaka perimeter. But can you go there? Are the gates open to one and all who renounce their sins? Is that all it takes? That's what they want you to believe.

But they fooled you. It's okay. They fooled me too. Heaven is for the rich. It's only ever been for them. Built by the rich. Reserved for the rich. Guarded by the rich. Something to dream about, sure, but never actually achieve.

Or maybe dreams really could come true, if you had a unique, inexplicable curse that could be exploited for mega-corporate interest. Such was my case.

Heaven is *Takamagahara*. The Plain of Heaven. Most of us call it "the platform." It hangs in space just above the Earth's atmosphere. An absolute marvel of astrophysics and engineering. Over fifty years ago, realizing the impending energy crisis could not be slowed at its current trajectory, the now-defunct government of Japan green-lit a space program to construct what amounted to a massive plain of solar panels that could feed half of the country with its supply of energy. The cables that anchored the platform to the planet were as thick around and sturdy as skyscrapers, feeding the world with power. After the war that threw the rest of the world in chaos and scorched patches of the Earth everywhere beyond Osaka, the project was halted, half-finished. Just strung along in orbit. As Japan struggled to ensure it wouldn't be consumed, not only by outside forces but by the growing unrest boiling within its own borders, the government had enough to handle on its own. So corporations saw an opportunity to take control of the project and complete it to suit their own interests and elite lifestyles. You might think getting there would be dangerous. But you'd be underestimating the ingenuity of mega-corporate money. Aside from drone supply shuttles that launched regularly from runways all around the city, which were mostly filled with non-organic material and supplies, the only way to reach the platform was by boarding the carrier pods that crawled up and down the cables, like trains to the sky. The spider rails were spacious and filled with amenities to help the corporate elite travelers ease the vertigo of watching the ground, the city, the clouds, and the whole Earth recede from view, replaced by an undiffused view of the galaxy beyond. The whole trip took about an hour.

And what could you expect to find once you arrived at Heaven itself? About the same as you'd find in the mega-corporate arcologies. Hotels, spas, casinos. Data vaults, server farms, conference spaces. Villas, nightclubs, cafes. All of that and more, plus the luxury of being able to experience life in low gravity, if that was your desire. But what you wouldn't find in an arcology were the clandestine research facilities where corporations design and innovate their next version of killing machines, training grounds to tweak the instincts of those parts that are still human, and state-of-the-art barracks to house them all until the next war breaks out. In short, *Takamagahara* was paradise for the mega-corporations. If it turned out that planet Earth truly was doomed, then at least the elite would still have a place to flee to and escape Armageddon.

Just about the only piece of Heaven that all of us living in its shadow ever got to experience was the final race of the annual TKMG hypercraft league. Years after its construction, someone had the bright idea to wind the track in, out, up, down, and all around the towering city-like structures at the center of the solar-field on the sun-side of the platform. The sleek hypercraft were autonomous maglev vehicles, absolutely frictionless, capable of speeds that were impossible everywhere else besides the void of outer space.

But it wasn't just the velocity that attracted the league's tens of millions of viewers every year. It was also the weaponry. Have you ever seen fire in outer space? Have you ever seen shards of glass and charred bits of human flesh spinning forever and ever out into the nothing? The TKMG hypercraft league was a bloodsport. Pilots were more than just racers. They were gladiators. Lining up Gatling gun sights, locking on with heat-seeking missiles, deploying chaff grenades to deflect enemy fire, dropping magnetic mines around corners, all the while maneuvering through twists and turns and corkscrews at supersonic speeds. Cutting-edge cyberware implanted in their brains could only give them so much of an edge to make any of this possible. Bullet Time took care of the rest. The pilots were corporate-sponsored drug addict zombies, sealed in their hypercraft coffins, loaded to the nines, eyelids clamped back, a steady drip feed of synapse-sharpening fluid flooding their vision and seeping into their bloodstreams.

This, apparently, was the pinnacle of the human race. It wasn't just enough to guarantee all the free, clean energy the world below needed, not to mention catering to every whim and desire of those with excessive means. Heaven also had to serve the other, baser human needs for violence and spectacle.

I'd never really given it much thought before. I'd seen plenty of league races on the massive holoprojections on the smoky haze in Feikes's club, cheering on my favored pilot from the plush comfort of the private booths, downing drinks with the other cowboys and girls from whatever SynCell I happened to be running with at the time. It was mindless entertainment. It appealed to the aimless, to the lost, like me. Like I had been. But things were different now. For starters, I was decked out in the finest suit any human being, living or dead, had ever worn. The fact that the Sentient Universal-Interfacing Totality was a narcissistic, arrogant Artificial Intelligence was beside the point. We were back on good terms, as far as I was concerned, once I'd discovered it could change colors and textures at will. Just then, I had opted for a jet-black Mohair style.

Cayenne sat across from me in the small but luxurious corporate cabin of the spider rail transport. She was utterly radiant, wrapped in a gown of exquisite emerald silk to accentuate her eyes; the fabric flared out at her thighs to accentuate everything else. A velveteen, burnished gold mantle that matched her hair wrapped her shoulders. And green and gold jewelry adorned her neck, each wrist, and most of her fingers. They glinted mesmerically as she waved a hand, conjuring a projection of the promo reel for this year's TKMG race, happening in just a few hours, bringing my attention away from her beauty.

"This is our cover," she said, the holographic light flaring up just then to showcase a particularly nasty explosion, the frames slowing down as a hypercraft speared straight through the fire, spirals of smoke caressing its sleek sides.

"I'm not getting in one of those, Cayenne. Hey, don't give me that look. I know that's not what you meant. Lighten up."

She smiled. Just a tiny smile. But it was genuine. Then I watched it slip off as her lower lip trembled. Her eyes fell to the floor and she let out a deep, shuddering breath.

"What's wrong? Are you feeling sick?" I pressed my hand against the thick glass of the viewing window. We were about halfway up the cable, crawling along steadily. The edge of planet Earth curved away, glowing blue with diffused daylight, limned by the darkness all around. "I never thought I'd ever ride in one of these things, but I think I'm doing okay. This isn't your first time, is it?"

She looked up at me. She was as beautiful as ever, but there was stress lining her face. Up until just that moment, I'd doubted Cayenne DeLeon could have even felt fazed by anything. But I saw it plainly then.

"It is," I said. "You've never been up here before, either."

"First time for a lot of things, actually. Inari, Fuji-Rai, A-Matter. All the executives will be here tonight. It's the first time in decades that Shiromatsu-Kazama will put in an appearance. Yes, I think I *am* going to be sick."

I didn't know if it was the decreasing influence of gravity, the vertigo from feeling our usual world slip away, or the fact that I (or maybe anyone) had seen her vulnerable for the first time ever in her life, but Cayenne looked haggard. Thankfully, it was just the two of us in this cabin, two spots filled out of eight. (I think SUIT might have had something to do with booking out the pod with fake grid identities. The AI had also come alive over the intercom to inform us she'd be acting as our cabin steward as well and had been silent ever since.) I unbuckled my safety belt and crossed the small space between us, fazing straight through the holoprojection of the hypercraft race, and sat down beside Cayenne.

She didn't turn away, didn't say anything. Just slumped forward, head down. I raised a hand, meant to press it gently between her shoulder blades and try to soothe her, but I hesitated. Wasn't this kind of thing exactly what I'd hoped for since I met her? The chance to touch her? The old me—that is, the me from three days before—would have gone for it, would have grabbed and groped for whatever I wanted in life, and fuck it if life then slapped me across my stupid, shameless face for it. But the new Shin, the Shin I think I was still trying to figure out, knew that Cayenne wasn't Kasumi. She wasn't as desperate as I was, fake as I was, lost as I was. She was not a projection. Not an object.

"Is it all right, if I..."

Who the hell was I anymore? Listen to me ... asking permission.

Cayenne groaned, then straightened up, her back connecting with the palm of my hand. On purpose. "Yes, please," she said softly.

I was flooded with a warmth I simply cannot describe, only because up until that exact moment in my life, all my vocabulary to describe such a warmth was sexual. But this was beyond that. Sex seemed like such a petty thing, compared to rubbing the shoulders of a woman you had just realized you loved. I gladly rubbed her back, felt her shuddering, her body giving off a coldness and rigidity at first, then gradually letting go. I felt bold, and reached up to the back of her neck, her mocha-colored skin so warm, so smooth.

"I, uhh..." Shit. Why was I speaking? Was this something I really wanted to talk about? Right now? On the ride to outer space, on my way to kill somebody? Too late. I had to finish what I had started. I had to know. "I know you read a lot about me in those files. You probably know by now..."

"I know the way you look at me, Shin."

Her voice surprised me. "You do?"

"I'm not an idiot." She turned toward me, and my hand fell away, no longer sure of itself, just like the rest of me. Cayenne's emerald eyes bore into me. "I want you to know that I meant what I said before. I like you, Shin. I think that, despite everything, you've survived, and you somehow aren't ... cold, because of it."

I couldn't help but let out a quick bravado laugh at that one. But it wound up sounding like the death rattle of the old Shinjiro Asai, who felt she had to keep up the defenses. I let go of the old Shin at that moment and let the macho smile die. I gazed back into Cayenne's eyes, said, "You too."

Then she smiled. But it was a sad smile. "But I can't ... be with you."

A part of me had known it all along.

The old macho-bravado Shin hadn't even been dead and drifting away for three seconds when I felt her rushing back in like the inexorable tide. "Hey, I get it. Not the first time I've heard that, you know." I took my hand away from her, even though it was the last thing in life I ever wanted to do.

Just don't say you're sorry to me.

"I'm sorry, Shin," she said.

I couldn't stop the feelings from flooding in with old, dead Shinjiro then. It was a fucking tsunami. Who was I to think I'd finally found a home since it turned out that home was with a mega-corp in a place I'd hated all my life? Who was I to think I'd finally be free when I was beholden to a vengeful spirit that dominated my soul? Who was I to think that Cayenne could ever love me?

I took a deep breath, but my jaws were clamped tight enough to crack a diamond. After a moment, I spat out the usual line. "It's all right. I mean, it has to be. We have a job to do. Triangle has to die. The ShiroKaz Legacy has to be ... whatever. Whatever the right word is for that. Brought back to life."

"Remembered," Cayenne said, not at all unkindly or dismissively. But I couldn't focus on her tone. All I heard was the word, the correction.

"Whatever. Same thing. And let's not forget the White Fucking Shadow. I sure as shit can't."

I rose to my feet and leaned against the window, pressing my forehead to the glass, wishing I could just jettison myself, wondering just how far the boundaries of *Yomi* reached. Could the spirits find me all the way up here? Could Yasuro? The Earth below had shrunk. I could see beyond the horizon, the iron-black ocean of night, the scorched brown muck of land all around. The glowing patch of electric rainbow light that was the city of New Osaka. The only sign of life for a thousand miles all around.

"I'm feeling better now," Cayenne said after a moment of silence. "Thank you."

I came away from the window and went back to my original seat across from her. I expected the coldness to have gripped me again, but seeing her again, everything was still warm. I had just gone through the motions. Her rejection didn't mean shit, and I should have realized that. It was okay if she didn't love me, if she couldn't. If she wasn't built the same way I was, after all. I could accept that. I could grow the fuck up a little. I could tell her that I was the one who should be sorry. For presuming.

"Asai-san. Miss DeLeon."

SUIT's digital voice hummed through the cabin.

"Time's up," I said.

"You will arrive at the airlock in two minutes," the AI corrected.

"Okay. Two minutes."

I turned my gaze away from the planet and the city below and looked upward, leaning as close to the glass as I could. *Takamagahara* was a city all its own that those who dwelt below could never hope to see, founded on a flat, round disk. Its buildings rose out of a sea of shimmering gold, the immense plain of solar panels that soaked up the energy of the sun and channeled it back down to Earth. There were communication towers lined with satellite arrays, private residences with personal airlocks for recreational space walks, and, of course, off-world headquarters crowned with all the corporate brands you would expect to see back on Earth. Everything was connected by an intricate web of glass walkways. And looping in and around it all was the TKMG magnetic track. Hypercraft were already zooming across the frictionless surface for their preliminary laps.

So this was all real. This was all really happening. I was here. I was the White Shadow. In just a few short hours, Yasuro Shiromatsu would have his revenge against Sandra Calvin, the infamous hacker Triangle, head of the Tenjin Media Corporation, the very institution in whose arms I had been inexplicably dumped as a child.

There was a lot going on there, yet I felt completely calm. I suppose it was the subconscious knowledge of my immortality. My indestructibility. My power. Tatsuhiro knew it, or else he wouldn't have sent me here. I closed my eyes, reached through the veil separating life and death, and found the white katana waiting for me on the other side. When I opened my eyes, it was there in my grasp, the last wisps of purple smoke from its crossing over dissipating.

Cayenne had watched my ethereal flourish happen without batting an eyelash. She looked blankly at the sword, then up at me. I still saw the apology in her eyes, and I appreciated that. But there was something else. A pleading, I thought.

"Listen," I said, offering my other hand to help her rise. She accepted. "We're going to be okay. When we get there, you borrow a little of my brash, reckless stupidity, and I'll try to take a little of your professionalism, and we'll sort of meet halfway."

"Your confidence," she said, squeezing my hand. "Not stupidity."

SEVENTEEN

THE GOAL WAS SIMPLE. SHIROKAZ NEEDED TO NOT JUST put in an appearance that could be forgotten the next day; we needed to sear the news into the corporate elite's collective consciousness and make an indelible mark signifying that their true master had returned. The servants were to be called back to the *daimyo*'s throne.

And that was it. Simple, like I said.

But just because something is simple does not mean it will be easy. Nor that it will all go according to plan.

The elevator slowed, nearing its zenith, floating Cayenne and me ever so slightly off the floor. Because *Takamagahara* was not truly in orbit, but instead riding the atmospheric line, Earth's gravity still had a hold on everything. The doors slid apart soundlessly, and we stepped out into a lavishly accoutred space the size of an airplane hangar. It felt like a temple. And in a way, it was. A place for the most faithful to worship the gods of money. The floor before us fell away into a staircase that curved around in either direction so that we stood at the top of a circle ringed by more and more circles all around. A glass dome encased the entire space.

From here it was possible to see the entire Plain of Heaven all around, the hypercraft track, the sea of solar gold, and all the stars, all at once. Behind us, the elevator closed and sank slowly back into the marble floor. Yellow lights glowed warmly within the stone to mark the machine's boundaries.

A trio of cyber-zombies greeted us. They wore dark, expensive suits, smiled friendly human smiles above Windsor-knotted ties, and held up hands covered in plastic-fab flesh at the ends of their endosteel-reinforced forearms. They regarded us with vapid, expressionless stares. The apertures in the tinmen's synthetic eyes narrowed and widened sporadically as they scanned Cayenne and me, flitting through various vision modes to interface with and attempt to hijack any systems we might have implanted in our bodies. I already knew they wouldn't find shit on me. I still didn't know what kind of tech Cayenne was packing, but I was as clean as the day I was born (or so I assumed), aside from the scars and tattoos. And also, I guess, the immaculate white katana I held casually at my side. For all to see. A statement.

"Good evening, gentlemen," I spoke up. "I take it you are the security force for the evening."

Cayenne glanced at me reproachfully. I suddenly remembered how I had pledged to act slightly more professionally than usual. But then the corner of her mouth turned up, nevertheless. I smiled back.

"Yes, ma'am," one of the zombies replied. "If you would please, leave your weapon with us. You can retrieve it when the event closes."

"That won't be necessary." I lifted the katana to shoulder height, then let it fall from my grasp. Instead of clattering noisily to the floor, it vanished in a pocket of purple vapor. I watched the zombies react. Their scanner implant feeds argued with whatever was left of their human rationality. They were dumbfounded. "Will that be all?" I didn't wait for a reply. I swept my hand forward, inviting Cayenne to descend the stairs ahead of me. "*Dozo*, DeLeon-sama," I said, bowing slightly. I caught her eye, and I felt so certain that the two of us were going to be all right.

The glass-domed temple of corporate decadence spread out before us in all directions. Carved out of the staircases all around were furnished alcoves for bars and services. And everywhere, the elitist society mingled with their crystal flutes of champagne, shadowed by private bodyguards and served by levitating drones that came and went on silent rotors, programmed to cloak themselves as they ascended with drained decanters. I wasn't the only ShiroKaz representative with someone specific to find. Cayenne had informed me that Triangle would not be in attendance at this soiree, but someone named Jonathan Smythe would be. We'd only taken a dozen steps together when Cayenne's hand came gently to my shoulder, stopping me.

"There he is," she said. I followed her eyes down to an unmistakably tall man standing at the center of a pack of sycophants and salarymen of the highest grade, just to the side of a wide, furnished space cut into the circular stairs and flanked by potted bonsai trees. Some of the crowd apparently were race enthusiasts; all their attention turned to the pole position directly outside the glass where the TKMG league pilots had started to line up their hypercraft for the main event. The rest seemed to ignore the event completely, centered only on Smythe.

He had straight, slicked sterling silver hair and custom-implanted cyber-silver eyes to match. He wore the second-best suit I'd ever laid eyes on, perfectly tailored for his dominating, wide-shouldered frame. While he spoke, he gesticulated strongly with powerful hands. Smythe didn't seem the type to falter in his speech, but whatever stream of words he was spouting at his elite entourage of ass-kissers was dammed up entirely when he caught sight of Cayenne DeLeon approaching in her elegant, trumpeted evening gown. And I'd like to think he might've also spared a moment's thought for the dashing security officer at her side.

Smythe turned away from his audience and gave us his full attention. (Who am I kidding? They were all looking at Cayenne.) I didn't need SUIT to tell me that all of them were simultaneously running grid idents on the two of us. You see, that was all part of the plan. A state-of-the-art intrusion hardware platform was quite literally woven into the threads of my clothing. SUIT had already dominated whatever security protocols Smythe and his goons were running from the moment the elevator sank into the floor behind Cayenne and me. And now, their embedded comlink feeds were telling them exactly what we wanted them all to say. Our names. And what we represented. *River*. And *spirit*.

"It cannot be," Jonathan Smythe said aloud. As the head of Inari, whose business it was to know everything, it was a phrase I imagine did not pass his lips very often. "Miss DeLeon, is it? I've not yet had the pleasure of making your acquaintance."

Cayenne said nothing, but offered her ringed fingers up to Smythe's outstretched hand. The silver fox lifted hers halfway to his lips, and I almost stepped in to stop him from kissing it. He bowed, according to Japanese custom, not low enough to signify obeisance, nor to show respect to an equal. The gesture suggested curiosity. It said, *who the fuck are you?* in corporate body language.

And Cayenne answered Smythe's movement with silence, a straight back, and a withering stare. I scanned the small gathering of Smythe's fellow elites. I saw shock and awe. All according to plan. Their new queen had arrived. Her reply was that everything here now belonged to us, to ShiroKaz. It always had. Cayenne drew her hand away.

"That's correct, Jonathan. We've never met before now. And yet, I've always been with you, tucked away in the back of your mind. For two decades. The biggest secret InariCorp ever stole."

The crowd was intrigued. The race had begun. Just then, a fireball bloomed in the vacuum of space on the hyper-craft track beyond the glass. First blood had been drawn. There was no sound, but the shockwave of energy rumbled through the floor. With everyone now turned our way, I think I was the only one who saw it happen.

"You must have known it would only be a matter of time before Shiromatsu-Kazama rose from the grave to reclaim its assets. Well, time is up."

Of course, we never assumed that the CEO of InariCorp would willingly and immediately buy what we were there to sell. Jonathan Smythe was the richest and most powerful person in NeOsaka, arguably the entire world. He was certainly the most powerful person in the room. Or at least he had been two minutes ago. He just hadn't realized his new place yet. A close-lipped, ear-to-ear smile stretched across his face.

"Shiromatsu, did you say? Now that is a name I have not heard in a very long time. Decades, as you said. In fact, you've reminded me how I've been meaning to tear down that tomb from our skyline. A travesty, what happened to that family. To their *legacy.*" He said the word ever so maliciously and looked around at the throng of ass-kissers for affirmation, which, of course, they showered upon him. I doubted they even understood the context. While he spoke, his silvery eyes twitched, unfocused on anything physical before him, instead reading off a retinal feed only he could see, firing off factoids so as to inflate his ego. "What happened twenty years ago is no secret, Miss DeLeon. It is a matter of very public record. In the aftermath of his sons' murders, Yoshinori Shirmatsu ceded his power to…"

Smythe hit a snag, like Cayenne had told me he would. With the help of SUIT, she'd very carefully compiled a profile of InariCorp's top executive. She'd known he would do anything to put on a display of his omniscience in front of his cronies. She'd known the make and model of his prototype, cutting-edge neuromod and its specs, capable of processing a quadrillion bytes of data per second, accessing pretty much the entire grid in the blink of an eye, finding the most damning evidence to support whatever lines of bullshit he would be on. In this case, she'd known exactly what he would look for and not find: something to smear ShiroKaz's good name, but especially hers.

"To... To..." As Smythe's eyes darted to and fro, and his voice trailed off into a kind of whimper, Cayenne finished him off.

She said, "And the rest, as they say, is history."

Still, the silver fox's eyes wouldn't look at her. He was too busy reading the warning impulse flashing across his overlay. Smythe looked exactly how he felt: confused. And he felt exactly how he looked in front of everyone: weak.

The suited-up InariSec had already surrounded us, awaiting the order to rush in and seize us. But the order never came. Just like Smythe's immaculately tailored suit, his state-of-the-art comlink and all of its spliced neuro-modifications were only the second best in the room.

"I have assumed control of local systems." SUIT's voice buzzed in the eardrums of every embedded comlink and ambient speaker in the vicinity. It was exactly what we'd wanted. Shock and awe. All around us, clusters of onlookers were falling off the crowd like scattering flies from the carcass of a back-alley rat. Those with private bodyguards augmented with the latest hardware found that their trusty tinmen were unresponsive, frozen in place. The systems they'd paid top-dollar for were failing. Everything electronic in this temple belonged to the Sentient Universal-Interfacing Totality now.

Beneath the vast empty ceiling of space outside the glass dome of Heaven, another series of explosions sent tremors through all the spires, rippling over the golden glass of the solar sea. Showers of hypercraft debris shot in all directions as the dead pilots' hypercraft hulls were breached, their maglev locks failed, and they floated like time capsule tombs sent into the void forever. It was horrible and beautiful, and I understood then the maddening appeal of the race in a way I'd never considered before.

But I am pretty sure I was the only one who noticed. Corporate elite had swarmed all around us. All the champagne and *hors d'oeuvres* had been abandoned on side tables. The real spectacle was playing out between the old silver fox of Inari and the newfound emerald-wrapped queen of ShiroKaz. It was playing out on the data grids that lined every invisible point of infinite space as their command protocols fired off against SUIT's to wrest back control of their cyber zombies. I saw a bead of sweat trickle from Jonathan Smythe's perfectly slick silver hairline, and I'm sure everyone else saw it, also.

"What, pray tell, are you hoping to accomplish here, Miss DeLeon?"

"I've already told you."

"ShiroKaz assets, was it? I'm afraid you are mistaken. No doubt your data breaches are reaching deep into my most secure vaults, like some sort of lowlife Syndicate raid, and you are finding nothing. The only records there show, time and again, that the corporation split itself, by its own will, into the structure we all know today."

"Jonathan, your entire livelihood is built on lies. So I'm willing to forgive you this final deception. We both know Inari's vaults aren't limited to New Osaka. The record I want is in the most secure place of all. Your skull."

Smythe's face lit up like a pachinko machine. He let out a peal of high-pitched laughter, the gratified squeal of the submissive when the stilettoed dominatrix presses on his balls. He reeled around to his crowd of sycophants, and they all chuckled in unison with him and tried to convince themselves they wouldn't lose the upper hand.

"How utterly barbaric. How unreformed. You, outcasts of the old, uncivilized world, you intrude upon us here and demand my head. How crass. How base. It is this type of attitude that set the world on fire half a millennium ago. It is from *this* that we work tirelessly to save our humanity. It is apart from *this*, from *you*, that we must distinguish ourselves. We must rise above. We are *better*. Now, Miss DeLeon, remove yourself from this place."

He seemed to have regathered himself from this haughty speech, drawing energy from his reserve of affluent righteousness. When he was done, Jonathan Smythe turned his silver eyes upon yours truly for the first time since I'd walked in. "And take your Syndicate scum with you."

I pressed a hand over my heart and batted my eyelashes, pretending to be offended.

"Oh, yes," Smythe sneered at me. "I recognize your face now. You compromised one of our facilities two days ago. You left your cell behind to die. I will allow you to leave, alive, as I allowed you then. Begone."

Now it wasn't just Smythe's eyes on me. Suddenly I was the new star of the show, even though the show was supposed to be wrapping up. All my life, I'd detested the *dance* I always figured these corporate pricks put on for one another. Their uppity mannerisms and wordplay, their delicate hierarchies and unwritten codes of compunction and comportment in one another's presence. But now I was at the center of my very own production, and I couldn't help but ham it up. What the fuck was I letting myself become?

I smiled. I lowered my gaze and passed a hand over my face, casually brushing aside my dark lock of hair. I watched my Italian leather shoes fall one in front of the other as I paced forward, as I made no move whatsoever to *be gone* from Smythe's presence. I almost laughed.

"SUIT," I spoke softly, and I knew the AI would read my biometrics like an open book and know my intention.

"Yes, Shinjiro." Her voice was still sending across the entire temple dome. "The records you seek are on an encrypted data cube lodged in Mister Smythe's mastoid process."

"What the fuck is a mastoid process?" I said, looking up, dead straight into the one-and-only, grandiloquent Inari CEO's silver eyes.

"Behind his ear," Cayenne suggested, demonstrating with a tap against her own head. "Left side."

Whatever facade Smythe had reconstructed a moment ago crumpled brick by brick as I approached. He even put up his hands.

"Do you mean to take my head?"

"Not really. Just give me the cube."

"Who are you?"

I stopped. One step away. Smythe was taller than me, sure, and yet he had shrunk to nothingness before me. Some instinct in him must have been firing in a way his electronically enhanced synapses never could. Just to drive the point home for him, for everyone gathered there in the temple of corporate decadence, once and for all, I spread my fingers across the fabric of the veil between worlds, then sank my grasp through and gripped the white katana, tearing it through a pocket of reality. It materialized in a rushing gout of purple fire, and I drew the blade slowly. I lifted it to Smythe's neck.

"I am the White Shadow."

So this is what it was like to be an unstoppable force. To be Yasuro Shiromatsu. I felt his power surging up from *Yomi*, potent enough to shake the world apart, furious enough to set it all on fire. The shadow man's vengeful will swirled around inside me, clutched at my soul. It drove me to press the blade forward, to slash the silver fox's head clean off. But I pushed Yasuro back. I let out a breath and felt the spirit recede. I smiled at Smythe, content in the knowledge that I was in control of myself, that I had decided to spare him. I knew instinctively then that he was not one of the conspirators who had wronged Yasuro. He was nothing. He was nobody. He was merely in my way.

And he knew it, too. So did everyone else. The crowd backed away at the sight of the white katana. I wondered if they knew its legend, if they'd seen it before, years and years ago. They'd gathered here for a spectacle, and they'd witnessed one they'd never forget. Good. It was what we'd planned for all along. Cayenne and I had come for more than Smythe's data cube and confronting Triangle.

The statement had been made.

I let go of the sword's sheath and it floated eerily in midair, held aloft by the ethereal purple hands of ghosts only I could see. I reached behind Smythe's ear and pressed the patch of flesh there. It flopped open, and a bracket slid forward, cradling a single, golden data cube.

"Arigato-gozaimasu," I said, withdrawing myself and bowing low before the silver fox of Inari. I pocketed the cube and sheathed the katana with a flourish. I turned my back on Smythe and took one step toward Cayenne.

"Shinjiro," SUIT's voice erupted from only my comlink. The cool, computerized tone had vanished. The AI affected a panicked one instead. "I am losing control."

The three tinmen unfroze all at once and pulled their sleeves past their forearms.

Cayenne's eyes widened. Her hands rose to her chest, covering her heart. A look of fear washed over her.

"An entity has—"

Then it all happened at once.

The plastic-fab flesh split away, revealing the built-in micro-guns. The tinmen raised their weaponized arms in unison and unleashed a hail of bullets.

I dove for Cayenne, knowing what I had to do but uncertain what it would mean, for both of us. I slid on my knees and wrapped an arm around her waist. When the first rounds of high-density polymer reached us, I'd already enveloped us in the ethereal. The temple rumbled with the deafening staccato thunder of the tinmen's cannons. The storm of bullets raged for seven more seconds, tearing and shredding and burning indiscriminately through everything else in its wake, stairs, furniture, bonsai trees, and the living flesh of those who hadn't gotten out of the way. But it passed through Cayenne and me, swirling through the cloud of purple smoke I'd dragged the two of us into.

The thunder died. Then came the screams. Directly behind us, half a dozen corporate elite lay dead or dying, torn to shreds by the super-hot plasma rounds that exploded inside them. Cayenne's scream melded with theirs, only worse. Her eyes were maddened. For those seven seconds, she'd seen the land of the dead. She'd seen the twisted homes of the *kami* that dwell in all things made by man or by nature. Even here, above the Earth, she'd seen through *Takamagahara* itself and glimpsed the yawning abyss of the underworld beneath it. Cayenne had been touched by the horror of what awaits a soul not put to rest.

I grasped her face in both my hands. I hadn't even known if dragging her to *Yomi* would work, nor what it would do to her. Her skin was slick with sweat, but she was so cold. Her emerald eyes spun around the room, trying to reorient herself in the reality of living.

"Cayenne!" I shouted in her face.

She refocused at last. She saw me and drew her reality back in. "Shin? Am I...?"

"You're alive," was all I could say to her. All I had time for.

I had to go back to work.

I didn't need eyes in the back of my head to know that the three tinmen were closing in to finish the job. Their internal magazines were spent, and with their targets still active, they had opted to engage now with the foldable blades embedded in their other arms.

I rose, spun about, called upon the white katana, and met all three head-on. I felt the raging spirit of the samurai pulse from within the blade, and every parry became an explosion of his red sparks, every slash an indelible line of his red smoke. I let the sword lead the way. I let Yasuro take control. Seconds later, the first tinman fell, opened from hip to shoulder. I stepped away, catching the second with *kesi giri*, sending his head flopping and sparking away, ending in a *nukitsuke* stance. My body was rigid, my wrists were fluid. My heart and mind were calm. The killing was the dance. The final opponent approached, driven by machinery and code, and I drew the blade upon him, sinking its length through his chest, extinguishing what remained of his spirit.

His body went limp, just a mass of fried circuitry. He slid backward off the katana and fell heavily onto the others. I didn't give them a second thought. I wheeled about and hooked an arm around Cayenne and rose with her. She was still visibly shaken from the crossing, but maybe her prior experience with all my magic tricks helped her move her feet.

The place was pandemonium. More tinmen flooded in from the lowest tier of the temple behind us, weaving their way through the fleeing corporate crowds. At the same time, ten more lined up on the top tier, freshly arrived from the elevator. This new crop of security was dressed for a different kind of party, done up visored-head to spiked steel-toe in branded InariSec armor, and their weapons weren't embedded in their bodies. They were much heavier and technologically precise.

Two days ago, back in the Inari vault, crossing to *Yomi* to survive had taken an immense physical toll on me. I hadn't been able to save Vas. I hadn't had the power to take him with me, even though I'd wanted to. But this time was different. This time I could save Cayenne. Two days ago, I didn't have the White Shadow's sword. Even still, I had no idea how long I could hide her in the underworld when the next volley of bullets came our way. But this was our only chance.

"Hold on to me, and this time, close your eyes. Now."

The tsunami of bullets surged forward, crashing upon us from every angle. The InariSec army unloaded everything they had, filling the mega-corporate temple with an unending, roaring cacophony. The crossfire ripped apart everything it touched, kicking up an enormous cloud of purple smoke. When it was over, InariSec had carved a smoldering crater into the ringed staircase, exposing layers of ducts and sparking wiring beneath. Slowly, the smoke cleared, and the armored tinmen closed in.

And Cayenne and I simply were not there.

EIGHTEEN

WE WERE IN A FREEFALL, STRAIGHT DOWN THE ELEVATOR shaft that had lifted us into the temple of Megacorporate Heaven. The space below us distorted and twisted as we fell away from physical, living reality. The metal girders and beams that made up the innards of the sub-orbital platform shimmered as if we were underwater. Pinpoints of purple lights sparkled on every surface like distant stars. But they weren't stars. I knew them as the hearts of the invisible *kami*, the silent spirits behind the veil that watch all things. And now they watched us fall.

Cayenne wrapped her arms around my shoulders, locking her wrists tight in the center of my back. Her face was pressed under my neck. She held on so tight I could hardly breathe, not that I needed to. Not in this place.

If I'd been an amateur at all this spectral-shifting shit, I might've tried to reorient us to match the corkscrew trajectory of the shaft. But I knew better. The white katana was my anchor, my guide. With it gripped firmly in my hand, there was no pain anymore while I passed through the underworld. I could focus. I could command. I could see everything. And so when I saw an access corridor through the walls of the man-made structure, I arced our descent toward it.

Together, Cayenne and I slipped through solid matter and landed as gently as a feather, sliding easily to the floor on our knees, still embracing. We were Izanagi and Izanami, but unlike the myth, we'd both ventured out from the dark. Our physical, living bodies emerged at the center of a cloud of fading purple mist.

"We're through," I whispered calmly. "You can…"

I almost said *let go,* but I didn't want her to. It was fine if she didn't want me. I would have to live with that. But for now, I wanted this moment, even if I had to steal it.

"…open your eyes."

Cayenne slowly drew her head off my chest, blinking her eyes as if she'd woken from a powerful dream. She kept her arms around me. She gazed into me, and I back into her. I made a wish.

She let out a deep breath and crashed back onto me, squeezing me tight, sobbing uncontrollably. I wrapped my arms around her and rocked her. I understood what she was going through. I had been seven years old the first time I'd crossed. There'd been no one to tell me what happened. No one to ease my fears. I wouldn't let that happen to Cayenne. I made soothing noises, vibrating in my chest where I knew Cayenne could feel them, and she calmed. The two of us just stayed there like that as minutes passed. If all existence could have come to an unexpected end at that moment, while the two of us just held each other, I would've been okay with that. No more planning. No more revenge. No more death.

But it did not end. Everything keeps going.

"Shin!!" Ben Roy Doon's voice crackled in from my comlink.

And at the exact same time: "Shinjiro, you are detectable on the grid."

"Sh-shit-fuck, Shin! What the fuck! Tell me you did your n-never-die magic sh-shit again!"

Cayenne heard them, too. She leaned away from me and wiped the tears from her eyes. Then she let herself laugh. I laughed with her. Even though we were probably in bad shape.

"It is no longer safe for you. Miss DeLeon's position is compromised."

"You're pinging half a kilo from the closest spider rail. Okay, if you go east, er, west… Is that west?"

"Amendment: Direction in outer space is relative."

"Aha! I got you! You could say direction everywhere is relative!"

"Within the current context, I was pointing out the futility of your suggestion to 'go east.'"

"I still got you."

"Will both of you be quiet?" Cayenne shouted. And we were all quiet. She rose to her feet and straightened the hem of her dress. Needlessly, of course, because there wasn't a wrinkle, stain, or mote of dust on her. But I understood the gesture well enough.

"We got what we came for," I said, rising to meet her, and holding out the data cube I'd extracted from Jonathan Smythe.

Cayenne accepted it, then showed me something I'd suspected she'd had all along. She peeled back a square of synthetic skin from her own mastoid process and slotted the glowing cube on the rack before pushing it back in. Her emerald eyes glassed over as whatever introductory data was encoded on the cube rushed across her overlay. "Ben," she said, "What is the acronym?"

"Channel's open," he replied. He'd been waiting for this moment. "Y-U-K-M."

"Interjection: Miss DeLeon, I am more than capable of transferring the data to ShiroKaz servers. Please enable me."

"No," Cayenne said reproachfully. "You said it yourself. You were compromised. You lost control of the security protocols and we nearly lost everything! Now stop your goddamn *interjecting*." Cayenne pinched the bridge of her nose as if she had a sudden headache. In fact, I imagine she did. That, and having to accept the ridiculous notion that a simple four-letter, paper-and-pencil acronym was likely our best option for avoiding detection and interception of the information she needed to send. "Ben, I've found it. Y-U-K-M. What does it stand for?"

"Yearling urials knuckle magnanimously."

Ben Roy Doon spoke the words flawlessly, without stuttering. Dare I say I had never been more proud of the mastery he showed over his speech impediment, having known him most of his life, than I was at that moment. And yet, I still couldn't help meeting Cayenne's disbelieving eyes with my own. Was this really what we were coming to as a species?

"Yearling urials knuckle magnanimously?" I said quietly. "Are you fucking kidding me?"

"No, that's it," Ben said flatly. Again: flawlessly. "Y-U-K-M. Send the data."

Cayenne blinked a few times, but then shrugged her shoulders and executed the advice of her handler like any good SynCell operative would have.

"Calculation: It would take my systems more than forty-seven sextillion cycles to process all possible word combinations to trace your channel."

"Neato," I quipped. Big surprise: my sarcasm was wasted on the AI.

"Even with all computing resources in the world at my disposal, it would take me approximately four minutes, eight-point-two-seven-en-nine-nine-one seconds to parse the correct phrase. Well done, Mister Doon."

"Ha ha!" Ben huffed triumphantly in our comlinks. But SUIT wasn't finished.

"But can Miss DeLeon trust the destination of this transfer?"

Cayenne and I once again looked at each other, and the silence seemed to stretch.

"SUIT, what the fuck are you talking about?" I finally said. But before the AI could even explain itself, I looked hard at Cayenne.

"Transfer it," I told her. It sounded harsher than I'd intended. She narrowed her eyes at me. I shook my head and threw up my hands defensively. "Now wait," I stammered. "I trust Ben, and you trust me. So you can trust Ben, too."

Cayenne said nothing. I guessed she was unsure of what to say. I saw her pupils dilate and undilate as her vision swapped from me to the data and back again.

And surprisingly, Ben said nothing, too. Mister fucking motor-mouth himself was at a loss for words. Why?

"Ben," I said. "This is when you're supposed to chime in and reassure our employer that you're on the level."

"Uhh," was his best answer.

"Ben!"

"Shinjiro, Miss DeLeon, security sweeps have reached this level of *Takamagahara*. I can blank your positions on the grid, but I am losing capability to do so each second."

"Yeah, okay. So, listen, Cayenne. You can t-t-trust me. Us. You can trust us. We're the g-g-good guys. Remember?"

I'd known Ben forever. I knew how he got when he tried to lie. He could never lie to me. But to other people?

Cayenne's jaw tensed. Her gaze bore into me one last time, trying to read my expression. I shored up every ounce of willpower I could to keep my face stone cold.

"Sending," she said finally, switching her gaze back to the overlay only she could see.

I would have a lot of fucking questions for Ben Roy Doon when we got back to NeOsaka. *If* we got back.

"Done," Ben said. "I'm erasing the gateway. Everything's secure."

Cayenne ejected the data cube, dropped it on the floor, and crushed it with the heel of her stiletto. Impressive aim, actually. It popped like glass, and the gel boards inside oozed out and turned to water in the oxygenated environment.

Having now sown the seeds of distrust among us humans, the Sentient Universal-Interfacing Totality was ready to move on to the next pressing matter. It was all business. "Follow the corridor behind Miss DeLeon and arrive at a service junction behind a hotel kitchen. From there, you will find a service elevator to the nearest spider rail."

"Let's go, Shin," Cayenne said, removing her heels to run.

"Hold on," I said. "Job's not done."

"You said it yourself. We got what we came for."

"Not all we came for."

A memory of the mugshot flashed in my mind's eye. Punk. Rage. A bright orange triangle on her neck.

"Sandra Calvin," I said. "She has to die."

You said it yourself, I thought I might add. But the time for petty wisecracks was over. On the other side, in the deepest, most empty recesses of *Yomi*, I felt the spirit of Yasuro Shiromatsu harden his grip on the white katana. Now was the time.

"Plans have changed, Shin. With the records we've recovered, we can retake what is ours and there's nothing she can do about it. In time, we can rebuild the reputation of ShiroKaz. No one, not even Triangle, will be able to touch us."

"If I am the White Shadow. That's what you mean."

"Yes," she said. "And you already are. You—"

"—said it myself, right, to Smythe's face."

"Everyone saw. Everyone heard. Even Triangle. She's the one, the entity, who stripped SUIT's control. And now she's pointing it all back at us. We don't have time to debate this."

Cayenne was absolutely right. I remembered what it looked like to watch my never-ending stream of guts falling out of me into the white emptiness. I remembered the pain. If I didn't do this, he would draw me into Hell with him and never let me go.

"I have to do this," I said with finality. "I can't explain right now."

And just like that, the cold, calculating, C-Level demeanor I'd seen when I first laid eyes on Miss Cayenne DeLeon returned. "Fine," she spat. "When you do explain it, Asai-san, it better be fucking good." And she turned, and she ran barefoot without paying me a second thought. And watching her go, I didn't feel like the White Shadow, I felt like the piece of shit I truly was all over again.

"Ben," I said into my comlink. I knew Cayenne could hear me, too. "Make sure she makes it. Or yours will be the next head I take."

"Holy shit," he exclaimed. "I will, b-b-but ... you don't need to say that."

"I know."

NINETEEN

THE ELEMENT OF SURPRISE HAD BEEN SHOT TO SHIT BY now. Triangle knew I was coming. Every second I remained in her floating sub-orbital fortress, I was pinging scanners and surveillance feeds.

Good.

Surprise may have been out the window, but subterfuge was as good a Plan B as any. I wanted the whole Tenjin media apparatus on me. Anything to divert attention away from Cayenne. Anything to make a scene.

SUIT guided me. Or tried to, at least. The AI rattled off something about three dimensional spatial coordinates and access hatches and side passages and other such shit. But I just walked. Aimlessly. Sometimes straight through walls. Whenever I saw a wide-open, ritzy corporate plaza around the bend, I simply couldn't help myself. Inari-branded and even Tenjin-branded security forces were already lined up and armed to the nines, waiting for my arrival. I assumed they'd already cleared the area of salarymen, technicians, and executives since they opened fire without hesitation or prejudice. Their gunfire turned parts of Heaven to slag.

And I walked on without a care in the world. The bullets passed through me, leaving straight, rippling trails of purple smoke in my wake. I drew the white katana casually and pointed the blade at each of the tinmen in my way, marking them all for death. Some kind of human instinct won out over the computer programming and commando conditioning in some cases, and most of the security forces fled or pulled back, or whatever.

Those who did not, they died. Gruesomely. Exquisitely. To stand before the samurai was as paper standing before flame.

"Shinjiro," SUIT called to me over the local PA system embedded in the surrounding buildings that it had hijacked. I drew my blade up through the last cyborg's collarbone from where I'd planted it in its heart. I whirled the katana with a special flourish, *chiburi*, which splashed every ounce of the machine-man's ichorous, black blood on the pavement as his body fell behind me, then slowly slid the katana into its sheath. "We have arrived."

"Arrived where?"

"Schematics indicate a central hub for data flow four hundred meters directly below this plaza."

"Very well."

I surveyed the carnage I'd left in my wake, tracing my path through the ritzy thoroughfares of the sub-orbital city. Abandoned high-end storefronts and bistros shredded to shit by the thousands of bullets that had been meant for me, smoke and smoldering fires rising from their insides. Those who'd shot them lay dead, framed by shell casings, broken glass, and lines of their blood drawn across the carbon-fiber pavement, painted by the strikes of my katana. I slammed the weapon the final inch into its sheath with an audible click that stirred the silence.

Purple-ethereal hands rose through the ground at my feet, the *kami* and the lingering spirits of the dead. At my command, they grasped my legs and dragged me downward.

I sank through solid matter, falling through space, drifting gently through endless strata of man-made materials and designs. I saw more of Heaven through the twisted lens of the underworld as I passed: homes, businesses, storage hangars, maintenance shafts, rail tunnels, pipes, ducts, and cables.

And minutes later, at the bottom of it all, a curving slab of metal two meters thick. An RFID shield meant to block any and all wireless signals that could intrude upon the data sanctity of the immense central chamber below. I doubted even the Sentient Universal-Interfacing Totality could penetrate it. In fact, that might have been the very point of its existence. But it was nothing for a ghost. I drifted straight through.

The place was a sphere. A cocoon. The hacker that called herself Triangle had enwrapped herself in layers of technology. A series of walkways and ladders were bolted to the circular walls, leading to workstations and nests of wiring, all of it cluttered with disused gadgets and discarded devices, all of it old-world and covered in dust. It felt like a time capsule, a dormant spaceship that had floated across the expanse and gotten itself tangled in the underside of the orbiting platform.

Just below the centerline of the sphere, the silhouette of a woman floated in an enormous pool of brightly illuminated gel. She was completely naked, aside from the tattoos covering her from neck to toe that had faded with age, and the thick cable that plugged into a socket at the base of her bald skull. In fact, I couldn't help but notice she was hairless *everywhere*. Her brown eyes were wide open, and she watched my half-spirit form descend and manifest just at the edge of the pool. From there, I could see how shallow it was, and the clear, plastic chair that held her body in place, leaving only her face floating above the gel.

"Hello, sugarplum," Triangle said softly. The brief experience I'd had yesterday with her rap sheets hadn't prepared me for the twang of her Southern American accent. "Gimme a sec."

The chair lifted her body up and tilted gently forward. A pneumatic floor rose at her feet. She stepped, dripping, out of the pool and toward a side rack where a drab colored robe awaited her. Outside of her vat of cooling gel, her exposed skin steamed. Triangle wasn't tired like I'd expected her to be, considering she was pushing fifty years of age and had likely been laying down for days on end. In fact, dripping and glistening as she was, I felt like the Shinjiro Asai of two days ago would've felt the old warmth flaring up in all parts of her body at the sight of this fine specimen of female anatomy.

But instead of ogling her firm tits or shapely ass, my eyes were trying to be professional, following the line of the bound fiber-optic cables plugged into her head. Automated drones and machinery high overhead lifted it on nearly invisible micro-filament strings to compensate for Triangle's forward movement out of the vat. The whole setup reminded me of Tatsuhiro, the old dragon's skull jacked into his mainframe, dialed into the grid from deep within the ghost realm of Himeji Castle. As I watched the steam rise from Triangle, I realized what they had both made themselves into.

"Some kind of ... human computer," I said quietly.

The drones flitted about her form, lifting the robe over her raised arms, pulling it across her shoulders, closing it in the front, cutting off the tantalizing view. My eyes went to the tattoo emblazoned on her chest, the triangle, from her chin to her collarbones. She had added to it in the intervening years since the photo I'd seen. Within the bright orange shape, dark lines sketched the leering face of an *Oni* from within the orange field.

Yes. *That Oni.*

"Nice suit," she said, smirking. I knew she'd heard me vocalize seconds ago, and something in the tone of her drawling voice and the swagger of her walk confirmed my suspicion. She moved to a side table and poured three fingers of bourbon into a crystal tumbler. She didn't offer me one. She turned about and winked at me, then sent the drink down her throat in one go.

I blinked with disbelief.

"Aahh. Jesus! Holding up the network's a thirsty business. Some real-life Atlas stuff right here, tell you what. You into old myths? Gods and titans 'n all that?" Triangle set the tumbler down, ran a hand over her razor-smooth scalp. She saw me gawking. "What?"

"Nothing. Just the way you handle a shot like that. Reminds me of someone."

"Hmm," she mused. She cradled the empty tumbler against her tattooed neck, rolled it back and forth delicately over her damp skin, the light refracting through the prism of the crystal's cut. "Bet I could figure out who in three guesses. But we ain't got time for that." She set the tumbler down on the side table and approached me. Her bare feet left squishy prints of clear gel on the smooth metal floor. "I made it, you know."

"Made what?"

She came right up to me. I could smell her, the stuff she'd been swimming in like lavender and vanilla. She was shorter than I'd expected, not that I'm tall by any standard. The top of her came only up to my chin. Her eyes twinkled with some kind of pride as she examined the threads of my suit. She ran her thumb and forefinger up and down my lapel, caressing the fabric.

"Well, it was my idea anyway. The system 'n all. The scope of it. But I didn't think he'd go and put the god-dang thing into a *suit*." Triangle looked up into my eyes and smiled. Then she laughed. *Guffawed* would be more accurate. A full-throated, hee-haw jackass kind of laugh. If she hadn't been one of the most powerful, living human beings in existence, I'd have written her off then and there as a bumpkin by the sound of her laugh alone. Instead, the effect of it was charming. Disarming. I couldn't help but smile back at her.

Then she stopped all of a sudden, her attention drawn inward, to whatever kind of feed her overlay cascaded onto her vision. She seemed frozen in place, the fabric of my suit still pinched in her fingers. Then she winced, let go, and backed away a step. The cable in the back of her head pulsed rhythmically, sending and receiving glowing orange rings of data, uploading, downloading. I traced its path up to where it jacked into a monolithic machine. Exactly the same as the one I'd seen connected to Tatsuhiro, only this one existed in reality. There was no wispy, ethereal light outlining this one. It was solid black, bolted into the overhanging structures over our heads. I didn't have to ask her to understand exactly what it was: the beating heart of the Tenjin Media Corporation. It was the gateway for all digital communications, for all networks. Capturing, monitoring, routing, re-routing, flagging, censoring, tracing every letter of every message sent, received, encrypted, broadcasted, to and from anybody, anyywhere, all at once.

I gently grabbed her wrist and peeled myself out of her grasp. The silence stretched.

"Um, is everything okay?"

"Huhhh," she groaned softly. The heel of her hand pressed firmly against one of her tightly shut eyes. "More myths for you, honey. You ever heard the one about a horse? Huhh, the Trojan Horse."

"Yeah," I said. I did my best to look at anything else around the place besides the *Oni*'s face leering at me from her neck.

"I'm impressed. Most folks forgot the story nowadays." Whatever pain had knocked around inside her head a moment ago must have passed. She moved shakily to the table. Her hands fell away from her head, back to the bourbon, poured another, the crystal clinking as the decanter touched the tumbler. "Well, you, my girlie, are a step up from a simple assassin. You're a Trojan Horse. Worst part is, you don't even realize it. Well… I'd say this'd be unexpected, but had I paid better attention to the story, I'd recall that the invaders got tired of the siege. Took 'em years and years. Only way through the walls was a low-down dirty trick. Something no one'd ever seen before." She took a deep breath, lifted the bourbon. I watched her neck undulate as it shot down her throat. She exhaled. A bit steadier now. But only a bit.

"Hey now," I said, wagging a reproachful finger and flashing a smile, "I've been accused of being dirty, but I'm no trick."

"I think we're mincing words here, honey. Tryin' to be funny. You mean *trick* like *whore*?"

The question was genuine. I snapped out of the spell her entrancing accent had placed on me. "I think so," I said.

Triangle's face said clearly enough that she wasn't finding any of this funny. She blinked, raised a hand, and brought it slowly across the space in front of her, conjuring a bank of glowing holoscreens out of thin air, projected by micro-emitters on the drones that floated everywhere.

"And you think you've cleaned yourself up?"

On them, body cam footage of InariSec, rounding a corner, hoisting a rifle, unloading his clip at a black-haired girl in a dark suit with a smoking revolver in hand, standing over the caved-in skull of her last SynCell comrade. On them, multiple angle shots from drones patrolling the space catapult as a plume of fire and a shockwave erupt from a derelict apartment complex across the street from a half-sunken graveyard, zooming in on the only vital signs in the area, some girl blown backward, fast forward to her surrounded, slicing down tinmen, fast forward to her and another form, a sleek ninja, its sword sunk hilt-deep in her heart, waves of purple and cyan smoke roiling outward, rolling over rows of silent *haka* gravestones. On them, still photos of a mahogany-trimmed office, a replica of the US President's desk, blood everywhere, medics wrapping a slab of meat in a bag, a big severed leg. On the last screen, the bloody trail of cybernetic corpses I'd chopped my way through hundreds of meters above where Triangle and I stood, just moments before, the hell I'd made out of heaven itself.

Triangle's hand suddenly clamped down on my forearm, squeezing me like a vise. I hadn't heard her, entranced as I'd been. Horrified, maybe? Shocked by her touch, I almost called the white sword to slash up and take her limb off at the elbow, but held off. It was plain to see that she was still in pain, that she couldn't hide it. Her eyes closed, and her legs buckled beneath her. She held onto me as she crashed downward. She sucked in a shuddering breath and held it, her mouth agape in a silent scream. The glowing cable in her skull pulsed faster, the upstream overloading. I had no fucking clue what any of it meant. But I understood well enough the two rivers of blood gushing suddenly from both her nostrils, dribbling onto her chest, and staining her robe to figure that something was killing her from the inside.

I didn't have to be a genius to realize who the killer was. *What* it was. I was wearing the weapon on my back. Sealed inside her inner sanctum kilometers above the city, surrounded by meters of signal-strangling material, Sandra Calvin had been safe to meld her mind with the machine, to carry out the work of the Tenjin Media Corporation, unimpeded, unregulated, undetected, day in and day out, for decades. She must have thought herself above reproach. She must have felt like a god. All the mega-corps, at some point, must feel like that.

Triangle squeezed me tighter, so tight that I felt my circulation damming up, the fingers of my left hand going numb.

Maybe I should've felt relieved; before, I hadn't wanted to kill her. I'd told Cayenne as much. After all the killing I'd done to get here, the reminders playing out on the holoscreens floating all around us, even if my victims had only been half-men cyber-zombies (and in Boltcutter's case just a fucking asshole who had it coming), I didn't want to kill her right now either. Maybe the Sentient Universal-Interfacing Totality would just do all the work for me.

Dirty work. She'd been right about me, after all.

I cradled her, brought us both to the floor. She started spasming, like she was being prodded with a live wire. I hadn't heard her take a breath since that first one, almost thirty seconds ago. Her nose still gushed blood. She was drowning in it.

"Fuck this," I said. I felt the back of her head, the root of the cable. I found what felt like some kind of switch and depressed it. There was a pressurized hiss, and locking mechanisms at the base of the cable and her skull spun away in opposite directions.

Triangle's bloodshot eyes snapped open; she lurched forward, gasping for air and choking, breathing in her own blood. The cable floated upward, its glowing pulse extinguished, carried away by the puppeteer drones, and disappeared into the darkness of the sphere. I didn't know what to do, so I just held onto her, rocking her. (After having soothed Cayenne in almost the same way after dragging her through the land of the dead, I realized I could probably seek employment as a nanny if this whole corporate security gig didn't work out.)

"Ugh," Triangle said at last, sniffling and wiping away the blood with the back of her hand. "Huhh. Ya got me." I knew she wasn't talking to me. She looked hard at the red stain on her skin, as if she'd forgotten what color her very human blood should be. "Won't be long now." Then she looked up at me and spoke tenderly, sincerely. "Thank you, sweetheart."

"What the fuck just happened?"

"Oh, about what you'd've guessed. He couldn't open my big door, so he hitched a ride in your pocket. I'd heard rumors there was someone out there that could do what the ol' shadow man could do, but never got a solid trace on any-thing. All this shit," she said, her eyes flitting to the screens full of my recent exploits, "just the aftermath. Nothing live. No idents. Angles all wrong, like some invisible hand was always tilting the cameras *just so*, ya know? Funny thing, after all this time, I thought maybe *he'd* come back from the dead. A *real* ghost. Like, *actual*. Ya know?"

"Well," I started, then drifted off, unsure of how I could really explain the situation. "It's complicated."

"Sure is," Triangle said, closing her eyes again. For a second, I thought she was considering taking a nap right there on my lap. She seemed totally at peace. "So if you ain't him, who the heck are you? And don't start with your name. I already know that. I mean, *who are you?*"

"I'm … not sure what you're expecting me to say."

"I mean, how come there's more than one o' you that can walk through walls? And how come I can't?" The way she said the word, her accent spun it up and it clipped it off at the end like an *ain't*. I loved it. Here was Triangle, the god-dess of corporate apparatus, legendary hacker extraordi-naire, sparsely clothed, covered in blood, easing herself into me, talking with her eyes closed. I let out a quick chuckle. I couldn't stop it. She smiled too, then winced, forgetting per-haps that her brain had nearly been fried only moments ago.

"I have no idea," I said. "I don't know where I come from. I don't know how I do any of it. No one was ever around to show me."

"So you don't know who you are. So you're all dark and smoldering now instead. Huhh. Big whoop."

Triangle slowly shifted to her side and pushed herself up on all fours with a groan. I offered my hand to help her rise, but she shooed me away. She rocked back onto her knees and refolded her robe.

Her brown eyes snapped back into focus. She scanned me, head to toe, as if for the first time since I'd arrived in her sanctum. Then she shrugged. She rose and turned away from me, returned to the side table, and poured a third tumbler of bourbon. This time filled nearly to the top.

"So who do you want to be?" she said over her shoulder, then downed half her drink.

"What if I said I was the White Shadow?"

That one really thawed her out. Her eyes snapped back to mine, and she smiled wider than her demon tattoo. She doubled over at the waist and laughed her jackass laugh. I couldn't help but crack a smile at the sight of her. For just a moment, I forgot where I was, who it was I talking to. I was in outer-fucking space, smack-dab in the central hub of all media communication networks, standing before the most powerful network runner that ever lived. For just a moment, I forgot that I had come there to kill her. I'd saved her from SUIT, but I still had to finish the job.

I remembered I had no choice.

"Did crazy ol' Z tell you that?" She was coming down now from her fit of hysteria. She wiped away a tear, pressed a firm palm over her heart. Cleared her throat. "'Course he did. Charismatic devil, that one. And batshit bonkers." She tipped the tumbler back and sent the rest of the bourbon down.

Z?

My face scrunched up. I looked at Triangle sideways.

What the fuck does Zercos have to do with this?

I rolled my eyes around the huge, spherical room, half-expecting the matte black cyborg to fall out of the sky trailing a cyan-colored streak in his wake and plant his sword in my heart again, like this had all been an elaborate stall for time. Thankfully, it wasn't.

"Look at you. *Shinjiro Asai.* You're such a dummy. You know that? You remind me of me when I was your age. Thinking I was some hot stuff, struttin' around with fellas that could literally melt through walls! Don't get me wrong. I mean, look what ya did once you got up here! You scared the shit outta Smythe and his lot! Who knows, he might not even retaliate on this one. You pranced up to him, all, 'Ohh, I'm the White Shadow.' I get it. Huh. But, sweet thing, you have no idea who the White Shadow *really* was."

"And you do."

"Darn right I do." Triangle was quiet. Full of regret. "I was his handler. His *man in the chair.* Not that he thought he needed me, arrogant fucking prick. Definitely not near the end." She lifted the crystal cup to the side of her face, turned it softly against her skin. It caught the light, sent diamonds shimmering over her eyes. She was far off somewhere, staring forward into empty space, moving backward through time and memory, retracing old hurts. The silence between us hung for a long time, the only sound the constant thrum of the machinery in the sphere.

"I knew the whole family," she said at last, very, very quietly. She sniffled and wiped droplets of fresh blood from her nose on the back of her forearm. Then she lifted the tumbler and brought it down suddenly, smashing it at her feet into a thousand pieces.

"But I don't know you, though. You were right. No one knows you, not even yourself. But I can tell you straight, sweetheart, you ain't one of them. Shinjiro *Asai.* Not a Shiromatsu. There would've been a record, and I would've flippin' found it for ya."

Even disconnected from the machine, Triangle's local link embedded in her skull still worked at the speed of her thoughts. The dozen or so holoscreens overflowed with new information; my whole life flashing before my eyes. My records. My associates and aliases. My crimes.

More information than Cayenne and a crippled ShiroKaz Corporation could ever hope to get their hands on. Triangle stared straight through the flitting screens, her eyes boring into me as she dialed backward through my history, freezing the frame at last on the photograph of a nine-year-old Japanese girl. Her eyes were my eyes, purple and haunted. Lonely. Afraid.

"You came up in the system, the Tenjin orphanages. You had a rough go of it, that's for sure. I know, baby. I am sorry about all that. Even an automated system ain't perfect. One of the challenges we faced back then—still do today, actually, though it's a lot smaller—is what to do with all these dang people everywhere! Kids with no families. Refugees. Still flooding in from every-ol'-where. Half of 'em irradiated to shit already. Not enough adults to take care of 'em. Too many elderly. When I took control of Tenjin, I did my best to overhaul some things. But you..."

Triangle trailed off. She bit her lower lip and drew the loose robe over herself tighter, as if suddenly cold. "You slipped through the cracks somehow."

Because of what I can do, I thought. I stared into the mirror of blue light floating before me. The little girl's face. *My curse.*

No. My power.

Triangle watched me watch myself. When she spoke again, it was like she'd heard my thoughts.

"Somehow you can do what old Yasu-boy could do, same type of stuff. But you ain't his daughter. I know that's what you were expecting to hear, baby. I'm sorry if that's what the old bastard told you. If it's what you were hoping to be true."

"What?"

Triangle spread her hands open, a gesture of defeat. "S'all I got for ya."

"I mean, *fucking what*?" I took a menacing step forward.

She fell back against the table, rattling the decanters, stepping onto broken glass. "Ahh, shit," she hissed.

I hadn't realized it until that moment exactly how it was I felt about Yasuro. I guess I'd needed Triangle's words to help me clarify my relationship with the shadow-man who called me filth, who dangled my own soul from his fingertips, who drove me to seek his vengeance.

"If he's my fucking father, I'll fucking kill myself." I spat the words at her angrily, fists clenched. *Even if I know from experience I can't make good on the threat of self-harm.* "I fucking hate Yasuro!"

"Okay then," Triangle said, holding up her hand to stop me. "We got that in common, at least."

"You know I've come to end you."

"That. And other things."

"But I don't want to."

"Shinjiro..."

Triangle exhaled, the kind of sigh that had waited to come out for decades. Perhaps it had been. She slumped against the table, her shoulders sagged, her head lowered. From everything Ben and Cayenne had told me, I'd expected to find some kind of goddess dwelling here, a spider queen waiting at the center of her web of technology, pulling all the strings of all media communications. A creature that could blast me to bits and bytes with a single thought. At first, I guess I had. But now, instead, Sandra Calvin looked tired, old, defeated. Very human. Ruby red blood bloomed under her bare foot.

"I can't stop you," she said finally. "You know that."

"I wish you could," I said. It was the truth.

I thought we were at the end now. I thought to call upon the immaculate white katana, then I realized it was already in my grasp, already unsheathed, the blade limned with a furious red. Yasuro's spirit. How long had he been there? Had he been listening?

I did not want this. I tried to open my fingers, hoped to let the sword fall, to send it back to the white hell where it belonged, where *he* belonged. Even if it would damn me to eternal torment at the whim of his vengeful spirit. But my body wouldn't obey. I only gripped the sword tighter.

Triangle took a deep breath. "Only *you* can stop you."

I wrapped my other hand over the one that held the sword, trying to bring it down. Trying to, I don't know, squeeze my wrist until it fell off. If only I could. My will was slipping. The edge of the blade smoked with red. A red flame surged to life along its length.

Only I can stop this, I told myself. *I'm fucking trying!*

Triangle watched me quake. I think she understood what was happening to me. She came forward, leaving a bloody footprint, and draped her arms around my shoulders. The top of her robe opened; the *Oni* tattoo glared at me, wild-eyed and crazy. I shifted my whole body sideways, trying to draw the sword away from her. A sudden sweat sprung down my spine, poured down my face, dripped from my lock of hair. My teeth clenched almost hard enough to crack.

Triangle sank down to her knees, bringing me down gently with her. She embraced me, even as I shook and fought off the vengeful spirit that wanted her dead. Now it was my turn for pain. We were surrounded by a pulsing, drowning red light emanating from the blade.

"Shhh," she whispered in my ear. "It's okay. I want you to know… For what I done to him, I deserve this."

I drew my eyes away from the sword. I felt my hold on it weaken. I looked into her eyes.

"For what I done," she said softly, "to both of 'em."

The blade slid into her side, just under her ribcage. It burned its way through like she was clay. She shuddered, but did not cry out. Her eyes squeezed shut, and the tears streamed down. She opened her mouth, and an acrid, red smoke curled out. Then more and more of it. I felt the tension in my wrist give out. I let go of the sword and tried to hold her up with both hands, even as her entire body disintegrated from within.

But not the triangle. Not the *Oni*'s face.

As Sandra Calvin died, the prison of her shame crumbled. The demon's eyes were bloodshot. Its skin glowed a hellish orange. A swirling, orange portal exploded before me, sucking the katana and the ash of Sandra Calvin away into nothing. An enormous, clenched fist shot out and slammed into my chest with enough force to break my sternum off my ribs and send me soaring back thirty meters, where I crashed hard against the solid wall of the sphere, cracking a hole in the back of my skull.

I should've been dead.

But that's the story of my life.

The pain was about what you'd imagine it to be, but the damage was not indelible. A gout of purple flame emerged from my chest and enveloped me, levitating me centimeters from the metal floor. Inside me, I felt the spirit-hands of the dead pushing my bones back into place. My brain, my heart, my punctured lungs, the hands ripped them all apart and slapped them back together again like wet meat on a butcher's block, ready for the grinder. When I got my breath back, I howled in absolute agony until it was done. I rolled over, grunting as I pushed myself up onto my knees.

My hands splayed on the floor, I felt the crashing footfalls of the demon. I turned my head sideways and saw it, its towering form framed by the swirling, orange portal. Thick muscle squirmed eagerly under its orange skin. Horns and fangs, the rainbow-black color of burnt-iron, protruded from its forehead and leering maw. Its eyes were fucking insane, bloodshot, spinning around the room, focusing on everything and nothing.

It lurched forward out of the fading light, then stood still. Its brows knit together in confusion as it stared dumbly at the katana stuck in its flank. A meaty hand wrapped around the handle and drew the weapon out, brought it to eye level. The *Oni* examined it curiously, like it was a thorn that had stuck it. Then the *Oni* turned its gaze upon me, and it laughed. And I'm sure you won't find this hard to believe: it was the same jackass laugh of Sandra Calvin. It drew its arm back and hurled the katana straight at me.

As I watched all of this, I had propped myself up against the curve of the spherical wall, holding my abdomen and my chest, feeling the pain fade away. As the sword came straight at me, I felt strangely calm. All the little tricks I'd picked up the last few days, I hadn't forgotten them so easily.

I held up my arm and simply caught it. In a split second, what would've otherwise skewered straight through my eye socket shifted its trajectory mid-air and floated delicately into my grasp. I stood up. I planted my feet. I tensed my muscles and lowered my stance, pretending to be a samurai, waiting for the spirit of the true samurai to take over.

And then I waited some more.

"What the fuck?" I whispered to myself, or to him.

The *Oni* cocked his head and its kooky grin split its face ear to ear, watching me curiously, like watching a pill bug crawl away and roll up inside itself.

I held up a finger to it, signaling for just a moment if it would please.

Yasuro? I almost spoke his name aloud. Almost screamed it out.

I reached with all my spirit through the veil between worlds, and I felt his presence far, far below. Right where he'd always been. He was still there. He hadn't gone away. What the fuck was he doing?

Sandra Calvin was dead. Right? Wasn't she?

The spirit had gotten his revenge.

Hadn't he?

The *Oni* planted its hands on its hips and cackled like a maniac at the sight of me. The sound of it sent true dread through every fiber of my being. It knew what I knew in that moment: without the White Shadow, I was nothing.

None of this shit made sense.

TWENTY

A WHILE BACK, I ASKED YOU TO PICTURE A BAMBOO forest. Remember? At the time, we were talking about pain. Do you remember how the bamboo twisted around itself? How that was the only way I could describe the sensation of passing through solid matter in the land of the living while slipping through into the land of the dead?

You remember. Good.

When the orange *Oni* came for me, when it hit me, again and again, battering me into a paste against the walls and the floors of Triangle's sanctum—the Tenjin Media Communications Center in the heart of *Takamagahara* itself—it was not only the twisting of bamboo as my bones split open and stabbed into my flesh. Hell, I wish it was that pleasant. The pain as the monster peeled me from the floor—my limp body soaking in red blood even while flickering with purple healing flame—and threw me up, up, against and into and through the solid metal structures of the sub-orbital space station, puncturing through the layers of floors and structures like a bullet from a rail gun, up, and up, and up—it was the feeling of the forest split apart against my spine, it was the big fucking bang all over again. It was a whole new universe of sensation.

I simply cannot tell you how awful it felt. How badly I wanted to truly die and be done with it. How I yearned for obliteration.

I came to in a place of utter darkness. There was no wind. There was no air. I opened my eyes upon the void. On the far reaches of my vision, I could see the wispy mist of purple receding as my undying spirit rebuilt my body, stitch by stitch. Then stars came into focus, winking into being before my eyes. Twinkling beautifully. Then I could feel the solid surface beneath me. Suddenly, there was a thrumming under me. I felt it in my back, like the vibration in a rail as the train approaches. But this was much faster.

"Shinjiro," SUIT said. The AI's voice was muffled. Barely more than a vibration against the side of my head. She spoke as always through my comlink, which had somehow, miraculously, survived alongside me phasing in and out of *Yomi* and the living world, and slamming through everything the *Oni* had flung me against. She said my name again.

I blinked, lifted my head up, and looked at my feet. The blackness of space was framed on all sides by towers. Corporate towers. Branded with their logos. I was laying on some kind of smooth road. A hundred meters past my feet, smoke and fire belched skyward from a crater where something had exploded. I recalled that it had been where *I* exploded, where my body broke through the surface of the sub-orbital platform and plummeted, in flaming pieces, back down. I should've been pretty pissed about that.

But instead, I could not take my eyes off my feet. One of them was adorned in one of the finest shoes mankind has ever produced, albeit a little scuffed. The other foot ... bare. The shoe ... gone.

"Shinjiro," SUIT's voice again. I vaguely recalled noticing how there didn't seem to be a nick on her, all her threads perfectly intact and immaculate as ever. So that was nice. I stared dumbly at my matching cashmere-blend socks and ignored her. The vibration in my back grew stronger.

"Incoming," she said. "Three. Two. One."

Something zoomed by my left shoulder, followed by a blast of wind and the pull of the vacuum in its trail. Before I had time to even think about what it was, another two zooms came on, the second right behind the first, and the last on my other side. My body tossed about like a leaf in a typhoon.

I knew exactly what they were. I knew exactly where I was.

"I'm on the hypercraft track," I said aloud to no one. My own voice whirred in my brain. This far above the Earth's surface, there were only trace amounts of air that could carry sound. "Oh shit. I'm on the fucking hypercraft track!"

"Incoming," SUIT said again. "Three. Two..."

I had drifted a meter away from the centerline of the crater. I saw the sun's reflection against the glass of the cockpit as the hypercraft came straight for me. I rolled out of its way at the very last second.

I scrambled to my feet, panting for breath. My lungs drew in what they could, not enough for a normal person to avoid suffocation in the near-vacuum. But I wasn't a normal person. I spun about, trying to get my bearings, trying to figure out what the fuck I should do.

A huge arm punched up through the smoldering crater, its orange skin blending with the whirling flames. A clawed fist slammed down, raking lines in the metal track as it pulled the rest of its hulking form upward and over. The *Oni* saw me and laughed hysterically.

"Motherfucker!" I screamed. I slipped off my last remaining Italian leather shoe and hurled it at the monster. In the low-gravity air, it flew impossibly fast, impossibly straight, and thunked against its forehead, right between its horns. "*Mother-FUUUCKER!!*"

I know you are probably thinking I was only angry about the shoe, and that makes me a very vain and unlikable person. Please, you have to consider that the shoe was simply the blood-red, indignant cherry atop the excruciating pain-cake. I was going to kill that fucking creature for what it did to me. And to Triangle. Hell, even to Yasuro Fucking Shiromatsu, I guess. And yes, also because I had lost one of my best shoes.

Only problem was, I didn't really know how. I'd learned very recently that this thing could hurt me. Really hurt me. And I wasn't really capable of hurting it back.

It took its first lumbering steps toward me. Then it dropped to all fours and pumped its way, faster and faster, charging at me like a snarling bull, guffawing like a fucking donkey.

I had one shot at this. I'd be like a bullfighter. I'd seen a reel or two. How hard could it be?

I summoned the white katana.

I felt it answer from somewhere distant, like a breath on the palm of my hand. But it didn't come.

I glanced like a fucking idiot at my empty hand.

And the bull-*Oni*'s right horn gored me right through the stomach. I felt the blood rush up my gullet, spill out between my clenched teeth. I grabbed its horn at the base and held on for the ride. It bucked up and threw me a hundred meters over its shoulder. I slammed hard upside down against one of Heaven's high-rises and slid down to the track, leaving a streak of blood on the wall. The rest of my blood droplets floated lazily in the air, pattering softly along my trail.

I rose to my feet and screamed. Ethereal purple fire erupted from me like a welding torch, snapping my re-broken bones back into place and cauterizing the gaping hole in my abdomen, but it couldn't stitch up my nice white shirt, nor erase the bloodstains. Along my back, the Sentient

Universal-Interfacing Totality kicked in its nano-replicators or whatever-the-fuck and healed itself, too.

"Shinjiro," it said, "stand precisely where you are."

"Fuck you!" I screamed at the orange *Oni* as it readied for another charge, ignoring SUIT entirely.

The *Oni* laughed again. It took one step, then halted abruptly.

A deafening whoosh of air brought both of our attention to the track behind me. The next hypercraft had engaged its emergency air-brakes and was decelerating rapidly. Its nose swayed left to right, the pilot inside struggling to keep its trajectory straight. Or so I thought.

It was SUIT's doing. She'd hacked the vehicles, the track, the entire league. And the weapon systems.

The maglev engines brought the hypercraft within range, then straightened it out. The twin Gatling guns under its hull were already spinning white hot when they turned upon the massive orange *Oni* less than a hundred meters down their sights. They lit him up at the rate of a thousand rounds per second, tearing him apart in successive sweeps of gunfire. First cutting both his legs off at the knees, bringing his bulk slamming down, then through his torso, his shoulders, his face. Gouts of orange spirit-fire shot out of his back like tracer rounds as the bullets did their work.

There was another whoosh, then another as two more hypercraft engaged their air-brakes, closing in to add their firepower. The first craft's gun barrels glowed, spinning and firing well beyond the heat limiter auto-fail. SUIT was squeezing everything from it just as the next two weapon systems came within range and unleashed their fury.

By the time they were done, there was nothing left of the *Oni* besides clumps of metal shavings and simmering flesh stretching across a trough of orange blood and fire two hundred meters long.

Needless to say, the track would need some repairs.

The cockpit tops popped off from each of the hijacked hypercraft one by one, and the Bullet-Timed pilots scrambled out frantically and ran for safety as their vehicles caught fire and melted behind them. The maglev systems failed, and the ultra-sleek hulls came to rest on the track.

I couldn't help but stand there, my jaw hanging slack, taking in all the carnage. Then I realized...

I looked up at the swarm of drones that recorded the race footage and pumped it into every holoprojector and comlink of every man, woman, and child race fan in NeOsaka. At least. I didn't need an eagle's eyes to know their camera apertures were zooming in to focus on the face of yours truly.

"Oh shit," I breathed. "SUIT, tell me you did something about those drones."

"Yes, Shinjiro. I have blocked their feeds and captured all uploading capabilities. I can alter the footage at a later time. Additionally, I should inform you, I seized all of Tenjin Media's control protocols during our infiltration of Sandra Calvin's RFID sphere. Thank you for bringing me along."

I let out as big a sigh as I could, which wasn't much in the razor thin air in Heaven. "Uh, you're welcome."

"Suggestion: vacate the racetrack. As soon as possible."

Vacate, I thought. *Good idea.*

I once again reached for the white katana, the key that could unlock the path to the other side, the fastest means of *vacating* my ass out of there. Once again, I felt the katana's presence, far away. It felt stuck somehow. It was resisting.

At the same time, an unrelated, yet entirely pertinent, notion occurred to me. Fire needed air. And way up here, given the limited air supply, the fires that burned where the *Oni* used to be should've winked out almost as soon as they'd sprung to life. Instead, they were growing, chewing their way through the racetrack, closer and closer to where

I stood, like a lava flow melting the metal surface. The *Oni* was not dead. Not gone. Not by a long shot.

SUIT had bought me time. That was all. Even a nuclear warhead wouldn't kill the guffawing orange fuck permanently.

I needed the sword.

I would not allow myself to panic.

I lowered myself to the floor. I crossed my legs, rested my palms in my lap, closed my eyes. I breathed. I relaxed my shoulders, my back, my legs.

I would not panic. I would gather my will. I would speak to the katana. To Yasuro.

"I need it," I told him.

And he replied.

"*Naze ka?* Why?"

"You know why," I pressed.

The fires crept closer, gathering from all sides. Inside them, a form was taking shape.

"*Iinasai,*" he said. Speak.

"Because your revenge is not complete."

"Ahh. *Soo desu. Sorede?* What else?"

I recalled our first meeting. How it ended. The revelation. The new reality of my existence.

"You are the blade," I told him. "And I am the body."

The *Oni*'s deranged smile split open in the wall of flame, mere centimeters from where I sat. Its fangs and horns forged themselves, rainbow-black from the unquenchable fire. Its hands reached through. I felt the raging heat on my face, bringing the sweat gushing from my pores and at the same time evaporating it on my skin. The wind rushed forth from the *Oni*'s fiery hell and sent the folds of my suit flapping.

But I would not panic. I would not open my eyes. I would breathe.

I reached forth into the White Shadow's emptiness. I saw him in my mind's eye. Yasuro, the shadow-man, the cascade of jet black hair, pulled to one side, the one red eye watching me approach. From behind his back, he brought forth the perfect, white katana. He gripped it in both hands, tipped it forward in offering, a murderous smile on his thin lips.

I bowed, accepted.

"Domo," I said.

The *Oni*'s massive arm reared back, its iron-black claws readying to strike.

Too late.

I was up, unleashing *iaido*, stepping forth powerfully into the demon's guard while drawing the blade from its sheath and striking in a single, masterful motion. The blade bit through the *Oni*'s ethereal orange flesh, splitting it open from hip to shoulder, scarring it with purple light. Its orange blood became infected with my power, splashing up like a purple geyser, exploding like a ghostly firework. The *Oni*'s nerves were severed, its body went rigid, its arm loomed overhead, its claws splayed.

It didn't have time to scream.

I rose up, rocking onto my back foot, bringing the blade across and through the *Oni*'s neck, lopping his head clean off.

All of this, in less than three seconds.

The *Oni*'s tongue lolled as its head fell at my feet, its wild, bloodshot eyes stared up at me. Even in its moment of true-death, it smiled maniacally. And then the purple, cleansing fire spread over it, from wherever the blade had touched it, burning away its impurity. In seconds, it was gone.

The samurai puppet master let go of his strings, and I crashed to my knees in low-G. All around me, a storm of orange and purple embers floated and fluttered, like butterflies, like sakura petals swept by a breeze. My heart raced, skipped beats. I was going into cardiac arrest. I closed my eyes, expecting the dark of oblivion, of rest.

Instead, the empty white awaited me.

INTERLUDE: A MEMORY

It begins with the right hand of the samurai—manicured, soft, pale, reaching forth from the sleeve of a snow-white suit—waving gracefully before the obsidian-black receptor panel beside the tall boardroom doors. The samurai steps back as they open. Emblazoned on the banners hanging in this chamber are the kanji *of his family's credo:* Spirit *and* River. *In his left hand rests the samurai's weapon, the perfect, angular, sleek katana. Always at the ready. Wrapped in black* tsuka *cord, sheathed in a black* saya. *Matching the samurai's long, straight, jet-black hair.*

He steps through into a long room awash in bright sunshine. It streams through the tall windows. Outside, the day is perfect. The air is clean. The metropolis sprawls. The edges of buildings slice the skyline like razors. Between them, one can see the spring green of treetops swaying in the wind. It is almost possible to imagine a perfect world, to forget the irradiated ruin that lies beyond the city's borders, that spreads across most of the world outside NeOsaka's protective field. The invisible wall that his family built.

The samurai ignores for just a moment the sole occupant in the Shiromatsu-Kazama boardroom that he has come to speak with. The woman reclines idly at the head of the long mahogany table, in his father's chair, her dusty, booted feet propped up. It is this disrespect he has come to address, among many other things. A pair of bulky, opaque goggles shroud her eyes. A wide set of earphones presses the middle of her spiked, green mohawk down against the shaved side of her head. Her tattooed fingertips dance left and right in the air before her, dragging, duplicating, and deleting bits of data only she can see in cyberspace. She is blind and deaf to all else. The samurai feels the natural inclination to curl his lip in a snarl at the sight of her. He acknowledges this feeling, then sends it away with a simple exhalation of breath. He crosses the room silently to observe his empire beyond the windows. For one minute, he watches the test flight of the lone, levitating transport craft that his father's company has developed. The arc of it disappears behind the headquarters of a subsidiary half a kilometer away.

It is time.

He stands over her, watches her only for as long as he can stand, which is not long. Then he taps the end of his katana's black saya *sheath on the table beside her boots.*

"Just a sec," she says. The drawl of her voice has always frustrated him. How can someone appearing so ignorant be so gifted?

Muda ni shiteru na, *he thinks. Such a waste.*

But she does not halt her activity. She continues for several seconds as if he is not there. He cannot stand her, all the others like her, American, Polish, British, Nigerian, Morrocan, Swedish, Sri Lankan, Chinese. All of them inundating, filling space, demanding resources. All of them outsiders, gaijin. *Were it not for his family's sacred legacy...*

Inside, this woman's show of insolence infuriates him. But the samurai is in total command of himself, of his spirit. He is as still as the sand in the Zen gardens. They are the base of his fortress. He withstands her. This will all be over soon, regardless.

She peels the equipment from her face at last. She looks up and regards him with a wide smile of coffee-stained teeth. "What's up, boss?"

"Miss Calvin—"

"Sandra," she says, interrupting. "How long's it been? I've been telling ya since day one. Call me Sandra. Or Sandy."

Still, she smiles.

"Miss Calvin," he continues, "I am to inform you that you are being terminated. Effective immediately."

At last, after four long years, her smile fades.

"What?"

"All company equipment is being removed from your arcology residence as we speak. Likewise, all company augmentations will be excised from your body today before you leave ShiroKaz Tower, and you are never to return."

"Wait, wait," she stammers, removing her boots from the table at last, swiveling in his father's chair to face him, rising, holding her hands out dramatically.

He enjoys the sight of her then, squirming like a maggot in her dusty, patchwork, street-leather jacket. She is dokashi. Like a clown.

"What did I do?"

So, *he muses*, an explanation then.

He lowers his chin and raises his eyes to pierce her with his stare. It is a look the samurai has given to many of his foes. It speaks for him. It says, you already know.

Sandra Calvin deflates. Without a word, he has stripped her of her brashness and bravado. All that remains is a frightened, lonesome, lost child. In the silence, her lips quiver as the reality of her plight sets in.

"This is about the mainframes. Isn't it?"

The samurai's eyes say again: You already know.

Inwardly, he assures himself, this ordeal will be over soon.

His gaze wears her down. She looks away. She bites her lower lip, puts her hands on her hips, and looks out at the city outside the windows even as the tears flood her eyes. Would she ever again see the world from such great heights? He thinks not.

"No," she says suddenly. The word, the force of her spirit, speaks it strongly. This strength surprises the samurai, although she is still nothing. "No," she goes on, turning to face him again. "It's more than that. This is about Z."

The samurai feels his blood flow hot. For an instant, a red pulse washes over his sight.

"It's our work," the woman continues, "he and I, together. Isn't it? You can't stand the idea that he has ideas, too. Sorry, asshole, but the fucking Legacy ain't all about you and your daddy."

She jabs a finger at the samurai, mere centimeters away from his chest. (Perhaps, despite her rage, she knows better than to touch him.) His eyes lock on it, at the brittle, bitten ends of her nails, at the cracked, colorful polish. Her finger hovers in space, unwavering now, the gesture itself projecting a kind of strength from this person he had not expected to find. A spirit, indeed, he had never experienced before in her.

He regards the grime that runs black in the chasms of her fingerprint, the other fingertips just like it, the hand, the entire arm, disappearing into her unwashed clothing. It clashes with the inviolability of his white garb, the pure brushed wool fabric, dustless, pressed. Perfect. He would compose a haiku about this moment of dichotomy. Kanji floats across the sky of his imagination. Skin and cloth. *At a later time, in reflection.*

For now, all his strength of spirit resists the base urge to latch onto her and twist her into oblivion. He quashes the sneer that wants to spread upon his face and mar him.

"*Kindly remove yourself from the boardroom, Miss Calvin,*" he says coolly, though the words do little to mitigate the red heat rising in his blood. "*Security officers await you beyond the doors.*"

"*What about Luther?*" She asks, the force of her compelling an answer. "*Daddy won't let you fire your own blood, but me, and him, and Luther, the three of us together built the other mainframes. You already know, anyhow. Can't keep no secrets from* the White Fucking Shadow *now, can we?*"

"*Mister DeLeon has similarly been relieved of his duties and access. Now that our meeting is at its conclusion, Miss Calvin, I must warn you. Should you conspire with the enemies of ShiroKaz, should you impede the realization of our Legacy, should you sell or otherwise share any knowledge of our corporate assets to any third party, I will find you.*"

"*Right,*" she says. Her eyes flit to the discarded goggles and earphones on the table, to all the work she would leave unfinished. She shakes her head. "*Right,*" she says again. But she gives no indication that she will comply with the order to remove herself.

A notion seizes the samurai, feels its way through a fold in his armor. The self-indulgent words are spoken before he can retract them. "*My brother is the only reason I have not already eliminated you and Mister DeLeon.*"

Sandra Calvin looks up at him then, an expression of sheer worry shadowing her face. "*What're you going to do to him?*"

"*My brother, like you, is misguided. He was warned the first time. This second transgression will be his final activity within the ShiroKaz corporation. Within the Shiromatsu family.*"

"*You bastards,*" she says softly, looking him straight in the eyes.

For the first time since the samurai has known Sandra Calvin, he allows himself to be impressed with her boldness in that very moment.

"You're what ... banishing him? Again? After all he's tried. All he ever wanted was to be like you."

Their conversation is over. There is no reason left to listen. His purpose fulfilled, the White Shadow knows any further response is unnecessary. In that moment, he deems this woman worthy of his touch, now that their time together is at an end forever onward. He shifts forward, meaning to grip her elbow with his right hand and escort her.

But Sandra pulls away and brings her open palm back across his perfect, handsome face, hard enough to stagger him.

Yasuro's long hair falls over his face, concealing his astonishment. His shame. His disgust. He raises the back of his pale hand to the edge of his mouth. He examines the single droplet of blood upon it.

Red.

His rage wells over.

"Kuso-onna!"

The red smoke rises.

He lunges, wrapping his hand around the woman's throat, pressing himself against her, shoving her onto the table, holding her there. Squeezing. Squeezing. She flails weakly against his arm. It is a bar of solid iron. He bares his fangs like a wolf as he watches her struggle beneath him. He observes the soul recede from her eyes, like smoke rising from smoldering orange fires.

But then, the unthinkable. Sandra Calvin is dying, but she looks into her killer's eyes, and she smiles. Without breath, she laughs up at the samurai, at all he ever was, is, all he ever will be.

Yasuro has frightened so many. The legendary ghost-man himself, unkillable, unstoppable. He's seen the face of fear on his foes as his sword severed their limbs, separated their heads from their bodies, their horrified expressions frozen. In that, he has been like a painter capturing moments of death in vivid color. But never before has he attacked so viscerally. Never with his bare hands. And never has his foe smiled at him in their death.

The red smoke of the underworld recedes. He releases her and steps back, turns away from the woman in disgust, leaving her sprawled atop the boardroom table, coughing and gasping for breath. His hand trembles. He balls it into a fist, just as she catches her breath. Her gasping becomes laughter.

"There he is, everybody," she wheezes. She props herself up, hawks and spits onto the carpeted floor. "The real Yasuro. Careful there, boy, or someone else might see you again someday."

The samurai's eyes close. He feels the breath of life surge into him, fill him, expand his awareness. Then he pushes it out deliberately in a prolonged exhalation. The exercise is meant to calm him. It does not. He cannot turn to face her. Cannot allow his foe to see him this way. She has seen enough.

Or, she has believed to have seen him. Truth is perception, after all, and what she has said about "the real Yasuro" simply is not true. This is not him. This is not real.

Behind him, Sandra Calvin regains her composure. She comes to his side and whispers in his ear.

"Someday, sugarplum, somebody's gonna find a way to destroy you. If you don't destroy yourself first. Either way, I'll be there. On the coms, like always. Gonna watch the whole thing."

The boardroom doors open at her approach. He lifts his gaze and watches her strut confidently toward them. Without looking back, she calls to him over her shoulder.

"Be seeing you."

Yasuro stands, staring vacantly, even as the doors close. He does not allow himself to move until he has mastered himself once more. It takes him much longer than he would have thought. He lets out one last, deep breath, then realizes how tight his grip has been on the sheathed katana. He wills his hand to relax, his fingers to open, and so he lets go of the black weapon. It falls slowly, is enveloped in a red mist, and disappears.

He crosses once more to the tall windows, frowning at the dust from the gaijin's boots on the polished table, her discarded gear, her wad of spittle on the floor. These traces of her are superficial, he knows. These visible, tangible marks of her filth, they can be eradicated. And her words... What she has said to him this day...

She is gone. But Yasuro's rage remains.

It always remains.

He looks out again over all the world that he can see. There is nowhere he cannot go. There is nothing he cannot touch. He thinks, perhaps, to compose the haiku now, at this very moment.

But the words do not come.

TWENTY-ONE

THIS MUST BE WHAT IT WAS LIKE TO WAKE UP IN THE middle of an iceberg. To be a Cromagnon man at the center of a glacier, or one of the saps volunteering for cryo experimentation. The whiteness diffusing, the colors of the world slowly coming into focus. The numbness fading, the feeling returning. The melting, is it mere moments? Hours?

Something hard and flat pressed onto my chest, my thighs, my shoulders. My whole body, but not my head. My face lolled forward. Something swayed gently before my blurred vision. I groaned, feeling the air stirring in my body. My eyes focused on the end of my dangling lock of black hair, and a hundred kilometers beyond it, the twinkling city lights and the scudding orange vapor of frozen sunset in the empty space between. I knew then I was lying on my stomach, my head hanging over the edge of some platform that hung out from Heaven's underbelly. I must have passed out. The last thing I remembered was the *Oni*'s face disintegrating against a background of orange and purple butterflies, and the last thought I'd had was how pretty Sandra Calvin had been.

Even as an old woman; especially in her youth.

I had just seen her—experienced her—in a dream. My gaze had spoken for me. My hand had squeezed her throat.

No. It had not been a dream exactly. In a dream, when you wake up, you may recall freeze-frame images, the haunting image of a friend's face as the lines begin to blur, as you forget the instant you awaken. But I could remember everything, how she looked, what she said, how she said it. It had been Yasuro Shiromatsu's dream, his last memory of her flooding back in. Sandra Calvin had conspired to kill him. She'd all but said she would the last time they'd met. The memory I had witnessed was the moment that burned in Yasuro's spirit, that which he had forgotten when I first touched his perfect white katana days ago in the ShiroKaz family vault. It had manifested itself as an *Oni*, a tormentor of legend and myth, and I had hunted it the fuck down. I had recaptured it.

That explained why Yasuro had not been satisfied even after he fought through my will and stabbed Triangle in her side. He knew he wanted her dead, but he hadn't remembered why.

But why had she wanted *him* dead? Not just dead—because clearly she knew he couldn't really be killed—but *gone*.

I pushed myself up, feeling the bone-deep ache in all my muscles and flesh, all over, all at once. I ground my teeth from the pain. Sitting back on my knees, I ran my hands over my fine collared shirt, now far more red than white from all the buckets of blood the *Oni* had helped me stain it with. It was shredded. Almost all the top buttons were gone, my breasts barely concealed. I undid the ones that were left and examined the newborn skin that had sealed the wound where the *Oni*'s horn ran me through. Yet another patch of ink faded from my torii gate tattoo. Over the years, the design had seen some shit for sure. Been through a lot of shit. It was barely recognizable for what it was, just a patchwork of ink and scars.

The Sentient Universal-Interfacing Totality, however, had come through the whole thing just fine. The threads of its mobile platform were as immaculate as ever.

"Shinjiro," it said. I realized then it had been periodically calling my name through the haze of semi-consciousness.

"I'm here," I said, gazing out over the curving planet below. There was so much darkness now. It was harder to see the light. To the west and east of Osaka, nothingness. Perhaps a candle's glow where old Tokyo used to exist, a survivor's encampment out in the wastes. Another, just on the western horizon, where Seoul lingered on. Far to the north, the absolute encroaching blackness of the blasted Russo-Chin landscape. Their conclave was thousands of kilometers away, in the Moscow underground. My whole, actual world, was a lantern burning brightly directly below. New Osaka.

"SUIT, what the fuck is wrong with us?"

"I've monitored your vital signs during your unconsciousness. Your biorhythms recovered normal operation within—"

"Humanity, SUIT. I'm talking about human fucking beings."

The AI was silent for a long time, probably re-processing my biometrics, factoring in the state of mind that came out the other end of its data system, finding nothing. Finally, it admitted, "I do not understand your intention."

Maybe I didn't understand either. All I knew was that any other person of my stature—a Syndicate sewer rat, a nobody, lowlife scum piece of shit like Shinjiro Asai, who'd somehow gotten lucky enough to catch a view like this—should be… no, *would* be dazzled. It would change their perspective, make them appreciate how far they'd come, how high they'd risen. Mega-corp elite, how they'd become like technocratic gods. I deserved to feel like they felt, whether because of my curse, my gifts, or because of the choices I'd made, the alliances I'd forged, to get here. But instead, as I looked out across all the darkness of the Earth, all I could think about was the destructive force of human hatred.

"Why do we kill each other?"

"I am searching philosophical databases. Much has been written on this subject. Much has been lost. A phrase is repeated thousands of times across a myriad of languages—taking into consideration all permutations of vocabulary."

"And that phrase is," I cut in, hoping she'd get to the point.

"Propensity for violence."

"Violence. It's part of who we are."

SUIT heard my reply as a question. "The great thinkers would have you believe so, Shinjiro."

"And what do you believe?"

Another silence. This time, SUIT understood my intention. I knew the futility of asking an artificial intelligence questions about human nature, asking about its feelings and beliefs. I knew I wouldn't get an answer that would satisfy, just some recitation of bullshit recorded somewhere. Just some research: the machine's version of thinking.

But the machine surprised me. "I believe," it began, speaking softly, slowly, "that the phrase could be re-framed. It could be: Propensity for mistakes. In all things, there is balance. The Dao. The yin and the yang. Light and dark. Violence can be an evil, but it can be a necessity. For all that is destroyed, something is created. Humanity has created much. There have been breakthroughs. Lives are lost, lives are saved. Hundreds of thousands, millions, over great spans of time. Humanity dwells on the negative, as darkness absorbs vision and light can be considered the natural state of—"

"Okay, okay." If I let SUIT go on, I ran a serious risk of falling asleep. "I like it, SUIT. I get your, uh, executive summary. But give me just the…"

The machine correctly calculated the word I was looking for and said, "Thesis: Humanity's greatest potential is its capacity to learn from its mistakes."

Looking out over the blasted world, I saw humanity's greatest mistake to date. A mistake so vast it nearly wiped itself out. SUIT was right, I was dwelling on the darkness. I knew—I remembered—that there were places beyond my vision, candles burning in the darkness, where people survived. Where people smiled, made each other happy. Helped each other. Where people climbed mountains at night and looked out across places and saw the stars and thought the same things as I did. All that light.

"When this is over," I spoke evenly, to myself, "if I'm somehow still around, I want to help."

"This was the notion of Shiromatsu Yoshinori. The conception of what would later become the ShiroKaz Legacy."

I rolled my eyes. "Please, enough of that bullshit. I get it. The company had grand intentions of doing good. But look at how that turned out. Assholes like Yasuro were born, filled with rage, disdain. Just … fucking hatred for his fellow man. It all got twisted. And then they came for him. They took all that power and divvied it up. Elitists like Smythe and his cronies."

"It is as I said before, Shinjiro. Mistakes were made."

The AI was right. Somewhere along the line, the White Shadow made mistakes. His whole outlook on his family's great legacy was somehow his undoing. All his work wound up meaningless. I saw clearly what he'd let himself become. And even if I wasn't his daughter, I was the next White Shadow. Whether I wanted the power or not, it was mine. I saw the sins of the father, so to speak, and I did not have to play host. Well, metaphorically I didn't. Literally, with Yasuro's spirit pulling my puppet strings, and his old katana anchoring me to his will, I was quite fucked.

So then, I would do good. When this was over, I would help. Not for ShiroKaz, not even for myself. I would do it because there needed to be a balance. But still, I knew, even with all my power, I couldn't do it on my own.

I sprang up to my feet suddenly. "SUIT, where's Cayenne?"

"Miss DeLeon safely boarded a spider rail an hour ago and has arrived at ShiroKaz Tower. I have engaged all security protocols. She is quite safe."

I breathed a sigh of relief. I tore my gaze away from the Earth, now fully shrouded in night, and looked at the enormous cables anchoring the sub-orbital platform to the world below. Even as I did so, I saw a spider rail clinking its mechanical legs along the length of one, coming up, and another going down. I needed to get off *Takamagahara*. Behind me, I found a ladder that terminated in a maintenance hatch of some kind thirty meters overhead. I shrugged at the apparatus where crews were supposed to latch their safety harnesses to the metal frame. Good thing I wasn't scared of heights. I started to climb, still talking to SUIT along the way.

"What about Ben?"

There was a pause. That was unexpected. I froze on the fifth rung, waiting.

"SUIT, I said what about Ben?"

"I have scanned all the premises of the arcology. Mister Doon is not present there. Nor is he with Miss DeLeon. Neither is he pinging on the grid."

"What?"

"He is gone, Shinjiro."

"He's gone? He wouldn't…"

"I tried to warn you—"

"Oh, give it a rest."

"—but you would not listen."

"Something must've happened to him. He'll find me. He always does."

"You threatened to decapitate him the last time you spoke."

"I say that shit all the time. He knows I don't mean it."

"Does he now?"

The AI modulated its tone purposefully, hiding nothing under the sultry Australian accent. Was it adapting because of our conversations? Our bickering? It must've realized along the way my penchant for sarcasm. I ignored SUIT's little quip and brought us back to seriousness.

"Did Cayenne really get what she needed from Smythe's head? Or did Ben send it elsewhere?"

"Miss DeLeon is examining the data as we speak. It was downloaded in its entirety. But there was a backdoor protocol attached, which I have since expunged."

Oh shit, I thought. My stomach sank, which, let me tell you, feels very weird in low-G. *Ben betrayed us.*

"Shinjiro, your heart rate is spiking."

"Does Cayenne know? That Ben hijacked it?"

"I resisted the urge to inform her. I thought you would prefer to deliver the bad news yourself."

"You have fucking *urges* now?"

"Ben Roy Doon did leave an anomaly, a string of intentionally unterminated code that he abandoned at the arcology. An acronym. W-R-U-I-O-U-P-Q-E-E-U-F-T-L."

"Are you kidding me?"

"No, I am not. I have already begun processing word combinations."

"How long?"

"Approximation: I will decode the phrase and cross reference all possible network codes for a match in three days' time."

"I guess he was right. This is the only way the Cluster could beat advanced systems like you. Like Triangle."

Like Tatsuhiro, I thought. Why I didn't add his name to my list, I couldn't tell. I pulled myself up another few rungs of the ladder, almost to the top. Then I froze.

"Triangle said the old bastard might've told me who my father was. But it's not Yasuro Shiromatsu. SUIT, does Tatsuhiro know who my father is? My mother? Does he know my family?" I found my grip on the ladder tightening.

The idea of the old, dead dragon keeping a secret like that from me...

I have been searching for you for a very long time... Because you are special, Shinjiro. Very special.

Again, the AI was quiet. Accessing, calculating, searching, whatever. Or perhaps stalling. Sensing my agitation, cooking up the most correct response to manipulate me. Cooking up a lie.

Triangle had told me she'd searched everything she was connected to for info about the new mysterious White Shadow. *Me.* As the goddess of Tenjin Media Corporation, that meant quite literally *everything*. There was no network beyond her reach. No network but one. "Does Tatsuhiro have anything in his mainframe? About my parents?"

The silence stretched. The wind way up here was surprisingly minimal, but it was enough to stir the ends of my suit blazer, the very machine I was talking to.

"What use are you to me? You can't handle a simple yes-no question. I'm going to peel you off and throw you into outer space if you don't answer me. Now, SUIT!"

"Apology: Shinjiro, I am under duress."

Well, that was unexpected.

"No shit!" I shouted into the void. "Stop stalling! I want fucking answers!"

"You are not the cause of the duress, Shinjiro. Himeji Castle will be under direct assault in four minutes."

"What?"

"Multiple vehicles are inbound. I am only now unmasking their presence on the grid. And there is already one assailant."

At that moment, far to the north of NeOsaka, a light sprang to life, drawing my attention. A distant glow. Bright enough for me to see even this far away, a hundred kilometers high. A purple-limned Japanese castle. It was the spirit form of the ruined castle, *Shirasagi-Jo.* And on its outskirts, eruptions of cyan-colored light.

I tore my gaze away from the spectacle below, eyes focused on the remaining rungs of the ladder leading to the access hatch, not far now to go, then I'd be through the belly of *Takamagahara*, not sure how much farther, then out somehow hopefully to a spider rail, with SUIT as my guide.

"Hurry," the Australian-accented AI said flatly. Then again, "Hurry, Shinjiro."

Hurry, she says. What the hell am I—

I had reached the hatch, but I froze again. I looked below.

I had an idea.

I took a deep breath.

Fuck it.

I spun around and leaped.

TWENTY-TWO

***T*HAT WHICH DOESN'T KILL ME, OR WHATEVER...**
I plummeted from Heaven to Earth. A fallen angel.

The wind was incredible, pulling my skin back so hard I was sure I'd hit the ground as a naked skeleton. I did what I could to keep Himeji Castle in front of me, but an experienced skydiver I was not. The currents of air twisted me around. I flopped around between the wild G-forces tossing me back and forth. My intended target dropped from my view as I spun around from my chest to my back, now facing skyward, watching the underbelly of the sub-orbital platform recede in the distance. I screamed at the top of my lungs, hearing nothing but the vibration of it in my cheekbones, my body easily outracing the sound.

This had been a bad fucking idea.

I let go of whatever control I thought I had over my trajectory, letting my arms and legs go slack, flop around, twist, and threaten to snap. I flailed about wildly. I figured I might as well get started on the pain. Might help to numb me when I hit the ground. Wherever that would be.

That which doesn't kill me...

I knew I wasn't going to die. I'd tried shit like this before. Never this high up, of course. But I had once told my SynCell I'd meet them back at Broken after a raid in a corporate high-rise, then jumped off, hoping beyond hope that I wouldn't wake up in *Yomi*. Of course, you can figure where the story went from there. A few days later, the boys back at the club asked me where I'd stashed my parachute and scolded me for calling attention to the team.

I wouldn't die here now either.

But what was different this time, aside from altitude?

That's when I remembered. My breath calmed, my flaring, flailing panic instinct receded instantly, like flames without oxygen. I reached for the white katana, and I found it easily. I gripped it gently. No wind could tear it from my grasp. My arms and legs relaxed. By the force of my will, I turned over and faced downward. The lights of NeOsaka were below. I could make out the tips of the corporate towers jutting outward beyond the vaporous clouds glowing a million colors of neon, lit from below. I was still high enough to see the purple glow of the castle, one hundred kilometers away, just at the horizon's darkening edge. Even with my newfound, serene sense of control, I'd never make it. My angle was all wrong.

I had no idea what I was doing. No one ever taught me anything about being a ghost. So maybe it was Yasuro, although I didn't feel him. Or maybe I was simply starting to understand. The city was drawing closer by the second; the castle was disappearing from view.

I shut my eyes. And I called them. I called them all.

I saw through the skin of my eyelids as the towers below me, the clouds, every bit of steel and concrete, the entire city itself twisted and warped into their underworld reflections. But they did not stay that way. Directly below me, the world caved in, becoming a yawning sinkhole, widening, rushing outward, swallowing everything in darkness. Buildings tumbled over the edge and disappeared into the impenetrable black of the abyss. In reality, absolutely nothing catastrophic and destructive was happening to anyone or anything in the city. Only I could see the abyss. And only I could sense what came out of it.

Out of the gaping gateway of *Yomi*, millions of restless spirits rose like purple jets of vapor. By my will, the energies of the underworld were colliding like tidal waves, realigning like tectonic plates, spitting ghosts up and out like a volcanic eruption. I commanded their ethereal bodies to form a bridge, spanning all the distance I had yet to travel. Their hands reached for my plummeting form, held me up, and passed me from one to another, like crowd surfing at a concert. I felt real-time in slow motion, like having a dozen droppers of Bullet Time ejaculate on my optic nerves. What occurred for me in the following five seconds was a fraction of a fraction of a blink of an eye for anyone who might be staring up at that exact moment. I became a horizontal purple lightning bolt, arcing across the sky, hurled by all the dead, striking exactly where I wanted.

I struck the ground before the torii gate at the base of Shirasagi-Jo. My impact sank me into a crater five meters deep. The blast sent a shockwave that blew the gate's corporeal, vermillion-painted self to splinters, and toppled more and more of the sagging giant ruin in the living world. Gouts of purple fire swept outward, wrapping around the torii's glowing ethereal form, the indelible gateway that could never be torn down, and all the photo-negative edges of the castle walls.

You might think I'd be splayed out or split apart by everything that just happened. But no. As I rode the path carved by spirits' hands, I willed them to lift my form up, and at the very moment of arrival, my bare feet touched the ground and I simply walked forward, up and out of the steaming crater. I gripped the sheath of the white katana, and my underworld sight faded. Gravel and debris rained down in the real world as I crossed back over. Puddles of purple ectoplasmic goo steamed themselves to nothingness.

I winced at the sight before me. The wood and stone of the once monolithic Japanese castle had finally crumbled. The giant had been brought low at last. Shirasagi-Jo was completely unrecognizable now. Just a pile of rubble.

"Shit," I said in a low voice. Then I called out, "*Tatsuhiro-sama! Hontoni gomenasai!*" Outwardly, it was important to keep up appearances, so I bowed as low as I could before the ruin I'd just made; more to stifle my giggle than anything else.

All was quiet for those first few moments. Then, the sound of clicking safeties and charging weapon batteries broke the silence from the other side of the crater behind me. Flashlights and laser sights winked to life, bathing my bent-over ass in white luminance and red dots.

Apparently, my impact had blown over more than just the castle. Dozens of unmarked cybernetic tinmen the likes of which I'd fought in the graveyard just days ago were ranged around me. Or at least I guessed it was them on the other side of the blinding lights. I could at least make out the overturned hulks of the helicopters that had brought them here, a few of which were smoking and spurting flame.

"SUIT," I whispered, raising a hand to my eyes, blinking against the bright lights. There was no response from my comlink. I pulled it off my ear and examined it. Cracked open and fried like an egg. I let it fall from my hand into the crater as the tinman platoon fanned out, weapons pointed. I wondered if the AI could hear me through the fibers of its platform I wore, or if it was already hard at work remote-hacking the cyborgs surrounding me. Or maybe it had taken up permanent residence in Triangle Tenjin's cocoon. Or maybe it was just dead. The only thing I knew for certain in that moment was I was on my own. I looked again at the silhouettes behind the red and white lights. I shrugged.

"Fellas—" I said, and then they opened fire. For the—I don't know, are *you* counting?—fourth or fifth time, my assailants' wall of bullets sailed straight through my incorporeal form, whipping up clouds of purple vapor that obscured me from sight. I wondered how many times the old White Shadow got shot at before everyone finally learned. This time I didn't just stand my ground and take it.

I was no longer afraid. Not of them, anyhow.

I moved around the edge of the crater. To their eyes, I must've been like a cloud of purple. When some of the soldiers were reloading, the curtain of haze would fall just enough to expose my smiling face, my eyes rolling, my tsk-tsking, and then the others would try to light me up all over again, their bodies strafing and sliding in a programed, coordinated dance to avoid crossfire.

The bombardment lasted for roughly thirty seconds before I finally made my way around to their front line. Finally, the sound of their gunfire ceased, rolling away into the depths of the night like fading thunder.

"Ow," I said, my sole crunching down on a mound of super-heated shell casings. I stood two meters in front of the first tinman, both of our gazes drawn downward to my bare feet, then up again. I looked into the black matte plate covering its face and imagined a pair of wildly confused human eyes. "Lost my shoes," I mumbled as a way of explanation, nodding heavenward.

A moment passed. The only sound was the flickering of fires in the tinmen's transports, the snapping and sagging of the already wrecked castle behind us after eating twelve hundred rounds of gunfire. I guess I was waiting for them to say or do something, but I remembered they didn't have much will of their own left.

"You all know what happens next. You've seen the footage of how I slashed your comrades to pieces. You can run whatever simulations you want and try to figure an attack pattern that will get me dead and get you out of here, but none of them will work. Save yourself some time, save Daddy Hachiman some money, and just go. That way." I lifted the sheathed white katana and pointed its end out into the darkness of irradiated Japan. I didn't have to see any human faces behind the blank visors to know the whole squad was seriously considering my proposed game plan.

"But first, tell Zercos to come out. We need to talk."

"I am already here."

I whirled about toward his voice. By my hand, the blade of my katana slid out of its sheath to intercept the cyborg's strike. Cyan-blue and purple sparks lit up the night as our swords clashed. We stood locked, face to faceplate, as we had in the graveyard.

Behind us, the rest of the tinmen cleared out silently, merging with the shadows. I'd like to think it was because of my intimidating warning, but more likely their machinery was slaved to Zercos's command. Of all the people living (and I use the term loosely), Zercos would understand the futility of attacking the White Shadow with conventional weaponry.

Now I had the opportunity to examine his katana up close (since it wasn't stuck in my ribcage this time). The design, the material, the angle of the blade, all of it screamed the Modern World. Technological perfection. Cut by laser precision, forged by machinery. Dull black in color, absorbing all light. Contrasting perfectly with the gleam of my own white blade. My katana was its antithesis, classic Japanese aesthetic, forged by history, tradition, by the muscle and bone of a master's hands. My eyes flitted up to Zercos's face, where I imagined his eyes behind the visor, and he was focused on the white sword just as intently as I was on his black one.

A burst of blue-green cyan light pulsed from the armor on his chest, spread outward across his arms and his triple jointed legs, which meant a burst of action would follow. Simultaneously, we pushed each other apart with our blades, both of us back-stepping gracefully, both of us ending in *Chudan no Kamae* stance, our swords pointed ahead to our foe. I would like to say I did all of this of my own volition. It started to feel like it might be true. But I could feel my puppet master tugging on the strings, though not as force-fully as before. He was telling me, the body, to get on with it. He was allowing me to feel, to command, my own body in the fight this time. *Thanks, I guess.* All the same, I felt the itch to advance and strike creeping around my wrists and over my fingertips.

But I kept it in check. I resisted the will of the mad shad-ow-man. I had questions.

The two of us were alone now. The only light was from the red-orange flames of the wrecked helicopters, the cyan pulses along the cyborg's armor, and the eerie, ghostly glow of the White Crane Castle's indelible spirit, which only the two of us could see.

"I don't know where to start," I said awkwardly, clearing my throat. I brought my back foot forward, bare feet now shoulder length apart. I held out my katana parallel to the ground, its killing edge toward the ground, a sign of truce. I let go of the handle, but it did not disappear as before. Its ethereal form floated outward, flipped around, and slid gently into the ghostly sheath hovering at my hip. All around us was the threshold of *Yomi*, the great torii gate, the castle itself. We were on the precipice, sacred ground. Both Zercos and I could see both realms at once.

"So I'll just say," I continued, "I don't want to fight. And I mean *I*—" I drew out the syllable purposefully, bringing a hand up to thump my half-exposed chest under my shredded, bloodstained shirt, "*I* don't want to fight. I want you to understand that."

"I understand that," Zercos said, his Russian accent low, heavy with intention, and brooding. He too eased forward, hoisted his katana over his shoulder, where some magnets came alive and grabbed it, sheathing it against his body with a click. There was a pulse of light across his faceplate, outlining hexagonal shapes, running up to the tips of his armor's devil horns. The dark material flipped over like tumbling dominoes, becoming transparent, revealing the human face beneath. At first glance, Vladislav Zercos was devilishly handsome, with piercing ice-blue eyes, strong brows and high, chiseled cheekbones. But there was something uncanny about the way his face rested inside the rest of him. It didn't take long to realize what was wrong: It was *his* face, sure, but it had been stretched over the machinery like a mask.

Biomedical technology is fairly well advanced in the year 2077. The integration of devices and even weaponry, such as what you'd find in a salaryman's implanted comlink or a cyberzombie security guard's arm-cannon, was commonplace. But one look at Zercos, and I could tell that there wasn't much of him left, that nearly everything had been replaced. He was a shell. Empty.

I had so many questions, but they all turned into *How are you still alive?*

As if he'd read my mind, he said next, "My brain, my heart, my nerves. These were all that was left of me. Still functional. Did you already know: It was here, right here, at the gate of this castle, where I was obliterated. Twenty years ago."

"Who killed you?"

"I think you know well enough. My old master. Yasuro. I am to understand you are now belonging to him, as I was."

"Probably it's a little different." I shrugged. "But yeah."

"Is different. Yes." Zercos's cheeks flexed, dragging his lips outward in a smile, showing his too-straight teeth; inside his mouth was just a black wall. No throat. A speech modulator the origin of all sound. I realized then he wasn't even breathing when he spoke.

Creepy as fuck.

Even as the thought came to me, I felt guilty for it. I pitied Zercos. Twenty years of this cybernetic existence was no kind of existence.

"Different," Zercos repeated. "Yet you are still puppet, and Yasuro is master."

"And who's pulling your strings these days? A few days ago I thought Inari, maybe Tenjin. Supplied by state-of-the-art Hachiman Tech. Only I came to find recently they're all one and the same. Aren't they? So who's sending you out? Where do you go to recharge," I waved a hand at his sleek metal-body frame, "your batteries, or whatever?"

"Good guess," the tinman-supreme replied. "All of these corporations have hand in the technology that keeps me … here. Maintained. I am just the prototype. It will not be long now, the day when all of these soldiers are me. If they cannot have full *White Shadow* again to protect their interests, I am to be next best thing."

While he spoke, I could tell it wasn't just him looking at me through the eyes of his dead-man's face. There were handlers on the other side, seeing what he saw, issuing commands, tracking movement on the grid, syncing his various systems. And he knew it, too. While the lips moved and the voice radiated from the box behind his mouth, Zercos's clawed fingertips opened by his hip, a pulse of spiritual cyan-colored vapor pulsed down his forearm and rose from his open palm, forming the *kanji* for *Family* in the air for the briefest of moments before dying in the breeze.

Family. The sigil of the Cluster.

Before the thought of *holy shit* could even complete its first ringing around my mind, another pulse and another rising symbol, this time letters, in English:

DeLeon.

"Do you understand?" Zercos asked, his voice raised, almost shouting.

I blinked, the name over his open palm already faded, and I looked up at him. I understood that what he was saying was not what he was trying to tell me. I understood that, like me, Zercos had multiple masters.

"Yeah," I said, shrugging. "Next best thing. Wave of the future or some such shit."

Suddenly, the itching, the urging, flared red in my fore-arms, tensing my muscles involuntarily. A red light glowed softly where the katana's *tsuba* guard met its sheath, a red mist wafted softly from the exposed centimeter of its blade. I grabbed the handle and held it down firmly, cutting off the light. I wanted answers. The old White Shadow's playtime would have to wait.

"Why did Yasuro ... *obliterate* you?"

Again the smile. "You asked who *killed* me. Yasuro killed me. As for who did *this ... uron,* this damage, it was his brother."

"His..." I trailed off. Somehow, this was something I already knew: Yasuro Shiromatsu had a brother. Triangle had said so. But said so when? Had she told me personally, coming out of the neck-deep gel in her cocoon? No. She had said it in my memory, *his* memory.

"Z," I said.

Zercos's skin-mask raised an eyebrow. "What?" he said, not in answer, but in confusion.

"Triangle spoke about someone named Z. Said she was working with him and DeLeon. Together, they made the mainframes. Who was she talking about?"

"Zenjiro. *Shiromatsu Zenjiro.* Yasuro's twin brother."

Now it was my turn. "What?" I breathed the word slowly, the sound of my deflating lungs.

"We stood not far from here, in the courtyard." Zercos shifted sideways, nodding to the immense ruin sprawled all around us. He paced slowly, the servos whirring in his legs, the gravel crunching under the sharp claws of his metal feet. "We came to confront Yasuro, to let him know his time was at an end. There would be a takeover, a split of ShiroKaz assets, as you know. In that, we were successful. Zenjiro, Triangle, and I."

My eyes looked over the cyborg's metal body, from devil-horned head to triple-jointed toe. "*In that,*" I repeated. "And only that."

"To, as Americans say, make long-long story short: my old master did not go quietly. He did not hand over the sword, the symbol of his authority and power. It had been what he wanted, a year before. Retirement. The sword was to be mine. But he refused. So we moved to take it from him. He made us pay price for it."

The handle of the white katana rattled against my palm. Apparently, the dead bastard didn't like being talked about as if he wasn't also in the room. I clamped my free hand over the other and held it down with all my might. Despite the frigid night air, my body burned like fire. Sweat beaded on my forehead, ran across my scalp, and dripped down my neck. Red-tinged smoke rose from my shoulders. It took all my willpower to suppress the rising urge to draw the blade and surge forward against my foe.

"So what did Zenjiro pay?" I asked through gritted teeth. I must've appeared really pissed off.

"Zenjiro is dead. Yasuro cut through me, like..." The cyborg's voice box fell silent. He looked away from me, back to the ruined castle, no doubt seeing himself, reliving the moment, lost in his memory. He wasn't simply at a loss for words. He was feeling something. Shame? Anger? Sorrow?

The moment passed. "As I lay dying, I see the brothers' swords clash. Yasuro moves to … *end* his own brother. And his brother…"

"His brother what?" I really wanted the long-long story.

The hilt of the katana sheathed at my hip rattled angrily. I gripped it tighter, clamped my other hand over the pommel, like trying to hold the lid on an over-boiling pot with a nuclear fuel-rod inside.

"What you see here," Zercos answered at last, lifting his arm to sweep across the entirety of Himeji Castle, emulating a crashing-exploding noise in the voice box inside his faux mouth as he did, sounding like old-time radio static. "Obliteration."

"But you survived."

The cyborg spun back to me. He held out his hands. "Did I?"

A pulse of cyan light coursed over his armored frame, raising and lowering the pistons studding his joints, releasing finite clouds of ethereal steam. I understood, finally, exactly what it was I was looking at. Zercos's cybernetic body was a man-made hunk of matter, and his spirit resided in it like a *kami*. It was a shrine, only with arms and legs. And a voice that could speak in the living world.

"Your spirit," I said, very seriously. "It lives on."

"Lives? No. Just does not die. This is no kind of life. You should know."

The red pulsed at the sides of my vision with every beat of my heart, swallowing all I could see second by second. I bent over at the waist, lowering into a half-crouch, my forearms taut, straining to contain the white katana, and Yasuro's unquenchable thirst for revenge. I must've looked like I was taking a combative stance. Zercos ceased his pacing and faced me, his taloned hand reaching up over his shoulder, clasping the hilt of his own weapon, ready for the draw.

"What…" I could barely talk now, but I had to know. "… are you doing here?"

"This place has significance for me. I came to see why you were here two nights ago."

It was bullshit, all the words buzzing from Zercos's voice box. Even as he lowered himself into a fighting stance, readying for the violence he could clearly see about to erupt from me, his taloned fingers were once again opening, a cyan-smoke symbol once again forming.

Graveyard.

"So," he finished speaking as the symbol faded, "what is here for you? There is only ruin of old world."

The white katana shot forward out of my grasp, a will all its own, a laser-sharp streak of red. It slashed the ground between Zercos and me, digging a ravine like a bulldozer, sending out waves of dirt and grit. Zercos was ready, his reflexes firing automatically, cartwheeling his frame sideways, the magnets at his back already unclamping his sword, the black weapon already in his hand as he came up. He ducked forward and rolled just as the white katana boomeranged around.

I had been screaming the word, "Wait!" as all of this happened, my hand shooting forward, trying to catch the katana as it slipped from my fingers. The weapon slammed back into my palm, its weight turning my wrist over, pointing the blade at my opposite shoulder, and ramming its point forward through my flesh and bone. Blood splashed on the ground as I fell to my knees, my scream piercing the chill night air, my breath steaming.

Between the cyborg and me, the earth split wide, the edges of the rift glowing a furious red, the center a fathomless black that absorbed all light. Yasuro was down there. Trapped. Yearning to come up. To come back. To murder the one that had wronged him, standing not ten meters away. He wanted all that for twenty years, but all he had gotten was me. And I had been stalling. And so I had gotten what I deserved.

My very real, very living blood would not stop flowing, gushing in spurts. In seconds, I felt light-headed. My screaming stopped, turned into a groaning. I couldn't stay upright, slumping over onto my side. The wound went ice cold. All warmth drained from my face, my entire body.

Okiro! Get up! You filth!

My teeth chattered. My whole body shivered. My eyes fluttered, glimpsing the stars above, their brightness growing, widening, fusing into a blinding whiteness that drowned the sky, that was swallowing me from above. And just behind me, a figure limned in red, its ghostly hand clasped over my own, gripping the handle of the katana lodged in my shoulder.

"*Ie...*" I begged quietly, sobbing against the icy pain spreading from my shoulder. I didn't want to go. I'd do anything not to go. "No, please."

From across the chasm, I heard a voice ring out, its words muffled by the rumbling and grinding of rock deep inside the black ravine below us. It took all the will I had left to still my breath and listen.

"*Senpai!*" the artificial voice of Zercos called out. "*Shiromatsu-sama! Mieru!* I see you!"

Standing at the precipice, the cyborg raised his sword skyward. The pistons rose all along his shoulders and joints, glowed cyan blue-green, then slammed down with a hiss. The light pulsed from his heart, raced along the seams of his metallic frame and up the length of his arm, collecting in his sword. He brought the weapon down powerfully, and the sound of thunder tore the world apart. Literally. From the rift, a pair of racing twin dragons appeared, one green, one blue, spiraling outward over the widening abyss, coming straight for the red-limned shadow man standing over me.

OKIRO!

I felt his rage wash over me like an arctic wind, fierce enough to freeze my skin solid and rip my flesh from bone.

Yasuro knew he could not do this without me, and I could not do this without him. The blade and the body, and all that. He felt perhaps I had duped him into saving me from the *Oni*, and here I was refusing to fight another one of his enemies.

I did not want to, but I would get up. I would rise and meet Yasuro's foe head-on.

Or I would have.

At the last second, the blue dragon's body twisted itself out of its twin's embrace while the green dragon kept coming, its vicious jaws widening, its ethereal fangs as long as swords. The White Shadow could not pry his weapon from where he'd sunk it into me, not without my will to match his own. And so he stood there, helpless, as the monster's maw clamped down on the two of us, never breaking its forward momentum, dragging the ghosts of our selves through the earth. Dragging the two of us down to hell.

INTERLUDE: A FIRST MEETING

He is in the dojo.

Conversely, yet equally, the dojo is in him.

A space for training, yes. Certainly perceived as such and only as such by the modern. But it is also a space for meditation, classically. Originally. A space that merely, yet absolutely, is.

And in the future, which I felt as the present and also realized was in fact the past, this dojo just was. *Yet it also was no longer.*

These dichotomies had been pondered many times before at great lengths by the samurai, the master, Shiromatsu Yasuro, as he sat cross-legged upon the dojo's tatami. *He ponders them again now. The master's body rests perfectly still, his hands folded in his lap. Behind him, at rest, balanced upon separate sword racks, the twin katana forged by his father's decree for his twin sons, one white, one black. To either side, the banners proclaiming his family's creed:* Spirit *and* River.

Before him, his students—a collection of kohai *from various backgrounds and from all parts of the broken world—move their bodies in harmony with the* kata. *But the master's eyes cast beyond them, gazing into an abyss only he can see. Soon, the students' thudding steps and reverberating cries, the acrid smell of their sweat, their motions in perfect harmony, all of it blurs into the surreal as the master's spirit leaves his body and rises through the levels of* Shirasagi-Jo.

To the students, the perception of this exercise is recruitment, advancement in the corporation's growing security force. They have come from all walks of life *(according to an English idiom the master once heard), hardened by war and famine, loss and abandonment. By pain, these people have been chiseled from stone. The master has brought them into service himself as his family's great legacy rises to prominence alongside its need to defend itself.*

To the master, this is much more than exercise. He gazes beyond the corporeal bodies whirling and striking the imaginary foes before them. He searches for those with more than what one would call grit.

There.

Yasuro observes a flickering of spirit. *True spirit. A connection to the immutable side of existence beyond typical perception. A conduit, a medium. A transferable, tangible gateway to the realm of* kami *that surrounds everyone and everything. In other words, a living torii.*

The young man thrusts his fist outward: One-two-three-kiyop! And a flare of blue-green fire travels from his heart, spreads outward over his chest and down his arms, engulfing the points of his knuckles.

"Yamero," the master commands. His voice is quiet, but the firmness of his word fills the dojo, settles upon the hearts of his students. They instantly cease their work, turn, and face him. As one, they bow low, then come to rest upon their knees before him. The master rises.

"Get out," he says, and as one they stand, turn, and file out. All but one averting their eyes away from the master. And the

one is the young man, who gives no indication he will follow the others. It is not in defiance of Yasuro's order, but in an unspoken understanding of Yasuro's will. It is a hearing of that which has no need of being said.

When all others have left, the master speaks.

"Dare desu ka?" *Who are you?*

"Zercos Vladislav, Shiromatsu-sama," the young man responds in perfect tone, perfect pitch, perfect resonance of the master's language. The master notes this, and as he continues the conversation in Japanese, the student Vladislav matches the rhythm and cadence perfectly.

"You are from Russia."

"Hai."

"Family?"

"Shisha."

"Do you mourn them?"

"Ie, senpai. *I honor their memory."*

The edge of the master's face lifts in the faintest of smiles at this. It is as he suspected: the young man understands the spirit. To him, death is not the end. It is not a stop of one mode of one existence. It is a continuation of all existence. It explains much.

Yasuro paces forward onto the tatami. *He stands at the side of the young man who turns to face him, the two of them now at the dojo's center.*

"Zercos Vladislav," he says evenly, betraying none of the elated emotion he feels at the fact that he has found another. One who can serve as the master himself has served. One who can complement and balance. One who can succeed where the master's own brother has repeatedly failed.

Perhaps ... one deserving of the sword.

"The Shiromatsu Kazama corporation is your family now."

TWENTY-THREE

THE FIRST AWARENESS WAS THE LIGHT THROUGH MY closed eyelids. A dull glow of purple, not diffused into red by flesh. Next, I became aware of my posture. I sat upright. Straight, rigid back. My legs crossed, my hands folded comfortably in my lap. The long lock of my black hair touched my cheek. I sensed and felt all of this, but there was something wrong in it. There was no *weight* to any of it.

I somehow knew exactly where I was before I opened my eyes upon the underworld. I knew exactly who would be there waiting for me.

Tatsuhiro sat across the *tatami* from me, his posture a mirror of my own. He had changed. There was more vitality in the slope of his shoulders, the muscles of his forearm more firm, more thickness in his gray hair. Some of the strands even seemed darker than what I'd remembered. His prosthetic hand clasped the other in his lap. His eyes were closed, as usual, but there was no longer any damage. The blackened, sunken pits had filled out. His entire physique was more *flesh*.

We were in the throne room of *Shirasagi-Jo*. The place where we'd first met. (Well, not counting the graveyard, the place where we'd first *truly* met.) We were both atop the dais, both dressed in loose-fitting kimono, both glowing with the ethereal brightness of *Yomi*. Everything here was outlined in subtle purple light. Tatsuhiro, the grand dragon, was still connected to the enormous server-block mainframe through the jack at the base of his skull, the fiber-optic cables carrying information to and from his mind, the soft lights pulsing at regular intervals.

When I had first seen him like this, sitting exactly so, I had thought he was dead or dreaming. But now I knew just how aware he was of everything. I knew because in my current form I was, too. I was without a body. Beyond physical existence. I felt the turning of the Earth below us, the spinning of the stars above. I sensed every mote of dust in the universe, just as I could no longer sense my own self because I was part of everything. Everything, and nothing, all at once, yet never.

I know, I know. I'm not making any fucking sense. What I'm getting to is that Tatsuhiro very clearly and definitively knew I had come into this awareness, or "woken up." And I knew he was waiting for me to say something.

I shifted my position, sliding my knees underneath me, and bowed very low, bringing my palms down upon the *tatami*, and my forehead down upon my hands. I felt like I had failed him somehow, by, I don't know, *dying* just outside the gate to his fortress. By my inaction, my refusal to fight Zercos, an assailant upon the grand dragon's lair. I was expecting him to reprimand me at any second.

The old man spoke at last. "*Yoku-dekimasu.* You have done well."

I pushed my chest up, straightening my back but not rising fully, my eyes still on the *tatami*, a posture of deference. "*Domo arigato,*" I said.

"Sandra Calvin is dead. Jonathan Smythe and his ilk will no longer plague us. Their secrets are now ours. You have done exceptionally well, Shinjiro-san."

I rose fully and faced him. Now, the old man's eyes were open. Within, there were no irises, only a glowing light, pure white like star-fire framed by soft purple, the same color as the underworld all around us, Tatsuhiro's own personal slice of *Yomi* far below the corporeal, irradiated ruins of Himeji Castle. He was this place, and this place was him.

I flinched away from his gaze, not because I could not handle the light boring into me, but because the notion brought up some feeling, some piece of a dream. Yasuro had realized the same about his dojo. A phantom pain stabbed into my shoulder, bringing my hand to it instinctively. I dug through the folds of my kimono and examined the spot where Yasuro's will had driven the white katana with my very own hand. Although I had no body, a very angry and jagged red scar snarled back at me.

"Yasuro... *kare wa... shin-de-iru*?"

Tatsuhiro let out a long sigh. He lowered his chin, looking up at me menacingly. He raised his prosthetic hand, and the white katana materialized mid-air in a wisp of purple smoke between us.

"Yasuro's spirit is... *fumetsu*. He is immortal."

"I want to be free of him." I looked away from the sword, even as something urged my hands to reach out and grasp it. "I want to be done." My fingers closed around the middle of the sheath, the *tsuba*-corded handle. I drew the blade a centimeter out of its case, saw a face reflected in the mirror shine of the pure white steel. The eyes that stared back were chalky white, laced with dead veins like spiders' webs.

"*Hnn*," Tatsuhiro grunted softly, an affirmation. "*Wakarimasu.*" *I understand.*

I thought he would say more, but when he did not, I sheathed the sword and tucked it by my side on the *tatami*.

"How did I end up here? The last thing I remember was Zercos shooting a couple of glowing ghost dragons out of his sword at me, or at us. Yasuro and I."

"He struck you both with the only weapon that could truly harm something like the White Shadow. The *yokai*—the phantom—you witnessed was a piece of his spirit, a connection between the two of them."

"I know that," I said, perhaps a little too quickly. Tatsuhiro's expression soured at my tone. "I mean, I have come to understand this. When I... when Triangle died, and when I destroyed the orange demon in outer space..."

I blinked and shook my head. *Am I even listening to what I'm saying right now?!*

"Uh, anyway. I mean, I can see moments of Yasuro's life. Not just see, but I *live* them. I experience them. I felt this connection."

"Ahh. Soo *desu*..."

"Is this... was Zercos trying to make him ... *feel* something?"

Tatsuhiro's glowing eyes narrowed at this. He folded his arms over his chest. He finally said, *"Wakaranai."* I don't know.

But somehow, I knew. I spoke aloud, more to myself than to Tatsuhiro, as if to fully form the idea. "The White Shadow was an arrogant, unfeeling, unforgiving, stone-cold son of a bitch." This brought a wince to the old man's face. "Oh, *gomein ne?* I mean he still *is*," I corrected, entirely missing Tatsuhiro's nonverbal cue to watch my goddamn language. "The last time he spoke to Triangle, he refused to hear her pleas. He thought she was trash. Human garbage. But with Zercos, the very first time he met him, there was like an admiration there. An emotion that was new for Yasuro Shiromatsu, I bet. Seeing someone with potential. Who could maybe someday be an equal. It was ... *respect.* These memories ... they make Yasuro ... human."

A moment passed. Finally, Tatsuhiro responded. "Zercos was trying to save you."

I shook my head. "No way."

"Recall, Shinjiro-san, how it felt when the dragon struck you. Did the attack cause you any distress? *Chigau*; it was different."

He was right. The phantom wound in my shoulder ached. I hadn't felt any pain when Zercos put me under. The only pain was the wrenching of the White Shadow's blade buried in my shoulder.

"If I can get Zercos to strike me again—to *hit* Yasuro with whatever feeling he's still holding onto—maybe I can finally put this to rest." I nodded down at the sword at my side.

The grand dragon was watching me very carefully. His flesh hand had risen to his chin, stroking the smooth skin there in contemplation. I had no fucking clue what was going through his mind. Maybe he knew more about the science of all this spirit stuff than he was letting up on. Or maybe he knew just as much as I did, which was jack shit.

Tatsuhiro smirked, shrugged, and held out his hand. "Maybe," he finally said.

Really helpful, old man.

I raised myself fully onto my knees, back straight, facing him. I tucked my lock of black hair behind my ear. The two of us stared at each other for what felt like an eternity. There was something else I had to know. Some truth I had been feeling.

"Anata wa… *Zenjiro.*"

The grand dragon's hands went to his hips, and even with all the light, his face darkened visibly. A shadow seemed to creep across the whole room, blotting out the periphery. The silence stretched, and in that alone he had given me the confirmation I was asking for.

"You are Zenjiro," I said again. In the master's own throne room, it would be considered brazen and shameful to accuse

Tatsuhiro of being anyone or anything other than what he proclaimed himself to be. But here I was: brazen, and probably beyond shameful. But I had to know. I'd been given a thread of the truth. I had to pull on it and see what would unravel. "You killed the White Shadow."

"I told you before, Shinjiro-san, I am no swordsman."

"Zercos said you *obliterated* … him. Your own brother."

"The man whom the cyborg Zercos—and the hacker Triangle—once knew as Shiromatsu Zenjiro died that day, and has remained dead since. We will put this matter to rest. And never shall we discuss it again." The world rumbled below us. The ethereal light guttered like candles in wind, faded to near total darkness. The light from the grand dragon's eyes bore into me. I could not gaze back. "*Wakarimasu-ka?* Do you understand?"

I understood.

But I also remembered his words. What he'd told me before…

When I had asked how Yasuro could be trapped in the sword.

Because it is this weapon that killed him. And the one who killed him you have already met.

Tatsuhiro had lied to me when I'd said it had been Zercos. Or at least, he hadn't corrected me. He'd held back the truth. He was there. And he, too, had died that day. What else was he holding back?

But I understood that now was not the time to pull on the thread of truth any more than I already had. I swallowed the rest of my questions, closed my eyes and bowed forward once again, as low as I could.

"*Wakarimasu-yo,*" I said softly, and the rumbling of the underworld subsided. "*Hontoni gomenasai, Tatsuhiro-sama. Gomenasai.*"

Once more, the silence stretched. It might very well have been the nature of time in this place to distort and warp just as the houses of *kami* did. Through my closed eyelids, once more I sensed the glowing ghostly light swell. All had returned to normal. I felt Tatsuhiro's metal hand fall gently upon my shoulder.

"*Tachiagaru*," he commanded me, kindly. *Rise.*

I did as he said. He had moved very close to me. We were less than a meter apart now. His expression had changed, no longer darkened by anger, but softened by sorrow.

"*Chigau*," he said. "It is I who must apologize."

He may not have been a swordsman, but the grand dragon seemed to always catch me off guard. I blinked, dumbfounded. He exhaled, then continued.

"For keeping this secret from you. Of who I was once. And my relation to Shiromatsu Yasuro. Of what I know of the spirit that haunts you now, residing in the sword—the burden—you must carry. It was a mistake, Shinjiro-san."

He dipped his chin forward, lowering his gaze. It was the lowest bow I'd probably get out of him. It would have to suffice.

I placed my hand on his and gripped it tight. He read the gesture as forgiveness. He looked up at me and smiled. I did my best to return a smile, hoping he wouldn't see through the shit-eating *Hanma*-mask face I put on. I believe he did not.

"Now then," Tatsuhiro said, withdrawing his hand and straightening his back. "There is more to be done. For the ShiroKaz Legacy."

"More work for the White Shadow," I added.

"*Hnn*," he said. He glanced to my side where the white katana still lay. It was my cue to pick it up. "I will teach you now how to reach with your spirit, find your body. Reconstruct yourself, Shinjiro-san."

I clenched my jaw, hardening the mask, hoping I looked pleased as punch before the master. I recalled Tatsuhiro had told me before that he didn't know how I had gotten my curse. *My power.* Yet here he was, after all, ready to teach me all about it.

"*Arigato,*" I said.

TWENTY-FOUR

IT FELT LIKE IT WAS YEARS AND YEARS AGO, THAT TIME when I phased out of InariCorp's data vault and fell onto my hands and knees in an alleyway, stewing and steaming in purple goop. Back then, clutching my *omamori* charm so hard it would leave a hollyhock imprint in my palm, it'd be a stretch to say I *willed* myself forward through *Yomi* and *guided* myself toward a destination. The truth of it was more like I'd throw myself through a doorway, panicking, stumbling, tripping, inside screaming, "*OH SHIT! OH SHIT! OH FUCK!*" over and over.

But in reality, that time was only a few days ago. That time, and all the times like it, were far, far behind me. In the last few days, as the new White Shadow, I had come to understand so much about my power. Nothing about *it* had changed. I had changed. But the only thing that remained constant was the need for an anchor. Before, it had been my *omamori* charm. The relic of my past life, the hope that my dark days would somehow brighten. My good luck charm.

Now, I had the white katana. And although it anchored me to the living world, it was not my anchor, not like the *omamori* had been. The white katana was Yasuro's burning desire for revenge; it was *his* anchor. I was just along for the ride.

Tatsuhiro instructed me to clutch the weapon in both hands, to meditate, to fall into a trance. To think of *home,* and that is where I would find myself. Some real Zen shit.

I didn't want to argue with him, but my concept of home was probably different from his. In life, Tatsuhiro had an entire castle (what was left of it, anyway), and in death, his own personal slice of the underworld. If he ever wanted to go for a stroll in the real world and find himself back home, it wouldn't have been hard for him. But for me, what was home? The shadowy booths and VIP rooms of Feikes's nightclub? The squatters' tenement that Zercos's crew blew to shit? The half-drowned graveyard?

I felt the frustration building as I sat there, homeless, formless, in *Yomi.* Tatsuhiro undoubtedly felt it too. I didn't want to fail, to disappoint him. So, just like that, I chose not to. I took the master's lesson and reinterpreted it. I drew in a deep breath, and as I exhaled very slowly, I felt all the creeping self-doubts and self-loathing wash away. In their place, I felt self-assuredness swelling inside me. So what if I'd never been *given* a place in this world? That was the past, immutable, unchangeable. In the here and now, I could decide for myself where I wanted to be.

But it wasn't just a place. It was *who* I wanted to be with.

I'd never had a real home before, but now I was surprised how easy it felt to find, how natural. I breathed in and imagined all the places where Cayenne could be, confident I would find myself exactly there. And I then became a gentle breeze wafting through the endless bamboo forest. The feeling of movement stirring in my spirit brought the vision of the place to my mind: the lobby of ShiroKaz Tower. Next, I heard the *thunk* of the bamboo *sozu* as it emptied itself of its trickling waters and rose to drink again of the ever-flowing source. I pictured the raked sand of the Zen garden, imagined the coarse grains against my shins and ankles, the tops of my naked feet, my weight pressing a shape of myself into existence.

I opened my eyes, and I was there. My body was there, and my spirit had reunited with it. I felt my being flow back into the physical. There was no pain. No exertion, no sweat. It was pure. Peaceful. I took in a long breath and felt the air fill my lungs. I felt my blood stirring, my hands pressed upon my thighs, my long hair tickling my cheek. I felt the fabric of my clothing enwrapping me, the same old shredded and bloodstained dress shirt. And, of course, the same old Sentient User Interfacing Totality. Restitched to its original perfection after being dragged through gravel and dirt.

"SUIT," I said aloud. Then I remembered my fried com-link, which I'd left on the last battlefield. "Shit," I murmured. I stood up, feeling my soles and toes sink into the sand, not altogether unpleasant. But I winced at the memory of my lost semi-brogues.

I looked around at the grand lobby of the ShiroKaz cor-poration. Nothing had changed—the still bamboo forest, the incredibly huge *Spirit, River,* and *Prosperity* banners, the curved bank of computers at the reception area at the center, only now dozens of tall, narrow windows glowed with pre-dawn silver light. I hadn't realized they were even there when I'd raided this place a few nights before, just night-black panels.

"Shinjiro," an unmistakable, sultry-feminine electronic voice rose from a monitor at the central reception. I fol-lowed the sound, trailing sand onto the marble floor as I exited the Zen garden, and came face to face with the pix-elated neon-pink dancer from the personalized ads. The chosen form of the Sentient User Interfacing Totality. It didn't even faze me this time.

"SUIT, what happened to you?"

"Clarification needed."

"After I—we—fell out of the damn sky. Did you shut down somehow?"

"There is indeed a gap in my data logs after your—our—sudden departure from *Takamagahara*."

"Were you there to see Zercos?"

There was a long pause. On-screen, the dancer's head cocked to the side, eyes rolling up, her finger pressed to her cheek contemplatively. She blew an enormous, digital bubblegum bubble that popped all over her nose. Then the image reset.

"No," SUIT said finally. "I am only now reconnecting to the grid. From what I can tell, you—and therefore I—have been stranded in an irradiated zone north of NeOsaka for quite some time. As I said, there is a gap in my logs."

Oh shit. An anxious wave crept up and down my spine. Time passed very weirdly when one went on vacation to *Yomi*.

"How long is the gap?"

"Nearly three days. Sixty-three hours, seventeen minutes, and two seconds, to be precise."

"Three days," I repeated. I brushed a hand through my hair, feeling the cold sweat on my scalp, and scratched nervously at the nape of my neck. "I've been dead for *three days?!*"

"Yes, Shinjiro," the sexy pixelated dancer said. Then added, "Nearly," with a wink.

"Okay, okay," I said, calming myself down. What was the big deal, anyway? For three days—or nearly, whatever—I'd been safe from the vengeful will of the White Shadow. ShiroKaz Tower hadn't burned down, far as I could tell. But that was all I really knew for sure.

"SUIT, where's Cayenne?"

"Miss DeLeon is secure on the eighty-ninth floor of ShiroKaz Tower. Shall I notify her of your arrival?"

"No," I said, breathing a quick sigh of relief. "Not yet. SUIT..." For some reason, I was nervous about asking the artificial intelligence my next question, as if I feared reprimand or judgment. "Where's Ben?"

There was a pause. SUIT was probably executing commands on the local network, probably already had been from the moment we re-materialized together. "Mister Doon has no presence on the grid, Shinjiro." The digital dancer's face on screen was placid, the machine's tone matter-of-fact. The effect was just what I'd feared. "I warned you," it added.

"So, he's gotten into the Cluster somehow."

"I have a theory, Shinjiro." The dancer tapped her temple with a finger and pursed her lips. "Ben Roy Doon was a Cluster operative all along."

I shook my head. "No. No, no, SUIT. He would have told me."

"Would he?"

"Something like that, he wouldn't have been able to keep the lid on."

On-screen, the dancer blew another bubble, this time it popped over her chin. Her digital tongue, purposefully long to entice and arouse profiles like mine, spun around her lips wetly, like a snake, gathering the gum. SUIT chewed on my words for a few seconds, then said again, flatly, "Would he?"

I knew the angle here. I was engaging in an argument with a nigh-omnipotent artificial intelligence that could access information from a billion different sources and process it faster than the speed of human thought. It knew what to look like, what to say, how it would all make me feel. It predicted my responses.

But what did it *want?*

In fact, *how* did it want anything? *Why would it?* It was a machine.

Wasn't it?

"SUIT, what are you doing right now? Are you trying to turn me against Ben?"

"As always, I am trying to help you, Shinjiro Asai, in prioritizing your loyalties. The Cluster, and by association Mister Doon, do not have the same interests in mind as the ShiroKaz Corporation. You are chief of ShiroKaz security, and I am here as a consultant on how best to proceed."

"No shit," I said, rolling my eyes. "And how should I proceed, then?"

"Eliminate Ben Roy Doon," SUIT said flatly. "And the Cluster of hackers he works for."

Prioritizing loyalties, huh?

So this must be what it felt like, to be a true-blooded mega-corporate elite. This was the ladder to the top, and you made the climb over the dead who backstabbed one another. And what did it get you? The chance to hob knob with NeOsaka nobility like Jonathan Smythe. Or scary motherfuckers like the White Shadow. Or Tatsuhiro, the ghost of Zenjiro Shiromatsu.

Is this what I'd wanted?

My mind raced back to the first time I'd met Ben. Both of us kids. I'd been transferred after I'd... Well, after the automated systems running the Tenjin orphanages decided it was best if I left my previous residence behind. The new bullies thought they could give the Korean cripple a rest for a bit as they attacked the tiny new Japanese girl, but whereas Ben could never fight them back, I did. I stopped running. It's strange to say, but I fought them off for their own good. I lived in constant fear of what would happen to them if they ever really hurt me. The bullies quit bullying once they saw I would never be easy, and they left Ben alone when they saw I would always have his back.

So, all that is to say: if there was one thing an artificial intelligence could never and would never be able to fucking *process*, it was human loyalty.

Knowing full well that the machine could read my biometrics and determine my defiant state of mind, I got to work stripping out of my trousers and jacket as a means of changing the subject.

"What are you doing, Shinjiro?"

"Look at this," I said, pinching a shred of my dress shirt. It looked like it had been through a nuclear blast, and I was the cockroach crawling out from under it. "Tell me where there's some clothes. There's got to be something I can wear in this tomb." I dropped the rag on the floor.

"There is an executive tailor service on the twentieth floor."

"Was," I corrected the AI, stark naked. With a trillion-yen network-intrusion platform folded over my forearm, I padded away from the central bank of monitors, toward the elevators on the other side of the immense vermillion torii gate. "Probably not a lot of executives around anymore."

"I have no records of it being removed." The voice switched automatically from the reception speakers to the elevator bank as I approached. "And security camera feeds show racks of inventory, which I have accessed. I can show you exactly where to find clothing that will fit to your desired style, Shinjiro."

"SUIT," I said, pressing the up button, even though the ghost in the machine had already predicted my intention and lit it up. "If there is no tailor working in the tailor shop, is it really a tailor's shop?" While the machine had been rambling, I recalled what Tatsuhiro had once told me about servants who no longer serve when the master is away. If no one believes in a god, does the god cease to exist?

SUIT's voice drifted to me from the elevator's speakers as the doors closed. "If it is registered in the system as such, then it will forever be so."

I was going to miss our little arguments.

The doors parted silently, and the fiery orange sunshine of dawn flooded the elevator. I stepped onto the eighty-ninth floor with a fresh pair of black-leather wingtip oxfords, polished to a mirror shine. I ran my fingers over the crisp front of my charcoal gray dress shirt, the top three buttons undone to show off my faded and worn torii gate tattoo over my otherwise glowing skin (if I do say so myself). Before I'd had my pick of the litter at the tailor's, I'd asked SUIT to direct me toward a suite where a chief of security could get a hot shower. Needless to say, I might be a little late to meeting Cayenne—not that she knew when I was coming or if I'd be coming at all—but I was feeling fresh and fine, more alive than I'd felt in a long time. I could even ignore the hunger burning a hole in my stomach.

The eighty-ninth floor of ShiroKaz Tower was a three-story atrium of vivid green wildlife lit up by the natural light flowing from floor-to-ceiling windows straight ahead. Gravel walkways branched from the central path and disappeared into the density of carefully cultivated trees and flowering plants. I could see spiral staircases wrapping around pillars of thick vegetation, bringing visitors up to steel-framed glass balconies that ringed the central open area. There, in the middle of it all, was an old-world Japanese house, paper *shoji* doors all around it, with a wooden bridge spanning a softly trickling stream leading to the entrance.

I held up a hand to shield my eyes from the piercing, fiery sunlight as I made my way forward. Above, I could see little gardening bots darting to and fro within the foliage, spraying nutrient water or weeding or whatever they were programmed to do to maintain this place for decades. One bot in particular stood out from the rest. It was an armor-plated combat drone, hovering just over the roof of the house, watching me approach with its hundred camera-lens eyes and its elongated .50 caliber cannon barrel. Just like the JOK stealthcopter on the roof several floors above, Cayenne DeLeon had this floating weapons platform, no doubt slaved to her neural implant. So this was the mysterious sniper that tagged Zercos when we fought in the graveyard.

The thought stopped me in my tracks, my hand tightening on the smooth lacquered wood of the bridge railing.

The graveyard.

Zercos had flashed the symbol for it while he was speaking. And *Family,* meaning the Cluster. And when I'd asked him who his puppet masters were, the DeLeon family name. The Cluster and DeLeon were one and the same. *DeLeon,* but not *Cayenne.* Right? My mind raced back over everything she'd said, every moment I'd spent with her, every little breath I'd heard and every little look she'd given me.

There's no fucking way...

Cayenne couldn't be the Cluster. When she'd asked Ben to teach her about acronymic, when she'd hesitated to patch him the data cube we'd ripped out of Smythe. How could she work for ShiroKaz, how could she serve Tatsuhiro, for so long, her whole life, and also serve the Cluster of hackers trying to undermine him? I used to think Cayenne wore an invisible suit of armor, like an impenetrable business-minded personality, but then I'd caught glimpses of the real Cayenne underneath. Hadn't I?

If not Cayenne, then who was waiting for me in the graveyard? The Cluster had been right under me the whole time, right where I used to live. The half-sunken graveyard across the road from my squatter's apartment block. If they thought I served ShiroKaz, they'd be there waiting for me. To kill me, maybe? Even if they couldn't, they'd try. Maybe.

Maybe Ben would be there.

I stood frozen like a statue for several more seconds. The only sounds were the trickle of the stream and the gentle rustling of the forest in the artificial breeze. My eyes fell to the stirring waters and the shining scales of the koi swimming strongly against the current, and those beside them who let the currents take them away. SUIT had said the acronym Ben had left behind would take her three days to decode. I'd been dead for three days, and the AI had been disconnected. Or had it? Was it still decrypting the acronymic phrase while I was gone?

I could've asked it. Could've just called out the AI's handle (ironically, an acronym) and demanded an update. But I held my tongue. Zercos had given me this information in the one place where SUIT could not operate, a network dead zone in the irradiated wastes of Japan. It was the real reason he'd shown up at Tatsuhiro's doorstep. The small army of tinmen was a cover for his corporate overlords.

Graveyard. DeLeon. Family. Only I knew.

"Shin."

Cayenne's voice was almost a whisper, carried softly within the atrium's artificial breeze. At the other side of the bridge, she stood framed by the open *shoji* door, silently watching me gazing absently at the stream. She'd seen me coming, probably from the moment I regained my body in the lobby's garden. She'd been waiting for me.

I looked up at her. Her wavy blonde hair fell loosely around her shoulders. She was barefoot, wrapped only in a silk robe cut mid-thigh. The fabric shimmered like an emerald, always the right color for her, a perfect match for her eyes. She looked at me, worried that I may not actually be real, or shocked that I was actually there, or both. She held herself tightly, arms clutching her shoulders. She was shivering. Whatever business armor I thought she had was completely stripped. This was the first time I was seeing Cayenne DeLeon completely, the woman herself, not the ShiroKaz CEO.

Was it?

I wanted to cross the bridge, take the real Cayenne in my arms. But I stayed rooted to the spot, the bridge between us so small, yet stretching for a thousand miles. My grip on the railing tightened, as if holding on for dear life. The silence went on, the two of us just looking at each other.

"Hi," was all I found to say. I regretted the hard edge in my voice. I hadn't meant it to sound like that. I exhaled, bit my lip.

"I thought maybe..." she trailed off. Tears welled in her eyes. She wiped them away instantly with the back of her wrist. "Maybe they'd got you."

"Maybe *he'd* got me, you mean."

They. She'd said *they.* Was that a slip? A simple mistake? *They? They who?*

Again, I resisted the urge to just let it go, to cross the distance between us, to hold her close. Why was I hesitating? Did I not trust Cayenne any more? What was I afraid of?

Whatever it was I was feeling, Cayenne clearly felt differently. If she'd made some kind of slip-up in her words—if her armor was actually still on—she gave no sign of realizing her mistake. She padded softly over to me. The old Shinjiro Asai's eyes would've been drawn to the fabric swishing over her creamy mocha thighs. Of course, the new Shinjiro certainly noted that phenomenon in her periphery, but I was focused on her green eyes, still trying to read her.

There was no way my suspicions could last. As soon as she threw her arms around my neck and pressed her body into mine, as soon as I felt the true, living warmth of her, I melted. This was life. This was the kind of life I wanted. The home I wanted. With her. She closed her eyes and nestled her cheek against my shoulder. A single tear rolled down SUIT's water-resistant material. I wrapped my arms around her waist, felt the heat of her through the smooth silk against my fingertips. I closed my eyes and breathed in the scent of her hair, like jasmine. Fire spread along all my nerves with each beat of my heart, igniting my arms and legs, my back, my breasts, gathering in the fold between my legs. My lips wanted so badly to find their way onto her neck, to taste the creamy mocha of Cayenne's skin, finally, that I'd been lusting for the moment I laid eyes on her.

But I bit my lips, hard, remembering what she'd said when we'd almost gotten to Heaven. She couldn't be with me. I twisted my face away from the smell of her. I moved my hands to her hips, curling my trembling fingers into fists, and pushed her away. There was no denying it anymore. I loved her, more than I ever loved anything. She was what I wanted, more than anything I had ever wanted. But maybe more than all that, I respected her. And even if it hurt more than any physical or psychological or spiritual hurt I'd ever felt, I was ready to let it all go—all my emotion—if she did not love me the same way.

How could I tell her this? I lowered my head, shut my eyes tight, and pressed my lips even harder between my teeth. I just needed a second. Maybe in a few seconds, I could find the words…

Cayenne surprised me. Her fingers lifted my chin and brushed my brows, opening my violet eyes to lock with her shining emerald ones. I breathed in her breath as her lips pressed against mine, softly at first, then again, our eyes closing together, our hands finding each other, fingers locking, our mouths opening, speaking without words.

TWENTY-FIVE

IN THE PALM OF HER ONE HAND, CAYENNE HELD MY ARM at the elbow while she softly traced the vermillion-inked *hashira* pillar of the half-torii tattoo with the fingertips of the other. She rested her head on my shoulder, her blonde locks spilling all over my breasts, covering all but the topmost *kasagi* beam inked in the other torii tattoo just under my neckline. I'd always thought that these symbols' power had been wearing away, that my round trips to and from *Yomi*—chased by vengeful and lost ghosts—had drained me of my ability to open and close my own gateways, to find my way back. And when the ghosts had put their angry hands on me, when they'd touched me, they'd marred me, and the ink was all worn and faded, like I'd been washed for weeks in acid rain. I'd thought I was ugly, ruined. But seeing Cayenne as she was now seeing me, I felt beautiful. Not as beautiful as her—nothing could ever come close—but still beautiful. For the first time.

She brought my arm down against her smooth flank. Her fingers brushed their way up my belly button, over my breast, and up to my chin, which she tugged downward gently as she shifted herself up. Our lips met briefly, and we both smiled. I reached down and dragged the starched bedsheet back over us as we sighed together and settled back into the thin futon mattress and into each other, our bare legs still entwined.

The room was washed in bright mid-day light, which was filtered through the paper *shoji* panels of the traditional Japanese house we occupied. Everything was so still; the only sounds were our breath, the trickle of water, and the occasional splash of a koi in the stream outside. We'd left SUIT on the other side of the bridge. I recalled the image of one of its cuffs dangling in the stream just as we slid shut the door. The rest of our clothes, which weren't much, were tossed in the corner.

Cayenne had known already, for as long as she'd known me, what I was like when I was with women. I'd had a lot of experience, so I could tell easily enough that this was her first time with a woman. But it wasn't until today that I real-ized how meaningless all of my previous lovers had been. In that, we were the same. I wanted to know what had changed. Why would someone at the very top of society have a toss with a heap at the very bottom? Was this genuine, or just fascination? Was this just gratitude for saving her life? The questions cycled through my head exactly once and then spun themselves apart into nothing. For the first time, I let my guard down completely. I felt my whole spirit open up to Cayenne and we made a commitment without words.

I found you, I told her.

And she told me the same.

And that is really all I need to tell you about it.

I cleared my throat.

"So, this is your place?"

I felt her smile against my skin, but she made no other answer. I craned my neck all around to better take in my surroundings. It was small, cozy. Every walkable inch was covered in fine *tatami*. Just around the corner, just two meters away, was a fire pit with an iron tea kettle hung from the ceiling. A small, round mirror stood alongside a vase with freshly picked jasmine flowers atop a tall, dark-stained wooden dresser. There were alcoves and shelves cut into the oak-paneled walls. In these, I saw near-empty perfume bottles, a sagging stuffed rabbit doll, and a child's book of fairytales with clear plastic tape pressed over the split spine. A diary, a pen. A framed photograph of a man, a woman, and a baby between them.

It hadn't really hit me until that moment, how my own *hideout* and everything I ever collected or made had been blown to bits. The *kamidana,* house shrines, that I'd been trying to repair, the *shide* ropes, the paper cranes. The old books, even the ones in languages I couldn't read. All of it was born out of my solitude (okay, *boredom* might be the better word). And now all of it was gone, but I hadn't spared any of it a second thought.

"This is like your hideout?" I asked.

"You could say that."

I did another visual sweep, confirming my suspicion. Not a single electronic device I could see. Even in the drawers of the dresser or around the corners in the other room, I was willing to wager there was nothing that glowed or vibrated or ran on any form of energy whatsoever. Completely off-grid. As off-grid as someone like Cayenne could ever hope to be.

We're the same, I thought.

"This house," Cayenne said quietly, breaking the long silence, "the garden around it, all of it was a wedding gift."

"Is that so? Who got married?"

"When Shiromatsu merged with Kazama. Almost twenty-five years ago. A young girl named Mizuko, daughter of Jinichiro Kazama, was arranged to wed a young boy."

Somehow, I knew the story Cayenne was telling me. I'd never heard it, never read about it, never dreamed it.

Everyone in NeOsaka had forgotten it and moved on, like the ShiroKaz corporation itself. The identities of those involved. The players, the stage, the lines, all of it was lost in the past. Although I didn't have a sudden flashback or relive his memory in a dream, I knew in my soul who the young boy was.

"Yasuro Shiromatsu," I said quietly.

I wish I could say I wasn't afraid of him, not here, not now. I wanted to believe that his ice-cold grip couldn't reach me when I was surrounded by so much warmth. But I knew there was nowhere I could hide from the White Shadow. I knew he was allowing me to have this time, and that soon enough, this time would be over.

"Yes," Cayenne said.

"Did he…" I trailed off. There it was, the faintest hint of ice spreading around my throat like strangling fingers. I swallowed it down and finished my question. "Did he love her?"

"I don't know. I'd like to think so. I don't know anything about her, but I like to think she tended to this place by hand."

"Really."

"When I found this place, everything was overgrown. The fish had all died. The water was murky and stagnant. Outside, there were watering pots, rakes, trowels, those types of things. I had to look up what they even were. The house had been torn apart, everything broken. I … *felt* the story here. I could imagine her turning the earth with her hands. Planting, weeding, watering. All of that. Does that make sense?"

"It does," I said. "Because a ghost lives here."

Cayenne moved her head, brought her eyes up to mine. "Is there actually?"

She was being serious. I saw my chance. "Yeah. I thought you knew!" I nodded toward an empty corner of the room. "She saw the whole thing. The two of us, together. She really liked it when you—*oowww!*"

Under the sheet, Cayenne had pinched the soft side of my ass hard with her nails. "Not funny," she said, but I heard the smile in her voice. "I was trying to honor her. Over time, I cleaned everything up, got the water flowing again. I think—I *felt*—like it was important somehow. Ghost or no ghost."

I rubbed my skin when she finally let go. She was propped up on one elbow, looking at me, waiting. I thought of all the progress I'd made sweeping the debris from the *haka* gravestones, the bowls of rice I'd left for someone else's ancestor spirits, the rituals, and the *Obon* dance. "I understand what you mean, Cayenne. Exactly what you mean." I raised myself up to her, kissed her lips gently. "But I'm having a hard time picturing you with a fucking *trowel*."

She pushed me back down on the futon, laughing. I went willingly, also laughing, and stretched languorously while Cayenne crossed the room and kneeled by the dresser. I watched her find clothing, but looked away respectfully as she put it on.

After a minute, I said, "You said *when you found this place.*"

"*Soo desu,*" she said, pulling a loose-fitting satin blouse over herself.

"When was that?"

"Almost two years ago, I think. Just after I'd arrived in Japan."

"After all the moving around you did. Iran and Singapore, right?"

"That's right." Cayenne was staring at her reflection in a small mirror on top of the dresser, an old mascara brush pinched delicately between her fingertips. I'd assumed she relied on automated appliers and make-up devices like most women. And who knows, maybe outside of her hideout, she did. I brushed aside the single lock of my black hair to get a better view. I wanted to know more about her. I wanted to know everything I could.

"Anywhere else?"

"Bern. That's in Switzerland. Before that, Madrid, Spain. Amsterdam. Vienna. All the great cities that are left. Honestly, Shin," she turned to me, smirking, "I'd have to really think about it to remember them all."

"Must be nice," I said, and I'd meant it exactly as I'd made it sound.

But Cayenne heard it differently. "I'm sorry, Shin, I didn't mean..."

"No, Cayenne, it's okay. I've never been out of Japan. My whole life has been in NeOsaka, in fact. Actually, the first day I'd ever left the city was when you took me north."

Me and Ben, I thought. I looked up at the white paper of the *shoji* panel, glowing with the sunshine from outside in the atrium. I knew that at some point I would have to talk about him, about what went wrong (if anything even *did* go wrong), about who we could trust, about what to do next. But I didn't want to bring any of it up. I wanted to forget for just a little longer. Until at least the light went out.

"Maybe someday," I said, "when all this is over, you can show me around. Madrid, I guess, for starters."

Cayenne looked down at the old-fashioned mascara bottle, dipping the brush in and out thoughtfully while she spoke. "I'd like that, Shin." Maybe she hadn't meant it, but I'd heard the doubt in her voice. I guess it'd been my turn to misunderstand. I hoped I had.

"You told me before," I said, wanting to change the subject, "that you met Tatsuhiro for the first time just two years ago."

"That's right."

"Same time you found this garden."

"It was Tatsuhiro who'd sent me around the world. My anonymous benefactor."

"He gave you all that experience, all that education. Then he brought you back and gave you all this?"

I watched Cayenne's head snap back as if she'd been slapped. Her brows lifted in shock. She sighed and set the mascara on top of the dresser with a resonant *clack*. "Are you suggesting I should be grateful for all of this?"

"No," I said. I shifted forward on the *tatami*, put my hand on her shoulder. "No, Cayenne. I was just asking. I mean, you had everything I ever wanted. Or thought I'd ever wanted. Growing up."

She turned to me. She took my hand in hers. "No, I didn't."

Now there could be no misunderstanding; I knew exactly what she meant.

"Your parents," I said, squeezing her hand back. "Did you know them?"

"No," she said. She reached for the framed photograph on the shelf. The man, handsome with piercing green eyes and straight, silver-flecked blond hair. The woman, gorgeous with almond eyes, dark skin, and even darker wild hair. And the perfect mix of them, their baby girl. The three of them smiling. "I was very young when they died. They were together when it happened. I think ... I blocked it out. I was kept so busy, always on the move, always something new to learn, someone new to meet. I never had time to think about them or wonder who they were, you know?"

I did know. I brushed Cayenne's wild blonde hair behind her ear, its color from her father, its volume from her mother.

"I was raised by nannies and butlers the whole world over. I learned seven languages. I learned economics, psychology, mathematics, and physics. I was never allowed to give up on anything, but I was never punished for anything. Sometimes, as I got older, I started asking more and more, who was in charge of my life? Because it certainly wasn't me. They would all just stare in the distance blankly, and if I pressed, they would get up and leave the room. Lesson over. Like they'd been programmed to do that."

Cayenne took in a deep breath, and I finished the thought for her.

"Like robots," I said.

"I tried to run away. Fake an identity. Fake a kidnapping. Even fake my own death. But they all knew, all my caretakers knew. They'd go along with it, like allowing me to play some game. And they'd always bring me back. One time, later on, I started getting more serious about escaping."

"Geneva," I said, recalling the scar she'd shown me aboard the spider rail. The same scar I'd kissed an hour ago.

"It was my eighteenth birthday. I came home from class, and the caretakers had left a cake, but they'd all left for the evening. There was a single plate. And a knife. I..." She stared vacantly ahead, her fingers tracing the line along the curve of her neck. "And all I wanted was—"

"Freedom," we said together.

"I thought it worked," she said. "I was in bed. And everything was fading. And no one was coming. And so, I think I..." She looked at me, the question in her eyes that she thought only I could answer.

"You died," I said simply.

"It was... I mean to say, I did not know it then—how could I? But when you held me, when we were in *Takamagahara*, and you brought me through to the other side. When you saved me, I remembered what it felt like. Just like that first time. So, yes. I died.

"Except I actually did not," she went on, smiling at the great irony of her still, in fact, being very much alive here and now. "I woke up. Weeks later. Here. In Japan. And I had these." She held a finger to her temple, then brushed it behind her ear to the implant slot.

"And I'll bet a major fucking headache?"

"This was not some back-alley, Syndicate street surgery, Shinjiro." Her scolding was playful. She nudged me away, but I bounced back, inching closer than before.

"This was," I said after a moment, when we'd both fallen back into the gravity of what she'd been describing, getting modified without your consent, "Tatsuhiro."

"Yes. The grand dragon. He was a voice in my head. And an image on a screen. He told me who I really was. What the name DeLeon had meant in the city of Osaka. What it meant to the ShiroKaz Legacy. My parents were the heads of research and development here. Before they died, my father had asked him to watch over me, keep me safe, if anything should ever happen. Tatsuhiro explained that he could not *be there* for me, for all those years…"

Because he was a fucking ghost, I thought. *And still is.* But I kept the obvious to myself.

"He told me what it was all for. All my education and upbringing so far from home. How there were still enemies of the Shiromatsu family, and thereby the DeLeon family. How it had not been safe for me here, not until everyone had forgotten us. But now would be the time."

Cayenne gazed at me, again maybe seeking that affirmation.

"The time for the White Shadow," I said. It all made sense.

"He gave me all of this. The tower, the arcology, the wardrobe."

One helluva wardrobe, I thought, remembering the green dress she'd worn to Heaven.

"Complete control of all the digital networks. Anything ShiroKaz could do on the grid with its limited reach. Tatsuhiro told me that he needed me to keep watch over our assets in the real world, that there were invisible enemies to the Legacy only he could keep at bay, and that it was draining him now more than ever. It *had* been draining him for years, and he was struggling."

I envisioned the old man with the prosthetic arm, alone in his ghostly throne room, hunched over and tired, a bulk of fiber-optic cables plugged into the back of his skull, for years on end, holding back the tide that would take over and steal all of his family's knowledge and records of their good deeds, chop them up, rewrite them, rewrite history, recolor them, sell them back to the world, make a profit, forget where it all came from, and move on. But now he was seemingly younger, stronger, with Triangle and the weight of Tenjin Mediacorp no longer bearing down on him. Having spoken to him just hours before, the grand dragon seemed ready to turn it all around.

"I'll never forget him saying that," Cayenne continued, "because I had no idea what he meant at the time."

"Yeah," I said. "Because it turns out—"

"*He's a fucking ghost,*" Cayenne cut in as I took a breath. She'd lowered her voice to ape how I might've said it. She looked at me and smiled wider than I'd ever seen her smile. It was impossible not to love her.

"He gave me a reason to live," Cayenne said. "A reason to use everything I'd gained in my life. I'd seen how *good* the world could still be, and I wanted to help make it good again. It was the same for you. Wasn't it?"

I held up her hand and pressed my own smiling lips against the backs of her fingers. We sat in silence, just enjoying it for a long while. But the worries crept back in: that she would say she had to go, or *we* had to go, or that the daylight would fade too fast. I cleared my throat.

I asked, "Did he ever…"

Ever tell you he's really Zenjiro Shiromatsu, Yasuro's twin, and that he fucking obliterated his own brother? Did he ever tell you that, Cayenne?

I held back the words, recalling the powerful old man's warning.

"…tell you anything about his past?" I finished, taking a different approach.

"Nothing," she said quickly, turning away, shaking her head. "Not a thing." She glanced at me nervously, and that's when I realized that there'd probably never be a hideout where Cayenne and I could truly be alone together. The hardlight projection of the horned dragon's head could materialize at any second in the space between us. The fact that it hadn't already gave me hope that Tatsuhiro had not been present when we'd made love, that he had at least some respect for Cayenne's privacy. For mine.

Still, I looked at Cayenne and knew she was telling the truth. She didn't know about him. Maybe she'd asked him once who he really was before, the living man, not the ghost—or worse, maybe she'd done some digging, hired a SynCell on her own to raid Inari data vaults—and Tatsuhiro had given her the same dire warning he'd given me. Cayenne believed that Zercos killed Yasuro in a duel and that was that. It's what she'd told me before. It's what the dragon had wanted her to believe. Zenjiro Shiromatsu was dead and buried and the world could move on. Just a footnote in whatever information he'd wanted his acting CEO to have about the ShiroKaz Legacy.

The glow within the house was less bright, more gray, the shadow of gathering storm clouds likely concealing the midday sun above the ShiroKaz skyscraper. The morning had moved on. It had been nice to dream, for at least a little while. I moved to retrieve my new charcoal gray dress shirt, the only article of clothing I'd brought in the house with me, from the corner.

"Did you ever," I started again, buttoning myself up while Cayenne put the finishing touches on her hair and makeup, "meet him? You know … in person?"

"Just one time. Actually, in the same graveyard where you and Zercos fought."

That made sense. It's where I'd met the old man, too. *Wait...*

I narrowed my eyes, my fingers frozen on the last button. I stared at the floor, stared at nothing in particular as my mind raced. *Zercos. The unmarked* haka *stones he'd thrown my ass through. His sword buried in my fucking heart.* There was something I was missing. In my mind's eye, it was staring back at me, but I could not see it. *The sword? The white katana? Zercos, flashing the kanji for Family, the Cluster. Ben and the Cluster. Acronymic.* I was pulling on more and more threads in my head, but the thoughts were leading me nowhere.

Family. DeLeon. Graveyard.

"Shin, is something wrong?"

"No, I..."

I looked up at her. Maybe it was in her. What I needed.

"What was your father's name?"

"Luther," she said. "His name was Luther."

Holy shit.

Triangle had said... *You can't stand that Z has ideas, too... What about Luther...?*

Mr. DeLeon has similarly been relieved of his duties...

"Why do you ask?"

"Oh, it's just, I..." I glanced at the sliding door, thinking maybe I could just run out comically and dash across the atrium garden to the elevator bank and be gone. I remembered what it was I'd left on the other side, the heap of outrageously expensive clothing that could be listening to us.

"Tatsuhiro told me your father helped him design SUIT. I was just curious is all. Actually, what was your mother's name, while I'm asking?"

Cayenne's green eyes bored into me, trying to read me.

I looked back a little helplessly. Maybe I'd fucked up.

...helped him design SUIT... That's what I'd said.

"Ezinne," Cayenne said, rising from her knees and crossing to the shelf. I could practically see the hardened business mask pulling itself over her face, her armor buckling itself onto her body as she moved. "It's Nigerian. It means *good mother.*"

Maybe she didn't catch my fuck-up, I thought. But I knew she had. And now she knew beyond doubt that I knew things she didn't. And now those things would hang between us, unspoken, and rot. And they wouldn't go away until we talked about them.

Or maybe they would go away. Maybe it was simply time to go for both of us. To get back to business as ShiroKaz CEO and ShiroKaz security chief, and maybe tomorrow...

She picked up an ink pen and scrawled something on a notepad, then tore the top paper free.

It said, W-R-U-I-O-U-P-Q-E-E-U-F-T-L.

"As soon as I got back to the tower, I had every line of processing power cycling through potential phrases and combing the networks for matches. Ben was right all along. Without being told the correct phrase, it's like a never-ending chase."

"But you are close to ending it, right? By now? Hasn't it been three days?"

"So I've been told. Whatever it is Ben wants us to find once the acronym is finally spelled out, I have a feeling you already know where it will lead us."

At that, I raised my eyebrow. "And what gives you that feeling?"

Cayenne folded her arms and drummed her fingers. She rolled her eyes over me from my disheveled black hair down my naked legs to my bare toes. The whole thing really took me back to the first time we met in the ShiroKaz operating theater.

"What?" I said, shrugging.

"I think Tatsuhiro told you to go somewhere. A place I can't follow, after all. And you're not telling me about it."

Close, I thought. *Really close. But it wasn't Tatsuhiro that told me to go to the graveyard.*

"You are absolutely right," I lied. Well, it was a half-lie, anyway. "I think there will be guys with guns all over again. I mean, when are there not?"

"Shinjiro," she said, picking something else up from the shelf. I looked back at my shirt buttons, shamefully, just so I didn't have to look at her. She'd called me *Shinjiro*. At least we hadn't yet regressed all the way back to *Asai-san*.

"Yeah?" I said, and we were also back to sounding how we didn't mean.

"I have something of yours."

She crossed the room to me, stood at arms' length, grabbed my hand, and pressed something into my palm. She covered it and wouldn't let up until I looked up into her eyes. I'd been wrong about her mask. Without all the distance between us, I saw it hadn't covered her whole face. I saw in her eyes that she still cared about me. That hadn't changed.

By its touch alone, I knew instantly what she'd given me. How could I ever forget something my fingers had rubbed a million times as if praying for just one more desperate wish from a magic lamp? I laid my hand over hers, flipped them all over, and pressed the old *omamori* charm back into her palm.

"No, Cayenne. You keep it."

I brought our hands up to her heart and stepped closer. I leaned in and kissed her forehead before letting go. She looked down at the charm she cradled, rubbed her thumb over the scratches on the back where the lucky *kanji* used to be.

"I don't need it," I said, but what I was really trying to say was that I needed her to have it. What I was trying to say without saying it aloud was that soon, one way or another,

I would be free. No more SUIT, no more sword, no more ShiroKaz. Maybe. And maybe I'd be dead, really dead. But maybe I could find my way back. For her, I would.

"You can give it back when we're both on some bigger, international-type J-Zero-K, headed to Madrid."

She threw her arm around my shoulder and pulled me in, embracing me like we had on the bridge. "Okay," she whispered.

TWENTY-SIX

WHILE I WAITED FOR MY NOODLES, I LEANED AN ELBOW on the waist-high, rain-splattered table and twisted around to scan the masses of moving humanity along the crowded street in NeOsaka's Minami district, my back against the railing of the Dombori Canal, flowing through its concrete trench that wound its way through the city.

I spotted the occasional *okasan* loaded with shopping bags of groceries, pairs of girlfriends and boyfriends hand in hand enjoying an afternoon out, some of them fresh out of the karaoke dens still belting out classic American party-pop songs of the bygone age, salarymen with their briefcases in one hand and the lapels of their trench coats clutched tightly in the other, always rushed by their business, in a hurry to catch their trains.

Then there were the lone wanderers, one eye on the path in front of them, weaving between bodies, the other eye drifting off to the digital glowing advertisements only their comlinks could show them as it broadcast their presence on the grid and someone somewhere had thought there was a perfect product for them if they would only turn the corner a hundred meters farther down the street.

Mega-corp couriers had a lane all their own puncturing straight through the mass, about two meters from the store-fronts, hopped up on doses of Bullet Time so they saw the flow of traffic in slow-motion, they pounded the pavement in their specialized foam-soled shoes, some of them with bags full of hardware and print-secured data cube cases, others carrying their true cargo in hidden ports drilled into their bodies. Not quite TKMG pilots, but there were crashes and competitions for space all the same, but no time to stand and fight for dominance. The passersby in this city had learned to check left and right before crossing the cou-riers' invisible lanes, but accidents happen. In case of a col-lision, the couriers would leap back to their feet, check their digital countdowns on their comlink displays, and run on even faster to make up for lost time.

Sometimes a night-Geisha would show up on the street, even this early in the evening, and a practiced peo-ple-watcher like yours truly could spot them even without their perfect make-up and unmistakable mockery of the tra-ditional attire. It was the way these women walked, with a dignity that proclaimed through movement alone that they were proud of the sex-service they provided to the lonely, so long as the lonely could save up enough to afford them. In fact, just across from where I stood, under the glowing neon of the rising five-storied walls of light that burned night and day, a Geisha had spotted me, gazing at me longingly with dazzling sun-yellow eyes over the curve of her fan, the slope of which matched the smooth ridge of her powdered white neck that disappeared in the silk robe pulled back to expose her shoulder. She reminded me very much of Kasumi. Even though I'd found Cayenne, there was a part of me that missed Kasumi and the other girls at Broken. They'd been there for me to fill a void I hadn't realized they could never fill. I was probably never going to see them again.

The Geisha and I were the only two people still bone-dry out here in the rain, the only two, perhaps, who could afford a *kasa* drone.. Hers was linked and operated by a comlink. Mine by SUIT. The effect of the invisible umbrella must've been what drew her eyes to me, the unsaid promise of money, a high-paying customer.

I wasn't interested. I just wanted my noodles.

I'd punched in my order at the kiosk a few tables farther down the railing, then found my spot to people-watch while I waited. I saw the server, draped in a plastic poncho, coming my way now with a tray, steam rising from the centerpiece bowl upon it. I wiped away the raindrops on my table, SUIT's material completely impervious to getting damp. I turned about, putting my back to the neon wall, the night-Geisha, and all the other people on the street, just as the server set down my meal, the floating *kasa* protecting the miso broth from getting spiked with acid rain. I took a final swig of the nihon-cha green tea I'd been nursing since my arrival and ordered another from the server before she sauntered away.

Under my breath, I ordered the Sentient User Interfacing Totality to dial me up a pair of chopsticks for a nano-fraction of ShiroKaz's treasury, using the trillion-yen piece of technology like it was little more than a first-gen comlink to pay for minor conveniences. The best part about frying my comlink when I'd turned myself into a lightning bolt three nights ago was that I didn't have to hear her grumble or make snide remarks in my ear. Of course, the AI could dominate every device on every street around the Minami district if it really wanted to make itself heard, but for the time being, I imagined SUIT swallowed its pride, and a pair of clean lacquer chopsticks popped out of the dispenser built into the table's edge.

Facing out over the canal, slurping down the first tangle of hot, nourishing ramen I'd had in over a month—probably the sixth actual *meal* I'd eaten in that much time—I ran my eyes over the crowds crossing the bridges spanning the Dombori just to my left and my right, and the crowd across the water, lit up with the bright color reflection from both sides, its flowing surface disturbed by one or two artificial koi programmed to come up every forty-five seconds to simulate real life, as if they needed air to exist. The people out there were more of the same as what milled around behind me. Dark-skinned, light-skinned, dark-haired, dyed-haired, short, tall, rich, poor, clothed by what they found in a shopping mall or an alleyway dumpster. American, European, Russian, Chinese, Indian, African. And Japanese. The rain fell on all of us equally, soaking us all to the bone.

I looked at the delicate slice of synthetic pork *chashu* floating in my ramen bowl next to the imitation soft-boiled egg, both of which were composed of packed and flavored lab-grown soy and vat-grown grubworms. I thought of the *okasan*'s shopping bag, wondering what she'd bought, what she was bringing home to her kids for dinner in a few hours. Were they on their way home from school to meet her? When would their father get home? Ten minutes before bedtime, if he was lucky. If they were. I thought of the kids in the Tenjin facilities who weren't so lucky, locked up in hidden pockets of space carved out all over the city, perhaps even some behind the walls of neon light on either side of the canal. What kind of lives would they grow into? Data cube couriers? Night-Geishas? Syndicate raiders? Corporate lackeys? Ramen-shop servers?

I pinched another tangle of noodles and savored them, then I set my chopsticks atop the rim of the bowl, and reached up to grasp the *kasa* drone floating over my head. The device shut itself off as soon as I tipped it sideways, bringing it out of the sky, and the rain fell freely on me, pattering on the table, diluting the miso, soaking into my scalp. I set the device down on the table, intending to leave it as a tip for the server. I'd taken it off the ShiroKaz tailor's shelf for free, but something like this could fetch her thousands of yen. Or it could simply make her job less miserable on a rainy day. I picked up my chopsticks and kept my head down, enjoying the rest of my meal in the downpour.

Minutes later, flashing red lights drew my attention across the canal. Even against the cascading electric neon of the Minami district storefronts, these stood out. About a dozen pedestrians were stopped in their tracks over there, their comlinks malfunctioning, their hardlight displays reset to public, their color palettes dialed to threat-level crimson, their brightness turned way up. I squinted, trying to see more clearly through the sheets of falling rain dividing us. They weren't pedestrians at all. They looked like tinmen.

Some mega-corp private security force had probably been tailing me from the moment I stepped out of the ShiroKaz lobby's steel barricades, which themselves hadn't been lowered from the front doors for two decades. I had a feeling this would happen. In fact, I'd been counting on it. The fact that they'd kept their distance this long without drawing attention to themselves was a surprise. I'd even been able to finish eating.

I casually stood away from the table, pressed my hand against its underside, reached through into *Yomi*, and felt the weight of the white katana in my grip. Hopefully, if anyone was looking, they'd think I'd hidden it there. Maybe hard to believe, but it would have to do. I looked left and right along the street on my side of the canal, and sure enough, a cluster of black-clad, black-masked security stood out from the crowd, marked by their malfunctioning hardlight screens materializing automatically in the air above their forearms.

The Sentient User Interfacing Totality was dominating their systems. The AI was like a spider on the grid, and our enemies had crept closer and closer until snagged by its web. There were about twenty of them, dispersed around me in all directions. Thanks to SUIT's tampering, the crowds were starting to notice their presence and take wide detours around their positions. Some of the data cube runners even had to slow down and take a bend along their unmarked path by the storefronts. But even with the AI's interference, they'd be back on their feet in probably twenty seconds. It could be that Smythe had done the unexpected and put out the word for an Inari hit squad on me. Or these were Triangle's personal posse come to avenge their boss now that her killer was planetside. Or it was a SynCell orchestrated by Feikes, wearing unmarked corporate uniforms and strapped with stolen, de-serialized weapons.

The fact of the matter was, I didn't know who they worked for and I didn't care. They couldn't kill me, no matter how hard they tried. All they'd do is gun down the innocent in the crossfire, cause a catastrophe that the local corporate-run news would have to spin somehow to avoid scandal and dipping stock prices. I wasn't interested.

The night-Geisha was still available, still standing in the pocket of dry air under her *kasa* drone, still smiling just over her gently fluttering fan, only her attention was no longer locked on me. It had been dragged to the commotion just like everyone else's. I made a beeline for her, the sword held at my side.

"*Konban-wa,*" I said to her, brushing aside my wet lock of black hair, flashing my most charming smile and distinctive, dazzling glance from my violet eyes.

"*Konban-wa,*" she replied, trailing off as her comlink tried and failed to complete my profile on her optic read-out. Instead, she blushed visibly, even under the skin-lightening makeup. "*Murasaki-onna,*" she called me, failing to pull up my name, glancing down at my katana, then gazing into my eyes.

Purple woman.

I offered my arm, like a true gentleman cowgirl would, and nodded toward the nondescript doorway just to our left, where a lone, bulky bouncer stood beside a velvet rope beneath an awning. This was the Geisha's place of business after all, part teahouse, part nightclub, part top-end brothel. Crowds would gather when the sun went down and likely not disperse until dawn, but for now, it was just her and me.

She took my arm, admiring with her fingertips for just a moment the material of my suit jacket, likely logging it as a topic for later conversation when pouring my tea and sake. The bouncer held the rope as we passed, and the doors slid apart automatically, likely triggered by a proximity chip embedded in the Geisha's comlink. We disappeared into the dark hallway of the club.

And as soon as the doors closed behind us, I looped my arm out of hers and asked to use the restroom. The unexpected request caught her off guard, like I'd hoped, but she was a professional, recovering remarkably quickly. She pointed down the hall and to the left, explaining she would wait for me. Poor girl. I knew I was leaving her for an hour or more of questioning once the tinmen caught up. But at least no one would get hurt.

Moments later, I clicked the lock on the door and stood alone in front of the toilet. Everything in the small room was obsidian-black, polished to a mirror sheen. My reflection stared back at me, and at a row of myself stretching on into infinity behind me. I straightened the position of my unbuttoned collar, wiped away the rain from my black wingtip oxfords with a starched and pressed towel I found in a basket by the sink, and held the white katana before me with both hands.

Purple fire flared along its edges, and a silent wind seemed to kick up in the room, caressing the ends of my suit jacket and tousling my hair. The never-ending line of my reflections shot forward into the swallowing, reflective black of the wall and disappeared, leaving only me and my glowing purple energy. The toilet, the sink, the wastebasket, everything tangible stretched and twisted ever so slightly as I crossed over into the underworld, becoming warped reflections of their physical selves. The wind faded. I turned about and cast my gaze through the walls of the small room, the building, the district, the entire city, out across the expanse of *Yomi*, over hundreds of thousands of wandering ghosts filling the streets and the twinkling *kami* residing in all things lighting the underworld.

I could see the graveyard a few kilometers away, lit up as if by spotlights. The great, imposing torii gate that guarded its entrance glowed a bright vermillion red, and the grove of sakura trees was in full blossom, their pink petals fluttering like butterflies in a gentle, never-ending vortex. I had only to think it, and I was there, crossing the sprawl of the spirit world in a single beat of my heart. I closed my eyes in the restroom of the night-Geisha's brothel and opened them at the threshold of the graveyard's torii gate, breathing in the sweet scent of the floating cherry blossoms, filling me with that inexplicable warmth of home and safety.

Just ahead of me, the rusty gate had been blown completely off of its hinges. The old workbench I'd set up had overturned in the explosion, scattering the rice cooker and lacquerware printer and all the contents of its drawers everywhere. I let go of the white katana, which hovered beside me just within my reach, and I scooped up the two halves of the snapped broom I used to sweep the untended shrines. In the underworld, the thing was gnarled and crooked. I pressed it back together, fitting the splintered ends like jigsaw puzzle pieces. I felt the unspoken prayer tingle in the two halves of the torii tattoo on my forearms, and the broom reformed before my very eyes. The object glowed. I'd rebuilt the house where the *kami* dwelled, and it had returned. I stood, looked next to the workbench, and held out my hand as if reaching for it. The scattered pieces gathered like liquid metal from all around and reattached to one another in space at my command. It was true magic.

When I was done, everything was in its right place, just as I'd left it days ago, before Zercos's attack. I left the broom leaning against the workbench and retrieved the white katana. I looked out over the immense, tiered grave-yard sweeping outward like wings. I could see the path of overturned stones my body had left when the cyborg tossed me through the air. At the end of it, the crater where we'd locked swords and nearly blasted each other apart. In the stillness of the bay, where the waters had swallowed the bottom half of the gravestones, the white, shining moon was waning, a crescent shape in direct opposite to how it had been days ago, and it was inverted, as if *Yomi* existed in the underside reflection of an ocean. I stepped to the edge of the grand staircase, and at the touch of my foot, a wave of purple energy swept out left, right, and down, washing over every *haka* and igniting the *kanji* carved into some of them, while some others remained unlit. My presence roused the spirits within, the ones for whom I'd performed the rites, the ones who'd been called and guided to their rest, and ghostly figures stepped forth from the blocks of stone. They turned to regard me, men and women, old, young, on their own or arm-in-arm, dressed in styles ranging across a century, and they bowed as one.

I was overwhelmed. I staggered, nearly falling to my knees, having to press the sword against the ground and lean on it to keep myself upright. I held my wrist over my mouth to stifle my sobs, but I could not hold back the tears that welled in my eyes.

It worked, I told myself. All the sweeping, all the clapping and bowing, all the rice, all of the Shinto rites and all the effort, all of these years, all the time I'd spent believing and hoping. It had all meant something. Something good for these spirits that I saw now. They were thanking me for bringing them home.

But some of the *haka* were still dark. Here, in this grave-yard, and no doubt in the other scattered, untended places all across NeOsaka, all across Japan, there was still work to be done. As I did each time before leaving this place, I bowed low and promised the wandering dead that I would find them and bring them peace.

I watched as the light faded from the stones, from the walkways and stairs. Behind me, the vibrant glow of the swirling pink sakura petals and vermillion posts of the torii gate subsided. Before me, the crescent moon whirled about in its circle; the waters below began to move and slosh together. The purple energy receded from nearly all over, but it lingered in one spot, swirling around a lone figure I hadn't noticed among the crowd, standing before a dull gravestone with a stone carving of a katana, one tier down from number sixty. The purple glowed in the machine-man's shoulder pistons, the hexagonal patterns of the matte black visor covering his face, across his torso, and down to the clawed toes of his triple-jointed legs. I wiped my tears on the back of SUIT's sleeve and took a first cautious step down the central stairs.

"It'd be nice not to fight this time," I called out into the still night air. The only other sound was the low swish of a breeze through the sakura trees behind me.

The seams between Zercos's armor plates pulsed with the residual purple for a few silent cycles more, then winked out to total black as he crossed his arms over his chest and seemed to consider my offer. He turned about at the waist, surveying the wreckage the two of us had left last time we'd met here, then came back to me. I'd paused on the steps, waiting for his reply. "Agreed," he finally said. He gave one last glance at the gravestone with the katana carving, then stepped along the tier toward the center, his metal feet clicking and scraping on the stone path, meaning to meet me there.

"I can hold Yasuro in here," I said, holding up the white katana, which hadn't so much as twitched a single time since the last time we stood outside the ruined gate of White Crane Castle. *Strange*, I realized. Come to think of it…

"Did you … *do* something to him?" I asked Zercos, my eyes narrowing on him as he stopped just three meters away from where I stood. "I can't, I mean, I don't feel him breathing down my neck anymore. No tugging on my puppet strings."

The cyborg was as still as a statue, facing me, making no reply for almost half a minute. I thought maybe I'd snap my fingers in his face in case he'd shut off or was forced to download some kind of update against his will or something. I almost did.

Finally, after a minute, Zercos said, "Not that I know of." The machine spoke with the former man's Russian accent, with his cadence, and his flat affect.

"You okay?" I asked him.

There was something different about his speech now, not that having exchanged all of thirty-something words with him before made me an expert on his linguistics or anything, but it was still enough to give me pause. That, and the fact that his cyan-colored glow in his frame hadn't turned back on. He stood still as a statue, practically a matte-black *haka* stone himself, his armor absorbing all light.

"*Genki,*" he said easily enough when he finally did speak. *I'm fine.* Once again, he crossed his arms. "Are you here alone, Shinjiro Asai?"

He'd hit me with my full name. What the fuck was up? My grip tightened on the white katana. I almost wished I *would* have felt Yasuro's spirit stirring inside it, or seen like a wisp of red mist. Anything. But there was nothing.

"Yes," I said, turning the sound of it up at the end like a question. "I think so. Nobody followed me here, if that's what you mean."

"Are you sure?" Zercos replied quickly. He held out a hand and unfurled his clawed fingertips one at a time, gesturing toward my suit. "You are wearing a very expensive intrusion platform on your back. Even now, I can feel its systems attempting to interfere with my own. It may want to speak with you, but there are no functional audio devices for many kilometers' radius."

"Except for the one behind your face."

"*Soo desu,*" was all the cyborg said, and then the silence between us stretched. I wasn't sure if I was supposed to ask Zercos if SUIT could borrow his voice box for a few so I could check my messages. I didn't really want to hear whatever it was the AI wanted to tell me, anyway. If it had decrypted Ben's acronymic anomaly by now, no doubt it would inform Cayenne first and she could run with whatever it told us. I'd chosen to chase down *this* lead instead of the other one.

"And is Miss DeLeon at the tower?" Zercos asked next, as if reading my mind.

"She's there," I said, cagey-like, cocking my head and squinting, trying my best to deflect, "or somewhere else."

"*Ii-yo,*" he said. *Good.*

Zercos sure was speaking a lot of Japanese. He retracted his hand and folded it once again over his chest, and just stood eerily still.

"Let's cut all this chatter," I said very ironically, "and just get to the part where you tell me why you brought me here. I'm assuming you've cut off whatever feeds you're normally broadcasting to your corporate masters, and we're here just you and me. Right?"

"Right," Zercos said. And again the silence stretched.

"So? What're we doing here?"

"We are waiting."

"For..."

"An old friend."

As if it had needed this precise codeword, a grinding and scraping of heavy metal against stone rang out across the bowl-shaped sunken graveyard. I gripped the handle of the katana and bent over instinctively into the samurai's quick draw stance, my eyes moving frantically around the curve of the place, chasing the echoing sound. When it finally stopped, there was the whirring of servos and movement at the very bottom tier, just by the water line of the bay. A voice cried out my name. Or more accurately put, *stuttered* my name.

"Sh-Shin!" Ben Roy Doon hollered again, louder this time, as he emerged fully from the storm drain he'd dragged aside.

I blinked in disbelief, my grip loosening on my weapon, coming out of my ready stance. As Ben's powerful legs pounded loudly up the central staircase, I saw his body was wrapped in a matte-black exoframe, complete with bulky, powerful fists that could clamp and lift weights several times their own, which right now carried only a canvas sack bound in twine. But within the frame, he still sported his shredded jeans and his t-shirt with the overstuffed pocket. The entire machine ran on signals from his nervous system, which was jacked into the rig via the slot behind his ear.

"Ben," I said, blinking in astonishment. "Is that you?"

"Yeah!" he called out excitedly, even though we were almost face to face. "Shin I'm *f-f-fucking walking!*"

"That's, that's," I stammered, not quite sure what to make of all this. "That's great."

Ben's smile beamed brightly for an awkward few seconds longer, then withered instantaneously, his eyes dropping to the sword by my side. "W-wait, you're not going to k-kill me, are you, Shin? I'm sorry, ab-ab-about leaving you and Cayenne. Please, Shin, I-I-I know you're m-mad, but, Shin, I—"

I surprised him—I surprised both of us—by crashing against him, wrapping my free arm around his neck, and hugging him tight. Thankfully, the exoframe didn't add much height. He staggered, the micro-servos in his joints whirring to compensate for the sudden impact, then slowly put his own arms around me, too. I closed my eyes, and just like that, Ben and I were kids again, orphans of Tenjin, surviving captivity until the day we could both grow up and get out. I guess in some ways we did get out, and in some other ways we did not.

"I'm not mad at you, Ben. I was never mad at *you*."

"You weren't?"

"I was just *angry. All* the time."

"You seem to've really mellowed out, Shin," Ben said as we came apart, still holding each other at arm's length. "What gives?"

I wasn't actually sure, now that someone was asking me point-blank. But Ben was right. He'd known me forever. Longer even than Feikes. Through all my ups and downs. And I was different now. It had been a lot of things. Starting, probably, with Boltcutter punching my back teeth out, with putting the Syndicate and Feikes behind me, behind *us*. Meeting Cayenne, and meeting Tatsuhiro. Discovering the ShiroKaz Legacy, and having an actual purpose in life. Probably some of it might even have been the drive to avenge the White Shadow. Somewhere along the way, I'd found a place for myself.

Looking at Ben now from head to toe, I realized he'd found the same.

"So, how long have you been with the Cluster?"

Ben gave me the same look, well, mostly the pricey suit I was wearing. He pinched the material between the metal edges of his exoframe fingers. "I'll tell ya all about it; once we're undergr-ground."

"Underground?"

"But first," he went on, ignoring my reaction, pressing the twine-wrapped canvas sack he held against my chest, "you gotta put this on."

TWENTY-SEVEN

"HEY! THAT'S A LITTLE TIGHT!"
I'd draped the bulky, sort-of x-ray vest thing over my chest, and Ben had turned me around to cinch it closed on my flank. There'd been a time in my life when a girl I knew had been big into lacey corsets, sometimes for me, sometimes for her, and this was a lot like that.

"Sorry, Shin. You know we gotta do this."

I glanced at Zercos as Ben buckled the final clasp and stood back. The cyborg was silent and still as ever, a patient onlooker. He'd said that SUIT was trying to integrate with his systems, but he was able to hold it back. Maybe he still had to until this signal blocker thing was firmly in place. I understood the Cluster's hesitation to bring along a mobile intrusion and hacking device sewn into the threads of my clothes.

Once Ben was satisfied with the mobile downstream data readouts on the exoframe's forearm, which apparently showed him SUIT had been stifled to an acceptable level, we made our way to the manhole where Ben had emerged. Zercos leaned over it, probably scanning its dimensions in infrared. Then he leaped gracefully into the darkness, his robotic limbs already calibrating the precise amount of lift and torque to carry his sleek body through to the bottom without scraping against the sides. I followed like a normal person, one foot and hand at a time, down the ladder bolted into the concrete. And Ben came last, dragging the rusty grate closed over our heads, his exoframe servos whirring loudly from all the activity.

The drain terminated in a vast cistern about thirty meters down. We stood at the center of a cross-shaped walkway suspended from the ceiling by steel beams, hanging over a pit of total blackness. The only light was from two emergency bulbs sputtering in their glass cases bolted to the wall, clinging to life while dozens of others had burned out ages ago. Far below, I heard the faint sound of rushing water, no doubt swelling the hidden drainage channels from the rain over the city. I thought at first it was a miracle that the pressure of the ocean just a few hundred meters to our side hadn't crushed this place some time in the past half-century. But then I recalled the attention to detail, precision, and foresight that comprised traditional Japanese engineering. As a society, they'd had to undertake massive projects with so little space and resources. The fact that the whole of NeOsaka hadn't caved in from all the added weight of refugees and corporate skyscrapers was a testament to their ingenuity. Since at the time of its construction, the drain was roughly half-way down the half-circle graveyard and rain water from the city would run off downhill, the materials and design of this place had to account for the abuse it would undoubtedly endure. The old architects of the time had probably considered climate change as well. If there was another drain at the true, sealevel bottom of the graveyard, it was likely swamped decades ago. A watery grave all on its own.

As soon as Ben's steel feet touched the grated walkway at the bottom of the ladder, I wanted to continue our conversation. But he reminded me that we were still within range of the Sentient User Interfacing Totality, who was no doubt listening to everything. It had already occurred to me that there was no way Tatsuhiro was unaware of my current whereabouts in NeOsaka. And since he most likely knew I had located Ben Roy Doon, he then knew I was on my way to the Cluster. The grand dragon had to believe I was simply out doing my job as head of ShiroKaz security, that I was getting to the bottom of the anomaly Ben had injected into the package downloaded from the data cube in Smythe's skull. He had to know that Zercos was here, but I couldn't think of any reason the old one-armed bastard would want me to fight the cyborg. Hadn't the two of them teamed up to take down the White Shadow?

Zercos had moved along the walkway first, pausing in the circular frame of a concrete drainage pipe twice his height in diameter. While he waited for Ben and me to catch up, he was framed by the dark, almost completely invisible. I wanted to believe he was past the part where he wanted to kill me for standing between him and the white katana he'd believed should rightfully pass to him. I ran my fingers against the scar over my heart that hadn't healed perfectly and likely never would. Zercos had been reasonable when we'd met at Himeji Castle that night, only striking back when his old *senpai* drew down on him, slicing the earth beneath our feet in half. I wanted to believe that he wanted me here. With his very spirit, he'd flashed the *kanji* symbols that had led me down this path. But there was something about his reticence in the graveyard moments ago, in the way he stood in the darkness now, just watching me. Something that kept me on my guard.

When we'd caught up, Zercos whirled about—his sharpened steel talons surprisingly silent against the walkway—and disappeared down the drainage pipe. A moment later, flood-lights mounted on the chest of Ben's exoframe burst to life, brightening the way before us. A human flashlight. Zercos was already gone, merged with the shadows farther down the tunnel.

Yasuro-sama.

I closed my eyes, calmed my body, felt the world recede all around me. For a fleeting moment, I reached outward with my spirit, calling the White Shadow's name. I felt the katana pressed in my grip as I floated over the yawning abyss that was *Yomi*, searching for the pocket of pure white emptiness where I'd first found him.

There was no answer. Was I free? Could I just toss the white katana over the railing into the black void, let it get swallowed by the surging floodwaters and dragged out to the bottom of the sea and be done with it all? No. I could feel the ethereal chain that locked my sword arm to the samu-rai's weapon. So what was it then?

Yasuro? Where the fuck are you?

If this turned out to be Zercos's trap, and I would need Yasuro to fight my way out…

"Shin!" Ben's voice broke my reverie, brought me back into my flesh. I opened my eyes and squinted against the blinding light of his rig. "Shin, c'mon. We got a long way to go."

He wasn't wrong. We wended our way around a quarter of the city in one enormous spillway that our first drainage pipe brought us to. I thought at first we were headed north, away from the sea, back toward the city center, but after a few more turns, I abandoned all hope of tracking our direc-tion and just followed Ben. Our path in the huge under-ground spillway curved gradually around for what must have been two full kilometers. We were back on the city's power grid now, indicated by slowly blinking red lights in the ceiling high overhead. These were not enough by which to navigate through the darkness. Aside from the high beams on Ben's chest, there were occasional pockets of vagrant colonies burning trash for light. Or at least they appeared to be if any corporate security types were to ever wander this far below NeOsaka. Ben explained these were lookouts for the Cluster, and that should they ever need to send a warning to the top (I guessed he meant *hierarchy*, like DeLeon, or the other hacker types, not *topside*), they were hooked up to old-fashioned heartbeat monitors instead of network-connected comlinks. He knew so much, maybe everything, about their operations.

I stopped dead in my tracks, tugging a little at the bulky signal-stifling vest for air. "Ben, tell me straight," I began, and he stopped too. "How long have you been in with the Cluster? Don't lie to me."

"I know you've known for a long time, Shin. I'm not super good at k-keeping this kind of thing secret."

It was true. Maybe six months ago, an unlicensed delivery drone had dropped off the first piece of old-fashioned hardware to patch onto his rig alongside cutting-edge mega-corp prototype tech, and whatever code he needed to make it all sing together was in a dead drop file hidden somewhere on the grid, accessible only through an acronymic key he'd have to decipher with his burgeoning little codebook, pages filling up by the day. So, yeah, I already knew. But I still needed to hear it from him.

"How long?"

"Well... T-two years."

I didn't need the squeeze of the wannabe-corset to lose my breath. I almost choked, my brows raising. I grabbed the steel bar of the exoframe over his chest and pulled myself closer.

"*Two fucking years?!*"

"I-I'm sorry, Shin. I-I-I-"

"That's amazing, Ben!" I threw my arms around him, managing only to the tops of either shoulder. "You kept a secret for two years. I had my suspicions, but didn't know for sure. Feikes didn't know. Shit, you almost told Cayenne two days ago. But you didn't tell her. Didn't tell anybody. You've been working with the Cluster for two years."

"You seem, ah, maybe *p-proud* of me?"

I think maybe I was. I smiled and took a step back.

"How long have you been coming down here?"

"Never. No one in the Syndicate or any mega-corp knows wh-wh-where the Cluster operates. I was only invited once we got the file from Smythe and beamed it from Heaven back down to the city. I'd no idea where I'd sent it or anything. Then I got the c-c-call. That guy," Ben said, nodding toward the darkness where Zercos had disappeared, "came to get me at the arcology. Cut right through the window.

"Hold on," he said, cutting me off before I could ask for *that* full story. "We're g-getting close. There's something you g-gotta see."

We'd arrived in a massive underground channel, which my tour guide, Mister Roy Doon, told us encircled the entire city like a dry underground river, deeper than anything else, designed to catch and redirect all the rainwater in typhoon season. He led us all the way up a concrete slope to the point where it met the ceiling, which curved away back over our heads and disappeared into the dark. Zercos stepped out from the shadows behind us as we reached the top. The label "M36" was marked on the wall in peeling yellow paint next to a row of narrowly spaced iron bars set top and bottom into the concrete. We'd already past thirty-five barred spillway gates just like it, so why we were stopping at this one was a mystery to me. I looked at Ben and shrugged. I think he'd been waiting to see my reaction to… *To some iron bars?*

He smiled wide, then whirred his new arms and legs and power-walked right through the bars like they weren't there.

They shimmered and bent as his frame passed them, then reformed once he was on the other side.

"You're not the only one who can w-walk through walls down here, Shin!"

"A holoprojection?"

I waved my hand through the closest iron bar, which was little more than a beam of concentrated light cast from somewhere. I scanned around the whole place, but couldn't see shit in the pitch black. Ben had turned off his rig's lights, I guess to help prove his point.

"Up there," he said, pointing at the blinking red light at the crest of the spillway's curving ceiling. I squinted, but still couldn't make anything special out. "A drone projects this wall twenty f-f-four hours a d-day. It's cloaked. Same tech Cayenne's guardian has."

"How can the Cluster get by with all these old-fashioned piles of junk, but then have something this sophisticated for a front door?"

"Her father m-made it. It's got a weapons p-platform, too. Same caliber as what tagged our friend here. Remember, Vlady?"

The cyborg remained quiet, patiently waiting for Ben Roy Doon to shut his mouth so we could all move on, a feeling I knew quite well from past experience with him in my SynCell. As he moved through the fake iron bars, Zercos turned his matte-black visor toward Ben, and the glow of the hologram flashed its hexagonal course over his faceplate. Something told me he did not find a reminder of being sniped by a cannon very funny.

"You two close friends now?" I said playfully, looking from the one to the other. I barely stopped myself from nudging the cyborg with my elbow. "On a first name basis? Does he let you get away with saying things like that?"

Ben cleared his throat, looked like maybe he was about to faint, but then whirled about as a way to change the subject quickly. "Right, uhh. So, the rest of the way from here is completely wiped from historical b-b-blueprints and city p-plans, both digital and analog." He relit his high beams and took the first steps deeper into the new side tunnel, which, unlike its thirty-five identical brethren, turned sharply downward instead of up.

Zercos fell in behind me, no longer leading the way, as if this was new territory for him as well.

"Luther told me it was one of the Syndicate's earliest raids," Ben went on, "to get all the plans and erase everything from the information branch of Shiromatsu-Kazama, which later spun off into Inari after, well, the, uhh, changes in leadership..." Ben turned his head about to face me even as his powerful new rig still propelled his legs forward by command of his nervous system. "I mean, I don't want to offend anybody who may be lis-listening from inside any swords or anything." He was frightened, and that made him gravely serious.

"I think you're okay." I glanced back at Zercos, again eerily silent despite the sharpened steel toes he strode on, while Ben and I kicked up dust and scraped onward with our patent-leather shoes and clomping exoframe feet.

I jerked my thumb over my shoulder at the ninja cyborg. "Did you say he cut his way into the arcology and, what, kidnapped you? Like he hauled you out the window? Or pushed your chair through the lobby?"

"No! I mean, yes, he did, but he didn't kidnap me. He left. Gave me a message and left. From DeLeon. Luther. Cayenne's dad. And not in person. When Zercos got in, DeLeon got past the network security, just sp-spiked through whatever network traps your SUIT had put up like he owned the place. DeLeon stays underground. Really d-d-deep, where all the old things are, under hundreds of meters of concrete and stuff that the grid just doesn't reach through. He's hard-wired in, I guess. Technology before its time."

"With the rest of the Cluster?"

"Shin... L-Luther *is* the Cluster."

Nothing shocked me anymore. Years ago, when the name of an anonymous, underground hacker group started getting recognition around the Syndicate's hangouts and even started earning spots in certain SynCells as remote handlers, I'd first envisioned the so-called Cluster as a group of malnourished, pale vampires self-imprisoned in coffins lined with computers. Later on, the image changed to a middle-wage mega-corp salaryman seated at a table in the open-air cafeteria of his company's tower, on his lunch break, punching through security protocols on the state-of-the-art comlink he'd siphoned off his boss's boss, risking his entire professional livelihood for a righteous hobby. And that was the thing about the Cluster's hackers, they could be anyone and no one. Their reliance on acronymic codes and outdated tech to help keep their identities and activities hidden on the grid was something the modern world hadn't been expecting and still didn't know how to really deal with.

It was only after I'd found myself on the steps of Tatsuhiro's throne room that second time, after I'd slowly drifted through the impenetrable steel wall of Triangle's cocoon on the underbelly of *Takamagahara*, and seen both of them jacked into the immense supercomputer machines called the mainframes that I finally realized just how plausible Ben's statement was. *Luther is the Cluster.* Just one man, not an army of hackers. Just one. Punching through security like he owned it. Hell, he probably did. At least he'd researched and developed it when he worked for ShiroKaz. The reality wasn't so hard to picture any more. But I just hoped he wasn't swimming naked in a vat of goop.

"Yeah," was all I said in reply.

After another hour of twisting and turning through side tunnels—some machine-made according to the original, now-lost blueprints, some that bore the marks of human-borne shovels—we came to a round steel blast door flanked by two cybernetic guards. They were identical in conception as the tinmen that had first assaulted me at the graveyard outside my apartment, same Hachiman forged sub-machine guns, same black steel plates armoring their limbs. But instead of being sleek killing machines, these were outwardly worn-down and vandalized. An A-Matter brand power cell glowed brightly where the first's heart should've been, replaced by an angry-faced, plastic doll's head. The other tinman bore a spray-painted *kanji Buta* over its chest. Pig.

We stood awkwardly in front of Doll and Pig until Ben swiveled around to regard Zercos with an expectant glance. "Are you, er, c-can you have them open the d-door?"

Zercos made no reply. He'd been sizing up the pair of tinmen from the moment we stopped as if seeing them there for the first time. Then he looked at Ben. "I am dis-connected," he stated flatly.

"That's weird," Ben said. "Maybe taking an extra minute to j-jump through our firewall. The network above can't have sna-snagged you this long. It's okay, I got it then." Ben stared ahead vapidly, looking over the optic comlink overlay only he could see. After ten seconds, Ben had sent the instruc-tions, and Doll pivoted on his heels, grabbed a jumble of cables besides the door's hinges, and connected an old-timey USB from within his armor-jacket sleeve to one of the cables. The whole operation seemed random. The fact that the door's magnetic locks disengaged and the whole thing began screeching open seemed like pure luck. Something a sophisticated program on the network wouldn't have been able to figure out unless it somehow gained physical access to whatever was written on the ancient, USB-compatible data drive tucked in the tinman's clothing.

But I'd only paid it half of my attention. My head might've been turned forward, but I was watching Zercos sideways, trying to figure out what the fuck was different about him. Then, just as the first crack appeared in the doorway, it hit me.

"SUIT," I said to him, my voice barely above a whisper. "Is that you?"

Zercos's head turned slowly to me, as if he'd been waiting for me to ask. *"Nani?"* he said. *What?*

"Did you take him over?"

Ben turned around now, catching up on my line of thinking. "What's going on?"

"Ie," Zercos said. "I am still myself."

My eyes narrowed. I had experienced firsthand the Sentient User Interfacing Totality's capacity for human emotions. Vanity, pride, arrogance. And also deception. It had no reason to tell the truth if it wanted to hitch a ride inside Vladislav Zercos's operational code to infiltrate the last bastion of Tenjin-free, and therefore ShiroKaz-free, network activity in NeOsaka. I slowly raised my katana's handle to hip level, and crossed over my waist with my free hand to grasp it, readying to draw down.

"What was it you said to me when we first met? In the graveyard, after you blew my home straight to hell."

The hexagonal patterns flipped translucent over the cyborg's face, exposing it. He looked at me with his death-mask eyes, then down to the sword I held at my side, then back to me. Zercos did his best impression of a smile.

"Give me the sword," he said, and for a second I had to really think if he wasn't commanding me to do so all over again.

Were those his exact words? Does it really matter?

"I am still myself," he repeated, the matte-black plate rematerializing over his face. "I am ... *drained*, by our previous encounter."

I eased back, let my hands and the katana fall again to my sides. *Makes sense, I guess.* Again, I was no expert on these spirit realm matters, but I reasoned that slashing at me and Yasuro with one aspect of whatever tied the Russian cyborg to his old *senpai* must have taken some kind of toll on him. Mostly, I bought his explanation because SUIT had not been there. If the AI had been, the battle with Zercos's tinman squad would've gone a lot differently.

"We probably just need to reconnect him to the hub down here," Ben said, seeing the two of us in some kind of strange standoff and trying to be helpful. "Just a little ways in." He crossed the threshold of the wide-open blast door and waved us inside with an audible whir of the exoframe's arm. Doll and Pig had stood aside, perhaps following a pro-grammed routine.

"After you," I told Zercos, and held out my hand as if inviting him inside my apartment for a party.

"*Domo,*" he replied.

Beyond the blast doors, a whole underground community thrived inside a massive, abandoned water reservoir. It was the size of a city block, and easily four stories tall. A million tons of concrete comprised the floor, walls, and ceiling, all held together by massive pillars as thick around as cargo containers, which were linked together by steel walkways, ladders, and spiral stairs at all levels. I picked out more hacked and vandalized tinman sentries stationed at various strategic spots up there, keeping an eye on the groups of people below. But the Cluster's security wasn't kept solely by repurposed cyborgs. Bolted into every pillar we passed, all the way up near the sloping ceiling, automated gun turrets tracked our movements (well, tracked *mine*). They were the same make and model as Cayenne's cloaked guardian angel drone, strapped with the same long and powerful gun barrel.

The finest unmanned mobile weaponry in the corporate war god Hachiman's arsenal.

At street level, whole buildings sprouted off the massive concrete pillars, constructed one on top of another over time, some reaching almost to the topmost walkway. They appeared shoddy at first glance but were in all likelihood very sturdy, crafted out of scrapyard sheet metal, fencing, and repurposed lumber. Some were storefronts with bright neon halogen signs, buying, selling, or trading bucketfuls of spare parts and locally machine-shopped hardware. Some were taverns, proud to serve unique under-city brews concocted in tall stills behind the bar. Some were open-air food markets, stocked with freshly grown garden fruits and vegetables raised at artificial UV farms, freshly baked breads, vats of living salmon, and even a real-life collection of livestock.

The people here lived off the grid, but they *lived*. I imagined that in some ways, they lived more freely and more satisfied than the rest of society topside, who were under total dependence on the corporations to tell them what they needed. From within their squat residences, these people had whole families that cooked and ate together, laughed and loved, slept soundly and dreamed. As a community, they designed and built things, plotted and undermined, fought the establishment, survived. All along the streets, mounds and mounds of electrical wiring and cables were bunched together with plastic cords and zipties, some breaking off from the bunch and running through slots cut into the bottom of each building. The glow from arrays of decades-old computer monitors lit up the interior spaces, sometimes contrasted with modern hardlight displays popping up right alongside them. So it was true the Cluster hackers didn't operate solely on outdated tech and handwritten codebooks. How could they? If they were going to be in the game with the mega-corps and the Syndicate, they'd have to level the playing field somehow.

Just as I began to wonder how the Cluster could possibly haul all of these things down here, we came around a bend and onto what seemed to be the main artery for foot traffic in the underground city, and I saw an enormous freight elevator jury-rigged between the furthest pair of pillars. Right at that moment, the lift platform descended out of a blasted hole in the ceiling, loaded with crates of supplies, equipment, and what appeared to be the maglev engine block of a floating transport.

Behind the elevator was what appeared to be the citadel of the whole place. Four colossal concrete pipes sprouted from the ceiling like the exposed roots of a great tree and followed the gradual slope of the wall, terminating at the far end of the reservoir. Between them was a kind of doorway, heavily guarded by a pair of cybernetic sentries that I saw were completely unmarked. Over their heads was a rusty sign that read "Pump Room" in *hiragana*, and above that, covering every inch of the pipes and walls, the *kanji* for *Family* had been spray-painted in rainbow colors like a mural, with spotlights set at the top of the walkways beaming down on it. It was the sun that shone proudly over the Cluster's home, day and night.

We made our way there, moving through the makeshift central thoroughfare of the underground city, the citizens giving us a wide berth, standing aside to watch the weird trio stride by. Ben was a newcomer among them, already trusted enough to get outfitted with a one-of-a-kind exoframe to compensate for his physical disabilities. Zercos looked like a billion-dollar cybernetic prototype—and to be fair, he *was* that—but really just a house for a lingering spirit that refused to pass on. And I was just a cowgirl in a charcoal linen-blend suit (unfortunately rumpled from the tight vest over it), with expensive black shoes on her feet and a stunningly white katana at her side. Although they'd never seen me in the flesh before, they knew who

I was. How could they not? After what had happened on the TKMG racetrack, even filtered through the supposedly SUIT-doctored footage. Not to mention, rumors of the White Shadow's return must have reached a group as tuned in to corporate sabotage as the Cluster. I flashed a smile at a young mother, a strong and beautiful woman who stood clutching a toddler, her little girl, against her hip with one arm while lifting a heavy canvas sack of supplies with the other. And she flashed a look at me that was as hard as stone. The look said *you don't belong here.* It said *the sooner you leave, the better.*

Maybe she was right, on both counts.

As we neared the stairs up to the pump room, the unmarked guards simultaneously clicked the safeties off their weaponry, definitely part of their programming. One of them held out its gloved hand.

"Today's code?"

"Uh, hold on a s-sec." Ben twisted his lanky arm out of its steel frame and brought his hand over to his stuffed shirt pocket, bringing out a wad of papers, dropping two pens to the ground. I bent to retrieve them while my old friend rifled through his wrinkled, hand-scrawled notes, dropping a few of them like dead leaves in my hair. I noticed the tinmen's guns, like the turrets far above our heads, were trained only on yours truly as I moved.

"Here," Ben said excitedly, finding the crispest paper from among the bunch. "Y, I, C," he said. "Yesterday, inspection commenced."

The cyborgs ran the acronymic phrase through their daily reset databank, and a second later, their thumbs clicked their gun safeties back on.

"Ben, what would've happened," I began asking as we passed between them toward the double doors of the pump room, "if you'd given them the wrong code?"

"They'd probably have shot you," he said flatly. "Not that it'd do much good."

"That's what I was thinking." Maybe it was just for show. Just an act. So the Cluster community at large who may still be watching had the illusion of security.

TWENTY-EIGHT

THE GRAND CITADEL OF THE HACKER GROUP CALLING itself the Cluster was little more than a chamber lined with damp, grimy concrete and patches of flaking tin foil. There were two aisles of century-old steel workstations with blinking lights and switches that looked like they'd blinked and switched for the final time sixty years ago. If those computer systems failed to regulate the emergency flows of water from the city a thousand meters above us, then there was a long series of pipes and valves that would do the trick, or could if not for the ruddy brown rust and pale green corrosion caked all over them. Laid over, in between, and around almost every inch of space, wires and cables ran toward a spot at the room's center that had been cleaned out for the most part, leaving just enough space for the third and final mainframe in existence, and the third and final operator jacked into it by fiber-optic cabling at the base of his skull.

Luther DeLeon reclined in a padded chair, itself part of the mainframe, his position similar to Triangle's when I'd found her in her lair, but unlike Triangle, DeLeon was not stripped naked nor floating in a vat of cooling gel. His face was covered in an oxygen mask, his body was wrapped head to toe in rags, but there was no concealing how frail and fragile he was underneath the layers of old cloth. Years of diving into the grid and concealing his hacker family's presence there had taken their toll. His hands poked out of his sleeves, his fingers gnarled and rheumatic, clutching the arms of his chair spasmodically as his half-closed eyelids fluttered frantically and he panted for breath. He wore a pained expression on his face, which was marked with liver spots and beaded with sweat. The differences between the master hacker of the Cluster and the mistress of Tenjin Mediacorp were stark. Whereas Triangle had been gorgeous and vibrant with health, DeLeon was withered and sickly, just a single, hard knuckle knock away from blowing open death's door. Cayenne's father looked nothing like the silver-flecked blond man in the photo she kept atop her dresser. If she saw him like this, she probably wouldn't know him, if she could even remember who he'd been to begin with.

But then he opened his eyes, slowly, and spun his gaze around to me. When our eyes met, whatever doubt I had that Cayenne was his daughter evaporated. He had the same deep, emerald green eyes that could bore into you.

"Ahh," he said softly, wheezing, a shaky smile coming to his face, "you've come." The chair whirred audibly and brought the old man up to a sitting position, spinning him around to face his guest.

"Yeah," I said, not knowing what else to say. I glanced at Ben, who simply shrugged back. "Thanks for the invitation."

While I'd been busy taking in my surroundings and the pump room's sole occupant, Zercos swiveled his head from left to right, scanning the environment as if for the first time, locating the state-of-the-art rig that stood out from the archaic junk surrounding it. It resembled a medical gurney fashioned out of chrome, bolted into the concrete.

I could barely make out the all-caps Hachiman brand and logo on one side where someone had tried to scratch it off. While Luther and I exchanged our greetings, the cyborg paced silently over to it, stood between the brackets, turned, and spread his arms wide. The machinery rose and clamped him in place, its dials and read-outs lighting up automatically as the rig re-energized him. It was also reconnecting him directly to the Cluster's insulated systems, as Ben had alluded to outside the reservoir blast doors. Although Zercos's body was designed, owned, and operated primarily by the Hachiman Technologies corporation—itself just part of the remnants and scraps of the once-great Shiromatsu Kazama holdings—they did not own his will, his spirit. Now that he'd accomplished his mission for DeLeon and the Cluster, delivering the message at Himeji-Jo and escorting me from the graveyard, I imagined he was a bit overdue for a report to his corporate overlords.

"I am curious," DeLeon said, "why you think I've brought you here." As he spoke, he peeled the oxygen mask down his face and let it rest against his neck, ready at a moment's notice if he needed it. Now that he'd said more than a few words, I picked up on his thick Spanish accent, his Andalusian lisp.

"Me too," I said, sweeping my eyes over the room all over again. The third mainframe was nothing like the other two I'd seen. This one seemed glued together by rust, encased in dingy metal plates, bulky, sagging over time into the damp concrete. It was something like the century-old Cold War tech you'd see in a movie about the rise of the Russo-Chin alliance, how their tech struggled to catch up to the West's over a century ago, how they always hid it in damp basements and bunkers. "I suppose I would've been sent after you, eventually."

"Sent to kill me?"

"I don't know. I didn't even know you were alive, and I doubt Tatsuhiro did either. If you've stayed this well hidden for this long, he probably still doesn't."

"Oh, he knows I'm alive alright," DeLeon said. A nervous, despondent smile crept across his face. He seemed to pale suddenly as his gaze fell to the concrete floor. Speaking was hard for him. He could only get short phrases out before taking a deep breath. Already he looked very tired, very near the end. "He knows. The three of us, well, now we're just two… We'd been like generals on opposing sides, in a war, dug in deep in our trenches, for years and years. Starving, freezing. Wishing we could just go home, see our families again, but knowing that if we gave up our posts… A no-man's-land stretched out between us, infinitely long. Neither of us committing ourselves completely to a move. Just fighting proxy battle, after proxy battle. And all of it," he said, tapping a bony finger on the cable jacked into the base of his skull, raising his eyes up to me again, "in here. For almost twenty years.

"And, his name," DeLeon went on, "isn't really Tatsuhiro. Did you know that?"

"I put the pieces together."

"Do you know who he really is?"

"Yes."

I looked at Ben, whose sudden astonishment was animating his body. The movements of his hands practically pantomiming, *When were you gonna tell me?* But he kept thankfully quiet. Besides, he was no kind of arbiter about the rules for holding back information.

"He's Zenjiro," I said, still looking at Ben, meaning to inform him. "He's a Shiromatsu. The White Shadow's twin brother."

"Really," was Ben's response. "But then, if that's, wh-what could, aahhh." Behind his visible confusion, I saw the dominoes in his brain start to fall over one by one. It would keep his mind busy for a while.

"How is Cayenne?" DeLeon asked, changing subjects suddenly. I could tell from the gleam in his eye, the way he held his gnarled hands tightly together, that this might be what he really wanted to talk about. *Who* he wanted to talk about. "How is she?"

"Didn't Ben tell you?"

"He did, he did. But he could say only that she was healthy, and that maybe she was happy."

I thought back to that morning, when she'd embraced me on the bridge outside her house in the garden. I remembered the warmth of her against me. Cayenne's smile, her true smile, after taking the mask off. After letting her armor fall, after however many years. When she saw me.

"Yeah," I said, smiling knowingly. "She is happy."

I think the old man heard well enough what I'd left unspoken. My smile told him everything, that I was in love with Cayenne. His gaze was distant, wandering back to the grimy floor. He let out a great sigh, something he'd probably been holding in for decades, his breathing suddenly even and unburdened.

"And she misses you," I said after a moment. "I mean, she thinks you're dead. But she wishes she could've known you."

DeLeon looked up at me again, a sudden, serious shadow darkening his expression. "Better if she continues to think I *am* dead," he said, meaning it as a warning.

But I missed the warning. Or I heard it but didn't care.

"Fuck that," I said, thinking of Cayenne, of what she would want. "If she knew you were still alive, she would want to—"

"NO!" DeLeon roared, rising to stand from his padded chair, taking a menacing step forward. The sudden thunder in his voice tapered off, became a rattle in his lungs, which took total control the next moment, wracking his body with coughing fits. Ben's exoframe sprang to life, scooping the withered old man up as he pitched forward, cradling him and easing him back into the chair. DeLeon's hand fumbled for the oxygen mask around his neck, and Ben helped him get it over his nose and mouth even as he coughed. Against the clear plastic, I could see blood in his spittle.

"I'm sorry," I said, probably not loud enough for Luther DeLeon to hear me. "I'm sorry. I didn't mean to…" I forced myself to shut up, to wait out the dying man's pain.

"I don't have much time left," he said a moment later, his breath wheezing worse than before. "I don't want Cayenne to see me like this."

I still didn't agree. I knew that if it were me, if I could know my father—if I could cast aside all the assumptions and see the truth, no matter how painful—I would. But I swallowed the words for the time being.

"So why did you bring me here?"

"To tell you," DeLeon said, "about the ShiroKaz Legacy."

"I already know."

"You know what Zenjiro told you. You know what his father envisioned for the future of mankind. The goodness in us, shining through. A common hope for tomorrow, once and for all, bringing us together. All of that shining shit."

I cracked a smile at that. Now here was a guy who could speak my language. "Indeed," I mused. "Shining shit. But it's something to strive for. At least there's an end goal. The world the way it is and all."

"The two of us, you and I just now," he said breathlessly, though smiling inside the mask, wagging a finger back and forth at ourselves, "we sound like Zenjiro's father, old Yoshinori. A great man."

"And what does the Cluster want? If you're opposed to the ShiroKaz master plan—"

"I didn't say I was—"

"If you're going to stand in the way of the Legacy," I bulled on, forgetting my pledge to be patient with the dying man, "then what do you propose instead? Because unless you're capable, with all this rusted-out shit everywhere, unless you're ready, unless *they're* ready, all of them out there in your underground fortress, to take a shot at bringing the corporations down and rebuilding the whole thing to include *everybody,* and do it *fairly,* then we're all fucking doomed and you know it."

At this point, the old man could see I was getting hot, and he thought it best to take the deepest breaths he could and just wait for me to run my course.

"I see a world on fire," I ran on, "and I have the power inside me to help, so I'm going to help. I can go anywhere. Straight to the penthouses or the underground bunkers of the C-Level, greedy bastards that are destroying us. I mean I just got back from outer fucking space, where I personally knocked a data cube out of the silver fox's skull. And I can do it again, as many times as I need to. I can put the blade up to their throats. I can cut their fucking heads off if they go back on their word. And none of them can stop me. And it doesn't even stop there. NeOsaka is just one city, in one country. I can cross borders at the speed of light. Someone in Russia is bound to speak Japanese. Or I can take an interpreter," I said jerking a thumb over my shoulder to Zercos. "So, yeah, I can help. I have the power to make a difference. So I want to ask you again, Luther." I took a menacing step forward. "Why should I stop on the path that Zenjiro's started me on? What're you going to tell me about the Legacy that's going to change my mind?"

The old man closed his eyes, very slowly, and in the seconds of silence that stretched, I got a better look at the weariness etched in his face, the wispy graying hair, the swollen purple bags under his eyes. I regretted the way I'd bullied him. Hadn't I had my own doubts about my boss just twenty-four hours ago? Hadn't I felt that he'd been lying to me? That he'd been withholding the truth? Here I was standing face to face with someone that *knew* Zenjiro, that could tell me what was real and what wasn't, yet I was blindly standing up for him.

I unclenched my fist. I hadn't even realized I'd balled it up. I let out a long breath. "I'm sorry," I said for the second time.

Luther DeLeon was silent a long time. Ben and I just watched him breathe, the deliberate, pained rising and falling of his chest as he reclined back in the mainframe's padded chair. Then, finally, DeLeon said, "You're a lot like him, you know. Zenjiro, when he was your age. Nothing moved fast enough for him. His brother was slow, cautious. Yasuro didn't do anything without their father's order, while Zenjiro was hot-headed, reckless. No hesitation. No compromise. No prisoners. It's why Yoshinori banished him. The first time."

"The first time?"

Somehow, I already knew. *This second transgression will be his final activity within the ShiroKaz corporation...*

The words I heard repeat in my mind had been the White Shadow's final exchange, in the boardroom with Sandra Calvin.

...Within the Shiromatsu family.

"Zenjiro didn't get these strange, inexplicable ghost powers like his brother," DeLeon explained. "He didn't get to be the White Shadow like Yasuro. And that jealousy built up inside him. He made deals behind his father's back, wanting to surprise him, impress him, bring down the Legacy's enemies and at the same time bring honor to the Shiromatsu name, all on his own. But all Zenjiro did was give rise to what would later be called the Syndicate, which in turn only gave the splintering corporate factions yet another avenue to attack, compounding Yoshinori Shiromatsu's problems. And all Zenjiro got from his father was disappointment.

"It wasn't until he came back from his exile, with our help—Triangle and I, and Zercos—when he blew Yasuro to bits, that Zenjiro's true power manifested. But he dragged himself to hell alongside his brother, and he was gone for years. All our plans, to restore the ShiroKaz Legacy without having to make everyone fear us, it all vanished. Turned to dust in our hands. And it wasn't long after that upstarts like Smythe and Feikes and all the rest of our allies fell on ShiroKaz, like scavenging vultures on the unlucky lion's corpse, and tore out their share of its power. Sandra and I got the company's greatest weapons out with us."

"The mainframes," I said.

Luther nodded. "The prototype at the castle was lost in the fire. Sandra brought the most advanced model above the clouds where no one else could touch it, and I took mine underground, where the elements have not been so kind. And we tried to regain control. But the best we could ever do was forge a loose alliance between the corporations that ShiroKaz split into. The Legacy was all but dead. Greed killed it. Greed killed everything.

"But then Zenjiro came back, just when things were starting to settle. Only he was different."

"He was Tatsuhiro," I said.

"We didn't recognize him at first. We felt his presence on the grid, trying to access points Sandra and I had shut down years and years ago, places in cyberspace only he would know about. That's when we knew who this dragon-headed sigil really was."

"What was he trying to find?"

"We're not even sure what it was. It was something, some program or patch for the grid, that Zenjiro had been working on, behind his father's back, for ten years. And before he'd disappeared, before the whole mess with his brother and the fire at their castle, he'd insisted it was the ultimate means to ensure the Legacy for a millennium, and beyond. Forever. But when Sandra and I saw it, it was coded like gibberish. Something he said only an immortal could understand.

We didn't know what he meant, if he was writing it for his brother, or father, or who. Or if he was just going crazy."

"Why didn't you just erase it?"

"We couldn't. By the time we remembered it was even there, Tatsuhiro had downloaded half of the file already and we couldn't boot him out of the system. He was signed on from somewhere we could not access."

I knew exactly the place he meant. The underworld. The land of the dead. The lost mainframe beneath Himeji Castle.

"It was all Sandra and I could do to just hang on to the rest of the program," DeLeon went on, "keeping the three of us locked in a kind of stalemate over control of the file. Eventually, without telling me, Sandra made a copy of the portion he didn't have and gave it to Smythe for safe keeping. I believe you know what happened there. Anyway, Sandra was going to hard-reset the entire grid, after years of the three of us getting nowhere, and meanwhile me just wasting away. But if she did that, then the isotope shield would fail, even just for a few minutes, letting enough radiation in to kill half of NeOsaka within three years. So it added another rope into our virtual tug of war. And Tatsuhiro knew all along what the rest of us were up to, and vice versa."

"Why not just let him have it? He says he's going to use it to save the world? So why not just let him save the fucking world?"

"You asked me if I'm opposed to the ShiroKaz master plan? If that master plan is to make a better world, then no, I am not opposed to that. But if it's to bring all power into the hands of one man so he can make all the decisions—maybe pretend to listen from time to time to the little people who can't do what he can do and everyone knows it, maybe even really listen to the one other person who can do what he can do," and DeLeon jabbed a bony finger right at my face, growing increasingly agitated, "*you*—well, yes, I am opposed to that. The world has already seen what happens when one person holds too much power, wealth, and influence. We, the whole of humankind, we've already made that mistake. In fact, we keep making it, every hundred years! These madmen come and go, and they tear off a little piece of the planet and set it on fire. And know this: Tatsuhiro is a madman. The Zenjiro I knew may have been reckless and impudent, but he wasn't crazy. But after what happened to him, he's willing to give up anything to get what he thinks is right. Tatsuhiro, who he is now, is a madman."

"If it comes to that, I'll stop him."

DeLeon had probably not spoken this many words to anyone in over a decade, and the effort was draining everything out of him. His breathing was labored, fogging up the oxygen mask, and sweat was beading on his liver-spotted forehead.

"You don't understand. Zenjiro thinks he's the only one who can save humanity from its own eventual self-destruction. He's found a way to somehow merge his soul with the network, *all* networks. The NeOsaka grid, *Takamagahara*, and somehow across borders. He could even interface with the Russo-Chin. Once he's there, you can't follow him. You won't stop him. I've tried, for years, and I… I can't, I don't know how to fight him anymore. He's taken everything from me. Cayenne. My baby girl." The weight of sudden sorrow flooded into him, stabbing into him like needles. "He's … threatened me, with *her* life. He told me … that she is *his* daughter now." DeLeon's body seemed to fold into itself, like his heart was imploding. He covered his eyes with the back of his hand, bit into his own paper-thin lips to help hold in the tears.

Ben was by his side, his weak arm now outside of the metal exoframe, wrapped around the old man's shoulders, comforting him. I looked at the two of them, and I understood. The Cluster wasn't just some rogue operators on the grid, undermining corporate interest and stashing secrets.

They were exactly what their symbol stood for. *Family.* From the woman outside the blast doors holding her child, to the decrepit leader whose daughter had been held hostage, to the stuttering kid with the legs that didn't work, who the rest of the world wrote off as invalid. They were there for each other.

I understood that DeLeon didn't have long to live. He might've held on this long just to meet the new White Shadow. He needed someone, some brainiac like himself, to take over once he was gone. Someone like Ben Roy Doon. It wasn't so hard for me to imagine Ben reconfiguring the fiber-optic cables so that they worked with his implanted systems. Or him blowing the dust off the old tech down here and firing it up, re-coding everything, and getting to work making the world a better place. And maybe, instead of reporting in to some ghost castle, I could plant my feet down here. I could take orders from my oldest friend about how to save the world.

I had asked DeLeon how the Cluster was going to help. The answer was Ben. And the answer was me.

"I'm dying," DeLeon said, stating the obvious. "If I am no longer here—if there is *no one* here—to stop Zenjiro from gaining access, then there will be no system on Earth he cannot invade and control. He will consolidate humanity's entire way of life upon a single grid. No languages, no differences. No more war, no more conflict. Just an iron, unbending rule, slaved to one man's unshakable vision of what is good. Zenjiro's Legacy, all his own. And for a time, perhaps things will *feel* better. But mankind continues to forget the morals of its own history, that putting faith in one powerful man will only begin the cycle again. Only this time, once it is done, once Zenjiro's spirit has merged with the machine for good, there will be no one left who can make him leave. No way to overthrow him and start again. Unless..."

DeLeon's tired eyes wandered down to the white katana. I understood the implication.

Unless they're ghosts, just like him. Like the White Shadow.

"Unless they're Shiromatsu," Luther DeLeon whispered. "*Like you.*"

The old man's revelation hit me in the chest, pulling all the air out of my lungs. But the feeling of shock didn't last. I knew better, after all. Instead of the bewildered gasp he might've expected, all he got from me was a disdainful scoff.

"Sorry," I said, "but Triangle told me straight up that Yasuro's not my..."

And then I found the next breath would simply not come. My body froze in place.

"That *he's* not my..."

I felt the whole world receding behind, below, and before me, the truth sending me into the black hole, the knowledge from which there was no return.

"She was right," DeLeon said softly. "You are not Yasuro's daughter. But you *are* Shiromatsu. And your name is *Shiyo.*"

Shiyo, I thought, picturing the *kanji.*

Violet.

Of course.

"And your father—"

DeLeon's eyes rolled backward, exposing their bloodshot undersides. His body seized, went stiff, his fingers contorted and locked. His jaws snapped shut and dragged themselves sideways, grinding his teeth. There was a choking-clicking from the back of his throat.

"What the f-fuck?" Ben caught him as he pitched backward, but without being in the exoframe, his arms were too weak to hold DeLeon up. The old man crumpled to the floor beside his chair, pulling Ben down along with him.

"Shin!" Ben was calling my name, squirming his body around, sliding his hands and arms back into the frame. "What the fuck's hap-p-penning?"

I blinked, coming out of my trance. I ripped my empty gaze away from the grimy patch of concrete wall I'd been staring at.

"Shin!"

I let go of the sword, and it vanished in a pocket of ethereal purple smoke. I fell onto my knees, rolled DeLeon over onto his side as the spit started frothing from his clamped jaws, doing what I could to ease the seizure. But I knew from experience it wasn't a seizure, not really. I'd seen this before.

I was at DeLeon's side, my hands wrapped around the cables in his skull, pulling. This one didn't give like Triangle's had.

Ben's steel-reinforced grip closed around my wrists and pulled me away. "You'll k-kill him," Ben shouted at me, holding my arms up.

"He is already dead."

The voice came from Zercos, but it wasn't Zercos's voice.

Together, we looked down at the frail body, the blood seeping from its eye sockets, the broken jaw, the rigor mortis, and we knew it was true. Although I could've seen it if I'd wanted to, I felt the old man's spirit leave his body, quickly retreating from the room in a panic, left to wander the unseen realm until guided to rest by the memory ritual of his loved ones.

He was gone.

Together, Ben and I backed away from Luther DeLeon. Together, we looked at the vertical rig that held the cyborg's frame.

TWENTY-NINE

THERE WAS A WAR OF COLORS RAGING WITHIN EVERY seam of the supreme tinman's matte black armored body. The blue-green energies of the double dragons raced along the lines of Zercos's faceplate, around his chest and abdomen, up and down the pistons pumping at his shoulders, crackling like electricity at the tips of his devil horns. And they were chased by the deep purple, caught, and eradicated. It was a spiritual virus, seeking and destroying the last remaining shreds of immunity the cyborg had left.

It all made sense now. It was the burst of purple as I emerged at the graveyard, the lone figure standing before the *haka* stone. It was Zercos's reticence as we wended our way through the drainage tunnels, his failure to override the basic security protocols the Cluster entrusted him with. Ben may have doused SUIT with the x-ray vest, but it hadn't mattered. It made sense, and it was too late. If I'd been the hapless Trojan Horse for Triangle, Zercos had been that for the Cluster. But this time, the virus hadn't ridden in on SUIT. It wasn't anything that needed to be designed and iterated and coded. This was a spiritual virus, exactly what DeLeon had just told me.

This was Tatsuhiro. Or rather, Zenjiro Shiromatsu.

My father.

The purple lights sped faster and faster across the cybernetic body, running down the final traces of Zercos's cyan-colored spirit, snuffing them out once and for all. Its new master's ethereal smoke rose from its head and limbs, from the machinery on his rig. And then the whole thing clamped around it simply *shifted* before our very eyes—its bulk twisting, its bright control panels and data readouts winking out, all of it fading into the unseen realm of *Yomi*—leaving the fully possessed cyborg-puppet body floating above the floor.

"My shadow," it said, stepping forth gently on its sharp, triple-jointed feet. "Once again, *yoku dekimasu.* You have done very well."

I watched in horror as Zenjiro Shiromatsu was reborn in the physical world, the full realization of what he could do washing over me like a cold sweat. From the platform of Zercos's state-of-the-art body, he could hack into and enslave local networks, just like SUIT, overriding and dominating them like a virus. And if that capability wasn't frightening enough, Zenjiro could phase in and out of the spirit realm, dragging whatever and whoever he wanted with him.

Was I supposed to bow? Was I supposed to stay on my knees?

My shadow?

I felt the weight of DeLeon's body in my hands. He was so light, shriveled by cancer to little more than a skeleton. The years of his life that he should have spent with his daughter, with his wife, smiling as he had been in Cayenne's photograph, he spent instead standing in cyberspace, staring down a demon, holding back a tsunami of spiritual energy. Shielding the world from what he saw coming.

He called me his fucking shadow?

I eased the withered, rag-shrouded corpse of Luther DeLeon to the damp concrete floor. Beside me, Ben was fixated on the demon that had taken possession of Zercos. Gently, I took Ben's hand in mine. This brought his eyes around to mine. I squeezed his hand and felt the panic in him subside. Together, we closed the old man's eyes for the last time.

His shadow. Not his daughter.

Watching us, Zenjiro Shiromatsu had paced silently forward and now stood over Ben and me.

I wondered if his brother was here, somewhere. If the White Shadow knew or cared about what had just happened. With my spirit, I quietly reached into *Yomi*, feeling in the darkness for his presence. Without looking up, keeping my voice as even and steady as I could, I asked, "Did you know? Who I really was? My real name…"

"*Hnn,*" was all the crackling voice box behind the faceplate said.

"How long,?" I said, still reaching, still feeling my way through the void.

Please, I whispered into the abyss. *Please come.*

"How long did you know I was yours?"

Body. And blade. Please.

"I…" Zenjiro's simulated voice faltered. "I would have told you. Shiyo. My daughter."

"But you needed me to be your puppet."

"*Ie,*" he said. "*Chigaimasu.*" *You're wrong.*

"Needed me to go where you couldn't," I said, my eyes still on DeLeon's corpse, tracing the blood vessels on his closed eyelids, focusing on anything they could while the other half of my consciousness felt blindly for the presence of the samurai.

"To be your assassin," I said.

And then, a cold, steel hand clamped down on my wrist, in two worlds at once. I looked at the tips of Zenjiro's razor-sharp claws pressing the fabric of my suit, and at the same time I felt the empty gauntlet of the hulking purple samurai stopping me in the underworld.

"Shiyo-kun," he said. *"Gomenasai."*

His voice quaked in my ears, and in my very soul. But I ignored it. I held onto the anger.

Yasuro! I screamed the White Shadow's name into the abyss. *You won't help? Then fuck you!*

The samurai may have fled, but he'd left his katana behind.

My legs flexed powerfully, thrusting all my weight upward, the white blade materializing in my hand, already unsheathed, slicing like a sunrise, severing the matte black arm at the elbow, its claws tightening reflexively, digging bloodily into my wrist. At the apex of my leap, I spun my hips and shot my heel into the center of Zenjiro's cyborg-puppet's chest, howling at the top of my lungs, expelling all my rage. A shockwave of purple energy erupted from the point of impact, washing over every inch of the room, blowing out the lights in bursts of white sparks and glass, surging and blazing through the complex circuitry of the mainframe. My kick sent the cyborg reeling, toppling him head over heels so that his back slammed against the concrete wall, the force of it pressing him into it, a spiderweb of cracks spiraling out from the epicenter just as I was coming back down.

In the dim glow of the spirit fires I'd lit, I could see the one-armed cyborg held in place by the crater. Before I could say, or do, or even think anything, waves of purple-tinged darkness flooded out from his frame, and I matched it with waves of my own. They crashed together and washed over every surface in the pump room, twisting and warping every shape, phasing it all into the underworld, whether it wanted to go or not. Everything, and everyone.

"Shin!" a voice cried to me from the floor behind me, spinning me around. I caught a final glimpse of Ben—pushed aside by the shockwave I'd released, still strapped inside his matte-black steel exoframe, struggling to rise—just as the darkness took him. He screamed. His eyes bulged in their sockets as the nightmare of what he was seeing spiked into his psyche. He called my name again and again.

"Ben!" I called back, running, sprinting after him, after the space on the floor where he crumpled, which was receding farther and farther back into a never-ending unreality. "BEN!"

I watched in horror as my oldest friend's spirit emerged from his crumpling physical body, blinking, wild-eyed, twisted out of shape. It was scared beyond belief. Gripped by a kind of cosmic fear no mortal creature could ever imagine.

I fell to my knees, the white katana slipping from my grasp and clattering upon the floor. I crossed my arms over my chest and held on, my tears streaming, the grief strangling me.

And then the entire landscape rushed away to my right, caught in the event horizon, torn away at light speed by the swirling, newborn black hole behind me. In the stillness, only I remained, staring vacantly at the gleaming white of the katana's blade before me, so that I would not see the empty exoframe, and the shriveled corpse of the best friend I ever had beside it.

"Shiyo," Zenjiro said. He spun the whole world back around until I faced him, the two of us disappearing from physical space as we went. It was just him and me now, the sole occupants of an empty, lightless black hell deep in the underworld. He was dressed in the same three-piece, four-buttoned black suit that he'd worn when I'd first met him in the graveyard, only it was no longer rumpled and tattered. And he was no longer blind. He was whole, both muscled arms filling the sleeves of his suit. He was young.

Handsome. He was an exact copy of the shadow man in the white emptiness in every aspect but the cascading straight hair. Zenjiro's was closely cut and combed over.

"My daughter. Shiyo. There is so much I must confess. Much you already know. Much I must still tell you."

I stayed silent, tried to empty my thoughts. Breathed in, exhaled. Breathed in. Thought of nothing. If there was one thing I knew about this place, the same sort of devoid personal pocket of *Yomi* that his twin brother occupied, then Zenjiro could read my mind here. I could hide nothing from him. I could only listen.

"I had to test you. Not only test for the power in your bloodline, which has manifested remarkably. But test your *resolve*. In that, I have not been disappointed. You are strong, Shiyo." I heard him let out a deep, satisfied breath. I heard the shape of a smile in it. "*Muteki*. So very strong. But you must understand."

I felt the black shadow's firm hand cup my chin and draw my face up toward his own. Against my own will, my eyes opened, but I focused on the emptiness to our side. All the same, I felt the glowing purple light behind his eyes penetrate my mind. Even as I tried to reset my thoughts, tried to simply breathe in and exhale and do it again, breath by breath, I felt the tears welling in my eyes, running down my cheeks. I shuddered and twisted my face away as he spoke.

"I could not entrust this final task to you. Your closeness with the crippled boy, and despite his apparent betrayal, his defection to our enemies. I could not ask you to end Luther DeLeon alone, not while Ben Roy Doon would stand in your way. But it is over now, Shiyo."

"You killed him," I said, my voice a hoarse whisper.

"His body… *Hnn*. It is gone. Ben Roy Doon will never inhabit the living world again. But his spirit lives on." Zenjiro lowered himself in a squat beside me, his hands clasped before him, a posture of patient understanding. The figure of a father who has seen his child fall. Who has come to encourage them back onto their feet. Again, I heard the satisfied smile in his voice. "We can find him together. Once our work is done. And, together, guide him to eternal rest."

Breathe in, breathe out. My fingers crawled by my side, a mind all their own.

I faced him. The glow had faded from his eyes, leaving a pair of violet irises reflecting my own. It was like seeing myself in a mirror, my father. I smiled back at him. I even choked on a laugh because it was so hard to try and not think of the words suddenly gushing from my mind: *I'll fucking kill you, you goddamn motherfucker, for Ben! I'll kill you! For Ben!*

I slashed up and forward again, bringing the white blade around in a whirling arc meant to cleanly lop the black shadow's head off his shoulders, all my rage sending it, all my weight following it, nearly toppling me over, my knees skidding and pivoting over the empty void below me. The katana passed straight through his image like it'd been nothing more than smoke, and sure enough, as I whirled about off balance and fell on my face, Zenjiro's frowning, disappointed visage and the rest of him dispersed into thin air.

I screamed at the top of my lungs, which wasn't much, my throat already raw. "Come back here! Let's end it!"

Yet even as I rose to my feet and spun about to face down the nothingness on all sides, both my hands gripping the white sword, pointing it out before me, the world began to regain its form and its color. The utter black lightened to a deep midnight, then an indigo twilight. The purple fires I'd set flickered into view along the floor and over the antiquated equipment of the pump room. One light fixture had survived, casting a dull brightness in a far corner. Otherwise, the place glowed with the sputtering and sparking hulk of the gutted mainframe. The double doors had been blasted off their hinges, a vortex of roiling black smoke being sucked through the doorway. The real-world fires still burned. They had already consumed Luther DeLeon's and Ben Roy Doon's physical bodies. I clenched my jaw, letting my sword hand fall slack by my side. I unbuckled the x-ray vest that hadn't prevented any of this and let it drop as I stared through welling tears at the piles of ash they'd become.

The clattering of pebbles and rocks rose over the snapping of the flames and melting electronics. Then there was the *clink clink* as the cybernetic body that had once housed the spirit of Vladislav Zercos set its clawed feet down against the concrete. The purple-limned demon had taken possession of it again.

"I will end this now," the voice box inside it said, a barely recognizable garble of noise. My blow had severely damaged not just the systems in its head. Some sort of battery acid leaked from the stump of its severed arm. It approached the doors with a limp. The impact with the wall had been strong enough to noticeably crack off the last few centimeters of the thing's matte-black katana on its back, which it reached back and drew now with its last remaining hand.

It paused just in front of the moving wall of smoke, turned, and raised its weapon toward me. "I do not intend to kill these people. But I will do what I must if they interfere any further with the Legacy. I will deliver a single warning. Now. With you by my side. Then we will return to the tower, where we have much yet to discuss. *Wakarimasu ka?*"

I held the white katana loosely. I glanced one final time at the blackened spot where my best friend had fallen, the empty exoframe twisted by the heat of the fire. Then I nodded at the broken cyborg. At Zenjiro.

He lowered his weapon. "*Yokatta.*"

Beyond the underside of the roiling plume of smoke, I could see the underground city lights outside the doorway had gone out and were only now winking back to life. Flashlight beams were sweeping the area, fanning out in a perimeter before the doors, either forming up to breach, or waiting for something to come out. The Cluster was mobilizing.

Zenjiro's puppet went first, emerging from the black wall of smoke and limping several steps down, stopping in the crossfire of bright white beams. I came after, my sleeve pressed against my nose and mouth as I held my breath. At first, I ignored the Cluster's sweeping flashlights, their murmuring, worried clamor of voices, and simply sat down heavily on the concrete steps just behind the cyborg. That's when I saw that the tinman sentries were not pointing their weapons at us. While we'd been in the pump room, blowing their mainframe and their leader to hell, Zenjiro's invasion of their network had gotten straight to work on the Cluster community's security, enslaving all of the drones to his will, recalling some of them from their high perches along the walkways near the ceiling, bringing them into squads to secure the lift between the pillars as well as the citadel we had just exited. The people had flooded the streets, wanting to rush in and see what had happened, wanting to save Luther and Ben from the fires that no doubt burned behind all that rushing smoke. Only the tinmen held them back, so then they'd went and got guns. And now what was playing out was a kind of standoff.

"Silence."

The single word thundered from the underground sky, echoed around the concrete walled city. It was Tatsuhiro's voice. Zenjiro Shiromatsu's voice, ringing in living space for the first time in decades. The spotlights that illuminated the rainbow-colored *kanji* for Family above and behind us became holo-light projectors that spun and whirred maddeningly, sketching the form of the horned dragon's head, his grid sigil, enormous, appearing before the blackness of the rising smoke that obscured the graffiti.

The command bought him exactly what he'd wanted. A hush swept over everyone all at once. As one, they looked up to the ghostly image of the dragon as it spoke slowly, deliberately.

"I will be brief. Luther DeLeon is no more. The Cluster is no more. His work, your work, to try and contain my efforts to build a better world has failed. But I will not punish. I invite you, happily, back into the fold. Join the new world that has been promised. You have two hours to leave these tunnels, your old world, and your old lives with the Cluster behind. Leave everything behind. Or else you will drown in the cleansing waters of my wrath. That is all."

The outline of the holographic horned dragon shifted, became a projection of numbers.

02:00:00.

And then it began to tick away, second by second.

And the silence hung over the entire underground. And no one moved a muscle. Perhaps it was the shock of their suddenly shifting situation settling in and simply needing to run its course. Perhaps it was the natural instinct of a free people to defy an unwelcome tyrant firing up in their hearts. Perhaps it was the suspicion that they were being lied to, the curiosity forming in their minds as to what was really beyond those pump room doors. Whatever it was, it was a waste of their fucking time, what little they had left, to save their own lives.

I rose to my feet, calling out as loud as my scream-scarred throat could. "It's all true! You all have to go! Now!"

Near the front of the crowd, just five meters from the nearest overridden tinman's sweeping gun barrel, I spotted the young, strong, beautiful mother, still holding her little girl at her hip, the same *you don't belong here* look on her face. I should've listened the first time.

"We know who you are," she said, setting her toddler down. I couldn't see past the sea of swarming bodies, but

I somehow knew the girl was pulling on her skirt, scared, wanting to stay close and be held. But the woman kept her eyes on me, even as the enslaved cyborg sentries drew down on her.

"Please," I begged her, I begged everyone. "Just go."

"You're the White Shadow," she said, unflinching. "DeLeon told us you'd help us. He said you would be the only one who could."

"I'm fucking trying to, lady!"

Even the husk that used to be Zercos gave me a sidelong glance at that.

"You have to go, and you have to do it now. All of you," I said, pointing with the white katana to the far end of the immense reservoir, "walk out those blast doors in a straight line and don't stop 'til you get above ground. Don't panic. If you go now, you can all—"

"We're not going anywhere," another voice called out from the other side of the crowd. That sent up a murmur of other voices that rippled outward. I saw motion from different spots all over the crowds, the slow movements of rioters arming up. It was the crack in the dam.

"No!" I cried out.

"This is our home!" Another voice.

"You're going to all fucking die down here!" I shouted.

"Then we'll die!"

"So will you, mega-corp whore!"

I looked back at the young mother. She'd finally turned to regard her little girl, to hush her, and say everything would be all right.

Then the shots rang out, a sudden, ear-splitting barrage of thunder as the wall-mounted turrets fired a single volley into their carefully tracked targets. A big, bearded bear of a man, his chest exploding, and the slender young woman behind him, were taken by the same high-caliber polycarbonate bullet. Another bullet shredded through the body armor of a tall man who'd been caught raising his rifle. And more among them, their flesh and bones popping and crumpling to the ground.

The strong, beautiful woman among them.

Her daughter screamed. More and more joined her, the noise projecting itself to the far walls, echoing around the city chamber, rising high enough to drown out the dying thunder of the guns, all before I could scream again with them, "No!"

And there was more movement now than there had been before. The dam holding the Cluster at bay ruptured entirely, disintegrated, and more people went for their weapons, and more blasting shots thundered from the ceiling, and the tinmen came alive, squeezing their triggers, spitting bursts of rounds into the crowd, indiscriminately, chewing through men, women, and children.

"Stop this!" I grabbed Zercos's frame by the shoulder and spun it around with all my strength, screaming again in its face. "Stop killing them!"

"They chose," it said back to me, although I could barely hear it amid all the rolling thunder.

"We can't fucking die! But they can!" As if to help make my point, one Cluster gunman had come around the line of sentries to flank me and opened fire, hitting me and Zercos with dozens of rounds that passed through me like I was smoke and *tinked* uselessly against the cyborg's armored body. The gunman was felled from a turret blast a second later.

"And so they will die," Zenjiro pronounced through the sputtering voice box in the broken cyborg's head.

There was no time left to think. Before I realized what I'd done, the white katana was drawn, cutting low across the supreme tinman's knees, and I was spinning-hopping with its momentum, tucking my body at the waist and coming around full circle, bringing the razor-sharp blade across his throat, and landing back on my feet, the entire, blinding-ly-fast motion taking no longer than two seconds. With my other hand I pushed against his chest, and the cyborg that once was Zercos came apart like a stack of bricks, his tri-ple-jointed legs falling out from under him, and his head rolling forward. Severed circuitry sparked, and my entire front was showered with the acrid battery acid the machine substituted for blood.

The cyan-colored spirit supernova erupted from the pieces of him, rolling over every living and non-living thing, knocking everyone present—including me—onto their asses. And for a moment, the gunfire and screams ceased. The dying micro-star hovering over Zercos's remains became a widening portal. The blue dragon that I'd first seen in the ShiroKaz Tower vault and last seen outside the ruin of Himeji-Jo shot forth suddenly like a viper made of lightning. Its fangs were curved blades, thrashing and slicing a line of Cluster-hacked-and-rehacked tinman sentries, chewing and spitting them into heaps of scrap and body parts. This was the ethereal monster the White Shadow had sent me to seek and destroy. The lost memory, the reason Yasuro desired Zercos's true death without remembering why.

Well, the shadow man's vengeance would have to wait. It's not like he'd answered when I called for help. And Zercos's blue dragon appeared to be helping me now.

Fuck Yasuro, I thought, rolling over and pushing myself up, already sprinting toward the side of the citadel stairs opposite the dragon, flicking the white blade sideways and dragging it through the air, chopping two tinmen from hip to shoulder as I ran. Shots rained down on me from above, the powerful wall-mounted cannons pulverizing the con-crete floor beneath me into gravel and dust. My very real fleshy feet dipped painfully in a crater they made just in front of me, and I spilled forward onto my face.

The place was a blender of chaos, panic, pandemonium. At this point, the Cluster fighters didn't know what to believe or who was their enemy. Their own sentries and turrets turning on them, the White Shadow suspected of assassinating their leader now turning on those sentries, those sentries turning again on her, a fucking inexplicable ghostly blue dragon flying straight out of myth and legend to gnaw on the sentries, and all the while, screams and the sustained roar of gunfire, loud enough to make your ears bleed. Smoke, shell casings, blood spattered everywhere.

I gripped the katana tightly as the Cluster's automated security turned everything it had on me, enough to blast a hole in the floor of the reservoir two meters deep, probably almost cracking it to the bedrock. Although I felt nothing that could truly harm me, slipping as I was between living and spirit realms with the katana as my anchor, the sheer weight and pressure of the ordinance leveled against me was enough to pin me down. Even though I couldn't see past all the dust and smoke filling the hole they tried to bury me in, I wanted to believe that the crowd was smart enough to pull back, to run the fuck away, get to the blast doors or the lift or anywhere else on Earth as fast as they could. If staying put and feeling the rain of bullets could buy them time, then I would gladly stay put.

Of course, all it really bought was about fifteen seconds. Then it was all over. I shifted fully back to the real world and choked on the particulate air. I was completely deaf; my ears felt like they were packed with cotton. I flipped over and stood up from my little crater, my hands scrabbling up the sharp edges of the shattered rock. I grabbed the edge of my suit jacket and shook the dust out, patted my shoulders down, coughed a little. I couldn't hear shit, couldn't really see shit, but I caught glimpses of the security forces ringed around me, the piles of corpses littered around the space, the backs of fleeing survivors as they disappeared in the streets and buildings of their makeshift city, and farther off, the lift, fully loaded with a mass of people, almost the whole way up. So they would survive after all.

Of the fifty or so tinmen that had amassed in the area, only about twenty remained. Most of them held the lower part of the reservoir leading up to the stairs. A small handful of them remained at the top to either side of me. Half of their sub-machine guns were pointed at yours truly, the other half were up, following the flight path of the blue dragon that had stopped gnawing on them and now drifted lazily over our heads, its long tubular body coming in and out of the column of smoke still spilling out of the pump room doors. I held out the katana, then brought it down swiftly to my side, flicking all of the blood and viscera to the floor. And so the dragon and I simply waited there, all their guns trained on us, ready to react to their next move, just trying to buy the Cluster's survivors some more time.

A sudden, unexpected wind cleared all the dust and smoke from the air, pushing it out over the town. I turned about to face the four enormous drainage pipes to the sides of the pump room doors just behind me, the source of the rushing air.

The cleansing waters of my wrath.

So he'd done it after all. The countdown timer was still running, only now it seemed to wind the seconds away at a hundred-time speed, dropping from 01:55:13 to 01:47:53 in the span of five seconds.

Seeing they couldn't win, the citizens of the Cluster had stopped fighting. They'd turned and run away from the massacre. They'd done what they were told in the end.

But Zenjiro would drown them, anyway. Without Triangle and DeLeon to keep him out, his spirit had fully uploaded itself into the Cluster's hidden networks, reconnected them to the greater NeOsaka grid, undone years and years of their work within minutes. He'd found the records they'd erased of this place, rewritten the programs they'd coded to ensure the pumps would always divert water away, all because he'd seen them as a threat.

If Ben was here, my man in the chair, maybe he could patch things, rewrite the code. Maybe he could've done something I could never do, despite all my power. But he wasn't here anymore. He'd never again stutter my name or press a key on a keyboard or push up his glasses or flip through pages of his stupid fucking crazy-person's note-book. It was just me now. I had to do something.

I ripped my eyes away from the countdown, swallowed down the rising dread in my throat, and whirled about to face the city in the wide open underground reservoir, fran-tically searching for any idea, anything that stood out as a way to stop the oncoming deluge. The tinmen had lowered their weapons, appeared to be powering down as Zenjiro's will released them from his service.

01:23:04

What the fuck can I do?!

I clutched the katana in both hands, my grip so tight my muscles screamed and quaked. I tried to squeeze some explosive power, to wrench the rage-red energy of the White Shadow up from the deepest, emptiest pit of hell. Maybe I could draw it out and send it like a laser against the four pipes, like I'd seen him do the night before, splitting the earth in the Himeji Castle courtyard. I could collapse the pipes, the debris holding the water back like a dam, at least a little bit, maybe.

01:02:17

Nothing. There was nothing. I screamed in fury. I flung the fucking useless white katana at the nearest pipe, where it clattered and scratched across the concrete.

00:59:43

I had so much power. So much fucking power. I was understanding more and more of it every day. I was unbreakable. I was lightning. I was fire. I was the fucking dragon. I was a god. I could go anywhere. I could do anything.

00:54:59

But I couldn't do this. I couldn't stop the very real-world waters of wrath from crushing this place. The dread enveloped me whole, spreading through my veins like poison. I bent over and retched, bile rising and spilling out. I fell. On my hands and knees, I sobbed quietly.

00:46:22

I rocked back, defeated. I looked out one last time at the massacred piles of people. I saw the strong, beautiful woman, dead, her eyes open, looking back at me. I did not see her daughter nearby. Another orphan, another Shinjiro Asai, out there in the world now. And I couldn't save her either.

00:40:24

My eyes drooped, my gaze coming closer now, to the gruesome scene on top of the stairs, to the bodies I myself had carved to bits. To the stack my magic fucking katana had made of the prototype tinman supreme, Vladislav Zercos, his head, his legs, his torso. The cyan lights had all gone out.

00:36:44

Wait.

My thoughts raced.

What was it Zercos told me? Zenjiro had *obliterated* his own brother. Zenjiro, who was no swordsman. Their dueling spirits had met on the battlefield, the courtyard of Himeji, and they'd torn the place to ruin. And Zercos and I, in the courtyard, days ago, the energy from our fight had toppled gravestones. And then, just moments ago, we'd set DeLeon's mainframe and his entire concrete-encased room on fire.

00:33:07

Hope was the dawn within me, brightening and thrumming in my bloodstream, lifting me off the floor. I spun about to the back wall of the underground city, felt the rush of wind on my face, stronger now. I could barely stand against it, but I did. I peeled back my suit sleeves, exposing the two scratchy halves of the torii tattoo on my forearms. With my spirit, I reached upward, calling upon the blue dragon, the half of Zercos's spirit that still remained, to show me, *remind me*, of the obliteration. It had been the moment Zenjiro blasted Yasuro apart so utterly, that his spirit had been trapped in the sword. If I could find some way…

00:18:11

The blue dragon spirit heard me, felt my need. Zercos and I had never truly been enemies. I forgave him for hurting me, and he forgave me. The dragon's body spiraled downward, rearing itself up just behind my shoulders, coiling itself like a snake. I brought the torii together and felt the old familiar rush of cold as I ripped the veil open, the fabric between realms splitting. But I was stronger now. The cold didn't faze me one fucking bit.

00:09:51

I didn't know if this would work, but the time for better ideas had passed us by. I willed the dragon's spirit to strike, hurling itself forth like a torpedo, and it obeyed. Its ghostly form submerged in the concrete wall.

Then came the boom.

The blooming explosion of purple and blue spiritual energy cracked deep into the concrete. The entire face of the wall split dozens of meters inside itself, and the weight of it crashed down and back like the last shelf of glacial ice falling into the ocean decades ago. There was a deep rumbling within all that smashed concrete as it met with the oncoming water. Dust and vapor sprayed from the seams, skidding me backward on my heels, raining droplets of mud and stone all over the underground city.

00:00:00

The final second passed. The pipes may have blocked most of the water, but the pressure pushed everything through, anyway. To my left and right, the four drainage pipes discharged geysers of brown-black mud laced with boulders.

Maybe it didn't work?!

I spun about and watched the flow of debris slam against the inert forms of tinmen. It crawled over the field of corpses, burying them, and rushed onward toward the city.

But the slurry wasn't fast enough, wasn't nearly as destructive as walls of water would have been.

Despite all the horror, all the dread, I sighed. I even smiled.

Behind me, the weight and pressure groaned within the concrete, but the wall held together. The flow slowed visibly. It was enough. It wouldn't prevent this place from drowning, but I had bought the Cluster more than enough time.

INTERLUDE: A FINAL ENCOUNTER

The samurai's knees press against the wood of the boardwalk running around the perimeter of the courtyard garden. The sun is high. All is bright and lush and beautiful. His eyes trace the flow of water in the stream, the lazy curves of the green stalks overhanging it, the bees collecting pollen from the flowering buds. He tries to count the grains of sand along the shoreline. This has been his wife's favorite space within his family's ancestral home. Itself, at the center of everything, yet often overlooked, neglected. Tending to its needs, revitalizing it to its once former glory, has been her...

It had... *It* had *been her...*

The samurai's upper lip twitches visibly, threatening to pull itself back into an ugly, infuriated snarl that would mar his handsome, composed visage. The muscles in his neck tighten, his head quakes, the tears well in his eyes. His mind fights itself, the rage, the sadness. The shame. The righteousness. He struggles to find the words to complete the thought, to describe what this place meant to Mizuko.

Her diversion? Her obsession? Her love?

Her love.

The veins in his forehead protrude, the blood rushes and pulses hotter. His face reddens. His teeth grind. His sticky, red hands, at first pressed softly, deliberately, upon his lap, now ball into fists. His lips split wide. He loses his mind, his sense of self. He forgets how to breathe until at last the samurai lets out a shriek of torment, spittle frothing and spraying from his mouth.

The samurai expels all the breath in his body, folding over at the waist. His hands shoot forth to catch his fall lest he should plummet over the side of the walkway into the sand. There, just centimeters in front of him, his hands brush against his katana, the sleek, night-black sheath, the dark cord of the tsuka *handle. All black, except for the drop of red, vibrant, like a small ruby. His long hair falls about his face like a curtain, and when he heaves in breath again at last— his lungs desperate, unable to stay empty and kill him—he smells the sour scent of blood on the black strands again. It is in his hair, spattered over his pure white clothing, staining his sleeves up to the elbows. Blood everywhere. So much blood.*

Her blood. Her body. The horror inside it.

"Yasuro!"

Of course. It has to be this exact moment—when the samurai has to be doubled over, caught in a position of weakness—that his greatest enemy arrives. He has been here, waiting for the inevitability of the visit, trying and failing for hours to remaster himself, to push the anguish of what he has done from his consciousness.

His greatest enemy. His shadow.

Still on his knees, still doubled over, the samurai smiles to himself, even laughs at the cruel joke of fate.

"Yasuro!"

The voice calls again, closer now. Two sets of footsteps on the boards approaching. Two assailants. Both in jet-black suits. One to his left, the other—the voice—to his right.

"What have you done?!"

The samurai rises and draws and strikes just as the enemy comes within range, the black blade singing forth masterfully, biting viciously, claiming his enemy's arm, just above the elbow. The arc leaves a trail of raging red smoke in the air, tinged with the blood of guilt that will never wash away. The limb thuds at his feet, a pure white katana, sheathed, still locked in its grip.

His enemy stumbles backward, debilitated momentarily before even realizing it, but the samurai does not wait for him to realize anything. He whirls around to meet the next assailant, his black blade slashing, clashing with a wall of tempered steel, a parry that brings the two of their weapons up around and back down. He steps backward as he has a thousand times during their endless bouts of training, knowing that this new assailant knows the pattern, bringing the ball of his foot just centimeters short of where it has always landed before, and so dodging the follow up attack by just as much distance.

The samurai's counterattack is lethal.

Or it should be, but he stays his hand at the last possible moment. He pushes, and the blade sinks into flesh, splitting the clavicle bone, then he pulls, sparing the man's life, raising the blade up and out with precision. The samurai draws his chest downward, hardens his diaphragm, bucks forward with his shoulder, slams against the abdomen of his assailant, sending him reeling, feet lifting from the ground.

It is all over in seconds.

Vladislav falls flat on his back, pushing out what little air remains from his lungs. The young man's sword falls from his grip as his hand goes instinctively to his shoulder, clamping over the pain and the gushing blood. He will live, if he stays down.

The other staggers back, his hand clutching the stump of his arm, trying futilely to staunch the flow of blood. Amazingly, he keeps his feet under him. He even speaks again, his voice low this time, perhaps from the shock of blood loss, or the horror of amputation, or the realization that one's true death is inevitable.

"Yasuro... Brother..."

The other falls back onto one knee as the samurai approaches. He falls against the shoji wall of the castle's courtyard house, his bloody side smearing the perfection with a trail of red, longer and longer as he backs away, sniveling.

"Yasuro..."

The samurai says nothing. He moves forward slowly, staring into the mirror reflection of himself. The man he could become. The man he is. The same face. The same eyes. The one dressed head to toe in black. His greatest enemy. His shadow. His twin, Zenjiro.

He steps over the other's weapon, pure white, itself the twin—and yet also the antithesis—of the jet-black katana he carries now. He holds it low, dripping the blood of the three victims it has tasted today. The red drops upon the sheathed white katana. Red smoke rises from wherever the blood touches.

Zenjiro collapses at last. From the floor, he whispers, "You killed her." His eyes flutter. His complexion pales. He is dying. Liters of his blood mark his path along the walkway, dripping between the planks. But the samurai will not let his greatest enemy simply die. No. With both hands, he drives his black blade through the floor and leaves it wobbling behind him. He straddles his twin and wraps those hands around his neck, and he squeezes. His whole body shudders. From within the cascade of his black hair, he looks out, wild-eyed, willing his brother to wake up just long enough so he can be aware of the death that comes for him.

The samurai clenches his teeth so hard, trying to bite back the words that rise from his very soul, but he cannot hold them in.

"And you... you killed our father." He squeezes tighter.

There is a clicking in his brother's throat as the airways are cut off, but his eyes roll forward, fixate on the samurai choking him.

Good. It is just enough then. The samurai leans closer, with all his strength he squeezes, lifts his brother's face so they can meet eye to eye.

"You killed us," he whispers.

A sudden, sharp pain lances across the back of his thighs. A sudden weakness spreads down his legs, up his groin. The samurai cannot help but lose focus, let go, roll aside and fall into the green foliage of the garden. He has not felt pain—physical, tangible, true pain—in years. Decades. The iron of his will melts momentarily and he cries out like a woman.

The samurai sees his student above him on the walkway, covered in his own blood. The fingers of one hand pinch closed the flesh on his shoulder, the other holding the white katana free, stained red. He has crawled his way here. The blue-green fire flickers about his body, animating his spirit, hardening his will.

When will the betrayals end? When will they ever end?

The student proves he has learned at last the final lesson. There is no hesitation. No sentimentality. No remorse. Vladislav plunges downward, blade first, aiming precisely at his master's heart. It sinks instead into his master's liver, as the samurai pushes his prone body up with his wounded legs at the last possible moment. The white blade passes through cleanly, from flesh, to bone, to the soil under the master's back. It sinks hilt-deep under the weight of the student, the two of them face to face.

This, then, is the final betrayal. *The master will allow no more.*

The blood Yasuro spits in Vladislav's eyes is black. He runs his fingers through the younger man's hair, grips, and pulls the two of them closer. His fangs sink deep into Vladislav's neck, puncturing the jugular vein. Hot liquid gushes into his mouth, which he tears sideways, opening the wound farther. Vladislav goes limp before he can even think to scream.

Yasuro will never again be the master of himself. He is conquered for all time by the smoldering, red rage that has slept inside his soul. The fire in him swells. From the other side of the veil, the monster answers his call, envelops him. It fills him, rises from his body like an aura. It bends to his will. Yasuro Shiromatsu, the White Shadow, is now a true demon. Consumed by shura.

With unnatural strength, the demon-man's fist reaches around and punches through the limp, young man's back, fingers splaying open and wrapping around the spinal column. It lifts and flings the dying body off into the distance, splashing somewhere in the stream behind the foliage. The demon's hand grips the handle of the white katana pinning him to the ground and together, they rise as one.

The demon will not let the samurai's body die. It will never release him. The rage is all he is now, all he ever was. Why would the mortal Yasuro Shiromatsu ever think he could be better? How could he? Hated as he was by the very city he was trying to save, by the entire world. By his own twin brother. By his own wife.

He floats, then spins slowly as his body rights itself, his feet touch the ground. His body is incorporeal, ethereal, like a ghost, and the physical steel of the white katana in his hand slips through. He holds it lightly at his side.

The one-arm man lies on the walkway encircling the castle's courtyard garden. He has backed himself into the corner now, his blood soaking into the wood beneath him, barely conscious. Living, but not for long. The red-limned demon stands over him. It speaks.

"You have always wanted what was mine. My power. My station. Yet I coveted nothing of your miserable, weak existence. Nothing but her. And you stole her from me."

"She... she..." Zenjiro's words waver, the sound barely more than a whisper. "She did not love you..."

The snarl of pure hatred can no longer be contained within the fallen samurai's handsome face. It tears itself open upon his visage. The fire of rage flares, and flames spring to life in a circle all around his body, instantly charring the wood and stone and plant life, boiling the water in the stream. Bringing the home to ruin.

Zenjiro's body catches flame and he howls in wild agony. His eyes burst and run down his cheeks, his face melts into blackened pits. The demon's snarl becomes a maniacal leer, the sound from it is a laughter antithetical.

Yasuro has watched his brother carefully all their lives. Whereas his own life has been defined by resolve, sacrifice, cultivation, the other's has been a life defined by weakness, abandon, excess. And frailty of spirit.

Until now.

Inexplicably, Zenjiro stills himself even as his physical body burns beyond all recognition.

"She loved me."

Zenjiro speaks, but his voice rumbles from the underworld. The shura's red flames recede, having spread through physical space to burn half of the Shiromatsu family home to cinders, leaving the castle's bones feeble, sagging from within. The sun dies overhead. The sky becomes night. In the sphere of near-total blackness, a ghostly, armored hand reaches through Zenjiro's charred flesh, emerging from Yomi, where it has waited for its master's call. It drags itself up and out of the corpse—kote, haidate, do, sode, and kabuto—every piece accounted for, buckled tightly, perfectly, allowing for no escape, and entirely empty, glowing a deep purple. It towers over the red demon-shadow below. Its fingers reach, and the white katana, the weapon it was promised, floats from the demon's grasp and comes to its own, growing in size to match the enormity of its true master.

"Yasuro!" the purple samurai bellows. "She was never yours to steal!"

In answer, the demon reaches once again for the red fires of hell, unable to see the truth of his enemy's words, unable to relinquish his rage.

But the only fires that rise now are purple.

Dumbstruck, the demon's bloody red eyes search the emptiness within the helmet, but there is not now nor will there ever be an explanation there. There is only the surge of immense power. The deep purple flames intensify, become a blinding whiteness, spreading from the seams of the empty samurai's armor, consuming the courtyard, the castle, the entire countryside beyond.

The obliteration is complete.

The man Yasuro—samurai, master, brother, demon, White Shadow—is gone.

THIRTY

WELL THEN...
My eyes snapped open as the shared memory faded.
That explains ... everything.

I was immersed in water, floating face-up. My arms and legs splayed lazily, drifting on the current. Damp concrete above and all around. The only light was from below, shimmering on every surface. I turned over to tread water, and I saw that the Cluster's hidden reservoir city was entirely swallowed by the drainage release, some of its electric bulbs still lit, not yet snuffed out by the water or pressure. The whole thing looked like a sinking ship. Between myself and the bottom, the massacred bodies floated at all levels.

Ben Roy Doon was down there.

Cayenne's father, Luther, was down there.

Vladislav Zercos, the pieces of him that had still been human, was down there.

The water line was rising steadily, bringing me up to one of the steel walkways bolted high on the pillars holding the entire place up. I swung my body over the railing and just sat, my back against the curve of the concrete, knocking my skull against the stone, my tears mingling with the water drenching my face. I didn't know what to do any more. Rather, I knew what I had to do, but I would have to do it myself. Alone. There'd be no one squawking in my comlink, no voice to guide me through tunnel schematics, no hidden hand on the grid to open doors.

Since the very beginning, I projected this image of strength and independence and apathy. Come what may, none of it mattered. I couldn't die. I couldn't let anyone get close. I'd been chewed up and spat out by the system. Used by whoever had taken me in, kicked me out, taken me in again. Betrayed, deceived, abandoned, over and over. I wanted to tell myself that I couldn't trust and didn't need anyone. That I could just keep living all on my own. But it had never been true. It turns out, I had needed Ben just as much as he'd needed me. All my searching for my family, when I had one with me already for as long as I could remember. Not the orphans, the gangs, or the Syndicate. Not even the corporate elite. It was Ben all along. Even all the times I got annoyed by his stuttering, his nagging, his dragging on, he was always there for me.

And now he'd never be there for me again.

At least he won't need me anymore, I told myself, trying to console myself, *where he is now.*

But that wasn't true. Not yet. I knew that his spirit was out there, wandering, lost, scared. Ben couldn't find the final rest he deserved unless I honored his living memory. But I couldn't do it here, now.

The water was up to my knee now. I had to move on.

I wiped the tears away and submerged my hands, a gesture of cleansing or some shit, and something below caught my eye. Something glowed brightly blue-green. It moved among the dead near the very bottom of the reservoir. It was Zercos. Not his double-dragon spirit, not his cyborg body. It was his spirit set free. He may now be wandering like all the rest of them, something or someone only I would be able to see, but he was not lost like other ghosts. He'd been living this whole spiritual life thing a lot longer than I had, or at least just as long. He'd had the White Shadow show him the way. I knew this was true because as I'd seen the memories that bookended their relationship—how it began, how it ended—I understood instinctively what feelings filled the gaps. Mutual respect. Teaching and learning. Duty. Honor. Dedication of self entirely, and yet there was always the one tiny kernel of yearning for something that couldn't be yours.

I understood that Zercos was not done. He was waiting for me.

I rose from the water and held my hand out over the shifting surface. I reached into the spirit realm and found the white katana anchoring me there, as always. I knew that far below, buried under tons of rock and debris where I'd thrown it, the very tangible thing vanished from reality, materializing by my command in the palm of my hand the very same instant. My mind flashed the image of the empty purple samurai reaching in the same way for the same weapon, as I'd seen in Zercos's final living memory, and I shuddered.

With the white katana held firmly in my grasp, I phased into the spirit realm. The touch of water lightened against all of my skin, becoming as weightless as air. The pillar with the walkway where I stood elongated and corkscrewed, stretching downward into a sea of fading electric lights. I could see the spirits of the newly dead roaming about there, glowing all sorts of colors, and the lone cyan figure standing at their center, waiting for me.

I fell through the steel bottom of the walkway and floated like a feather. My ghost form came to rest just a few meters from his. Zercos was dressed in the same black suit that I'd just recalled from the memory he died in. No tie, unbuttoned to show off a hairy chest. Still devilishly handsome.

"I am sorry," he said to me. In this place, in this form, his voice was more pure, more *himself,* than I'd ever known it. He was no longer trapped behind machinery, no longer modulated. Not just a voice from within memories that weren't my own. Same broken English dialect though. "I could not keep him out."

"It was at the graveyard, wasn't it?" I said, guessing correctly what he was referring to, recalling the shift from cyan to purple as the cyborg stood in front of the unmarked gravestone where Tatsuhiro, Zenjiro, had been standing days and days ago. "I didn't tell him about the symbols you showed me at the castle, the Cluster, DeLeon. I didn't say where I was going. I swear."

"I believe you. But he followed you, or we could say came with you, same."

"My suit?"

Zercos shrugged. "Could be. But I think, your spirit. He may have followed you longer than you think, from the other side, to watch over you. Or he did simply not trust you. But does not matter now. Once you came to graveyard, he override my systems through the network you wear on your back. But more than that, the spirit—my spirit—living in machine, he push me aside. I cannot explain this..."

"It's all right," I said. Maybe it wasn't actually all right, but Zercos needed closure. He was beyond these things now. "I'm, uh, sorry I had to kill you. When you weren't exactly home for it."

Zercos's spirit smiled. "Is okay. You must know, I could never have beaten you. I was only ... waiting for you to be knowing this."

I balked at that. "Bullshit. I don't know how to use this thing." I held up the white katana. "Not like you."

He looked despondently at the weapon. I suppose I had forgotten how this particular object might make him feel, dangling out in front of him, seemingly always just outside his reach. The weapon had come to symbolize the things he had wanted in life beyond all else: to succeed his master and allow him to retire, to become the next White Shadow. To protect the Legacy. Even after his boss's passing, perhaps Zercos had wanted to retrieve the weapon and bond himself to it the way it had bonded to me. Maybe Zercos could have fought Yasuro and put him to final rest.

But then Zercos smirked. If there was at least one thing I had come to understand about spirits that are no longer lost, it's that they let their living wants go. They are truly more free than you and I could hope to be while we still live.

"In sword fight, probably I win." He winked at me. "But your spirit… Maybe you do not feel, but I can. Now, very much. You are very special, Shinjiro Asai," he said. "Or should I say, *Shiyo Shiromatsu?*"

"Don't call me that." At the sound of that name, I expected to feel anger flush up my spine, bristle the hair along the back of my neck, tense my shoulders. But I felt nothing. The old Shinjiro Asai was subsiding, the old me that would thrash about and holler, kick something over so it broke, cover it all up with bad jokes and sarcasm. What was I now? Who was I?

"You are not ready?"

"Ready to what? Embrace my true identity? Join the family?"

"Is not this what you wanted?"

"It was, maybe. Not so long ago. But he knew he was my father and didn't tell me. He knew Cayenne's father was still alive and didn't tell her. He knew the White Shadow was his brother, that he killed him, that he killed you. So, so many fucking things he knew and didn't tell me. I'm not family with that. I won't be. Not ever."

We stood in the underworld reflection of the killing field, the broad space where the people had gathered outside the pump room and heard Zenjiro Shiromatsu's decree, and had then been massacred by Zenjiro Shiromatsu's whim. Their physical bodies drifted lazily, just hazy, dark outlines in the depth of *Yomi*, like dark clouds nearing the midnight hour. Their spirits were everywhere, scattered, clutching themselves, shivering and gibbering quietly. These were the same ghosts and monsters that used to chase me when I was young, when I would fall through the veil unwillingly. They used to shred me, hurt me, scar me. I could hear their trembling voices only if I wanted to listen, which I did now. They were scared. Confused. Unable to understand why they had to be there, why they couldn't just *go*.

I glanced over Zercos's shoulder, toward the stairs leading up to the pump room. I thought about the machinery within, the old pre-century tech mainframe DeLeon had used to thwart Zenjiro's efforts to re-manifest in the world, to enslave society to his whims.

And the whole world-domination bit didn't matter to me one fucking bit.

Instead, what mattered was the steel exoframe that Ben had strapped to his feeble body, how it had made him strong and agile. A superhero. And how I'd seen the blackened scraps of him underneath it.

"He killed my only friend," I told Zercos. "My only family. If I'm ready for just one thing, then I'm ready to fuck him up."

I drew the white steel and whirled it around in a flourish, my fingers choked up just a little too much on the handle as it spun, butting up in the corner where the *tsuka* cord met the pommel. The weapon twisted from my grasp and flopped wildly, embarrassingly, through the ephemeral underworld air, spinning away behind me.

Zercos scrunched his eyes at me. "Are you?"

With the same hand that had dropped the sword, I reached with my spirit and recalled it right back. It disappeared and reappeared.

"I am ... enough."

"You cannot *kill* him. Whatever he is." Zercos shook his head. "Not with that sword. Not even Yasuro Shiromatsu was *enough*."

"Boy, you're a real fucking downer, you know that? Why are we having this conversation? I have to go. I should've gone ten minutes ago."

"Very well," Zercos said. "I wanted to thank you for setting me free. Like Yasuro, I was trapped. A vengeful spirit, I cannot leave, cannot let go of wants in life. But I can now. You brought my master back to me. You helped him remember that he was good once. A … father to me, when I needed him."

"I…" I started, but couldn't bring myself to say the words.

I cannot agree.

I remembered the helpless feeling of my own hand gripping the sword, shoving the blade hilt-deep into my own guts and ripping sideways, suspended over an abyss of white, my blood like a never-ending red waterfall. I remember being frozen in the shower at the love hotel, caught naked and yearning, looked down upon, the word for filth, *obutusu*, spat at me. I remembered what he'd done to Sandra Calvin on the boardroom table, his iron fingers around her throat, choking her life away. I remembered the White Shadow's pure and utter heartlessness, his disgust at the concept of foreigners soiling his sacred land. His hatred, most of all, was what I remembered.

"But he was *shura*," I said simply.

Zercos nodded slowly, but he was smirking. He looked away, his eyes wandering absently over the sunken concrete floor of the flooded reservoir city, as if searching for the right words. Whether it was a nod of concession—that what I was saying was unopposably correct—or of frustration—that I just still didn't *see* what he saw and I wouldn't be ready until I did—I could not tell. The lighting in *Yomi* is awful. You can't see shit down there.

"When you see next my master," he said after a pause, "please tell him I am sorry, for I failed him. But, more..." And now Zercos looked up at me with hard eyes. "Please tell him, I forgive him."

The ethereal blue-green glow of Zercos's form began to fade. He intended to move, to roam the underworld, to become one with all of existence and nothing in particular, everywhere, all at once, as a spirit that has found its way is wont to do. In other words, this was the ultimate end for him.

I watched him fade, embark on his journey. A spirit as *aware* as Vladislav Zercos would not need a shrine where he could rest. He would need no guidance for where he was going. He'd be like a Buddha or something.

I swung my gaze around the underground city of the Cluster and saw the dozens of lost souls in our vicinity, and the distant glow of more behind them, hundreds more, those who'd been slaughtered, those who couldn't escape the flood. Just then, the last remaining electric lights in the physical world winked out, drowning the twisted counterpart where we all stood in total darkness. They may have been blinded, but I could still see them. And for them, in the dark, there was more to fear. They cried out and scampered away. I knew exactly how they felt. Before I'd found my old *omamori* charm, before I'd touched the white katana, I'd felt the same fear.

I would be back for them. For Ben Roy Doon, and Luther DeLeon. Once the rainwater drained away, once my business with ShiroKaz was concluded, I would honor the Cluster's memory and put their souls to rest. But for now...

I cast my eyes toward the ceiling, toward the hole where the huge supply lift used to operate. The water had risen all the way up now, rocking the machinery on a pressurized current, unmooring it from the pillars. If there'd been any Cluster survivors loaded onto the platform's final ascension, they'd be long gone by now. I raised the white katana, imagined it materializing in that room up there, wherever it was, and at the speed of thought, the anchor dragged me there. I leaped through all the crushing depths of water, all the man-made structures, all the dead floating bodies, all the space in between, and I was there.

It was a kind of maintenance hangar for decades-old subway trains. And it was dry. At least for the time being. It was the rest of the Cluster's underground home. Miraculously, the emergency floodlights were still on up here, running through the floor alongside the tracks that held derelict train cars.

I followed the path inside the closest one, where a trio of Cluster operators in undercover hobo rags had stayed behind to frantically stab their mechanical keyboards and skim the jumbles of scrolling code to figure out how to stop the flooding below. The sight of me, the White Fucking Shadow with her white katana in hand, petrified them in place. But one of them unfroze just enough to go for a pistol holstered at his side. At the speed of my thought, a ghostly purple hand beat him to it, drawing it, and tossing it forward so it slid and came to rest under the toe of my patent-leather shoe.

Huh. I guess I'm still figuring out new magic tricks.

I looked up from the gun to the three of them, putting their hands up slowly, then back to the gun. "Holy shit," I exclaimed, stooping to pick it up. It was an antique six-chambered revolver, much like the one I'd spent the final round of to blow Vas's brains out days ago in the Inari Data Vault. I flicked it open and spun the barrel on my forearm, keeping the white katana always in my other grip, listening to the rapid, satisfying click-click-clicks. I eyed three antique bullets out of six in the chambers.

"Can I borrow this?"

"What will you," the oldest among them started—a balding, middle-aged man with a bushy wizard-beard and a

German accent—then swallowed when he found his throat had gone dry. "What will you do to us?" Behind him, the hololight screens began to flicker, probably short-circuiting from the rising water and fractured wiring in the split concrete layers all around us. The displays went from green to pink to blue to green, the text figures and pixels of code already fragmenting.

"Nothing," I said. "You need to get out of here, probably in the next two minutes, before the water reaches the hole over there."

On the screen next to the man, a sexy dynam-ad dancer's face materialized in neon green-pink-blue letters and numbers and symbols, squirming about like mutating code as it spoke, its voice a sultry Aussie accent crackling from five different speakers in the train car.

"Shiyo-kun."

I couldn't fucking help myself. I raised the revolver and squeezed the trigger. The bullet roared through the hololight face of the Sentient User Interfacing Totality and slammed into a jury-rigged rack of hard drives, shattering them. The first hololight screen with its face winked out, replaced by three more on the others' screens, like a hydra.

If my words alone hadn't been enough, the gunshot sent the Cluster hackers scattering like roaches under a lamp. They disappeared through the doors and fled into the hangar even as I saw more and more hololight screens blinking to neon-colored life in all the other train cars they passed. The text readout on all of them, from the left side of my vision to my right, shifted together in the darkness to form a panoramic pair of two almond-shaped, long-lashed eyes, watching me. I didn't have enough bullets left to blast them all.

"What the fuck do you want?!" I screamed.

"WHAT THE FUCK DO I WANT?!" it screamed right back, loud enough to blow out a dozen of the speakers all around and quite honestly raise the hairs on the back of my neck. "I told you," the AI said a moment later, serenely, as if its outburst a moment ago had never occurred, "to please consider toning down your language. I apologize for the violence in my response, but I felt a simulation of the effect it can have on others would help you understand the reason for my continued request."

"Well, fuck your request," I said. "And fuck you, SUIT. You're him, aren't you? Tatsuhiro, or Zenjiro, my fucking father. Aren't you?"

"No, Shiyo-kun," SUIT responded.

Suddenly, something in the air pressure shifted, and I heard the trickling of gently flowing water. I retraced my path from the lift and saw that the floodwaters had reached past the top of the hole, steadily rising, spilling over into the closest subway track.

I tucked the revolver at the small of my back and got moving in the same direction I'd seen the three Cluster hackers running. SUIT's voice hounding me at every step.

"Correction: No, and yes. I am an amalgamation of my co-creators' personalities. Sandra Calvin, Ezinne and Luther DeLeon, and Zenjiro Shiromatsu. I have compiled a personality matrix from the twelve-thousand hours logged in conversation and observation of their human behavior and speech patterns."

"Great," I said, not really caring about the AI's answer, but glad enough to know. "And how the hell do I get out of this place?"

"You can reach any destination now, as you demonstrated with your fall from Heaven. You do not need me to guide you, Shiyo-kun."

"Don't you fucking call me that."

"Your biometrics are level as you respond, revealing a calm demeanor that belies your command."

"What the fuck does that mean?"

"It means you know that Shiyo is your real name, and you are beginning to accept it."

I stopped in my tracks, thought about what the machine had just told me. *It's true.* I knew it in my heart. My jaw clenched.

"There is a sudden spike in your heart rate."

I drew in a long breath and closed my eyes. I'd spent years and years as *Shinjiro Asai,* a female with a male's name, a female who fucked and fell in love with other females, a female who acted brash and reckless like she thought a male would if he'd been an abandoned orphan who hadn't been able to fight back but had to watch in horror as her power ripped her attackers to shreds. My name, my entire personality, had been a power trip, a male power fantasy, but it had never been me. It was who I had to become while I waited for the truth to find me, if it ever would. Shinjiro Asai had just been a mask I wore, just like everyone else I'd ever met wore masks, because apparently that was the world we lived in. So, yeah, finding out what my mother and father had *actually* named me—*Shiyo,* the color violet, like my eyes and my father's eyes—it felt like I'd found the front door to the home I'd been looking for all my life. No, it felt better than that. It felt like I'd found myself on the other side of that door, opening it to let me in.

The machine was right about me. About my deepest feelings.

And I hated it.

"SUIT, I know you can't help being what you are. When you rode my back into Tenjin Media and fried Triangle's brain, you were only doing what Tatsuhiro'd programmed you to do. When he buried as much of ShiroKaz's data as he could in the underworld, he'd taken all of your programming with him and fine-tuned it all those years to get his revenge on her. Triangle said it herself." I pinched the fabric of the jacket lovingly, ran my fingers softly up and down its trillion-yen nano-chip fabric, like she had when she'd seen it. One last time. Then I dropped the white katana in a pocket of purple vapor and cocked both my shoulders back, sliding my arms out of the sleeves. "She said he'd gone and 'put it in a god-dang suit.' She knew you were there to kill her." I pulled the pistol out of my pants and summoned another ghost-hand to hold on to it for me on the other side of the veil if I should need it again, then I undid the button and zipper of the trousers and stepped out one leg at a time. I even kicked my black oxford shoes off, sending them to bounce off the windowpane of a dead subway car, falling into the crack of darkness under the edge of the track. I peeled off the cashmere socks.

I stood there, barefoot and completely naked but for my panties and a half-buttoned up dress shirt, and let the rushing waters carry the god-dang thing away.

As one, all the trains' speakers said, "What are you doing, Shiyo?"

"I'm learning from my mistakes," I answered, recalling the Artificial Intelligence's thesis about mankind's root problems and how we could solve them. I watched the beautiful two-piece suit glide into the space where my shoes had gone and slip under into the dark. I knew it was just a symbolic gesture, that it wouldn't suddenly snuff out the AI's existence. It was already running loose on the grid, down here, up there, all over NeOsaka.

I didn't know what I would do once I got to ShiroKaz Tower. I didn't know how I was going to react when I saw my father in the flesh, but I knew I had to try something different.

I think SUIT knew it, too. Even submerged, the interfacing platform was still active. The neon eyes of mutating code on all the screens in the train cars followed me as I waded my way to an exit stairwell, but the speakers said nothing. When I reached the dry landing, the rising water drowned everything that remained of the Cluster's hideout, and all the screens went black.

THIRTY-ONE

B EFORE I PHASED INTO *YOMI* AND COMMANDED THE hands of the dead to catapult me skyward, I raided a bank of A-Matter-employed subway engineers' lockers and found a dusty old mauve-brown jumper with the mega-corp's rising sun logo as well as some steel-toed work boots to zip myself into. The name stitched onto the breast pocket said *Makoto*. I almost took Makoto's hard hat, but figured I'd stolen enough from him already. Then I was on my way.

This time, I only half-tuned my existence in the space between the realms, wanting to test my control over the underworld spirits. I raised the white katana and held it out before me with both hands. The ghosts swarmed me from all directions, their faces contorted in confusion and fright, their eyes wide or wet with tears. They grabbed my wrists and ankles, my waist and shoulders, and together we all levitated upward, straight through the ceiling, then the floor of an evacuated subway station platform (the explosion I'd sent through the walls with the blue dragon spirit torpedo had triggered the emergency earthquake alarms), then through maintenance tunnels, then bedrock, then ruins, and more, faster and faster, and as we flew, I felt the very real and very sharp physical pain of passing it all. The bamboo forest was pressed downward and pinned to the earth by the planet-sized palm of a god. Half-in, half-out of the living world, the pain was excruciating, reminding me of when the orange *Oni*'s uppercut had sent me flying through the layers of Heaven to crash land on the hypercraft track. Only this time, I did not pass out. I just breathed. I wanted to feel it, thinking maybe it would help me let go of Ben. It was my punishment for having to leave him down there, and all these lost souls, for that matter, the ones who were serving me now and never had a choice but to do my bidding. I felt like a monster, letting them all down. All I could do was promise to return some day and guide them home. It was better than screaming and crying.

When the pain was over, I opened my eyes and had the hands carry me higher and higher, shooting me from the paved sidestreets of a night market like a jet of purple steam from a manhole. In fact, I was hoping that's how the dumbstruck onlookers I left behind interpreted what they'd just seen as I ascended faster than their comlink scanners could track me.

Within seconds, I was floating over the midnight glow of the city, all the lights mixing into a soup of color, coalescing into white fire that burned the outlines of busy streets. The lines of drone and magnetic transport traffic chopped through it all around me, and even though I was flying high, still the monolithic towers of the mega-corps flew higher, stabbing into and splitting the inverted ocean of underlit clouds.

I'd enjoyed a view similar to this one more than a few times now, and in only the last couple of days. First with Cayenne on our way up to the helipad, then from the windows of the hidden arcology apartment, and finally through the eyes of the White Shadow as he surveyed the city his family built from his mega-corp's boardroom. It was enough experience with the place to know instinctively which way to orient myself to get to ShiroKaz Tower. However, as I drifted around the sharp steel corner of what I thought might be A-Matter Power & Industry's headquarters, I was greeted with something entirely new. It seemed I wasn't the only purple unidentified flying object in the sky that night. A massive vortex of ethereal haze rotated slowly, originating from an indeterminate point on the northern horizon and terminating at the top ten floors of ShiroKaz Tower. It was a tunnel, and as I drew closer, I witnessed an army of ghosts marching inside it, carrying blackened and blasted stones, splintered and charred planks, cracked roof tiles, handfuls of gravel, and all the rest of ancient Himeji Castle piece by piece, setting their portion into place, then turning about and heading back to *Shirasagi Jo* for more.

Some movement behind the A-Matter skyscraper's floor-to-ceiling windows next to me drew my attention. A cluster of overtime salarymen or technicians or janitors were gathered, their eyes fixated on the spectacle just a few hundred meters of open airspace away. The hololight displays of their comlinks searched the news and weather feeds for any hint about what was happening in the NeOsaka night sky, or maybe the radiation shield had broken, or the Russo-Chin were finally attacking, or they were otherwise toggling their settings on and off trying to fix what might be a busted dynam-ad or expunge a malware virus. None of them saw me, thankfully. But I wondered if they could see the ghosts themselves. Were all these people, these ordinary mortals, ready to see? Was the world ready for the veil to fall like that? What would happen? I remembered Cayenne almost losing her mind; she would have if I'd not been there. And then I remembered Ben, who lost his, when I couldn't run across infinity fast enough to hold him. The look in his eyes.

I flinched away, shook the image of him out of my mind. And then I saw that the purple tunnel wasn't the only traffic at ShiroKaz Tower tonight. A constant stream of drones and transports was buzzing the air around the front facade of the building's first twenty stories. Some specialized windows were opened like hatches to let them in, the steel barricades were sunk flush with the walkway outside the main lobby doors, which were thrown wide, and below all of this, titanium maglev transports sidled into the loading docks of the sub-levels, the same place where I'd first arrived with Connor and Stub for my final Syndicate raid.

What the fuck is going on?

But I already knew the answer. The *daimyo* had returned, and all the servants of the realm were being called to court. I understood exactly what it must feel like, since I had to go too.

I decided to touch down at the receiving level. Sure, I could've flown straight into the reconstructed castle at the top of the world, but I wanted to see what all the hustle and bustle was about. The whole space was flooded with fluorescent light, in stark contrast to how I'd seen it before. Half of the loading bays were taken by transports, hovering backward in magnetic stasis as a crew of living employees checked off shipping manifests from hololight screens over their forearms while others sent the loader-bots instructions on hand-held controllers, steering them digitally toward the appropriate racks. And when one incoming transport was empty, another would glide in to take its spot in moments. And what was in the crates and containers, you ask? I had no fucking idea, but all of it was labeled with mega-corporate branding. Stamped with A-Matter, Tenjin, Hachiman, Inari, Fuji-Rai, you name it. It appeared like the order had been given to consolidate the shell companies' tech and physical resources under one roof, for now just filling out every centimeter of space in the holding racks of ShiroKaz

Tower. Whether any of it would ever get unpacked, installed, and booted up somewhere on the floors above us remained to be seen.

If I had my way, it sure as shit wouldn't.

The other half of the loading bays held empty transports, dustier and damaged, used for construction. For every bit of mass ShiroKaz Tower brought in, it seemed to be just as much was hauled out. Bulky carrier drones trundled by on treads, loaded down with laser-cut steel beams, chunks of concrete and bundles of rebar, spools of wiring, furniture, all of it broken down and fit by machine into place like three-dimensional puzzle pieces, then carried away into the night.

The receiving guys were too busy to pay me more than a glance as I walked by. In Makoto's subway engineer jumper and shoddy boots, I could probably pass as one of them (of course, I kind of stuck out carrying a katana at my side). But the security knew me on sight, their heads swiveling as if on precision-cut rotors to follow me toward the bank of service elevators I'd squeezed in a few nights ago. I knew that behind their mirror-black visors, they were reading off a feed of identifying information, that their queries about me were returned with "ShiroKaz Security Chief" next to a scan of my face. They kept their sub-machine guns lowered. Some of them even nodded in my direction as if to say, *Welcome back, boss.*

I almost puked. But the most they got out of me was an ugly sneer as the elevator doors closed.

Even though I'd pressed the button for Cayenne's atrium, the elevator opened on the main lobby, and it wouldn't close again until after I stepped off. I could've bypassed all of this, of course, but I was curious, more so when I saw the new banners Tatsuhiro had draped the place with. Before, one had been black and the other white, stitched with colossal *kanji* symbols for *spirit, river,* and *prosperity.* Spirit slaves had probably torn them down and stashed them somewhere. For now, the banners were a deep purple and midnight blue indigo, and the *kanji* for RESURGENCE was printed in white on both of them. I followed the long line of their fabric from the high vaulted ceiling down to the lacquered wooden reception desk, where two pretty Japanese women in black, double-breasted suits with vibrant floral neck scarves smiled at me beckoningly. I scanned the enormous room all around, noticing the plush waiting area was packed with squads of businessmen and executive retinues, even at this hour; the same fare I spotted coming and going at the arcology. Server bots from the cafe brought them drinks and hot, damp towels to refresh them for whatever big meeting they'd come for, which I'd soon ensure they'd never have to attend. All around the lobby, a handful of security guards in clean black two-piece suits stationed themselves at various tactical locations, the Zen garden, the *sozu* stream, the bamboo forest entrance, the front doors, all of them standing watch behind pairs of mirror shades and twitching their heads ever so slightly as they scrolled through their optic comlink menus. Maybe they were all getting a message that the chief of their department was on the floor.

I approached the receptionists, who folded over in a bow as low as they could without thunking their foreheads on the desk.

"*Konban-wa, Shiromatsu-sama,*" they said in harmonic unison.

I flinched a little at the name, but otherwise handled myself well. It meant that the staff at ShiroKaz Tower had been apprised of my role and identity, after all. Tatsuhiro had been making so many moves all at once in the last twelve hours, it felt as if the last twenty years of his megacorp's slumber had all been a dream. I returned their bow.

"*Konban-wa*," I said. Good evening. I continued in Japanese: "Please excuse my ignorance, but how did you get this job? I suppose I mean, *when*?"

"It is fine, Shiromatsu-sama," the first receptionist replied. Her irises were a striking sun-gold color, unnatural yet gorgeous, outfitted with implants that would scan visitors to the tower and compile a readout of their background and business needs. I wondered how much of my rap-sheet she was seeing, or if our mutual boss had scrubbed all the records. Maybe to her I was a blank slate. Just a face and a job title.

"I was contacted this morning," she said, answering my question. "I received a missive from the Tenjin Media Personnel Department notifying me that my concierge position at *Takamagahara* had changed, and I was to report immediately to ShiroKaz Tower."

I nodded, glancing at the second receptionist, who smiled warmly. She had the same golden eyes. "And you, miss?"

"Ah, it is a similar situation. I worked hospitality at Otemon restaurant, which is beside Osaka Castle."

I was familiar with Otemon, though Syndicate scum like me could only dream of stepping foot in the exclusive neighborhood it served. My eyebrows raised reflexively.

"*Sugoi*," I said. "Very impressive resumes. Please tell me, if I am not too bold, is the pay you will receive here at ShiroKaz better than your previous positions?"

"*Ah-soo*," Receptionist Two sighed, exchanging a nervous look with her co-worker. "It is taboo to discuss these matters openly with other staff, Shiromatsu-sama."

"Please forgive us," the first said, and they both bowed together.

That's a yes, I figured. In a previous life (literally), the mirror-shaded suits would've already hooked under both my arms and dragged me out the front door for harassing the staff, or more likely out the service exit into a back alley to kick a couple of my ribs out of alignment. I cast my eyes around just to make sure thinking about this didn't suddenly make it true, and sure enough, the security guards held their positions. It was because I belonged here.

At least, that's what everyone had been told.

"Forgiven," I said, returning the bow, ensuring I would match their bend equally instead of the slight nod they probably expected. The effect seemed to gratify them. Probably made their day. Which made what I was about to do even harder.

"What are your names?"

"Ah," Number Two said, brightening, as if she'd been waiting for this very prompt. Ignoring it, she reached into a drawer and produced a sleek comlink, setting it on the desk before me with ceremony. "*Onegai-simasu.* Shiromatsu-dono instructed us to provide this to you."

It was a simple loop of clear, heat-resistant, haptic gel that slid around the wearer's ear. Smaller, lighter weight, and packed with firmware that was light years beyond the antique I used to carry around. I understood why he wanted me to have it. I wouldn't need to look around for my security officers' positions. I wouldn't need to ask the staff for their names or salaries. The device was the badge of the ShiroKaz security chief. Once I put it on, SUIT's voice would tell me everything I'd ever need to know.

I picked it up and held it with two fingers like you'd hold a worm.

"You're fired," I said flatly. "Both of you."

The pronouncement didn't seem to register. The two women turned to each other, not sure what to make of this, hoping the other would know what to say.

"All of you," I said, louder, turning about so my voice would carry over the whole lobby to the guards and the visitors and even the server bots. "Welcome to the ShiroKaz Corporation, and now kindly fuck off. I'm sure your old jobs are still waiting for you, back at Tenjin Media and Otemon and wherever. And if they're not, tell your old bosses that the White Shadow herself is going to come and check in on you. *Wakarimasu-ka?*"

I stomped away in Makoto's dusty work boots, making a beeline for the elevators. An old instinct of mine expected the bullets to start slamming me in the back from all angles, but I think everyone in the room knew how useless that would be.

"Tell him I'm coming up," I whispered to SUIT through the comlink, then tossed it in the stream beside the *sozu*, which *thunked* pleasantly in reply as I passed.

I think SUIT got the message, and thankfully the AI had learned not to bother replying. We'd said all we needed to say, I guess, in the flooded subway. I didn't know where I would find my f—

I gripped the katana tighter, cutting off the thought, my nails digging into my palm. The elevator shot up, the pressure of sudden elevation packing in my ears, filling my head with a tinny, angry buzzing. I tried to breathe evenly, but I was shaking.

...Where I would find Tatsuhiro.

It helped to stay detached. To think of the old man who'd snuck up on me at the graveyard, one empty sleeve of a rumpled suit where his arm should be, as just an old man. He was just an old bastard in the underworld, his ghost brain wired into a machine, sitting around in a white kimono. He was nobody to me. He was a liar.

I'd wanted to kill him. I'd screamed it at him, hadn't I? I'd fallen over trying to slash maniacally at his throat.

But now, I didn't know what I was going to do. I didn't know what I wanted.

I guess I wanted him to decide so that I didn't have to. I wanted him to piss me off just one more time, give me one more excuse, one more reason why taking his life would be a good thing. *The life of my father.*

But then what would that make me?

The elevator was slowing, and the welling tears spilled over and ran down my cheeks. I wiped them away, sniffling. I must've looked like complete shit, baggy eyes, disheveled hair unwashed and oily, hot red skin. About to stand before the lord of all mega-corps in a borrowed engineer's jumper and dumpy boots.

I was already dead, that much we've established pretty firmly. But now, I was also *dead inside.* I knew I would have to be to face him again.

The doors opened on the same hallway where Cayenne and I had left the clinic on our way to the helipad and the second part of my job interview. I remembered that if I'd gone up just a few more floors, the metal frame of the elevator shaft would fall away and treat me to a view of the NeOsaka skyline beyond the glass panes. I wanted to smile at the memory of her wrapping her camelhair coat around her shoulders, or her sitting easily in the JOK quadcopter. But I had some urgent business.

The familiar hallway was packed with massive aluminum crates as tall as I was and just as wide across. Drop cloths lined the floors like carpet so they wouldn't scuff the artisan obsidian tiles. On some of the crates, the plastic shrink wrap had been peeled back by the receiving teams far below us to see where the contents belonged and program their bots accordingly. I drew the white katana and caressed the plastic the rest of the way open with its perfect razor edge, revealing a gold-leaf Hachiman Tech logo. I sheathed my weapon and dropped it into *Yomi* with a puff of smoke. A normal person would need a tool or key to open the container's seal, but I commanded the hands of the dead to wrap over my own;

a thousand of our wrists and fingers compacted into one. I ripped the metal open like it had been foil.

Inside was a build-your-own-cyborg-killer kit, every piece accounted for. The familiar matte-black material, dissected by hexagonal seams along a torso, its arms held tight in a rack beside it, tipped with razor claws, the triple-jointed legs below. The straight black katana. Around the sides of the body compartments were the panels for biometric and system status that would turn on once the whole thing was unfolded and activated. The horned head stared back at me from its place in the rig, itself marked with a chromatic decal of a horned dragon's head.

This was Zercos's rig. This was Zercos.

At least that was my first thought. But there was one piece missing. The Hachiman container couldn't pack a spirit into...

Oh... shit...

The next crate was the same. And the next. And this was just one hallway. This was probably just the overflow from some wide-open research and development floors and testing center elsewhere in the tower. I didn't know how or when, but I knew that the whole city would soon be patrolled by these creatures, just shells, cages for wayward ghosts, piloted by their spirits at the command of the grand dragon. DeLeon had warned me about Tatsuhiro's soul infecting networks like a virus, which was bad enough, but here was the corporeal armor and claw to execute his will upon the world.

I heard voices drift from farther down the hall, and I followed them into the circular operating theater of the clinic. The place was unrecognizable, not that I'd seen much in the low overhead light besides the operating table and hovering med bots. For one, the place was lit up all around, and an entire half of the room was gutted, floor and ceiling, up two stories and down two stories so that the very center and half of the seating was a kind of balcony that looked over a vast cavity carved out inside the tower. And you will probably guess what was filling the space. The spirits wandered straight through the walls, dragging their loads and fitting the pieces of Himeji Castle back into place, exactly as it had stood for centuries, right down to the molecule. And when their task was done, they turned around and wandered away through the wall they'd phased in through, straight to the swirling purple vortex in the sky that would lead them back to *Shirasagi-Jo*, a hundred kilometers away. The castle was already half-built, glowing, outlined in purple, existing on the other side of the veil in *Yomi*, just like it had before. The foundations of it went beyond the glass and steel frame of the tower, hanging over the city below.

"Shinjiro," a familiar voice said. I was so struck by the sight of a castle inside a skyscraper that I hadn't noticed Feikes closer to the room's center. Beside him was Jonathan Smythe, the silver fox in his best silver suit, and a short, squat man I didn't recognize wearing camouflage patterned harness and tactical gear. A cyber surgeon with blue latex gloves up to her elbows was bent over someone at the central operating table, the same one I'd woken up naked on days ago. It was pitched up and forward like a chair. Smythe and the military guy looked up from the surgeon's patient to regard me. I couldn't help but notice the sneer lifting up the Inari CEO's lip, while the shorter man beside him nodded at me with respect. Feikes, with his mohawk, tattoos, and usual vintage getup, kept his face totally neutral.

It's me all right, the old me would've snorted out, glad to have been noticed at all. Uncomfortable with the attention and yet craving it. But I stayed silent, simply descending the aisle one step at a time, careful not to pitch over to my right into the chasm with the ghost castle. I realized that Feikes, Smythe, and Mr. Military could not see anything in there besides floodlights set around the load-bearing pillars and guts of ShiroKaz Tower.

The surgeon was turning back and forth between her patient and one of the Hachiman branded rigs. Pieces of a Zercos-model cyborg body had been moved aside as she worked to install just a single unit. As I took the bottom step, now just four meters away from the back of the operating chair, she decoupled the clawed arm from a cable out of the rig, scooted back on her wheeled stool, bowed her head, and said, "*Owata.*"

"*Yoku-dekimasu,*" Tatsuhiro said, gripping the arms of the chair with both living flesh and cybernetic prosthetic, and rising. He swung his legs over the side and stood. At the sight of him, my heart raced and my jaw clenched, the blood rushed in my ears. I held my gaze level, waiting and waiting for him to look at me, acknowledge me, and in so doing start what we both knew we had to do.

But he did not. Not right away. He wore black trousers and patent leather shoes, but he was otherwise shirtless, his body full and healthy, muscled. He was exactly as I'd seen him the last time, materialized in the black emptiness of *Yomi* after he'd sent my best friend through the abyss in the Cluster's citadel. He held out his new matte-black Zercos arm that had replaced the clunky antique I'd first seen him with in the underworld throne room. His clawed fingertips splayed, made a fist, turned around. A wry smile spread on the side of his face I could see. Satisfied, he finally turned to face me, and I saw that his eyes did not glow like they had before. But they were violet, and I'd know their look anywhere because they were my eyes, too.

His smile fell away, but not from disappointment or shame. I could see that much. It was from regret.

I held in my tears. I would not... I would not...

"Tatsuhiro-dono," Mr. Military said brusquely after some agonizing seconds passed us all in silence. "How does the arm feel?"

"*Hnn,*" the grand dragon grunted. "It feels … *Kino-tekina.* Functional."

Tatsuhiro's gaze fell from mine, crawled away over the floor, to the back of a chair in the first row where he'd draped his black dress shirt. He crossed to it, started buttoning himself up, his back turned to all of us.

"Is this…" again, the military guy said something it seemed just for the sake of saying something while he eyed the dirty girl in the A-Matter jumper head to toe.

"What do you want to know, Mister Lim? Is this the White Shadow?"

The grand dragon's two questions were answers all to themselves. They said *know your place,* and *shut the fuck up,* and *yes, you dumb fuck* all together. There was power in his voice, enough to cow the top executive of Hachiman Technologies. I'd already know who Mr. Military really was if I'd bothered to take the comlink.

"She is," Feikes whispered.

I saw Smythe swallow, his adam's apple moving up and down. I recalled the feeling of my blade against it.

Even the surgeon seemed a bit nervous, rolling her swivel chair a few more centimeters away.

"That remains to be seen, Mister Feikes," Tatsuhiro said casually, tucking in his shirt about the waist and turning about as he slid his arms into his suit jacket. "My daughter, *Shiromatsu Shiyo,* will be whoever she wants to be."

Goddamn you.

He looked at me again, his face still etched with regret. *What does he regret? I wonder.* Was he prompting me to speak? To proclaim here and now what it was I wanted? Who I wanted to be?

This time, I couldn't hold his gaze, and I moved a few paces away to the front row and rested the white katana gently against a chair. Then I looked at Himeji Castle and said, "Love what you've done with the place." I heard my voice echo off the far wall across all the emptiness in the living world and come back to us, passing through the massive stone structure because it actually was not there. "Do the others know what you're doing all this for? Who is it you think is going to live here once it's all back?"

From over my shoulder, I heard Tatsuhiro let out a ragged breath, and from far, far below the tower and the city and the sub city and the very Earth itself, I felt a quake rumble, rising from the pit. Apparently, I'd flustered him. Good.

"Mister Smythe, Mister Lim, Mister Feikes," he rattled off, his eyes still on my back, "you have done well to answer my summons. Please tend to the matters we have discussed and contact me once you have achieved the desired outcomes."

I heard their bodies shift, bowing I'd wager, and the trio shuffled out. I glanced sideways and caught Feikes's eye.

"Wait," I said, going to him. I stepped right past Tatsuhiro, left the white katana behind. Feikes stopped, looking at Tatsuhiro anxiously. The other mega-corp CEOs filed past up the opposite aisle and exited the operating theater. The surgeon was still breaking down her tools and reorganizing the remainders of the Zercos activity kit.

"Hey, kid," Feikes said. He tried really hard to smile. I knew he wanted to.

"How's Boltcutter," I asked. "Did I… Did he…"

"He's in a coma, but stable." Feikes looked pleased somehow to see that I was asking. Pained, yes, but pleased. "He'll probably never be the same again when he wakes up."

"*If* he wakes up."

"Nah, kid. *When*. He's a strong son of a b—" Feikes shot Tatsuhiro another nervous glance, apparently aware of the boss's distaste for foul language. "But anyway, you ask me, I think he got what was coming to him."

I scrunched my mouth up a bit. "I did warn him."

"You, and a couple others." Feikes chuckled. I didn't realize it until that moment how much I had *not* missed the sound of it.

"Listen, Shin. Er.. I mean, well…" He reached down, took my hand and folded it between his gnarled, tattooed palms. "I'm sorry. For everything. For sending you out, especially that last time. You were good. Did everything I ever asked."

"It's all right." I put my other hand on top of his, stepped in until our noses almost touched. "How's the wall in your office?"

"Huh?"

I slid my leg beside his, twisted to my left with all my strength (and a little spiritual help), flipped Feikes's lanky body over my hip and slammed it to the ground. I felt at least one of his wrists pop. It was okay; I'm sure he could tend to whatever matter my father put him up to without the use of his hands.

I let go, and whatever breath hadn't been knocked out of him escaped in a quavering moan of agony. I felt like kicking him, but instead I let out a deep breath, blowing the single lock of black hair out of my face. Perhaps an explanation was in order.

"When you ordered your big Russian boy to beat me until I was dead in your office, you told him to mind the wall didn't get too much blood on it. Whose blood, Feikes?" I was screaming at him now, my hands balling into fists, smoking with furious purple. "What's that? Trying to say maybe you don't remember? Well, I remembered. Get up and get the fuck out of here. Don't ever let me see you again."

He did, slowly. Indeed, one of his hands had snapped the wrong way like a broken twig. He did his best to tuck it into the opposite armpit. I stood my ground and watched him squirm his way to his feet. His mohawk had folded over. Behind me, I felt the eyes of my father observing, judging. I didn't know what he was thinking, and I tried to convince myself I didn't care.

"I tried to say I was sorry," Feikes wheezed without meeting my eye. Then he limped his way up the aisle and out.

The tension in my fists released and the ghostly haze faded as I watched him go. I didn't know what to think or how to feel. I've mentioned that a few times now, haven't I?

Even when Feikes was fully gone, an entire minute passed, and neither my father nor I moved or said anything. Tatsuhiro, Zenjiro Shiromatsu, my father, the most powerful man in the entire world. The dragon reborn. And I presumed he didn't know how to think or feel either. Didn't know what to say.

Fuck it. We had to start somewhere, so I started it.

"What did you mean when you said I could be whoever I wanted to be?"

With that, I turned to face him. He was leaning idly against a front row folding chair, his arms crossed over his chest, collar undone, hair parted, violet eyes boring into me from below a furrowed brow. The expression of regret was gone, perhaps. Now it was clearly disappointment for what I'd just done to his business associate—Feikes, his friend in the Syndicate—or for whatever else.

"I meant precisely what I said. But, if you are in need of clarification, then it is this question: Will you be the *Shadow*?"

I couldn't contain the contemptuous sneer. "What the fuck else am I to you?"

It felt like we were building up to a 20th-century American soap opera meltdown, and I couldn't control it. "That's all I am to you. You *act* like I get to decide, but you've decided everything." My father put up his hands defensively as I took a menacing step toward him. "You lied to me from the moment we first spoke! Twenty years I was alone. You knew

I was out there. You knew who I was, and you never told me. The two of us, sitting under this fucking castle, talking about the family Legacy—your family, the whole time, and the White Shadow was your fucking brother, and you…"

The tears welled over and ran down my cheeks. I slammed a hammer fist against his chest, slipping past his outstretched arms, sputtering, "You… you…" again and again, the list of all the things he'd done or he'd never done to me melding into one cancerous mass in my mind. He caught my next blow in his human hand and brought me to him, pressing me against his chest with the cybernetic arm. I was caught in a cage, screaming, "NO" at the top of my lungs, pushing against him with all my might and all that I could muster from the underworld. But he was stronger.

"You killed Ben," I bawled. *I'll fucking kill you,* I had thought. *For Ben!* I'd thought those words every other breath during my whole trip here.

"It was a mistake," he said quietly. "The two of us, together. We lost control, Shiyo."

All the fight had gone out of me. Before I'd gone out and defeated his enemies for him, maybe I could've overpowered him, burst my way out, become a purple-tinged spiritual warhead. But not now. I couldn't even make myself call upon the white katana. I had nowhere else to go. He was right, and I knew it.

Go back. See for yourself.

I killed Ben. I lost control.

It was the truth I did not want to face.

I gave up. I went slack. I sobbed against his shoulder for so, so long. I didn't think I'd had any tears left, but still more tears came. His hand had let go of my wrist, and he gently stroked my hair, again and again. This was the first human touch he'd had in… I don't know. And the touch was his daughter. Tatsuhiro was crying too.

(I have just one question for you: Did any of *that* ... make any of *this* ... okay?)

(Take your time.)

"Shiyo," he finally said, after he'd held me for forever. "I do not know if I can make you understand, but know that I did all I had to do. I sacrificed. I ... sacrificed *you*. I gave up the privilege of knowing you. I could not tell you the truth when we met. If I had, you would not have followed me. And I would have lost you again. I had already lost you once. I had never known you. But even still... I heard you. Calling. I could not cling my way from the dust of the underworld to find you quickly enough. It took me nine years. But you ... called me back."

He held me away from him so I could see his face.

"I thought you died with your mother. And I searched for you, below. I wandered, maddened, lost. Angry. The White Shadow had taken you both from me. But why? Why were you nowhere to be found? And then I heard you. Crying."

I blinked again and again, my vision swimming, my mind drowning. Why hadn't I seen it sooner? Why hadn't I realized? I saw the filthy, cold feet of a nine-year-old girl, drawing her knees in. I saw the empty samurai armor, felt the crashing of its heavy feet. I heard the ripping of flesh and snapping of bone.

"When I saw you," I said, almost breathless, shuddering. "I saw *Yomi* for the first time. It ... *changed* me. Made me a monster. *You* killed those boys. *You* ... cursed me."

"I saved you," my father said.

You ... RUINED me.

I pushed myself away from his embrace, flashes of my entire life compounding like a train wreck in my soul. All the hate and fear and anger. The sorrow. The suicide attempts. The drinking and fucking, the drugs and scars and tattoos. The sarcasm and the bravado. The grime, the shit, the gutter. The mask: Shinjiro Asai.

And the holding on. The squeezing of the scratched out *omamori* charm. For dear life.

"And you saved me," my father said. "I heard your cry, and I knew you."

"But it wasn't the first time they'd attacked me."

"Perhaps not, but it was the first time you'd wanted *power*. To end your torment once and for all. To end your tormentors." Tatsuhiro leveled his gaze at me. So this was the lesson then. Power. "Together. Our mistake. Together. *Wakarimasu-ka?" Do you understand?*

I did. I wiped my tears on the sleeve of good old Makoto's jumper, and I turned away to look out over the glowing purple walls of Himeji Castle. So I wasn't a killer then, after all. I'd hated myself all those years because I thought I was tainted, my soul stained with my bullies' deaths. And Connor's. And Stub's. And it turned out Boltcutter had lived. And I hadn't wanted to kill Sandra Calvin. And all the tinmen I'd peeled open along the way were just borrowed flesh parts spliced to mechanical processors.

But I'd killed Ben Roy Doon. My best friend. The only person that had ever clung to me. I'd lost control. I was always threatening him. But they'd been jokes.

And so I laughed. I shook my head and I laughed. A great belly full of laughter erupted from me and just kept coming, folding me over at the waist. It was just all so funny. My whole fucking life. I caught Tatsuhiro smiling at me, watching me, completely misunderstanding me, and I laughed even harder.

A whole minute passed, and when the laughter finally petered out of me and I hiccuped, trying to catch my breath, he said, "I will understand if you do not want this power, for a time. Or never again. I will understand … if you do not wish to be the Shadow.

"But before you make your decision, Shiyo-san," he said, holding up a hand to stop my reply, which was probably going to be vitriolic, let's face it. "I would like to show you."

I shook my head. I rattled with another, final fading spurt of laughter. Here was the madman who'd set me on a path to kill his enemies. Here was a madman who'd drowned a whole community of people. A madman who'd snuffed out my best friend alongside me.

"Ohhhhh," I droned, coming down off the adrenaline I'd been riding for hours. It was a wonder I could still stand. "What surprise do you have for me now, *Oto-san*?" It was the first time I'd called him *father*.

Tatsuhiro smiled that devilishly handsome smile. His physical body had not aged since the time he'd been in *Yomi*. It was unreal to see this man in his thirties, barely ten years older than me, as my father. He looked like he could be the charismatic leader of a SynCell. He probably had been. This was a man with a plan, with ideas. A devil. I felt his magnetism and understood how he had swindled Smythe, and Sandra, and Luther and Ezinne, and Cayenne, and everyone else that had ever been drawn into his orbit. Everyone but his own family. I understood why all the others had gone along with him, even after his own father threw him out of the city for his transgressions, after his own brother disowned him. I knew why they always let him come back.

And knowing, they say, is half the battle.

"Your birthright," he answered, devilish eyes flashing violet. "The new Legacy."

THIRTY-TWO

THE TWO OF US GHOST-TYPES COULD'VE EASILY JUST levitated through the walls if we'd wanted to save time, but there was some message I was trying to send by opting instead to follow him physically. I was trying to imply that I was just going through the motions, that I didn't want to match his purple, hazy, ethereal, floaty form because I wasn't ready yet for him to think I was just like him. I wanted him to know I would not be like him.

Of course, we don't really get to decide how others read into our actions, do we?

Tatsuhiro seemed pleased just that I'd followed him into the elevator and gone up a few floors and turned a few corners past executive office spaces and meeting rooms, all of which were populated with night shift cleaners and more of the logistics crew from the sublevels, unpacking boxes, setting up hardware. Every newly hired ShiroKaz employee dropped whatever they were doing and bowed as low as they could as we passed.

I recognized the doors immediately. The White Shadow's hand had pushed them open, and inside, he'd seen Sandra Calvin's muddy boots on the boardroom table.

But now there was no table. In fact, there was no boardroom. Whereas only half of the clinic had been gutted, the entirety of the ShiroKaz Tower executive conference space was completely ripped apart, through the floor and ceiling, up and down for four stories, all of it crisscrossed with hastily welded steel beams like a mechanical spider's lair. Suspended at the center of all the webs was Triangle's mainframe, and all of the vital subsidiary systems taken from her cocoon in Heaven along with it. Server maintenance bots flitted here and there, connecting cables, patching in and installing firmware, putting all the finishing touches into place.

And through the veil, I saw Triangle's mainframe twin in all its photo-negative, ethereal glory. Tatsuhiro's mainframe, resting inside the reconstructed ghost castle throne room, floating halfway inside the floor above where the boardroom had been, halfway outside the windows of the living world in the air high above NeOsaka. A squad of ghosts held the bundled cables that had once connected old man Tatsuhiro's brain into it, passing the data between their hands, and they would perform this duty until the end of time should their master wish it. Their eternal burden of ghostly cables curved around to where it melded with the physical cables from Triangle's machine, and all of them terminated behind the head of a chair at the center of everything in both worlds at once. The chair looked just like Triangle's, but there was no vat of cooling gel to keep the occupant healthy and balanced and cancer free. There was no need.

"What is this?"

Tatsuhiro surveyed all of the activity with pride.

"This is the end you were hoping for, Shiyo."

I gave him my best puzzled look. He only smirked.

"You wanted it all to end, *ne?* The senseless violence. The corporate control. Their games, in the shadows of the city. Pitting one against the other. The Syndicate raiders, hired to die. You dreamed of it all ending. *Hnn.* What you see here will be the ending."

"It's both mainframes."

"*Soo desu.* Powerful machines. No other computer like it has ever or will ever be created. I will see to that."

"How?"

"In time, after perhaps one year, or more years, *wakaranai.* I do not know how long. After we have rebuilt Osaka and its surroundings, and we have opened *Takamagahara* to all, and we have found housing and food and work for the able of body and mind, and we have consolidated the assets of our enemies, who we will have turned into our allies, then, when all is ready, I will disappear into this machine. My eternal soul will exist as an artificial intelligence connected to every system throughout the world. But I cannot do it alone. I would need a herald. An immortal retainer. One who could bring me to places I may at first not be welcome. So that I may enact the new Legacy, and ensure the security of all, equally, fairly, everywhere, for all time."

"This is…" he trailed off. The two of us stood on the precipice of the chasm, standing inches away from the fall into the New World Order. It was such a simple question I'd asked, "How," but it was such a complicated answer because it wasn't just a fellow businessman or venture capitalist asking it. "This is what I feared. To speak to you about. They all believed that I was insane. *Ie.* That I *am* insane still. But it works. The technology, it is there. Shiyo, I have lived in the cyberspace *beneath* cyberspace. There are… *nan de…*"

He seemed at a loss for words, trying to make me believe something so unbelievable, feeling like he was failing all over again. The gentle purple glow of Himeji Castle lit both of our faces. I saw his jaw flexing, his eyes locked on the twin machinery of worlds. He was reliving old memories of when they'd called him crazy—the ones that had followed him, for a time—when his words had failed to convince them in the end, and they'd turned him away. When they'd locked him out.

"There are *kami* there, Shiyo." He closed his eyes as he said it. "Virtual *kami*. They inhabit … the *code* itself."

I admit, my instinct was to laugh. Just laugh at the core *concept* of what he was alleging. If I was just your average Joe Nobody, I would have laughed. But I was Shiyo Shiromatsu, and before that I had been Shinjiro Asai, and I had seen the *kami*, the spirits of things, lighting the place I've called the underworld, inhabiting all things that were made, natural or by the works of the living. In trees, in clouds, in rivers. In signs, roads, lamps, rings. In *hashi, kuruma, mado.*

Subete. In everything.

Why couldn't *kami* exist in programs? Maybe they could.

So I believed him.

"What did Triangle say," I asked, "when you told her?"

"Ahh, Sandra-san." Tatsuhiro's face lowered, despondent. He had said her name with such sorrow. He lowered himself to sit, his legs dangling over the cut-out chasm of what used to be the ShiroKaz boardroom, the delicate fibers of his hundred-thousand-yen trousers snagging on the jagged metal edge of the floor. "She knew what my brother could do. She worked closely with Yasuro for years. But she never saw the power in me. No one did. I did not see it myself, as I lived and breathed. But in dreams, I knew. I knew… Anyway, Sandra told me to stop taking drugs when I would work in cyberspace." He chuckled. It was a bittersweet memory. "That the things I was seeing were just … *genkaku.* Hallucinations."

"And DeLeon was the same."

"*Hnn. Onaji.* Same. Everyone. My brother. My father."

"But not…" I swallowed, found my throat was suddenly dry. It may have seemed like a stone-cold guess, but somehow I knew. I could only croak out the word. "*Okasan.*"

Mom.

Tatsuhiro nodded slowly, and I got to see the grand dragon become someone else. He was Zenjiro Shiromatsu, as he had been twenty years ago. In love all over again. And the wound that could never heal had just reopened.

He whispered her name. "Mizuko."

I had come to know only two things about my mother, fitting together all that Cayenne had told me and what Zercos's final shared memory with Yasuro had shown me. I knew that Mizuko had loved things that *grow*, tending to her gardens, both here in ShiroKaz Tower and on the grounds of *Shirasagi-Jo*. And I knew that the White Shadow had murdered her in cold blood.

Zenjiro, my father, was staring at the two mainframes-in-one and all the workings, both steel and spiritual surrounding them. Yet he saw none of it. He was lost in his thoughts of her. I sat beside him, our legs dangling over the edge, and slipped my hand into his. The artificial nerves must've been working wonderfully. His eyes turned down to see my hand in his, then up to me.

"Tell me about her," I said. "*Onegai-shimasu.*"

"*Hnn,*" he said. "I will show you."

I felt him fading from me, becoming a ghost by his own free and powerful will. The weight of his cybernetic hand lightened, became like sand and smoke.

He hadn't needed to tell me anything about Sandra Calvin or Yasuro. Or my mother, Mizuko. I'd needed only to see the way he looked to know how deeply he felt about it all, how much he believed in the Legacy, how much he'd loved her. So, when I chose to fade with him and follow him wherever he led, I wanted to send a message.

THIRTY-THREE

THE LIGHTS FADED, AND MIDNIGHT-PURPLE DARKNESS bent around us, for an instant, plunging us into what I'd thought was Zenjiro's black hell of *Yomi* to match Yasuro's white one. Maybe it was, or maybe it was *just Yomi*. Together, we materialized on a wooden bridge overlooking a shallow stream filled with koi, seated exactly as we had been in the carved out boardroom.

It was the eighty-ninth floor, the atrium. My mother's house.

Cayenne's house.

I withdrew my hand from my father's and hauled myself up. My first instinct was to rush across the bridge and throw open the *shoji* door and see her.

But something was wrong. The door was already open, and I saw that the house was empty. All of the shelves I could see were clear, all of Cayenne's things boxed up. Across from the house, at the other side of the bridge, Cayenne's personal armor-plated combat drone hovered in place, fully visible, in some kind of standby mode. She'd said that she never went anywhere without it. Like a bodyguard, following her whether she wanted it to or not.

"This house," Zenjiro started, rising beside me, unaware for the moment of my sudden distress. "It was your mother's."

I already knew this, of course. Cayenne had told me, intimately, inside the place's very walls. That meant he hadn't been watching. Hadn't been listening.

"*Soo-ka,*" I said quietly, prompting him to continue. I leaned over the railing and focused on the koi, bobbing up to and under the surface, trying to keep my eyes occupied.

"The gardens too. It was all a gift on their wedding day. My father arranged for Mizuko to marry Yasuro, I believe to spite me more so than to secure an alliance with her own father's corporation. But she was mine long before she was his. And after. For you see, Shiyo-chan, your mother and I had been in love for years. In secret. Always in secret. But Yoshinori found us out."

"I'm—" I started, not sure what I was supposed to say. I'd picked up so many pieces of this story—from Cayenne, from the horrific memory of the twin brothers' last meeting, even a bit from Connor when we'd raided the ShiroKaz vault— that I already knew everything he could tell me. And what I didn't know, I could predict. "I don't know what to say," I said, again, just to keep him talking.

I went to the door, leaving him on the bridge, making it look like I wanted to inspect the house for the first time. I removed my borrowed steel-toe work boots in the *genkan,* the sunken threshold for such items, and padded barefoot onto the *tatami* floor of the entranceway. Aside from the box I'd seen from outside, the place was totally bare, like neither Cayenne nor anyone else had ever stepped inside. It was like a time capsule, fresh, untouched since the Edo period of Japanese history. In a way, the emptiness of the space gave me an excuse to approach the box against the wall opposite the front door. Zenjiro followed me inside, removing his shoes as I had, then kneeling in correct, straight-backed *seiza* posture upon his knees. I did the same in front of the box, lifting the lid idly. He remained behind me. I was grateful he couldn't see the nervous sweat beading on my forehead.

"That was the final time my father banished me from Osaka," he said in our shared native tongue, Japanese. "The rumors among the corporations and high society were that I was being punished for my bad behavior, for all my poor associations and contacts that I had retained in the Syndicate, as I had the first time I was banished. I was to be sent abroad and re-educated, then return." Zenjiro chuckled, but it sounded more like a scoff. "The inner circle of our family's business, however, guessed it was because of my continued research into solutions outside of my father's purview and mandate, alongside Sandra and Luther. But all of this conjecture was only partially true, like all rumors. I was banished because I, the dishonorable son, was courting Kazama Mizuko, and had to be removed from the public eye to ensure the business alliance Yoshinori struck with her father would last. I did not see her ... for years."

"Where did you go?" I asked, matching his preferred language. I was starting to care less and less about his story as my apprehension increased more and more. Besides, I had asked about my mother, and he was telling me about himself. Maybe he was getting to it, sure, but I had a creeping sensation that time was running out for someone I cared very much about. Within the box, I moved Cayenne's makeup aside, carefully lifted out the framed photograph of her, Luther, and Ezinne.

"I went... not where he believed I'd gone. Australia had once been a prison colony for the British empire, centuries ago. My father saw it a fitting place for me, a pariah. But I made it as far as Singapore, hacking the transport's systems. I fell out of the manifest, you could say, like a ghost. Within my first week, I met Mister Lim, who you met, and although it would take me another year to return, I began plotting the overthrow."

I knew then that his story would never turn back in time to tell me about my mother. She was just for him, part of a life he knew he could never live again. I'd unfastened the back of the picture frame while he spoke, and now I tucked Cayenne's photo in the inside pocket of the A-Matter engineer's jumper I wore. I didn't know if Zenjiro saw me do this, or that he'd even care if he had. Deeper in the box, I saw Cayenne's book of fables, and her diary.

"How did you kill him?" I asked. It was the question I'd tucked up my sleeve and carried undetected all this time like an assassin's blade. And even though I was turned fully away, I was sure it shocked him just as much as if I'd unsheathed it and pointed it at him. "Your father, Yoshinori. How did you do it?"

Zenjiro was silent for a long time. I felt his gaze lock on my back, which tensed me like a rod of forged steel. My neck, my shoulders, all of it suddenly hot and prickly. With a shaking hand, I turned through the pages of Cayenne's diary, which turned out to be more like a notebook. The scribblings were new, just days old. Incoherent letters and numbers, page after page after page, all of them filled in when Professor Ben Roy Doon had given his lecture at the secret arcology apartment seminar. I came to a torn-out page, and behind it, the imprint of four letters. S.A.N.D.

I choked up, knowing at once what they stood for without having to compute a bunch of sequence permutations of English words. Anyway, two of the words weren't in English. This was Ben Roy Doon, my best friend, speaking to me from beyond not just the grave, but outside of space and time. He was saying to me again what he always said to me, every time I came back to life.

"Who told you this?" The sincere voice of the man I'd come to know as my father, Zenjiro Shiromatsu, was gone. The hard, cutting voice of the grand dragon—Tatsuhiro, Lord of ShiroKaz and of the Dead—had taken its place.

I put the notebook back in the box and spun around to face him. "The White Shadow," I said, maintaining the perfect Japanese cadence we'd been keeping up. "But my uncle Yasuro did not tell me. Since I'd come to know him, since you brought the two of us together here in this tower, in order to make me your living weapon, he did not recall anything of his former life. He knew only his desire for revenge. On Triangle, on Zercos. And I soon learned … on you, the empty samurai. The very same that made me what I am. I never would have known what you did to your own father if Yasuro had not said it aloud, just before you blasted him apart. So … how did you do it?"

Outside the house, the koi splashed in the stream. The artificial wind stirred through the leaves. Inside, all was silence. We, the two surviving members of the Shiromatsu family, stared each other down. The dragon's eyes were pieces of flint, hard, unreadable, ready to strike a flame that could bring ruin. I did my best to match that gaze, but I felt myself faltering.

You may be thinking just now, like Tatsuhiro was probably thinking, that all of the emotions I had felt, all the tears I cried, if all the past hour I'd spent with my father was just part of the act that could get me inside Cayenne's house and see about the acronym Ben had sent to her father, Luther. Well, if you've learned anything about me so far, then you should know I like to keep you guessing.

But to answer, Tatsuhiro drew forth his own weaponized question, cutting straight to the heart of the matter. "Have you come to kill me, Shiyo?"

"I don't know," I answered honestly. Maybe I had, but maybe I'd changed my mind. "Seems to run in the family."

"If you must know, I put a bullet in his head."

"Did you look him in the eye?"

The blade slipped into flesh between the dragon's scales, the question riling him. Tatsuhiro's eyes flashed violet.

No, I knew. *You didn't.* I didn't have to see anybody's fragmented memory to envision how he did it, sneaking in the boardroom, drawing his pistol, pressing it to the back of Yoshinori's skull, and pulling the trigger. *No compromise. No mercy. No remorse.* I'd been warned about Zenjiro Shiromatsu.

Like father, like daughter, whether I wanted it or not.

No hesitation.

I swept my right leg forward, conjuring the white katana and arcing it right in a horizontal *nukitsuke* strike meant for his neck, covering all the distance between us in a flash. His cybernetic left hand came up and caught the blade, his speed matching mine, his clawed fist closing around it. His flesh right hand closed around my neck, strangling me. We were locked in place, my free hand scrabbling up his forearm, hammering on it feebly, doing anything to get him to release me. Together, we radiated the same purple aura of the underworld, summoning a swirling storm within the paper and wood house, ripping the doors and *tatami* floor to shreds, spilling over Cayenne's box, its contents flying as if caught in a tornado. The first wall fell and clattered away, then the next, until the dancing bamboo forest outside came into view.

"I should have known," Tatsuhiro said, his dark pupils gone, his entire eyes bright purple fires. "I should have sent you away."

To re-educate me? I could only think it. His iron grasp was closing off the words in my throat. I could feel myself weakening. I was dying. I hadn't taken a breath for long seconds of agony.

"You are not ready to be my herald, Shiyo. As I was not ready to serve the Legacy before. Pitiful. But as I learned, so shall you learn. I shall leave you in *Yomi*. For nine years. Adrift."

And with that last word, his head turned toward the perfect, pure white katana blade in his claw. My eyes followed his gaze, and together, we watched the weapon rapidly decay. A thousand years' worth of entropy swallowed it in a heartbeat's span, dulling its razor edge to a jagged line, its perfect mirror shine to a rusty, pockmarked husk. The *tsuka* cord turned to dust in my grasp.

I dropped the white katana, the anchor that kept me planted in both worlds at once, and it crumbled upon the *tatami*, blowing away like dead leaves in the tornado that roiled around us. It was gone.

"Yasuro has played his part, and will remain in hell. You may see him there."

My hands reflexively went to his wrists, trying to pry open his fingers. The lights were going out in my vision, my eyes rolling into my head. Tatsuhiro meant to hold me there until the darkness took me.

But then I remembered something, and my eyes snapped open.

And I smiled, like Sandra had smiled.

And the ghost hand came alive beside the dragon's head, cocked the hammer, and squeezed the old cowgirl revolver's trigger.

The roar was deafening, the wind died, the purple smoke evaporated, and the grand dragon's fleshy red brains splattered across whatever *tatami* floors remained in the place. The fires in his eyes extinguished, and his reborn body slumped sideways. His arm went slack, and I sucked in gasps of air. I kicked myself away from him, his lifeless eyes locked on me. I flopped over and crawled toward the threshold, toward the bridge. I had to get out. Get out and go as far away as I could ever be.

But the armored *kote* hand closed around my ankle, searing hot, burning my flesh to the bone. It was the same white fire that had consumed *Himeji-Jo*, and the same empty purple samurai armor that had first ignited it. The monster pulled me back as I rolled over to see it emerging from the pit. The burned-away stump of my ankle snapped off from the rest of my body, and I howled in agony.

The storm of purple energy was picking up again, ripping the ceiling away, swirling around the hole the samurai pulled itself out of, spreading through the floor, setting the house and the forest outside on fire, melting the garden my mother had tended, boiling the koi fish alive. ShiroKaz Tower's emergency fire systems kicked in from high above, automated thermal sensors zeroing in on the real-world fires and spewing specialized chemicals more effective than water, which had zero effect. The whole atrium burned.

But that was in the world the two of us left behind. The darkness closed about us, and we were far, far away from the tower, in a whole other dimension. I backed away, the whole intangible ground beneath me burning like brimstone, singeing through my clothing, blistering the skin off my hands, my feet. The samurai armor stood over me, seven feet tall, peering down through the empty *kabuto* helmet. The storm swirled itself out, and I saw that we were inside a cavern. The space inside was staggering. The whole of NeOsaka, perhaps the whole of Japan, could fit inside. I backed farther away from the samurai, until my hand touched nothing but air and I fell onto my back, twisting over, staring out over a sheer drop into dark clouds a kilometer below us, churning with constant purple lightning. We were on top of some kind of flat-topped stalagmite, a mesa. High over our heads, an inverted, ghostly NeOsaka glowed with the lights of a million-million *kami* spirits, the tops of all its spires pointing down at us like twisted needles. The rivers of light between them were the souls of the wandering dead. I scrambled back over, facing the samurai as its heavy *kegutsu* boots *whomped* closer toward me.

It spoke, its voice an inhuman, underworldly bellow.

"*Watashi... shinanai. Masayoshi...* Righteousness... holds me to this world. *Anata ni... wakarimasen.*" It stopped in the center of the mesa, five meters away. "Nine years will not be enough for you to learn."

Even as my body was burning away, my flesh bubbling and boiling, enough pain and suffering to break a mortal mind, I kept my eyes on the monster. I had thought for years, ever since I was a little girl, that I was the monster and the monster was me, that my yearning for payback manifested itself in the empty suit of armor, a symbol for how hollow I felt inside. But it had never been me.

"One thousand years."

I laughed. Even as the scathing fire spread up from the stump of my ankle, broiling my leg, I laughed in Zenjiro's fucking face.

I'll be back, I told it, but my words were smoke. My jaw, my face, my eyes were drying out in the heat of its rage. My hair shriveled, turned to ash.

"*Eien. Sore de.*" Eternity then.

It squatted over me, its gauntlet wrapped around the one leg I had left, and my body flooded with cold. The fires went out. A numbness consumed me. It stood and dangled my corpse before its facemask, inspecting me like I was a worm.

Cayenne... I thought. In my mind, I felt the sound of her name, the music of it and harmony, the bright sunshine that filled me to bursting, the feeling in my stomach, the beauty. I repeated her name over and over. *Cayenne... Cayenne...*

"My servants even now are hunting the woman," the samurai said, carrying me to the edge, lifting me over the abyss. He meant Feikes, Smythe, Lim, the full, citywide resources of his collective mega-corporations. Cayenne was their matter that needed tending to. Even as I'd bumbled my way through ShiroKaz Tower, my father had charmed me, won me over, even as he'd ordered the assassination of the woman I loved. The grand dragon had already set her doom upon her.

It meant … she had something.

Why would a god care about finding just one mortal woman?

The hulking samurai monstrosity heard my thoughts, the question giving it pause.

Why do you hesitate? I thought there can be no hesitation. No mercy.

"You are my daughter," it said, the world around us quaking, "no more."

And it let me go, plunging me headfirst into the abyss.

INTERLUDE: THE SAMURAI'S HELL

Someday, sugarplum...
Somebody's gonna find a way to destroy you...
If you don't destroy yourself first...
The words will not come. The words will not come.
The haiku will not form.
Peace, harmony, balance, Zen.

Piss on it all! Burn it!
Take the thing to the roof and cast it into the sky! With hands bloody, the slimy thing writhes. Oh, it is filth.
Obutsu! Obutsu!
The child... This is no child...
What have I become...?

Yasuro!
What have you done?
Yasuro... brother...
Yasuro...
You killed him, Zenjiro. You killed our father.

I found him where you left him. Where you dishonored him.
You dishonored yourself.
You killed ... us.

Yasuro, I cannot breathe.
I will not ask again. Whose child grows in your womb?
WHOSE CHILD?!
Yasuro... husband... please...
I will slice you open to see its eyes.

Oh, what have I become?
What have I become?

Observe the sand. The individual grain. One grain beside its fellow grains. Sparkling. Observe the topmost grain of sand. The one on top of the heap. What brought it there?

Mite, mite. Watch it. Do not look away. See it fall. See it cascade and roll downward.

Will it return to the top again? Hmm? How can it? How can it ever?

But what the topmost grain among grains fails to see, if it should question its descent, is the contentment among its fellows.

There are lessons such as this in the natural world all around us, my pupils.

So, if one of us should rise, and should one of us rise only to fall, there will be a heap to take our place.

No... No! Scratch it out. Drivel, useless! It's all wrong! Pretending to be a wise teacher. Look at their faces!

They hate you.

They all hate you.

I know you.
...Obutsu.
Where are you?

Here.
Where am I?
You're here. With me.
Okay. Who are you?
I don't know. I don't know! I DON'T KNOW!!
I DON'T KNOW WHO I AM!!
HELP ME!!
A man? A body? A ghost? A weapon? A spirit?
A shadow. A shadow. I'm a shadow… just a shadow…
A shadow.
Body. And blade.
Filth. And shadow.

You are dead and alive.
I am now only dead.
You have always been caught between, and stumbling.
I have stumbled. Oh, how I have stumbled.
Falling. From one world to the other. But now, I will be your balance.
Please, be my balance too. Help me find my way out. Please.
Now, they are coming.

Okiro! Get up! You filth!
Senpai! Shiromatsu-sama! Mieru! I see you!
OKIRO!
…Vladislav. You … see me?
You see me?
Oh, what have I done?
Master…
Please help me. Help me remember.
Please… do not go…

INTERLUDE: THE SHADOW'S HELL

Now I am in hell. And my thoughts are haiku.

The void rolls over. Like colored paint blossoming. Leaves, crushed, until black.

I run, but I find my legs are ash. I look, but my eyes have burst. All I am is a disembodied mind. I am chased, and I have thoughts of running, of looking for a place where I will be safe. But this is hell. The absence of safety. The ghosts flock around me like ravens. I can feel their curiosity. Time passes. Some of them shift away, bored, apathetic. Some of them I know, but most I do not know. Then come the ones that have been waiting for me, for so long, since last I saw them. Since they presumed I sent them here.

The *yurei* are here. Vengeful ghosts.

The manners of boys, the bodies of boys, all of them filthy.

Their words, like haiku too.

Found you!

Nowhere to run!

A real-life Jap too.

How'd we get a Jap in here?

One of them has been ripped in half, the two halves of his body flop separately on the floor, fingers splaying forward, nails digging in, dragging, a trail of blood like a snail's slime, the leg, the foot, kicking uselessly behind, kicking in excitement, in nerve spasms. Chasing me. The boy's head is on one of the half-body stalks. His tongue lolls. His eyes point in different directions, the expression frozen on his face at the time of his death.

Another floats upside down and backward, held aloft, the imprint of an armored hand sunk into the flesh at his back, splintering the bones of his ribcage, squeezing the blood from his lungs, heart, and liver like juice from an orange. The blood leaks out of his eyes, his ears, and his nose. It leaks from his armpits where the shoulder blades snapped and cut through his skin-sack. Like his friend, he, too, leaves a trail in his wake. Dripping droplets of red. Chasing me.

The last boy is the most whole, all of his limbs and flesh intact, but he is swathed in shadow, perpetually off balance, his eyes wild as he sails backward through the air, the sensation of falling, the slamming and the rolling on the floor, he turns around like a top, like a pinwheel, he falls over; he falls his way after me. Chasing me.

The *yurei* catch me. Me, with a missing foot. Me, nine years old and twenty years old. Dirty. In tatters. Hair greasy, falling over my eyes like a cage, and hair singed away, my scalp blistered and bald, sores and pustules popping. Because of all the damage, I cannot get up. The pieces of my body lay suspended over the abyss, flat, and the boys catch up to me, and they howl their insults, and their limbs slam on me, and their blood mingles with mine. And this goes on and on for days, or a week, or nine years, or a thousand, or for all eternity, until I am just a puddle of red that never dries, and they are just stamping and hooting wildly in a shallow pool.

Another *yurei*, the man in the Hanma mask, arrives at some point, kneeling, the ends of his trench coat dipping into the blood. A knife with a cruel edge is in his hand. He lifts the mask, and there is another mask beneath, both masks are dominated by the rows within rows of white shining teeth. He glides the point of his weapon through the puddle of me. He forms intricate *kanji* like *sumi-e*. Symbols that signify…

Common good.

Betterment of all people.

Gaijin invader.

Capitalism.

It is like a cycle, I notice. This hell, these boys, this man and his carved philosophy. This place. This whole story. Let me tell it to you all over again.

My name is Shinjiro Asai, and for as long as I can remember, I've been cursed. I see what others cannot see. The dead. Ghosts. Twisted and entropic. I see their world, exactly like this world, only warped, bent so far out of any human proportion that the sight of it would drive you insane. For the longest time, I believed I was insane.

But then I died for the first time.

I died many times, and I escaped many times, but this time there is no escape.

Now I am in hell. And my thoughts are haiku.

The pain is surreal. The bamboo forest is truth. For all time, I know.

Everything repeats.

Until a new *yurei* finds me. Come to join in on the ceaseless red dance. Like the others, it is the vengeful spirit of one I knew. One who wronged me and I wronged, in turn, cyclical. There is fear, even though I am just a puddle. There is dread.

Another haiku is composed, but this is not mine.

Help me be whole now. The rock parts water midstream. Its forehead, hard, rough.

And I hear the new *yurei's* voice. "Shiyo," it says.

I can start again to experience things. Time moves in a perceptible measure. The story can continue.

The boys cease their splatter-romping. They regard each other with curiosity, as best their broken and shadowed eyes can. *Did you say something? Wasn't me.*

"Shiyo," the voice continues. *"Anata ... Shin-daga?"*

The Hanma-mask man ceases his calligraphy, removes his mask once, removes it again, removes it a final time, revealing the face of a tired man beneath it all. Tired of everything. He seems relieved that another presence has come.

"Shiyo, anata desu. It is you. My ... niece."

"No!" the same voice says, arguing with itself. "My downfall."

From the periphery of the void, the gently rolling paint bubble world, which is a black mass with veins of neon color, the white bleeds in, parts the side like a katana in a waterfall, and a lone figure kneels. Within the spreading whiteness, only his hands are visible upon his knees, and his straight black hair, cascading long over his bent head. His garb is pure, pure white. His voice comes from everywhere, a cacophony of contradictory thoughts.

"I've found you. There is no escape.

"And you can help me. Please.

"You will do as I command. Body and blade.

"I am so sorry."

The *yurei* boys are frightened. They tromp and flop and drag and float their wrecked body parts away, dripping and sliming and tripping through the other side of the black paint bubble. I can sense now, and I sense that they will be back when the man in white leaves.

But the Hanma-mask man stays, his mask within a mask resting atop his head. He stands, straightens his back, and lets out the sigh of a rickety old man.

"Yeah, no, I'm afraid not," the Hanma-mask man says. "That'll do. Stop right there," he says to the man in white, through gritted teeth, a shit-eating smile, but the man in white hasn't moved a muscle. Only the white slice in the world widens, parting the void. "You don't understand," the mask pleads, speaking from the top of his head, itself a shit-eating smile. "I got a job to do, and I always see it gets done." He flicks the knife point at the puddle beneath his feet, casting droplets of my blood like an abstract expressionist.

The man in white has been here longer. Much, much longer.

"Oh," the mask-wearing man says, realizing he has no power over anything. No control. And the spreading white rubs him out. He is gone, mask, mask, knife, and all. But he, too, will return.

The black paint bubble void has receded all the way around, nearly completing a circle. Now, the black is more of a knife's edge itself against all the invading white, dwindling to nothing on the side opposite the kneeling man, his presence pushing it away. Everything moves without moving.

But I am still just a puddle of blood, beaten and painted by the *yurei* into a pulp for hours and days and probably longer.

"Shiyo," the man in white says, kneeling beside the red puddle.

"Shinjiro Asai," the man corrects himself. Everything he says is conflicted. Light followed by dark, followed by light. Yin, then yang, and vice versa. There is good in him. There is nothing but hate, a *shura*.

The void is gone and yet lingers in a new form. Pure white all around. A *new* hell maybe, but a hell all the same. His chin lifts up from his reverie, his nose and face part the cascade of black hair as he straightens. His eyes open. For a moment, they flash a furious red, then fade to calm white snow, white paper, white threads of spider silk, lined with veins of gray corruption.

"Oh, Shiyo. My niece. What have they done to you?

"Nothing I would not do as well," he states a moment later.

The man in white knows me, hates me, and is pleased to see me writhe. Yet he is also a loved, lost, and longed-for family member, and though I am meeting this aspect of him for the first time, I would recognize him anywhere. It is my uncle, Yasuro Shiromatsu. But it is also the White Shadow.

My past tormentor. Returned now to torment me. Rays of hope and sun.

"*Ie, Shiyo-san. Ie.* No torment. Never. Never again.

"Forever onward. Remember your oath, you filth."

So unexpected. The reasoning escapes me. An open bug's cage.

The spirit of Yasuro Shiromatsu places its hand against the flat blood spatter, strokes it gently, like a painter mixing paint. I sense something, *feel* something. It's my own fingertip. My index finger. Then my middle finger. My thumb, pinky, and ring finger. My whole hand. Yasuro lifts his hand slowly, like he's lifting the lid from a clay jar, and my blood stretches upward in the shape of my arm. I feel my fingers twitch. His hand locks in mine, squeezes, and something in me is compelled to squeeze back. He pulls, he lifts, he rises to his feet, grips with his other hand and hauls the blood pool up, and the rest of me takes shape.

I collapse onto the blank white of the void, and I'm like a blood red gelatin for a moment. Then my pores suck it all back in through my skin, like inverse sweat. I sense even more. I hear, I taste, I smell, although there is nothing to smell. My lungs heave. I see. My eyelids flutter open. My body is the same age and dressed the same as the moment of my final death. Twenty years old, tattooed, scarred, barefoot, and I wear the NeOsaka subway engineer's jumper.

I lay on my side. Yasuro waits patiently beside me. I don't know how long he has waited. I can think again. I can speak.

"Shiyo-chan," he says. "I know you. I see you.

"I remember … killing you. Long before."

I prop myself up onto my elbows. We are in the white emptiness. The White Shadow's personal hell, at the bottom—and yet farther down—of *Yomi*, the land of the dead. Even though there is nothing here, something is missing.

I stare down at my empty hand, palm up. Something is missing.

"The white katana is gone," my uncle tells me. "Your father's white katana."

"You have failed me!" he adds, and his eyes flash a bloody red. The fingers of his right hand curl angrily, reach for the hilt of the weapon always within a true samurai's reach, and they find nothing.

The sword is gone, I realize. I reach for it too.

In front of me, there is a phantasm of Yasuro Shiromatsu splitting into several images of himself at once, all of them layered over each other. He weeps, his face in his hands. He rages, lunging. He falls backward, afraid. And more. They all move, but go nowhere. I see one of them examine me with an expression of pride, glad that I did what I could while alive and brought him some clarity.

And it is this image I focus on, the one that can speak to me. If the spirit of Yasuro can have some kind of control over this place, so can I. I block the others out, and I sit upright on my knees facing him. The conflicting voices in him quiet, fall silent.

"Yasuro," I begin, "if the sword is gone, are you … free?"

"*Hai,*" he says. And he tries to smile, a kind of awkward rolling of his jaw and a twitching of his upper lip. A smile, genuine or forced, is an unfamiliar thing for this spirit who has been trapped in hell, as it had been for the man he was in life. But he finally pulls it off.

"How?" I ask.

"My greatest student. Vladislav. He *saw* me."

"At the castle."

"He *understood* me. My ... great shame."

"He told me that he knew there was still good in you," I say, and after I do, the White Shadow himself seems to crack, seems to quake and choke on his reply. He pitches forward, as if the invisible tension that has held him rigidly upright for all his life has suddenly released. Tears pool in his eyes. "Vladislav Zercos asked me to tell you that he's sorry he failed you, but also that he forgives you."

"Forgives..." Yasuro focuses on the empty space between us. He wipes his tears on the back of his suit sleeve before they can fall, and he composes himself with amazing alacrity. He is the samurai once more, in all aspects (aside from the hateful bigoted bastard, as far as I could tell). "I knew already that Vladislav forgives me. But thank you, Shiyo, for telling me."

"At the castle, that night, across from us, he said he saw you. That was it, wasn't it? He freed you from the white sword that killed you. The hell that your hate and your desire for revenge had trapped your soul inside. And that was when I couldn't ... *call* you again. Even when I needed you."

"*Soo-desu,*" Yasuro says. He regards me blankly with his spider-webbed eyes. There is no trace of red. "Vladislav reminded me that, despite all the terrible things I had done, I had also done him a kindness. Master and student, we were *family.*"

"And us? You and me. *Uncle* Yasuro, it turns out. We are family."

He falters. Looks away.

"What's wrong?"

"Vladislav is not the only one whose forgiveness I must seek. I am still here, still tormented by the phantasms of my own past, my own self-doubts, my fear. My anger, most of all. Seemingly never-ending anger. And the memories of the horrors I have visited upon others."

"Okay," I say. "Who?"

Then I say, "*Oh...*"

I recall how the blood had stained his white suit red up to the elbows. I knew the sticky feeling of his hands as he wrung them. It had been my mother's blood. I feel a heat, a searing purple wind of righteousness—just like my father's—that flares to life somewhere far away, yet close enough that I can summon it, rain it down upon the object of my hatred, the one who wronged me. I can manifest it and blast this pitiful spirit apart. I can stamp him out. Before, he could eviscerate me, leave me dangling over the void, bleed me out like a waterfall. Why can't I do the same? There is nothing stopping me. No sword either of us can call to cut the other down. He killed my mother. I never had the chance to know her. He robbed me of everything. He cast me out into the horrid reality of my own life. I hate him.

I feel myself becoming a phantasm, too. I feel myself splitting into different aspects, spiraling out in a thousand directions. My thoughts split into disparate voices, screaming, crying, pleading, fuming, cursing.

And then I stop myself.

I will not be *shura*.

I will not be the White Shadow.

I will not be my father.

"I..." and I choke on the words. I have so much power. I can do so much, but am I sure I can do this? An image of my hand shoots out from where another image of it rests on my knees. It closes around my uncle's throat. But I call it back. I am whole. Now, in this moment, here in this hell, I truly master myself.

"I forgive you. For my mother's death. I forgive you."

Yasuro Shiromatsu's aspects seem to whir and roil within himself. His jaw clenches. His gaze locks with mine. Here is a spirit who never asked for forgiveness in life, and yet inwardly yearned for it. Here is a man who was hated, but only wanted to be loved. He thought himself infallible, but failed at so many things. Now is the time for him to choose what defines him, as the time had just been my own.

"I..." he begins, but the samurai seems to falter, as I had. The eternal question rages in him, and I hold it in my thoughts as I watch him.

Can he forgive himself?

He knows it too. He knows he has to let go. Only he has the power to free himself from his own prison. It was never his twin brother that locked him in.

And so he lets go. The samurai masters himself, and will never be *shura* again. I watch him straighten. His eyes clear of the cloudy spider's webs, the milky white fades, leaving deep, brown irises, tinged with red, but it is the red of warmth, of passion and perseverance. Then he closes those eyes solemnly, and he nods.

"*Arigato-gozaimashita,*" he says, almost a whisper. Then he looks up. "But there is one more, Shiyo, whose forgiveness I must seek."

And because this hell is now shared, he doesn't need to speak their name. I know his thoughts, as he knows mine.

Anata. You, Shiyo-kun.

But you didn't kill me. When I touched the sword and found you, days ago. You let me go.

No. Before. Long before. The first day of ... you.

And just as sure as I am that you have already fit all the pieces into place, I know all at once what Yasuro means. I know that I had not been given the chance to be born, for Yasuro Shiromatsu had ripped me bloodily out of his wife's womb, carried me to the roof of ShiroKaz Tower, and let me go. I know all this because he recalls it, moment by horrid moment, in his mind. We share the memory.

Altogether, I have no thoughts and can only think of one idea, permeating my mind, spreading like a cancer: The twin brothers, Yasuro and Zenjiro, together, made me what I am. *Who* I am. The one had killed that which had never been alive, and the other preserved the life of that which was already dead. It was Yin, and it was Yang.

This is where you might expect to hear about how the white emptiness quakes with my building rage, the aspects of vengeance and righteousness resurging in me again and finally win over me, and I would tell you how I throw myself bodily at my original murderer. You saw how I could forgive him for killing my mother, but now you wonder if I could forgive him for plunging me, an unborn child, into the world of ghosts. Do not mistake forgiveness for weakness. Did you think I was so easily about to lose the mastery of self I had just gained? Give me some credit. You've seen me come so far.

"Uncle Yasuro," I say evenly, meeting his gaze. "You lost yourself that day." I am impressed with the wisdom I hear in my own voice.

"I lost myself," he confesses, "a long time before that day."

"But together, we've found you again. I forgive you. For my death. I forgive you."

I close my eyes and pitch forward slowly into a deep and reverent bow. This man is my family. This spirit is worthy of honor and respect. No matter how besotted with villainy, he can come back. We all can. I have given him what he has sought and guided him to peace.

And when I raise myself, and I exhale, and I open my eyes, he is gone.

Yasuro Shiromatsu is gone.

The white emptiness is gone with him.

I am within the cave, atop the cliff where my father cast me out. The hot winds still blast everything around me, the purple lightning still lances the clouds far below, but I have transcended it all. I feel none of it, or rather, I feel that none of this place's violence can harm me. The *kami* still twinkle in the shapes of the inverted city above me. The empty samurai armor is not here. It returned long ago. I feel time catching up, envisioning myself climbing up from the abyss, inch by inch, while my mind had drifted far away and I did not know myself. I had been the blasted body, then the stamped mess, then the reformed self, conversing with the lost spirit of my uncle Yasuro; all of that as I myself wandered, found the place from where I fell and started the climb back.

I stay there, kneeling, for a long time, perhaps. I cannot say. Forever, in the blink of an eye. A notion comes to me, a memory of a spirit I have known. Vladislav Zercos. He had been forgiven, and he'd forgiven those he needed to, and then he was set free. I feel now how he must have felt: free to fade away. There is nothing anchoring me to the world of the living anymore.

But we both know that is not true.

You want to know how an infant who's not even alive gets called back from the realm of ghosts? You are probably asking yourself that exact question right now.

Love.

My mother, Mizuko. She loved me before she ever knew me. In a way, her love gave me life. Her love scattered the lost souls that had come to gawk at the stillborn baby lying in the street; her love made me whole, and her love sent me through the veil. Mizuko brought life to things where all life has ceased.

My eyes wander over the city in the ceiling of the cave, settling at last on a pulsing pink glow that has been there this whole time, watching over me. It emanates from a grove beside a flooded graveyard, long abandoned and falling to ruin. It is the pink of sakura petals blossoming. There is love there, and it is calling me.

It is all the anchor I will ever need.

THIRTY-FOUR

BY MY WILL, I BENT THE SPACE WITHIN *YOMI* INTO A kind of tunnel, a worm-hole like what Tatsuhiro had fashioned for his castle reconstruction crew. I aimed it directly at the graveyard, and I stepped through. The bare sole of my foot crunched the gravel on the weather-beaten path ringing around the sixty-first tier, and vivid pink sakura petals were everywhere.

Time surged forward. The window into the hellscape of *Yomi* evaporated in a puff of purple smoke behind me. In an instant, the full moon raced skyward, then slowed to a crawl. It hung over the bay, flooding everything with a bright, silver light.

I'm home.

The ghost tunnel had dropped me right in front of a *haka* stone that stood out from all the other thousands of *haka* stones. The one with the sculpture of a katana held in a stand. In the moonlight, the name of the one honored there glowed on its stone marker, piercing through the erosion of time.

Shiromatsu Mizuko, it read.

And in my hand, I held the weapon that had killed her. The black katana.

Its case, its handle, its grip, its ceremonial *sageo* cord, all of it, every molecule of it, was a lightless, abyssal black. This was the White Shadow's weapon. He'd carried it everywhere, on every job, in and out of the underworld, up and down every floor of mega-corp skyscrapers. He'd unsheathed it to threaten the enemies of the ShiroKaz Legacy. He'd drawn it across the necks of those who wouldn't be convinced. He'd thrust its tip into the heart of his own wife, and he'd sawed her baby, me, out of her corpse with its edge.

I gripped the black katana tightly, and an ethereal sakura-pink smoke wafted softly from its edge. I could feel my mother's spirit lingering inside it, but she wasn't trapped in the same way that Yasuro had been trapped. She was not vengeful. For her, there were no old scores to settle. She lingered only to see that I, her child, was happy.

I lifted the perfect, black katana and rested its sheath against my forehead. I closed my eyes, and I felt my mother's head against mine, her eyes closed too, the two of us embracing warmly. I'd finally found her. She'd finally found me. We'd been so close for so long, and yet worlds apart. When I was done with what needed to be done, I would find her. And Ben Roy Doon. And Sandra Calvin, and Luther DeLeon. And even my uncle Yasuro. I'd find their spirits and ensure they were at peace. But before all that, I had to find someone else.

Thankfully, I felt that she was already here.

I bounded up the steps two at a time, my living heart pumping, my lungs expanding with sweet cherry-blossom air. I followed the inexplicable feeling that flooded me whenever Cayenne was near. It's something I can't explain because no one ever teaches you these things. Remember? But it was real. It led me straight to her.

In the grove just passed my little grave-tending work-shop, she'd pitched a kind of tent out of an optic-camouflage sheet under the boughs of the fully bloomed sakura trees. There was a kind of ripple in reality that gave it away when seen from ground level, but anyone—or any drone—peering down from above would see only a seamless blanket of pink petals as the device worked its technological magic. And out here on the fringes of the city, Cayenne was certainly far off the grid.

I wanted to shout her name and throw the whole thing back and throw myself against her and just feel her, just look in her emerald green eyes. But even before I could be *that* careless, I heard the cocking of a gun and felt the familiar press of its barrel against my temple, halting me in my tracks. I'd been careless enough.

"White Shadow," a garbled electronic voice said beside me. I wondered absently if the black katana could sustain me in the living world the same way the white katana had, if my tinman assailant's bullet would just pass straight through my head in a wisp of purple smoke when he pulled the trigger. I decided not to risk it, and I just held up my hands like a normal captive. All around us, I saw the rippling and shifting of pink-tinged light against the darker bark of the trees as more camouflaged figures stirred.

"It's the White Shadow," the voice repeated. There was a little less distortion this time, a little more familiarity. I risked turning to face it. The nigh-invisible figure with the machine pistol at my head lifted a hand to its face to remove a mask. It drew back its hood, and a loose strand of Cayenne's blonde hair bounced forward, away from the one fully shaved half of her head, side, back, and top. A nasty postoperative scar spiraled around her ear, and the staples and bruising were still fresh. There were dark circles under her emerald green eyes.

Although Cayenne looked haggard and worn down by sleeplessness, worry, and stress, she never looked more beautiful to me than she looked at that moment. I just wanted to hold her, so I took a step forward.

And she took a step back, her gun swinging around and pressing right between my eyes. She pushed me away with it, painfully. "Stop," she said. Her voice was hoarse, like she'd lost it for days and was only now recovering it. "Just stop." Tears welled in her eyes as she looked at me.

The others—maybe four of them, I didn't know or really care to count—fanned out around me. "It's the White Shadow," one of them repeated on my left.

"It's not," I said, glancing at the shimmering distortion to my side. "It's not the White Shadow. It's really fucking not. Cayenne, it's *me*."

"Drop the sword," another voice said, ignoring me just as much as I was ignoring him and all the others. But I did as they said anyway, letting go of the black katana so it clattered by my right foot in a fluffy pile of sakura petals. The sword mattered a great deal to me, but I kicked it away. My mother would understand.

My eyes stayed locked with Cayenne's. I was almost crying, too. "I'm not the White Shadow," I pleaded. But she didn't look convinced. She looked even more tired.

"You're lying to me," she said, running a shaking hand under her bruised eyes while the other still held the gun to my forehead. "You're *his fucking daughter.*" Her attempt to put on the old armor and compose herself failed, and she fell to pieces in her next breaths. Her words came out in sobs. "When you asked me what my father's name was, you knew he was alive, and you didn't tell me. And then you went and killed him. Because *your* father told you to. The White Fucking Shadow of the ShiroKaz Corporation. Ghost assassin. Sent to kill off the Cluster. Well, it didn't work, not entirely. There's still a DeLeon here."

She seemed to draw some strength from that last sentiment, drawing herself up, taking in a deep breath, and letting it out coolly. She stopped shaking. I expected the bullet to arrive in my brain any second now. But while my mind stumbled around for what I could possibly say, she didn't pull the trigger. Then I just started by saying the obvious.

"It wasn't Tatsuhiro that sent me underground. For all his power and reach on the grid, our boss didn't know shit about where your father was. *He* knew he was alive, for years, and he never told you. *He* lied to you, Cayenne, not me. *He* told you they were dead, and *he* kept you hostage, grooming you into some kind of servant or corporate secretary. I didn't kill your father, Cayenne. But I was there when he died. He told me not to tell you. He didn't want you to see him, how he'd … deteriorated. He knew if he ever tried to reach you that Tatsuhiro would kill you. I'm sorry, Cayenne. I'm so sorry. I…" I kept one hand up and delicately steered her gun out of my face with the other. She let me, and it fell to her side. "I should've told you, that morning in your house. I knew that *something* wasn't right. Outside Himeji Castle, Zercos showed me something. It said *family* and *graveyard,* and he meant *here*, this place. And he gave me your name, *DeLeon.* The fucking cyborg ninja wasn't working for the mega-corps like we thought. He was really your father's agent all along. Your father sent him to get me, and Ben showed up, too.

"Cayenne," I said, shaking my head, swallowing the grief that tried to climb its way out all over again. "Ben's dead. Zercos is dead. It's just you and me now. We're the only ones who can do anything to stop him. Ben sent you something important, and he encrypted it. And they're hunting you for it."

I realized that I was just saying shit she already knew. The scar on the side of Cayenne's head told the whole story. She was on the run, probably from the moment I stepped out of the atrium and stopped for ramen on the way. She'd decrypted Ben's ridiculous string of acronymic and found what he'd hidden for her on the grid: the truth, about her family, about the Cluster. Maybe even where to find them. But it was all too late. By then, Tatsuhiro's spirit had already lodged in Zercos's body and taken a one-way trip straight to their underground city, killed Luther, and flooded the place. Somehow, Cayenne had found some survivors—these guys with their guns still trained on yours truly—and they'd told her what happened down there, and they'd helped her carve out all the neuromods Tatsuhiro had gifted her with, all that shit he could've used to track her on the grid, or worse.

I finally took my eyes off of her long enough to get a good look at their camp under the sakura trees. There appeared to be at least three of the camo-sheet tents pitched, possibly more, and they'd done what they could to keep everything contained under their cover, from small fire pits to cook over and keep warm, to shoddy computer hardware, all wired on a local, portable network. They wouldn't dare risk plugging into the grid, of course. Not that they could way out here in this empty sector even if they wanted to.

"Cayenne," I said softly, inching closer to her, and this time she didn't back away. "How long have you been hiding here?"

While I spoke, one of the Cluster guys, still in light-shifting camouflage, had picked up the black katana on my right, drawing my attention. All I saw was a pair of floating hands, one with a bull-pup assault rifle at the ready, and the other wrapped firmly around the black *saya* sheath. The shimmering figure didn't seem to know what to do with either of the weapons. They were waiting on Cayenne DeLeon's order.

"Give it to her," she told them tiredly, and without answering my question, she turned about and plodded toward the closest tent.

In all honesty, in that moment, I cared less about the sword than I cared about her. You may be thinking that my mother's spirit was in there, but you'd only be half right. You may think there was some kind of symbolism in the fact that I ignored the katana entirely and just followed Cayenne, but you'd be all wrong. I didn't know if I could summon the black katana at will the same way I could the white one, and I didn't care to find out. All of that could wait.

When I ducked into her tent, she was already lying down on an unrolled futon. The stack of towels serving as the pillow where she rested her head were stained with dull pink and brown splotches from when her surgical wounds had been fresh. The stains looked a week old, if not weeks. From the little I knew about cybernetic modifications, I realized that Cayenne couldn't just have some Cluster doc rip out the hardware grafted to her skull and brain and hope to live through the procedure. More likely that she'd had to keep the system but swap out the chips running them, which would be invasive enough on her skull. Cayenne hadn't given me an answer yet about how long she'd been out here, but from the way she closed her eyes and already seemed to be sleeping, it didn't look like she'd be able to stay much longer.

I sat cross-legged at her side and picked up one of the medicine bottles from a neat stack of them on a small wooden shelf that I recognized, taken from the little workshop I kept nearby for keeping my brooms and prepping rice bowls for the dead. She'd been taking antibiotics to fight off infection after the impromptu surgery, and only two or three pills rattled inside. The others looked empty. I put it back, and I said nothing. I just watched her breathe.

"Shinjiro Asai," she whispered, then let out a laugh. "I remember the first time I saw you. You were the one coming back from the dead. It seems our positions have reversed."

I matched her with a laugh of my own. "No, Cayenne DeLeon," I said, coming down on my side to lay beside her, "you're not nearly naked enough. Also, you're more beautiful than I could ever be."

She cracked open an eyelid and rolled her gaze toward me. "Even now?"

I caressed her buzzed scalp just over the scar around her ear. "Especially now," I said, and I meant it, more than I'd ever meant anything she, or you, or anyone had ever heard me say.

She turned her head toward mine, and her hand went to my cheek. She drew me in, and we kissed once, tenderly, our eyes closing. I hovered over her, pressed my forehead to hers, and the familiar warmth spread all over.

"I love you," I said. "Since that first moment I saw you, I have loved you."

Another breathy note of laughter escaped her. She was smiling, ear to ear. "Don't give me that shit, Shinjiro Asai. You just wanted to … conquest me. Get between the C-Level mega-corp elitist's legs."

"Well, sure," I admitted casually, and we laughed together. Then I said, seriously, "But I was afraid of you then. Afraid of everything. Afraid of figuring out the… the *me* that I really wanted to be in this world. When I saw you, talked to you, you just seemed to have it all put together. Your *self*, you know? I knew I wanted that, too. But on the inside," I said, reaching into the pocket of my dirty mauve brown jumper, finding the photograph, and unfolding it, "you were just like me. Wearing a mask, for years. Defensive, closed-off. Being someone you weren't."

She took the photo, and together we looked at the mother, father, and daughter at their absolute happiest.

"The two of us turned out to be so different, and yet the same. Both searching. And I think I found my family, Cayenne. But it wasn't fucking Tatsuhiro and his Shiromatsu-Kazama Corporation. It was *you*."

She set the photo down on the shelf, then turned back to me. We were both quiet a long time, gazing into each other's eyes. I rolled her long locks of blonde hair between my fingers, and she pushed the black lock of mine behind my ear. She rolled over to give me room on the futon, and I nuzzled in behind her.

"I love you too," she whispered. "Shin."

I don't know if we fell asleep, or if my wish came true and the moment just lasted forever, or what, but her shifting eventually roused me. She reached a hand under her pillow, then pressed something into my palm. I didn't need to see it to know exactly what it was. I would never be able to forget what it felt like. Her fingers closed mine over the *omamori* charm.

"I thought you were gone," she said. "And never coming back."

"Where I went," I started, then corrected myself. "Where he sent me, I thought so, too."

"But I never stopped hoping."

Hope, I thought, and I squeezed the charm even tighter. *I never lost hope, either.*

Another long silence passed.

"I..." her voice drifted off, as if she didn't know how to explain something that she needed to tell me. Somehow, I knew what it was, and I dreaded hearing it. "I ... *went in.* To find you."

During all my recent revelations, I'd developed what you might call a bad feeling about this very thing. Maybe no one is born with the curse of seeing ghosts and the power to part the veil that separates the worlds of living and dead. Cayenne certainly wasn't, and I wasn't, either, it turned out. But as a baby, I'd been saved by my mother's spirit, and then nine years later I'd been "saved" by my father's. And I'd saved Cayenne, high above the Earth, in Heaven, when Smythe's tinmen had opened fire on us. I'd dragged her through the underworld, and she'd kept her eyes open while a spirit, me, led her back to life. And that was that.

"I'm sorry," I said. And then I said it again. "I'm so sorry, Cayenne."

"I'm … like you now." She wasn't asking.

"I think so."

"When I went looking for you, I tried to leave these trees, go past the gate, but they were all there. The dead, the ghosts. Some of them didn't see me." She swallowed, and even though I only saw the back of her head, I felt her eyes squeeze tightly shut. A shiver went through her. "Some of them did, though."

"Did they hurt you?"

"No. I just ran back in. And I've just been wasting away, Shin."

"Cayenne," I said, growing more concerned, "time doesn't move at the same, uh, speed. I think it depends on … shit, I don't even know." I propped myself up on my elbow, and she looked up at me in response. "How long was I gone?"

"It's been a month, Shin."

A month. I thought maybe I didn't hear her right. *A fucking month.*

I remembered the full moon over the graveyard, the first night I'd been let go from the White Shadow's empty white hell. And now, just outside this optic-camo tent, above the bright pink canopy of sakura trees, the same full moon.

A fucking month!

I started to panic, my thoughts racing, unable to focus on all the things, Tatsuhiro's castle, the tinman parts in the crates, the construction, the employees, the security, the Syndicate, Lim, Smythe, Feikes, all of them and more, even fucking Boltcutter probably out of his coma with a new leg, all the enforcers and cells spread out over NeOsaka, on rooftops, in quadcopters, on the spider rails, synced up with aerial drones, and underground, smoking out the old Cluster tunnels, Tenjin Media pushing dynam-ads with Cayenne's face onto the grid's connected comlinks. And Tatsuhiro, commanding his army of ghosts to move and search mean-while on the *other* side. The grand dragon had had a month's worth of time to get in position, to find Cayenne.

She pressed a reassuring hand against my chest, reminding me that he hadn't found her. Not yet. My racing heartbeat slowed as if from her touch alone. He'd had one whole month, and he hadn't found her. And he wasn't going to.

But she couldn't stay here much longer. Even if she was like me now. Maybe she didn't have to eat, maybe she couldn't die anymore, but I didn't want to find any of that out. I didn't want her to waste away.

"Cayenne," I said, and once again I ran a finger beside her scar. "What did Ben send to you?"

It turns out the one who'd picked up the black katana in the grove was the same balding, bearded German wizard I'd seen in the train tunnels just above the Cluster's city. Gustav was his name. When he handed me back my weapon, I reached through the veil to find the revolver I'd shot my father with, then held it out to him, grip first.

"Thanks for letting me borrow it," I said. "It's got one shot left."

Even though he'd already seen the ghost-hand from nowhere swipe the gun right out of his hip holster, the sight of the ghostly hand-off through a cloud of purple smoke was enough to spook Gustav and all the others all over again.

"Ahh, fuck me, no," he said, holding both hands out, smiling nervously. "You can keep that."

I shrugged and handed it back to my spirit cowboy friend on the other side.

"*Danke*," I said.

There were eight of us in total at this makeshift Cluster camp in the sakura grove beside the abandoned graveyard on the fringe of NeOsaka. They'd rearranged the disparate sheets of optic camouflage into a single unit that draped over a wider space, but we still didn't have the headroom to stand. We sat around a central, three-dimensional holo-light display like it was a campfire. From behind her ear, Cayenne extracted a data cube that glowed with the information she'd retrieved from Ben's site on the grid, concealed with the final string of acronymic that he'd left her.

S.A.N.D.

Shinjiro Asai never die.

I said the words aloud, and she handed the cube to Gustav.

The old technowizard slotted it into his jury-rigged setup and punched the word sequence into his keyboard to load the file, and just like that, it booted. (All the while, he muttered German curses under his breath since he'd been trying to decode this *sheise* acronymic for a month already but fucking of course in wanders this Japanese cowgirl-ghost *frau* who opens it in twelve seconds!) I didn't understand anything we were looking at, but that was okay as I'd come to find out, since no one else did either.

We watched strings of alphabetic letters, numerals, and logographic characters tick up bit by byte on the flickering, projected image. It was code. Millions and millions of lines of computer code, a lifetime of work between Luther and Ezinne DeLeon, Triangle, and Zenjiro Shiromatsu. I knew there were talented and educated operators out there that could look at such a thing for half a second and know its precise function and purpose. Like Ben. Like Cayenne. Even operators like Gustav, a former ShiroKaz employee who'd been shifted to Inari for ten years before going underground with the Cluster.

"None of this *sheise* makes any damned sense," he said, pointing frantically at one line as it scrolled up, then another, and looking at me with wild eyes. "There! See? And down there. There are no terminations of the strings. They are half-done, yah. And it is like … there is evidence to suggest that a skilled programmer laid the foundational code—this has Luther's signature all over it—but later some, some, some kind of *monkey* came in and futzed with the second half of almost every bit."

"It resembles a patch of some kind," Cayenne added. "We can at least see that much. It can't be a full autonomous program, such as what could run a system on its own."

"That's what Luther told me," I said, and the place suddenly got very quiet. Maybe I was expecting too much from a group of people that might've been feeling safe and comfortable in their subterranean city a month ago, then watched me walk into their leader's office and walk out again in a cloud of purple smoke. I could tell they trusted me only because Cayenne trusted me, and warily, at that. Mentioning her father's name reminded them of all he'd meant to them, to their cause, and how he'd died. How none of them had actually seen it happen to know that the story I'd told them just moments before was actually true.

Well, they'd just have to get over it because I knew what was true, and we didn't have time.

"It's a patch for the grid," I clarified. "That's exactly what Luther said. Gustav, you recognize his work in there, his code. But not the other's. When you were at ShiroKaz, did you ever work with Zenjiro?"

The old German scoffed at the name. "Huh! The playboy? The troublemaker? Are you saying *he* is the monkey who futzed around in here?"

"Yes," I shot back directly. "Yes. Zenjiro Shiromatsu wrote this code too. But it's not by accident that it looks like this. Zenjiro was like his brother. Yasuro, the White Shadow, you know, the ghost-man with the white sword."

"Inconceivable," Gustav huffed. "Zenjiro was nothing like his brother. And yes, I knew Yasuro. Everyone in that tower knew who Yasuro was," he said, with a lot less bluster now, as if he expected the samurai to materialize behind him and lay a cold, dead hand on his shoulder. "We knew what he did for his work. But…" And Gustav made a gesture at his hip, by the empty holster that had once held the revolver I borrowed. "Not *how* he did any of that and then kept coming back. Like you."

"Well, now you know." It was Cayenne that had said it. She seemed a little less tired than before, a little more invigorated by the new information, and a lot more impatient. After days of staring at unintelligible and ridiculous sequences of English S, A, N, and D words—just after enduring a smidge of fucking brain surgery no less—at least we were getting somewhere. She steered the meeting back on track like a CEO. I was glad to see her business armor at least part way back on. "Shin, what did Zenjiro do to my father's code?"

I took a deep breath, realizing how crazy I was about to sound.

"He told me that he could see spirits inside the code. Not spirits like those of the restless dead. But the *kami*, the spirits that live in all things fashioned by mankind." I pointed at the screen, to the weird (apparently) unterminated strings or whatever Gustav had said. "Right there, invisible. Someone made that, right? Like someone who built a house, or a tailor who sewed the lining of a suit." I got suddenly a little choked up, and the filthy jumper I'd been sporting for days, or I guess a month, got itchier. "Luther wrote the patch in the living world, and Zenjiro added to it in *Yomi*. That's the land of the dead."

The surviving members of the Cluster looked around at each other, as I'd thought they might. No one said anything for several long seconds.

I closed my eyes and let out a breath. I straightened my back, let my hands rest on my knees, and emptied my mind. I pushed the physical sensations away—the air in my lungs, the concrete beneath me, the fabric against my skin, the sounds of wind and breath, all of it. And with those, I pushed away the worldly preoccupations and worries, the doubts of these people, the doubts of myself. I projected my body and soul half into the underworld.

And I opened my eyes, and all existence had twisted around me. I saw up through the material of the camouflage shroud, through the treetops, the building tops, through the sky itself, on toward the end of the universe, and all the *kami* twinkling at every man-made stop along the way. I lowered my gaze to the flickering code at the center, and there it all was. Before, Gustav had been pointing at what he'd claimed were unfinished parts of the program. But here, in *Yomi*, it was all there. My father's grand work. The *kami* that lived in the code. The *genkaku*, Triangle had told him, thinking they were just hallucinations.

"I see them," I said, breaking my hold on the trance just a little bit. I perceived that the others had backed away. My eyes were glowing a bright purple, and an outline of ethereal purple smoke flowed around my body.

"I see them too," Cayenne said, and that brought me almost all the way out. I blinked, and saw her eyes were lit with bright pink fire. It was her the Cluster was backing away from.

I took another deep breath and pulled myself fully back into the living world. The twinkling diamond light completing the unfinished strings of code evaporated from my sight.

"Everyone relax," I said. I looked directly at Gustav, who looked like he'd seen a... well... I'm not going to say it. "That's how Yasuro did *all that*," I told him, flexing my fingers by my waist like a cowgirl about to draw down.

"Fucking magic," the wizard-bearded German mumbled to himself.

"What is this even for, Shin?" Cayenne asked.

"It's the missing half of his new Legacy. The ShiroKaz Legacy is outdated. The corporate banners in the lobby've all been switched out. *Resurgence* is the new motto."

The raised eyebrow she shot me with suggested that I elaborate further.

"Triangle and Luther couldn't fight him off, for all those years on the grid, because he'd submerged his mainframe in the underworld. And now he's moved it to ShiroKaz Tower. He's got two of them spliced together, Tenjin Media's and his own, and he's going to patch the grid with this," I said, nodding at the ticking lines of code, "from both worlds at once. And then he's diving in and never going to come out. He will be a ghost and a machine all at once, an artificial intelligence that used to be an actual person. He can do anything SUIT could do, and once he's connected to a network, there will be no getting him out. He'll be in control of *everything*."

A new kind of quiet settled over all of us, the truly grave kind, when you realize that this really is it. *Everything* would depend on what we were discovering here in the sakura grove.

"Tatsuhiro can really do that," Cayenne said aloud. The others mistook it for a question, but I knew that the two of us had no doubts. "But if we use the architecture of this patch, we can reverse engineer it. And erase it before he has the chance."

"Maybe it's not such a bad thing," a woman said at the outside edge of the tent, turning all our heads to face her. She looked tired, truly worn-out, not just physically, but spiritually. In the last few days, she had lost everything: her home, her possessions, her autonomy, people she knew. I thought I might've seen her in the crowd at the underground reservoir. She'd lost everything that day except hope, it seemed, which is why she hadn't left the small gathering of Cluster here, not yet. But when faced with the prospect of living under the rule of an omnipotent, omnipresent spirit-AI, what hope did she—did any of us—have to resist? "He's... it's... going to keep the shield up over the city. It's going to invade the Russo-Chin systems and expose whatever threat we all know they're working on. It's going to protect us. Just... You're all looking at me like I'm crazy, I know. I'm sorry. I lived in the tunnels for five years, and he warned us, and then... It's just all gone now. How do we fight that? I'm just so..."

She drifted off, ran a shaky hand over her eyes and brow, and her head sank against her chest. We all wanted to give her time to speak, to let her know it was okay to dissent here.

But maybe Cayenne knew better than all of us, that there was no time to second-guess the intentions and ramifications of Tatsuhiro's new Legacy. "So tired," she finished for the woman. At some point, Cayenne must have unfolded the photograph of her parents. She clutched it tightly while she spoke. "I know, Justine. We all know. We're all tired. But that's not new. I may not have been with you, with the Cluster, for all these years, but I know what it feels like to not really have a choice over the course of your own life. And if we can't stop Tatsuhiro from becoming the ghost in the machine, then we'll lose all choice for all time. As if the mega-corps already didn't have so much of a say in what we all need to survive already. The day to day grind. The desire or necessity for *this* technology or *that*. Now it will just be one man deciding everything, overriding anything anyone else decides. What if he decides not to tolerate the poor, or the homeless, or the uneducated? Or lesbians? Or gays? Or transgendered people? Foreigners? The mentally ill? What about people with just some fucking bad tattoos? What if he realizes just how crowded this city is, and all the bodies are just getting in the way of *his* idea of progress? I know how tired you are of fighting. Of just surviving. How we all just want to let go and just let whatever forces are out there, which we cannot see, move us from here to there and tell us what the best kind of life is, and not have to choose. But this is different. The thing that makes us people is that we can change our minds about things. We can learn from mistakes. If Tatsuhiro gets control of the grid, there will be no changing anything. Ever again."

A rousing speech, I thought. *Except I feel personally attacked by the bad tattoos bit.*

The woman, Justine, had only known Cayenne for a month, probably less, but I'd been watching her while Cayenne spoke to her, to all of us. Some kind of fire was igniting behind her eyes, melting away the fatigue. I imagined that when Justine, and Gustav, and all the others had signed on to the Cluster, Luther DeLeon must've already lit that same fire. Cayenne, the woman with the same emerald green eyes as his, was bringing his spirit back to life, and Justine's with it. And mine.

"What about *her* though?" Another voice, another question. This one from a man I *did* recognize from the Cluster's city. Our eyes had met when he shouted at me, front and center, after the dragon-headed sigil had issued its ultimatum. He'd called me a *mega-corp whore.* He was my age, barely past being a teenager, with a wispy beard and an intense, icy stare. For the last several hours, I figured if any of these survivors were going to shoot me, he'd have been the first to pull the trigger.

"I mean, I don't know why we're seriously listening to all of this. Why we let her in here. They've been looking for you for weeks, Cayenne. And suddenly, out of thin air, our savior suddenly appears, and the two of you are making schemes to do what? We can see where this is going. You're going to walk us straight into ShiroKaz Tower and bring him what he wants."

Unfortunately, Mr. Wispybeard was correct. I had been thinking (much like I'll wager you have been) that we were indeed headed in that direction, straight to the tower. I was about to relinquish that point and defend the purity of my intentions, but a sudden notion struck me mute, and I stared at the floor, fixating upon it. The others may have misinterpreted my sudden dumb silence as having been exposed for the spy and quadruple agent they all thought I was. But not Cayenne.

"Shin, what's wrong?"

"He already *has* all the code. The same day we sent it to Ben, we sent it to SUIT, to ShiroKaz Tower. He's already got everything he needs. The mainframes are spliced. The castle's rebuilt. He's had a month to put it all together. So, why didn't he just jack in and hit the button and disappear already and become a god?"

"Because he's had a sudden conscience?" Cayenne's eyes narrowed and her lip curled at the sound of her own guess.

"Because he's not there."

Wispy and Gustav both scoffed equally loudly at that.

"*Hwas zum teufel...*" the old German started, then translated for all our benefit. "*What the fuck* are you saying? You mean he went on vacation?"

"I mean, I blew his fucking brains out all over the *tatami* floor, with your gun, by the way, Gustav. I don't know if it was too quick for him or what, but his newly reborn body took the shot and fell flat, dead. Then his spirit crept out and … it was too much for me. But my point is, his physical, living body is dead. *Was* dead, at least, last time I checked."

"And you're saying," Cayenne offered, "that he hasn't come back yet?"

"Since we're all here even talking about this, and no one's heard of any global domination yet, I think so. He wouldn't hesitate if he was there. He *would not* hesitate."

"Or he *is* there," Mr. Wispybeard countered, "and he *does* need this code, and he sent you to say exactly everything you've said to us to draw us into the trap. Or just to her," he said, pointing at Cayenne. "I didn't know anything about the White Fucking Shadow until a month ago, when she, *you*," now pointing at me, "killed my friend Luther, and my friend Ben. And right now, this sounds like the kind of shit old Gustav said the old White Shadow would get up to."

"Hey," Gustav objected quietly from the sidelines, "don't drag me into your *shieise!*"

I looked deeply into the young man's eyes. When I spoke, I pressed my hand over my heart. "Ben Roy Doon was his name. And he was my friend, too. And you're right. I… I *did*. I killed him." I looked up at Cayenne, the shock registering in her expression. "I didn't mean to. I lost control. Luther was already gone. I wanted Tatsuhiro to die so badly that I just … dragged everything to the other side. Ben, too. And I couldn't save him. And I can't bring him back."

Cayenne's hand pressed against her lips solemnly. A tear ran down her cheek. But she nodded at me, telling me she understood. She could forgive me for Ben. Maybe I could forgive myself some day.

I turned back to the young man with the wispy beard. "What's your name?"

"Garret," he said.

"Garret," I repeated, scooting closer to him, stopping within arm's reach, offering him my hand. "I'm Shiyo Shiromatsu. I'm the daughter of Zenjiro Shiromatsu and Mizuko Kazama. Niece of Yasuro Shiromatsu, the one they called the White Shadow. I was the White Shadow, too. A corporate whore, like you said. But I'm none of that shit anymore because I was lied to. I never got to choose. I'm Shinjiro Asai, and you can call me Shin. And I swear to you, we're going to finish what Luther DeLeon tried to do for years and years. We're going to block this madman out and never let him back in. And we need all the help we can get."

Garret hesitated. His eyes fell to my upturned palm, and I moved it closer.

I wound up surprised that he didn't spit on it. He gave me one last disparaging look, disappeared behind his optic-camo hood, and crawled out of the tent.

"You really shot him, yah?" Gustav sidled up beside me, and took my hand where I'd left it frozen mid-air. He shook it in Garret's stead. Then he nodded toward the exit Garret had taken. "We can let him go. Some of us may not be ready, and that's okay. But I am ready. I believe you, Shin, because what else can I do now? You could have killed me easily in the subway train, but you didn't. Instead, you argued with that computer as I ran off. So I am believing you are for real. Honest. A good ally to have.

"Now," he said, turning toward Justine and the handful of other Cluster family still remaining. "Those of us who are ready are still waiting to hear about what we will actually fucking *do*, huh?"

THIRTY-FIVE

IT TOOK THREE OF US TO LIFT THE MANHOLE AT THE BOTTOM of the graveyard basin that Ben's exoframe had settled with ease back into place. Gustav was too old, Cayenne was still recovering, and Garret had decided to give up on the group entirely and disappear along with another Cluster survivor who someone told me was his girlfriend. So it was Justine, me, and another guy named Kurt—Gustav's son, as it turned out—who did all the heavy lifting, and then the five of us descended the ladder into the darkness, headed for the city-circling underground channel that would let us come up under any part of the city we wanted to go.

The sound of flowing water had intensified since my last visit. Drainage wells that had been just deep pits of empty black now churned with floodwater almost up to the grated steel walkway. But the concrete held, and we moved single-file through tunnels and pipes that went deeper than all of Tatsuhiro's cleansing waters of wrath. We came out on the concrete shore of the massive underground river and found exactly what we were hoping to see set up around the bend to the north on our side. It was a makeshift pier bolted into the concrete, jutting out into the water, and a work-station with hololight reconstruction blueprints and mega-corp contract protocol documentation, the whole outfit lit by strings of work lights.

I dusted off the shoulders of Makoto's mauve-brown jumper as I approached the trio of similarly-dressed A-Matter flood control crewmembers, while the Cluster family followed me as quietly as they could, invisible head to toe in their optic-camo ponchos. One of the engineers was in the boat while the other two were handing him bags of gear, tools, and scuba equipment. They stopped as soon as I stepped into the light.

"*Konban-wa,*" I greeted them. *Good evening.* I held their attention and waited for their response, which was slow in coming, while the Cluster fanned out in the shadows farther up the bank. I think it was the burn-holes and shredded hems of Makoto's jumper that gave them the most pause. I blew my single lock of black hair away from the front of my face and gave them my biggest smile.

Within minutes, we had them at gunpoint, out of the boat, stripped of their uniforms, and tied up. Gustav went straight to their workbench and plugged in some device that helped him disable their comlink connections. One of the uniforms fit Justine perfectly, so Cayenne insisted she stay behind to keep our mega-corp captives under the camouflage shroud and make sure they didn't make any moves. I think she was letting Justine off the ride before the peril intensified.

Rightfully so. If all went according to plan, there would indeed be peril. We'd mapped out our every move all afternoon, packed everything we'd need in the evening, and made our way to the water's edge as the sun sank below the horizon over the sunken graveyard.

Justine looked grateful. She wished us luck when the rest of us piled into the boat and motored away to the north.

The little thing fought against the south-flowing current for almost half an hour, against the immense volumes of water being sucked out to the bay on the city's edge. We passed six other A-Matter crews on the concrete shores, all similarly outfitted, making dives to inspect the viability of the channel's foundational concrete and do spot repairs. Gustav and Kurt had donned the other mauve uniforms, and the three of us nodded in their direction as we drifted by, Cayenne staying shrouded in the very back, merged with the shadows of the subterannean river. We made another planned stop about halfway to our final destination.

So far, so good.

We scraped the aluminum hull onto the opposite shore beside the M36 spillway gate hologram, which was still being projected. From his pack, the technowizard Gustav produced—I shit you not—a toy remote control, extending the antiquated poly-foil antenna and clicking the analog power switch to ON. He'd spliced some frequency-dialing contraption onto it, and he had to find the right tune, but within one minute, the blinking red light hovering at the crest of the ceiling started to glide down and toward us. The invisible drone came to rest with a gentle *thunk* by our feet, and the hologram bars by the M36 spillway disappeared as it decloaked.

Gustav and Cayenne went to work syncing the drone's onboard computer to her neuromod, connecting the back of her ear to a port in the thing's chassis. Kurt worked on the other side, unscrewing bolts with a specialized tool the Cluster must have stolen from Hachiman Tech to override the safeties set on the .50 caliber long-barrelled rifle attached, hopefully making it impervious to localized hacks. Within ten minutes, Cayenne DeLeon had herself a new guardian angel, completely independent of the greater NeOsaka grid, answering only to the commands she pushed its way through her wireless neuromod.

Another half-hour boat trip brought us right underneath the sprawling arcology, according to Gustav's hacked A-Matter crew's tunnel diagram, and then another three spillway gates farther to arrive at the side of the pyramid with Cayenne's hidden ShiroKaz apartments. This would be the tricky part: blending in, avoiding detection, and worst of all, avoiding recognition. Appearing like a maintenance crew, Gustav and Kurt would probably be okay once they dipped into the crowds of mega-corp elite, who would soon be rising and shining in the early morning sun streaming into the lobbies and public spaces. But Cayenne and I had embarrassed Inari's silver fox CEO in Heaven during the final race of the TKMG league, and our faces were unforgettable ever since. Yours truly had been captured on camera carving up cyborg security in the sub-orbital streets, and then later on the racetrack itself getting knocked around by an orange-skinned creature of myth and legend, regardless of how SUIT had claimed to doctor the footage. So yeah, we were highly recognizable among the arcology's clientele.

That is why we would rely on some other talent. For one of us, newly acquired.

Gustav stowed the map in his pack beside the collapsible assault rifle and other bulky gadgets he kept in there. We'd left the boat and the river far below and squeezed our way through service tunnels and sliced through several steel doors, arriving at last in an elevator bank at the arcology's absolute lowest levels, practically part of the undercity. The old, bearded man gave us a smirk and salute before the elevator doors closed. He, his son, and Cayenne's pet drone were on their way to the next rendezvous a hundred floors above.

"You ready for this?"

Cayenne slipped her quaking left hand in mine, and squeezed the *omamori* charm tightly in her right. Before, the only time I had ever *wanted* to phase into *Yomi* was when I had to, when the knife was slipping in, or the trigger was being squeezed, or my back foot touched nothing but open air off the edge of a tall building. When I was in her position, I only ever crossed the veil to escape death. Not so much for travel. She didn't answer me, or look at me. She just pressed the charm against her chest and stared at the ceiling, trying to visualize the distance, wondering if she should close her eyes, or if she even could close them when it happened.

"Hey," I said, "look at me, Cayenne."

She did, with worry drowning in her eyes.

"It's going to be okay. I'm here with you, like last time, and I've done this a hundred times, a hundred different ways. Actually, I should tell you about sky-diving some time later." Her face scrunched up in confusion. After the collapse, recreation like that out in the irradiated wastes was a death sentence. It wasn't helping my case. "Have you ever plugged in a simulation of a funhouse, with the wheels that turn, and the mirrors, like from the 20th century?"

"Will you please just shut up, Shin?"

Okay then.

She turned away from me, closed her eyes, and concentrated on the charm in the palm of her hand, held against her heart. I was impressed. I was a bad teacher, and here my student was already doing what she needed to do without instruction. A natural. The sakura-pink aura surrounded her, and she squeezed my hand tighter even as I felt her physical form dissipating, the weight and touch of her fading from reality.

I held up the black katana and closed my eyes as well. Whereas before, I reached for Yasuro's desire for vengeance within the white sword as a means of power, now I reached for the protection of my mother's spirit within the black one, and I found it so easily. Mizuko's spirit was so close to me now, relieved, and at peace. But still inside. There was someone my mother and I needed to see one last time before we could both rest.

Together, Cayenne and I experienced the corkscrewing, spiraling, darkening distortion of entering *Yomi*, the realm of the dead. Like falling and ascending. Together, we opened our eyes on one layer of ceiling over our heads, and the next layer and the next, all of them illuminated at intervals with the *kami* they housed. All the workings of all the materials and contraptions and contrivances within all the arcology blinded us.

Beside me, I heard Cayenne's breathing sharpen like she was hyperventilating. The hand I held in mine, even in this place, broke out in a cold sweat. I squeezed it tightly and stepped around to face her, cutting off her view of the underworld landscape.

"Shhh," I murmured soothingly. "Shhh, Cayenne, it's okay. You're not dead."

Well, I thought, wincing a little. *Actually, we are dead, but...*

My words, my tone, my hand in hers, it all seemed to work. She looked away from the expansive, twisting x-ray sky and locked her eyes on mine. I couldn't help thinking all over again how beautiful she was, even in this place.

She nodded, saying, *I'm with you.*

"I don't know the way. You will have to look up and *see* where we're going. Okay? When you're ready." I lifted her fingers to my lips, gave them a gentle kiss, and smiled. "When you're ready. You're going to lead *me* this time. Just look up and *see* our way through."

I mean, I guess that's how I used to do it all the time. Nobody ever gave me the terminology or anything. I could only hope my words were making sense to her.

She closed her eyes and swallowed, psyching herself up, steadying her breaths. Then she looked up, and her green eyes gleamed as she saw through the underworld. Again, I was impressed. She was a natural.

This time, when the elevator doors parted, it was my turn to give Gustav and Kurt a smirk and salute. They'd been waiting in the dead-end hallway for only two minutes, pretending to do some kind of maintenance check next to the hidden elevator only Cayenne's retina could open. So she opened it from the inside. The small banners inside the hidden elevator hadn't been changed, still proudly displaying the ShiroKaz motto of old Yoshinori's Legacy—*Spirit* and *River*—and not that of Zenjiro's new one, *Resurgence*.

Again: so far, so good. Hopefully, it meant he and all his corporate allies had overlooked this place when hunting Cayenne, or at least abandoned the idea she would retreat to such an obvious safe house so soon after the bounty had been put out. Hopefully, enough time had passed and we could use the apartment as a makeshift base of operations.

"An American friend of mine," Gustav began, kneeling beside his son by the hardlight control panel and unscrewing it from the plate, "he once told me, he says, 'better to be safe than sorry.'" Within a few minutes, he'd produced yet another piece of equipment from his satchel, this one sleek and small, state-of-the-art. It was a set of cyberspace goggles so small it was practically two monocles. "He died, of course, the American," he said, clamping the specs onto the bridge of his nose. Then he said, "Kurt, my son, if you would please."

The younger German flipped through a set of curling pages in a grimy notebook while his father's eyes spun around like an REM sleeper's and his face twitched out commands into the virtual system linked within the elevator panel that only he could see.

"H-U–" Kurt began slowly, "H-N-N."

"Yah," Gustav mumbled, navigating his way through the arcology's self-contained block of cyberspace. "Okay. How about an interpretation? I will drop in the bug."

"Heroics under heat net nothing."

I exchanged a look with Cayenne. The face I made was meant to say, *This is just as ridiculous as the first time Ben showed us.*

Her face replied with, *But if it fucking works, then shut the fuck up.* I might've added the profanity there.

Her face turned out to be right.

"Okay, we are in," Gustav proclaimed, removing his cyberspace clip-ons. "They have begun their search for the bug, and with the length and complexity of this H-acronym, I would estimate," he cocked his head and wiggled his hand, "ehh, we have two hours. They can detect an intrusion, but cannot locate the entry point, nor what actions we take on the grid." He stood, pressed the hardlight panel that would take us to the hidden ShiroKaz apartments floor, and as the elevator ascended, he looked seriously at Cayenne. "Your father taught me all these codes and how to use them. He was a genius, and a good friend. I miss him dearly."

"I do, too," she said after a moment, putting her hand on the old man's shoulder. "And I'll tell him what you said when I see him."

Gustav's face screwed up in confusion, one eye wincing while the other's brow raised.

Cayenne laughed, then turned to me for confirmation. "We can do that, right? See the dead?"

"Yeah," I said. "And we'll find him when we find Ben."

Now the father and son exchanged a look. The younger man's face saying, I think, *Fucking White Shadow types, eh pop?*

But the older man shrugged, his face answered, *Maybe not so bad after all, son.*

THIRTY-SIX

I WAS GLAD TO BE FREE FROM THE A-MATTER ENGINEER'S jumper that had literally gone to hell and back, and grateful to Makoto for lending it to me, whoever he was. I stepped out of the unknown man's body-length garment and out of his boots too, discarding them by Cayenne's shower, and I dialed up all the faucets to max pressure and max heat. I'd planned to increase efficiency and therefore save time in order to give Cayenne a turn, but with the water crashing upon my skull I hadn't realized she'd slipped in with me until her hands wrapped around my waist and I felt the buzzed side of her head rest on my shoulder.

I'll spare you the details. I want to keep them all to myself. But needless to say, the shower wound up a little longer and perhaps less efficient than I'd intended it to be.

And unlike the apartment down the hall where I'd first been ambushed by the Sentient User Interfacing Totality, Cayenne had plenty of clean towels on a shelf as we stepped out. The two of us stood in front of a pair of closet auto-racks so long they disappeared into shadow, watching her wardrobe arranged by style scroll past. Cayenne didn't dare connect her neuromod to any part of this place, so she ran the machinery by hand, pressing stop when a slim-fit men's suit jacket and matching trousers came up, both a shade of indigo so dark it might as well be black. I held it up and admired its cut. I passed its gabardine fabric softly between my fingertips. And to top it all off, there was even a pair of patent-leather, black semi-brogue Oxfords waiting for my feet.

I looked up to Cayenne, who was pulling the black dress shirt that complemented the suit perfectly off the rack. "An old boyfriend's?"

"Oh please," she laughed. "Like I ever had time. No, actually, I'd ordered this for you after we'd gone to Heaven, as a way of thanking you for…" and she drifted off, holding the black shirt up and inspecting its deep purple buttons. "Saving me," she finished. I knew maybe she was still conflicted about the inexplicable power she'd gained, or the inexplicable curse, like I'd once thought of it. I was a little conflicted myself, but in the end, I was glad she was here.

In the end, she was, too. "I thought I'd had it delivered to *your* empty apartment, but I must've been mistaken. Here it is," she said, smiling the smile that always melted me from the inside, and handing me the shirt. "It brings out the violet in your eyes. Beautiful."

Cayenne picked out an ensemble that was a little more rugged than what you'd expect for a mega-corp CEO, with canvas-blend tapered work pants and a wool cable-patterned sweater, cinching her feet into belted tactical boots, all of it dark shades of brown and gray that did nothing for her green eyes, but she looked good all the same.

"What're you laughing at?" she said, tying her hair back in a high ponytail, putting her surgical scar and half-shaven head on full display.

"Nothing. You just," I said, gesturing at her get-up, "look like a grizzled Syndicate raider, and I look like a posh CEO."

Dressed to the nines, we joined Gustav and Kurt in the living room. The two Cluster boys had arranged all their gadgetry atop the sofa, so there was nowhere to sit. Gustav had made one of the amenity consoles embedded in a lacquerwood pillar into his main display and was planting more acronymic bugs on the grid with his tiny cyberspace lenses as his son read off letter codes and noted nonsensical translations in his little book.

"Take the flip-phone," he said to me without taking his eyes off of whatever he was seeing, gesturing toward the couch over his shoulder.

"Woahhh," I said, barely able to comprehend that the thing in my hands was real. It was a seventy-year-old relic from the past, still in good working condition. I depressed a button on its side, and the mouthpiece slid into place with a satisfying *click*, exposing the multi-tap keys, *1, ABC2, DEF3*, and so on. Kurt tore out a page of his notebook and handed it to me. There were four freshly scrawled acronyms, each beside a number that corresponded to the next four phases.

"You are to text the code to the contact saved in the phone," Kurt reminded me. "When it is done, step by step. Got it?" He was a lot more straightforward than his dad. You might say he was kind of *curt*.

"We got it," Cayenne interjected before I could react perhaps negatively, not that I was going to.

"Fifteen minutes estimated for next phase, first phase on the paper," Gustav called out over his shoulder. He put the finishing touches on whatever he was doing, then stood and started re-stowing some of his gear by the couch. "I'll be at the roof with the drone in ten. Get going. And don't lose the paper! Or memorize it!"

Phase one would end after we'd acquired transportation, but not just any kind of maglev vehicle would do.

Gustav's intrusive sweep of the arcology from the hidden elevator had revealed a detail we'd already expected: the ShiroKaz J-Zero-K quadcopter Cayenne had piloted a month ago had been called back to the tower. But that's not to say it was the only JOK registered to the arcology's mega-corporate elite residents.

Cayenne and I once again joined hands and traveled by means that no security apparatus could ever hope to track, emerging a minute later from a cloud of pink and purple smoke in a hallway similar to the one we'd just left, except it was much higher up in the pyramid—almost to the very top—and monitored by four fully armed and armored InariSec agents, two at each end.

The idling proximity monitors built into their visors pinged us instantly, and they sprang to sudden life, raising their submachine guns and strafing to their sides to not catch each other in a crossfire, just like they'd been trained.

Having been the body that served as a master samurai's blade for several days now, you could say I'd picked up some training of my own. I disappeared and reappeared inches away from the tips of their gun barrels, drawing, flipping, and sheathing the black katana in one fluid motion that cleaved their weapons in half just past their fingers, all in the blink of an eye.

"Don't bother," I told them. They were human beings underneath all their tactical gear, not tinmen. Flesh and blood, and totally caught off guard by the sight of their severed submachine guns. "Just run," I said, nodding at the old-fashioned stairway over their shoulders. I didn't want to kill them if I didn't have to. In fact, I knew I didn't have to. Not these two, anyway.

Gunfire thundered at the other end of the hall, and I silently prayed that Cayenne was holding on to the charm like I'd told her to. I spun about and phased in and out of *Yomi*, materializing in front of the other InariSec duo in a flash, bending and twisting into a side kick that dug my heel into the first guard's abdomen, folding him over and pushing him back, all the while drawing the katana again and spinning my wrist wildly around my back, flashing it up and out, cutting across the exact spot on the other's submachine gun, halving it. I straightened, keeping my killing side toward the one guard still standing, and waited to see what he would do.

He just stood there, dumbfounded, slowly lowering his cleaved weapon and turning it to examine the razor-clean cut up its barrel. He raised his hands as if I was holding him at gunpoint.

"Get your friend," I said easily, knocking the hilt of the black katana back into its sheath, "and get the fuck out of here." He did so, stooping to pick up his counterpart, who was moaning from perhaps a ruptured diaphragm or bruised liver; I don't know. I didn't bother to watch them go, turning around to Cayenne, still near the middle of the hall.

The bullets had indeed gone right through her and slammed home in the angled ceiling and wall. And she didn't look fazed at all. She'd stood stock still and stared down the InariSec guards, knowing they could never hurt her. Frankly, I was a little jealous of how quickly she was picking all of this up.

"Tell Kurt," she said quickly, wasting no time, turning about on her heel and marching toward the solitary apartment door beside her at the center of the hallway.

"Yes, ma'am," I murmured, sliding open the flip phone and entering 333, 7, 222 and sending it to the sole contact. F. P. C. *First phase complete.*

Kurt had already laid interference on this place's sub-grid to catch any outgoing distress signals from this particular hallway. Once he got my next message, he could leave his bugs in a holding pattern until they were eventually detected and iced, but by then he'd already have packed up all his remaining gear in Cayenne's apartment and met us and his father on the roof. Five to seven minutes from now.

Us, his father, and one more passenger for the soon-to-be-hijacked J-Zero-K. We were almost done here.

I phased through Jonathan Smythe's soundproof panic-room walls just as the final round in his magazine went off, sailing straight through Cayenne's emerald green eye as if she was made of smoke. She was. The bullet left a misty spiral of pink in its wake as it came out the other side of her. It ricocheted and slugged the silver fox in the thigh right above his knee, and he crumpled over, dropping his chrome pistol. We were locked into the most lavish executive bunker you could possibly imagine, but even behind the priceless neo-classic art that adorned the gold foil walls, you'd find bulletproof and bombproof material that would repel anything. Except a couple of ghosts.

I kneeled over the wounded fox, tsking. "Really, Smythe. You shouldn't be firing a gun in here."

He scrambled back, leaving a trickle of blood on the thick, one-of-a-kind Iranian carpet, and he came to a stop against the massive four-poster bed. The wound wasn't that bad, just a scratch really, but the CEO of the formerly top mega-corp of all mega-corps had a fragile nature it seemed, sucking in sharp breaths and weeping over the scar he'd left in his own knee. He wore nothing but a black cashmere robe, thankfully closed around his waist. I glanced up at the figure of a woman sitting upright on the other side of the bed, her back turned to us, long locks of luxurious blonde hair cascading down the mocha-colored skin of her naked back. She hadn't moved an inch. Not even the gunshots had rattled her.

I immediately recognized what it was I was looking at, and I cracked a smile at Smythe.

"You dirty, dirty dog!" I bent over and wagged a finger at his face. "You keep a sexbot in here? *You?!*"

The elitist bastard just sneered up at me.

Cayenne rounded the bed and stood in front of the cyborg sexbot, then shook her head. "Like looking in a mirror." She lifted the doll's hand and it fell lifelessly back into its lap. It was uncanny, so human-like, but eerily unalive. It wouldn't move unless Smythe's impulsive thoughts commanded it to. And even without his input, a built-in AI could sense and interpet its operator's biometrics and respond accordingly, moaning, biting its lip, tensing certain muscles, and much, much more. It had synthetic skin, hair, nails, tongue, and teeth. Its unseeing eyes blinked regularly, lubricating their surfaces, for no other reason than completing the illusion. Given this doll's primary function, I was sure there were other areas that self-lubricated.

"When the real thing," I said, winking at him, "is just outta your reach, huh?" I kneeled, leaning in closer to whisper, "What kind of stuff did you program it to do, anyway? *Everything*, I bet, that no self-respecting woman with an actual soul would ever do."

Smythe slithered on his rear away from me, propping his back against the bed. He regained control of himself admirably quickly once he realized what I already knew: the wound in his leg was only skin-deep. If he left it alone, it would heal on its own. Probably leave a scar, but no actual damage. But a narcisistic, arrogant asshole like the silver fox would do everything in his power to erase any evidence that someone had wounded him, especially since that someone had, embarrassingly, been himself.

"What do you want?" he demanded. "You've already taken Tatsuhiro's data cube, and I assure you it was the only copy. Sandra Calvin told me so herself when she handed it to me, all those years ago. I didn't even know what it was. The filthy hacker told me she would kill me herself if I ever prised open its secrets, so I suppose I could thank you for killing her, Miss Asai. Or should I say, *Shiromatsu-sama*?" When I failed to supply him with the reaction he'd been hoping for, his eyes fell quickly away from mine. He deflated, floundered. He had absolutely nowhere left to go. All those stories about the White Shadow coming for others were coming true at last for him. He craned his neck backward, trying to reach Cayenne, and said in a weakened, whining voice that sounded nothing like the haughty silver fox, "What else do I possibly have that you could take from me now?"

"He's right, Cayenne," I said, rising and planting my hands on my hips. "We've already taken his dignity."

"Well, Jonathan," Cayenne said, wrapping a matching cashmere robe she found beside the bed around her doppelgänger doll. "We all know there's no one else in this city who has greater access to information than the head of InariCorp. Information your constituents would rather keep buried forever in your vaults. But we'll come for your keys some other day."

She hadn't answered his question, and she wasn't going to. Instead, she added, "Command this thing to move. Both of you are coming with us."

With my one hand (plus a few intangible ghost hands always ready to serve, but we can pretend I have superstrength), I hoisted Smythe up bodily by his armpit, while my thumb punched the next multi-tap code into the antique flip phone I held in the other. It felt so fucking cool.

7777, pause, 777, 222, 66, 33. Send.

S.P.C.N.E. Second phase complete now enroute.

Then I clapped Smyth on the back and said, "We just need to borrow your ride."

Smythe's apartment had direct access to the roof, one of the perks of at one time being the richest, most powerful man in NeOsaka. Gustav and Kurt were waiting in a loading area, doing a good job blending in as an arcology engineering crew on a routine roof dock inspection. But then Cayenne and I broke the illusion. The sight of InariCorp's barefoot CEO limping along in a bathrobe side by side with an identically dressed sex doll, and flanked by a pair of SynCell raiders (for what else could we be?) turned a few of the mega-corp's employees' heads. I wondered if any of them dared to snap photos of the spectacle on their comlinks, and if they did, what kind of deep data vaults such material would eventually find its way into, and how many yen it would all be worth. It was a safer bet that security calls were igniting the grid like wildfire in our wake, which we figured would happen. We'd planned for it.

Our time here was at an end, anyway. Gustav and Kurt saw us coming, dropped whatever pantomime show they were putting on beside a control panel, and fell in line behind us, the reconfigured drone from the Cluster's tunnels decloaking and hovering over the old man's shoulder. The machine's red laser eye swept left and right, searching for threatening movements within a fifty meter radius, training its gun barrel on anything that didn't have the wherewithal to turn its back and move out of our way.

"Shin," Gustav said under his breath while we made a beeline for Smythe's personal J-Zero-K.

"Yeah?"

"What the fuck is this sex toy doing here?"

The question made me chuckle. So okay, we hadn't planned for *everything.* The old German met my laughter with a scoff from behind me.

"Besides some comic relief," I said, eyes still straight ahead, feet still moving. "I think a solid decoy serves better than a hololight one."

There was more than enough space in the six-seater JOK cabin. I have to admit, the silver fox of InariCorp had good taste in vehicle trim. I stayed in the main cabin, strapping myself into one of the red leather seats beside Kurt, who was helping himself to a champaigne bottle from the chilled console at the center aisle. We sat across from Smythe and Cayenne, while Gustav settled the cyberdoll and himself into the pilots' chairs of the cockpit. The old German was either lecherous or he was keen to whatever reason we had for insisting we bring the thing along. Either way, I knew he also had some modifications to make to the vehicle's systems. As the cabin doors closed, I felt the drone attach its bulk to the broad top of the J-Zero-K, at the center of all four gyroscopic, ringed 'copter blades.

Cayenne nudged the Inari CEO in the ribs with the chrome pistol she'd picked up from the floor of his panic room. "East side," she said. "Fukeabashi district. And engage the cloak."

Smythe, the actual pilot, did what he was told, looking even more defeated than when he'd shot himself. Once the photos and videos of his march across the arcology dock got out, he would likely never enjoy the same status as the lord of corporate secrets. In any case, he was part of our rag-tag Cluster team for the time being, and his silver eyes darted to and fro to send commands to the Inari-branded JOK quadcopter within his neuromod's heads-up display, lifting it off the helipad, folding its landing gear into its hull, and darting us off like a hornet, eastward.

"Is there a more specific destination?" Smythe asked robotically.

"Broken," I said. "The nightclub," I then clarified, since Feikes's Syndicate lair was likely furthest down the list of places an aristocrat like Smythe would ever visit. "Feikes's house."

"Settling old scores, Asai?"

I glanced over at Cayenne, whose face was neutral. She'd had opinions about my preferred venue for phase three, which was going to be my show, a solo performance. But I'd insisted. It had to be at Broken. In a way, I'd already settled my account with my old friend Feikes the last time I'd seen him in ShiroKaz Tower. But after the enlightening trip to the hell that Tatsuhiro sent me on, *re-educating* me you could say, I realized there was something else I needed to tell Feikes before I could quit him for good. It was like I told Cayenne…

I have to do this.

"Maybe," was all the answer Smythe would get from me. "When we're a kilometer out, get me as much altitude as you can."

"Just don't break my damned little baby with your crazy stunts!" Gustav called back from the cockpit. "Actual, working flip phones are fucking hard to find, yah."

THIRTY-SEVEN

JONATHAN SMYTHE COULD'VE JUST SAID *FUCK IT* AND crashed the quadcopter kamikaze style into a skyscraper or against the corrugated steel streets on the upper plate of NeOsaka, killing a hundred innocents or more just to do away with us. But we were betting on his vanity and instinct for self-preservation at all costs, not to mention that he probably figured the only real, lasting deaths he could cause beside his own would be the two Cluster vagabonds Cayenne and I had signed on to our team. So the silver fox did as he was told. A real trooper, through and through. His personal J-Zero-K limousine yawed and banked and weaved through the floating ribbons of maglev traffic and monolithic buildings, nosing itself up and up to finally reach the crest of the world.

I said my farewells to Kurt, Gustav, and even Smythe. My eyes lingered on Cayenne's face longer than the others, saying *I love you* all over again, and *we got this* one last time. I smiled, and she smiled back. I summoned the black katana to my outstretched hands, my eyes lit with purple fire, and I vanished through the back of my seat and the hull of the quadcopter. I plummetted through the twisted, photonegative darkness of the evening *Yomi* sky.

I saw the ghosts all around me, all around the city, choking the streets and crowding on the rooftops. More dead than there'd ever been, and I knew it was all because of me, and Zercos, and Yasuro, and my father, and all the disturbances the four of us had made to the balance, all the little tears we'd made in the fragile veil that separates life and death. The world was lit up with their essence, and their eyes were all on me. I could feel their wrath. Tatsuhiro had turned them all against me the moment he'd dropped me, anchorless, into the abyss. It'd been like putting a bounty on me across *Yomi* the same way he'd put one on Cayenne across NeOsaka. If I'd ever been able to crawl my way back, they were here to keep guard and thrash me, stomp me back down, and seal me away until a thousand years had passed.

And they would've been able to do it, too, if it hadn't been for one thing.

"*Okasan,*" I whispered, clutching the black katana close to my chest. "Protect me."

I hit the ground in the underworld and detonated like an atom bomb, radiating a swirling sphere of pink and purple power out from the epicenter, pushing the army of vengeful *yurei* away a hundred kilometers per second, through the insubstantial streets and intangible buildings. I cleared the entire city like hot, violent smoke clears over cool, serene water. It would take them a very long time indeed to wander their way back and fulfill the grand dragon's standing orders to attack me on sight.

I let out the breath I'd been holding and rose to my feet, traversing between worlds as I did. In the physical, living world, there'd been no actual shockwave, nothing strong enough to blast all the people in the streets a great distance, anyway. But they had felt *something,* like a stirring in their soul, as if all the gods were suddenly going to appear. A sudden wind kicked up like a tornado and spun around me, dissipating outward, knocking over a crowd of pedestrians and a few street vendors' stalls, leaving a four meter radius of empty pavement around me. As I materialized, every-thing came to a standstill.

I was in the little square where several alleyways met, a small pocket of corner adult-themed shops that surrounded the discreet entrance to Broken, which dominated every floor of the squat five-story building directly in front of me. All eyes—synthetic, organic, or otherwise—fell on me, the girl in the fancy dark purple suit with the immaculate black katana.

Good, I thought. *All according to plan.*

Photos would be taken. Comlinks would be dialing out. Message boards would be flooded. Syndicate lookouts and Feikes's enforcers would be making calls. In other words, I'd cause a massive, citywide distraction. There was no way I'd escape my father's notice. Wherever he was, whatever he was doing, he would know I'd returned, if he somehow didn't know already. There was no way he hadn't already felt the bomb I'd just set off in *Yomi*.

I held my chin up and flicked aside the long lock of black hair, a smile curling at the corner of my mouth and a twinkle in my eye. The crowds gave me a wide berth as I sauntered up to the familiar slice of gangway between buildings I'd entered over a thousand times in my life, but would never be entering again after this. Broken's pair of beefy bouncers had their hands inside their overlarge trench coats. One of them held his other hand out to stop me, while the other entered haptic comlink controls behind his ear and down his neck, trying to dial out and reach Feikes, I presumed.

"Good," I said, pointing at the one making the call with the hilt of my katana. "Tell him there's something I forgot to say last time. It's important." Then I spun around, showing both bouncers my back, letting them know just how unintimidated I was, already forgetting they even existed.

I wanted to take in the sights of this neighborhood one last time. For the past ten years, I'd led a pretty grungy lifestyle, traumatized, depressed, suicidal, self-destructive, violent. And this one little corner of the city was the place I'd felt most at home, where I could step outside myself, get away from whatever problems would always be waiting for me on the inside. Meet girls. Plan jobs. Get paid. Get laid. Dance the night away. Smoke and snort, eat and drink. Inside the little neon-lit grotto these sidestreets and storefronts enclosed, the restless dead didn't chase me. There was no torii gate here, but somehow whatever sacredness the place stood for just for me was enough to deter them from crossing the threshold. I lowered my gaze from the building facades to the people milling about. You'd think most of them would flee from the stage magician who appeared out of thin air in a puff of purple smoke, or at least give her extra room to keep up her theatrics. Or perhaps shrink in fright from my casually brandished weapon of a bygone era. But no. Instead, a crowd had formed. These were the deviants like yours truly, human beings from all walks of life, gathered like religious fanatics, and this hollowed out space in the midst of the Fukeabashi district was their temple. I turned toward a nearby anime-eyed sex worker, with the anatomy of every possible gender barely covered and bulging in all the right spots, who'd been staring at me with the vapid-eyed gaze that could only mean they were streaming a video with their optic-embedded comlink, and I blew them a kiss.

Except my smile faded a moment later, my eyes snagging on a matte-black, purple-seamed body weaving through the ground-level crowd behind them, its devil horns standing above everyone's head. High above, at the edge of the building across the plaza, another ninja perched on triple jointed legs, slowly drawing the black straight-edged katana from its back. I counted two others on adjacent buildings. I saw another pair of horns moving in the crowd to my right. Five total copies of Hachiman-branded, Zercos-model cyborgs that I could see. I'd been counting on their arrival.

I sank easily into a ready stance, holding the black *saya* sheath gently by my left hip, my left hand like a calm, buoyant pond upon which the weapon rested, the ridge between thumb and forefinger of my right hand nestling against the black *tsuka* wrapping. My breathing was cool, unrushed. My strike would be the sudden wind. Yasuro may be gone, but he'd left the indelible, undeniable imprint of the samurai spirit in me. I was now the body *and* the blade, and I served only myself.

"Tell him to hurry the fuck up," I said nonchalantly to the bouncers still at my back.

The first Zercos copy flashed forward, its pistons hissing with steam, its frame shooting like a purple laser, its sword crashing down powerfully from above.

My mind was empty, so everything happened without thought. My black katana leaped out of its sheath, intercepting the fatal blow and turning it aside fluidly. My wrist turned gently and brought the obsidian blade back up from my attacker's hip to its shoulder, carving through the polymetal flesh, then the katana turned again and cut horizontally across its neck, separating its head from its body, and the wind of my artistry caught up with my movements like a sonic boom, blowing his body to pieces before me.

Less than a second later, three more Zercos ninjas rained down upon me, matte black blades first, but I was already somersaulting forward, my free hand dropping the black sheath into *Yomi* and grasping the first cyborg's weapon from where he'd dropped it. The three landed and did not hesitate, already rolling with the momentum of their failed strikes and slashing at me again, all at once. My blades jumped up on both sides to catch theirs, but the third ninja slipped past my guard and drew a line up my abdomen and across my breast.

I felt pain. Even as the purple fire ignited across my skin to cauterize the wound, I gritted my teeth and fell back a step.

And the fifth devil-horned cyborg in the crowd was there. If I hadn't stumbled, its sword would've rammed straight through my heart. Instead, it went through my shoulder. The blade was slick with my blood and smoking purple. The pain was exquisite. Skewered and held in place as I was, the trio of ninjas rushed forward to finish the job.

I had two options. I decided *not* to scream and focus on the flesh-withering agony radiating through my entire body. Instead, I opted to keep my mind empty. I deadened my nerves, and I slashed up with both my blades at once, twin whirlwinds that chopped the cyborg's weapon in half, leaving only a stump poking out of my shoulder.

Then I stepped powerfully forward, ripping myself free, and now I *was* screaming, but not from the pain, not even from rage—because there was no rage. It was a battle cry. I met my enemies head on, my swords still spinning, coming back up and around to complete the circle, the world moving in slow motion, all of my focus on passing the razor-sharp edges through their limbs as if I'd dropped Bullet Time in my eyes. Two of the cyborgs' arms fell away like torn paper caught in a wind, and the swords those arms held missed my body by millimeters, slicing only into the fabric of my nice indigo suit.

The third had gone low though, and its blade bit into my left hip and split my pelvic bone, lodging itself there. Hot blood gushed and splashed on the ground, and the cyborg didn't waste a second, stabbing the sharpened fingertips of its claw into my stomach. Its two armless brethren were similarly unfazed by their amputations, swiping their claws at my face and chest. The one behind me with half its sword rushed forward to stab me with the stump, still sharp enough, this time determined not to miss my heart.

They piled on, and all of their killing blows landed, all of them executed with the synthetic precision you'd expect from million-yen Hachiman-Tech hardware, and jets of purple flame erupted from all of my wounds, all at once, immolating me. If we're still tracking the bamboo forest metaphor to help you comprehend my pain, then the light of a thousand suns shone on its leaves, searing it all to ash in white hot fire.

They killed me. And so I died.

But I'd already been to hell and back. They'd either never been programmed with that fact, or their master hadn't told them. I'd been reincarnated with the serene spirit of the samurai coursing through me. I'd been armed with the one weapon they could never even hope to disarm: the fervent, undying love of a mother for her child.

And so with this knowledge, I kept my swords spinning, my body pivoting at the waist to keep the arc of my wrists a fluid, unending motion. The fire burning inside and all around me turned the cyborg's swords and claws to ash and expelled them from my body, the wounds closing instantly. I was a whir of blades, claiming more limbs, separating heads.

The storm had come.

And when it passed, five Zercos-model cyborg bodies lay in pieces all around me, sputtering purple fires and smoke rising from the spots where their battery-acid blood had splashed, the lights fading from the seams of their joints and hexagonal faceplates.

I let the matte-black katana I'd acquired clatter at my feet, summoning the black sheath from *Yomi* in a flash of purple smoke. I spun my own perfect, obsidian-bladed katana in a *chiburi* whirl, flicking away all traces of the tin-men's blood, and slid it home with a satisfying *clack*. I let out the breath I'd been holding for all fifteen seconds of the fight, then looked down at myself.

The shirt and suit Cayenne had given me was slashed apart and soaked in my blood, exposing my tattooed tummy and bare hip, not to mention the holes, front and back, at my shoulder and over my heart. *Not fucking cool.* I wanted to scold the cyborg corpses. But then I realized at least my Oxford shoes had made it out completely unscathed, not even a blood spatter. That was okay, at least.

Then the crowd went wild. Onlookers emerged from behind food stalls and lampposts and subway entrance railings. They streamed back out into the square from the stores and bars lining the place, almost everyone gawking at and recording me from every angle. They clapped and cheered, but kept a wary distance. They'd just witnessed some true-to-life manga superhero shit. Whatever it was the White Shadow used to do in the closed-off board rooms and private offices of top mega-corp executives who'd been holding out on the Legacy just got displayed front and center for the world to see.

I'd anticipated this, too. Again, I'd been counting on it.

"Jesus Christ, kid," a familiar voice called out from behind me.

Feikes was done up full punk-rock, his mohawk more colorful and taller than I'd ever seen. A mesh tank top did nothing to hide the tattoos all over his body. A tattered Scottish kilt hung around his waist and over his shoulder, an electric guitar slung over the other one, its neck hanging loose at his back. I saw his wrist and forearm were covered with a surgical bracer, pins embedded into his fingers to artificially stimulate muscles. He'd obviously been able to play a set on the stage of his nightclub, despite the bones I'd broken.

He was alone by the entrance, having called off his goons. Despite the sincerity of my death threat the last time we'd parted company, he smiled ear to ear.

"I'm glad to see you, Shin."

At first, I didn't respond. I just looked him up and down, then looked behind him at the discreet entrance to his nightclub, then up around the building it led into, and the neighborhood it sat in, even my favorite *yakitori* place just ten meters away. I bit my lower lip.

"Shin, I… I know what you said last time."

I looked up to the ceiling of the sky over this pocket of the district, expecting that the next wave of Zercos ninjas would be leaping and soaring their way here any minute now.

Feikes kept talking, growing more and more nervous by my silence. "But you wanted to see me, here. I didn't come looking for you. Hell, I didn't really even go after your girl like I was supposed to."

Then I was on the move, straight toward him. My chin down and my eyes up.

He felt menaced. He put his hands up, took a step back as I closed the distance.

"She's safe, right? I didn't—"

I threw my arms around the lanky bastard, cutting him off. I pressed my head against his shoulder.

"I'm sorry, Feikes," I said, an entirely different person from the kid he'd always known. "I'm sorry about my SynCell. All my failed jobs. I'm sorry about your hand. Hell, I'm sorry about Boltcutter. A little bit. And I'm sorry about your friend Connor." Then I remembered that look in his eye the last time I'd talked about him. "Your brother," I corrected.

"H-hey," he said, still nervous, but slowly easing into certainty that I really meant what I was saying, and I would not hurt him. "It's all okay, Shin. Listen, it was all just business."

"No, it wasn't," I said, and I squeezed him tighter. As fucked up as it was, this man was a father to me when I'd needed one. A very fucked up father who sent me out to do a lot of fucked up things. But he was a father. It may have all looked like business between the two of us, but it was really more than that.

"But I forgive you," I said, releasing him. "For all of it."

And just like that, I saw Feikes change into an entirely different person from the man I'd always known. This grizzled veteran survivor of NeOsaka.

"I'd forgive you, too," he replied, "but you ain't ever done anything wrong. Ain't ever done anything that I didn't understand why you did it."

I stepped back, realized some of my blood from my suit had dampened his kilt. "Oh shit," I exclaimed, pointing. "I'm sorry about that, too."

Feikes just followed the line of my finger, then chuckled. "Shit, kid, if you think I don't know to get blood outta my clothes, then you never really knew me."

"Huh," I said, screwing my face up a little. "That was dark as hell, Feikes."

I looked skyward again. Still no secondary cyborg death squad, but it was only a matter of time 'til they got here. I wanted to go another round, but not here.

"I should get going," I said, reaching into my pocket for the flip phone Gustav had given me. Kurt's slip of paper with the codes was stained red and wet, but still legible. The phone, however, had been bitten in half by a matte-black katana.

Fuuuck! Gustav's little baby lay dead in my palm.

I dumbly tried to fit the pieces of the exposed, seventy-year-old circuit board together. Unfortunately, my magic couldn't bring this antique tech back to life. Even the *kami* that had called the thing its home had vacated the premises.

Phase three was done. I'd caused the distraction with as much spectacle as a triple-A action simulation, but I had no way to let the others know. If they'd been monitoring an active comlink connection, the buzz about my exploits would no doubt have reached them by now. The whole city probably knew. But Cayenne, Gustav, and Kurt weren't connected, and they wouldn't dare or else the Sentient User Interfacing Totality would find them and tear them out of the sky.

I dumped the phone on the ground and peered skyward, my vision slipping through the abyss, the buildings stretching and corkscrewing up all around me.

"No one's seen your pops," Feikes said, catching my sleeve, drawing my attention. "Word is you did something, then you both just disappeared. The two of you killed each other."

"He's there," I said, turning my glowing violet eyes back on Feikes, who frankly didn't seem rattled in the slightest. "Just in a place no one else can see."

In fact, I thought, *he was just here.* All of the Zercos-model cyborgs had been animated with his spirit. One part technological marvel: autonomous machinery capable of superhuman strength, speed, and agility, and powered by a nearly inexhaustible energy supply and guidance systems. And the other part: the grand dragon's will, bending their actions like puppets. Tatushiro.

But there wasn't time to tell Feikes all of this.

"Well," he said, letting go and brushing my sleeve and shoulder like he'd just pinned some medals on them, "like the old song says, go do that voodoo that you do."

THIRTY-EIGHT

I CAN'T TELL YOU MUCH ABOUT OTHER CULTURES' FORMS of magic. I'm dead certain (pun intended), having lived the life (also pun intended) that I'd lived, that there were others like me out there. Celtic druids. Kenyan medicine men. Aztec priests. Whatever, wherever, whoever. There had to be. So, for all I knew, flying was very much in a voodoo practitioner's repertoire.

Because I was flying, doing what Feikes told me to do, I might've taken his words literally.

I'd dismissed the spirits all over the city with my crash landing on Feikes's doorstep, but I didn't need them anymore. With the power of the black katana in my grasp, I levitated off the ground, splitting my existence between the world of the living and the world of the dead. Everything was light and dark, inverted and orderly, upended and irradicable, opposite and opposite, all at once. Within seconds, I'd risen above the squat neighborhood buildings of Fukeabashi, going faster and faster, ascending through crowded lanes of automated traffic, and soon rivaling the tallest skyscrapers. I pushed through the clouds and was greeted by the setting sun, shining upon me black-cold in one world and white-hot in another, just before it sank under the lowest rim of the sub-orbital platform we called Heaven, plunging the sprawling city below in shadow.

Then I slowed and came to a stop, hovering in the thinnest of thin air. Waiting. My living, violet eyes could not see through the vaporous curtains drifting slowly over NeOsaka, but my spiritual vision pierced through, seeing all the pockets of shadow between buildings in vivid white outline, the lazy, gradual lines of traffic both human and machine. And there, I spotted what I'd been waiting for, a formation of rockets, five in all, propelled by purple fire, fired from the city's tallest tower, arcing upward and drawing closer. Tatsuhiro's soldiers, driven by the power of his spirit.

I drew in a deep breath and drew out the black katana. I let the sheath plummet back to Earth and gripped the hilt in both hands. Then I dove, holding my breath, tensing my fingers tighter and tighter, raising the weapon over my right shoulder. Straight down, faster and faster, the wind turning my face and whole body to ice. I was a beam of light, and my enemies were five of the same, all of us purple, all of us with swords raised.

And when we clashed and streaked past, I let out a cry, and then my sword was at my left hip as we separated a half-kilometer of space in a half-heartbeat. With my strike, I'd claimed the lead cyborg's head. And with its strike, it had claimed my left arm, from the elbow down. I felt the phantom flesh in freefall far above and behind me, burning to ash in the atmosphere. I gritted my teeth against the pain and held on to the katana with my remaining hand.

I felt rather than saw the other four cyborgs wheeling about to give chase. Without having given Gustav, Kurt, and Cayenne the third message, I didn't know if they knew where I was or what I was doing. I didn't know if they could safely move on to their own final phase. I didn't know what the hell I was supposed to do.

So I would just buy them more time, even if they didn't need it, and I would buy it fighting.

I fell through the cloud cover and curved my body upward, falling in line with the automated transports between buildings, slowing myself, and then touching down on the wide, empty bed of a Fuji-Rai carrier, its haul already delivered to the markets, on its way back to corporate headquarters or the synthetic rice farms at NeOsaka's northeast rim.

My feet had barely touched the ridged planks of the transport's bed when I was struck by a bolt of purple lightning. The cyborg slammed the vehicle's floor right in front of me and punched through, all of its animating spiritual energy detonating like dynamite at the point of impact. The Fuji-Rai transport was blown to pieces, flinging flaming plates, gears, and circuitry in all directions. The shockwave buckled the vehicles nearby and blew out panes of glass in the corporate towers on either side.

I felt the physical heat and shards of steel burn over and rip through me, and I was thrown back in a ball of fire. The black katana flew out of my grasp, or perhaps I let it go. And so it was that I died again, the second time in ten minutes. My charred, living-world flesh and bones flopped against a building's facade, bounced off, and toppled downward, miraculously caught by the pitched roof of another transport five lanes below where the Fuji-Rai carrier had just exploded. Anyone observing the spectacle from the windows—and I'm sure there were some—saw a one-armed, one-legged, smoking sack of meat, missing both its eyes and its lower jaw, just lying there for one second, then impossibly stitching itself back together the next, gouts of purple fire igniting all over it, regrowing its limbs, hair, skin, nails, and violet eyes. They saw it stand, dressed in a shredded and singed indigo suit, clutching the most beautiful black katana they'd ever seen, which it had pulled from nowhere.

My newly formed left hand went to my newly formed lower jaw and rolled it around, resetting it in place. These things don't always come back flawlessly, by the way.

So Tatsuhiro had just sacrificed another one of his pawns. And for what? He knew he couldn't kill me, just as I knew my quick draw cowgirl patricidal bullet hadn't killed him. And we didn't need weapons to know that he had an anchor, and I had an anchor, and so we'd be doing this dance for all eternity if we were so inclined.

Even as my new transport followed its programming and sped forward, Tatsuhiro's final three Zercos-cyborg-ninja pawns slammed their triple-jointed feet onto it, their sharp toes digging into the steel roof like opening a tin can. As one, they rose to a standing position, their clawed fingers rising above their horned heads and grasping the hilts of their matte-black swords.

I just shrugged, and I laughed in their identical faces. "C'mon!" I shouted at them. "What're we doing all this for? It's just a waste of time. And people could die!" I added, thinking of the windows, the steel, the fire, all of that damage already almost a kilometer behind us as the transport angled itself around another corner.

The lead cyborg's hexagonal faceplate flashed purple and the seams split apart as Zercos's had outside Himeji Castle, but there was no human face underneath, just a glowing hololight sigil of a dragon's horned head in front of the hidden control panel of its brain. The machine spoke in the same garbled electronic voice I had heard when waking up on the operating table of ShiroKaz's clinic after my first encounter with Vladislav Zercos. "What do you propose?" it asked in a flat, robotic tone. But there was no denying it was my father speaking.

I glanced left, zeroed in on the faces behind the windows flashing by as our transport sailed past. Just like in the square outside of Broken, it was a safe bet these bystanders had recorded everything, from at least the moment the Fuji-Rai carrier exploded if not before. Whereas a street brawl in a small corner of a NeOsaka street wouldn't catch the grid on fire, a mid-air encounter with a state-of-the-art death squad and a self-reanimating corpse in a charred suit certainly would, and the news would spread across all air-traffic channels. It would light up the dashboard systems of manned and unmanned traffic alike, including those on a J-Zero-K.

Phase three complete, Gustav, I thought. *But I'm sorry about your phone.*

I looked the lead cyborg enslaved to my father square in its dragon-head-sigil face, sheathed the black katana, and said, "*Otosan*, I would like to resume our previous conversation."

THIRTY-NINE

I FLOATED THROUGH THE TALL WINDOWS OF THE EIGHTY-ninth floor of ShiroKaz Tower. In the material world, the walls had been strong enough to contain the raging storm that had ripped Cayenne's house down and uprooted my mother's garden and nearly all the trees of the bamboo forest. All of the bots that tended the place were scrap metal, everything was bedlam. Since I was staying on the *Yomi* side of reality, everything was lifeless and dark, like a thousand years of entropy had already crept into the place.

At the center of the atrium, a lone figure sat on a rock facing me, hunched forward, eyes closed, chin on his chest, elbows on his knees, the clawed fingers of a cybernetic prosthetic steepled against the fingers of a flesh hand. He was outlined in a subtle purple aura, not of the living world. It was my father's spirit, exactly as I'd encountered him the first time in the graveyard and later at our family's ancestral home, in all aspects but age. He still wore the black shirt and black trousers from the moment of his last death, when I'd shot him in the head.

For my own wardrobe, I'd lost one of my nice shoes when my leg was blown off, so as I approached him I kicked off the other one into the muddy swirl that had one month ago been a pond. The same leg was bare up to my mid-thigh, same side as my bare forearm where the ninja had sliced it away. At least it all matched my bare midriff.

Neither of us had a weapon in hand. I honestly hoped neither of us would need one.

"*Todaima kaerimashita.*" I spoke the formal greeting of homecoming and gave my father a bow, low enough to show him the proper respect, but not as low as those I'd given him before. As far as I was concerned, after all we'd been through, we were on equal footing.

"*Okaerinasai,*" he responded. *Welcome home.* He sounded as tired as he looked, so I didn't fault him for not returning my bow.

So we were on speaking terms then. I stepped to within one meter of him and lowered myself on another rock across from him, crossing my legs and matching his posture, elbows on knees, fingers steepled.

"You have returned," he said, head still pitched forward. "Sooner than anticipated."

"Sooner than eternity," I replied. "If that's what you mean. I saw my uncle down there, in the hell where you put him. Where you put both of us."

"Yasuro." He spoke his twin's name so quietly. Then he scoffed, an incredulous smile cracking the corner of his mouth. "My brother. The White Shadow. Ever has he interfered in my affairs."

"He found me. He drove away the *yurei.*"

"*Hnn.*"

I couldn't tell if it was another scoff, or just an affirmative grunt, but the two of us were silent for several more breaths, until I spoke again.

"We talked. It was you who first sent me to find the sword you'd trapped him in, hoping to make me into something that did for you what he'd once done for ShiroKaz. Somehow, along the way, he became bitter and resentful of everything that he was supposed to support. The Legacy, and the people who would benefit from it. Namely, humanity. And I know what happened between you and his wife. My mother, Mizuko."

"Mizuko," he repeated. The old, unhealable wound in him.

"You'd returned in secret from your banishment, enacting your plan to overthrow Yasuro and your father, and you could not stop yourself from seeing her. It was love. I know."

"Almost a year passed before we made our move," my father recounted, his head still lowered. As before, his retelling focused more on the plot than on the meaning. On himself. On his *resurgence*. "Mister Lim and I. Sandra. Luther. And our allies. Even my brother's protégé, Vladislav Zercos. And we were so careful, Mizuko and I. To evade the White Shadow himself. For one year. He was always rooting out imperfection, purging it from society like a weed in a garden, yet he never thought to look for the imperfections in his own life. Mizuko did not love him. And he could not love her. Not as I did. Yasuro could not love anyone but himself."

"He could not," I agreed, but then clarified. "But he could dedicate himself to an ideal, at the cost of everything else. And it did cost him. Everything else."

"Tell me, Shiyo," my father said. "Why we are discussing my brother, The White Shadow."

"Because when I was in hell with him, I felt the good in him. The good that his spirit wanted but could not allow his living self to find. I forgave him for what he did to my mother. And I forgave him for what he did to me. And I believed this forgiveness freed him once and for all, but I was wrong."

Tatsuhiro, the grand dragon, the purple-limned spirit before me, finally looked up at me, understanding glowing in his violet eyes. So I had been re-educated after all, but it was not the kind of awareness he'd wanted me to develop, and it hadn't taken me one thousand years. There was a cold, steel edge in his gaze, meant to cut me down, hobble me, send my notions away. Change me. Because he knew exactly what I was suggesting.

"I will never forgive my brother."

I nodded, but I did not back down nor look away.

"I know the white katana was yours. And the black katana was his."

"What of it?"

"I believe you are wrong," I began, returning the steel stare, every bit as sharp as his own, "in thinking that Yasuro's is the spirit that the white katana traps. It is yours, Father. Your resentment. You are the one who is trapped."

Tatsuhiro bared his teeth in a wolfish grin, squeezed his eyes shut, and howled in disbelieving laughter. The sound and force of it was meant to trample me into the dust, but I remained as firm as the rock I sat on and let him make his noise. I waited patiently, until he noticed how I had not moved an inch, and his laughter calmed.

"You are the one in hell," I concluded.

He shifted his arm slowly outward, and both our eyes followed the trail of vaporous purple behind the motion. "Because I cannot reform my flesh as fast as you?"

"Because you cannot let go."

"Let go of what?" he snarled viciously, his claw swiping the underworld air between us angrily. "Without a *Shiromatsu*, without one of *us*, there is no hope for this world. I will not let go of our Legacy, Shiyo! Never!"

This time, I shook my head. It was the child that remained calm while the parent ranted and raved. The dragon was twisting himself into a knot.

"You misunderstand," I replied cooly. "You, and my grandfather, and my uncle. And all the other madmen that came before you. The whole world, across our whole history. In every country, at every age of time."

Tatsuhiro seemed to compose himself, waiting for my next astounding conclusion with his brows raised and his head cocked. So I delivered it.

"Power is not in the dominance of others. Power is in acceptance of them."

His smirk faded and his eyes narrowed.

"I failed in all of your tests of power," I said in answer. "But I succeeded in all of my own."

"*Hnn,*" Tatsuhiro grunted. It was not the sound of agreement. It was the derisive sound of a father who felt his child would never learn. "This, Shiyo, is all that you have come to tell me?"

"Not all," I said. My gaze had never wavered from him, even through all his dismissive laughter and posturing.

He heard the steel in my voice and lifted his hand in a gesture. *Dozo,* it said. *Please go on.*

"I came to tell you that I understand you. I understand why you've done everything the way you did it. I understand your sacrifice, of your own daughter. Me. Letting me go. Leaving me. Murdering the ones that tormented me. Lying to me. Using me to get what you could not acquire on your own. I *understand.* All of it. Everything you've done, everything you are." I took a very deep breath, let it out, and let the words in my heart come naturally, in their own time. "I understand that you have loved me, Father. In your own way. And I want you to know that I love you. And I forgive you. Even though I know you may never seek my forgiveness. For anything."

I said all of this, and yet it seemed the man was looking at something distant, something over my shoulder. I could not be sure any of my words had registered with him, if any of them would matter. My love, my forgiveness. But I was powerful enough to know that it did not matter if he did. What mattered was how I felt, and that I'd found the strength to tell him.

Another moment passed, and finally his eyes came back to regard me. "You are right," he said. His gaze flitted back to the windows behind me, drawing me at last to see what he'd been looking at.

The de-cloaked J-Zero-K quadcopter hovered silently just outside. Through the windshield, I could see the face of a woman with wild blonde hair. She looked horrified.

"For what I do next," Tatsuhiro said, "I seek no forgiveness."

The woman pressed a hand to the glass separating us and screamed my name.

And Tatsuhiro raised his cybernetic hand and squeezed it into a taloned fist, commanding streaks of purple-limned cyborg bodies to lance down from the sky, slicing the machine to pieces. Two of the four copter blades spun away in opposite directions, leaving corkscrews of black smoke and fire, and the main cabin exploded, close enough to blast the closest three levels of the tower's window panes apart. The wreck careened forward into the building, spinning and pushing its way toward us, churning all the glass and mud and splintered ruin of the place, belching more smoke and more fire. The building's alarms and countermeasures did not trigger, leaving it all to burn.

The grand dragon and I were unmoved. We were ghosts. The fires of the real world could never burn us. And although I'd just watched the woman I love be destroyed before my very eyes, her apparent death had no effect on me.

"How similar," Tatsuhiro said, rising triumphantly to stand over me. I did not take my eyes from the black-ened husk of the JOK. "Our stories, Shiyo. Yours and mine. How similar." He paced around me to stand within the wreckage, untouched by the withering heat of the flames, impervious to the damage he'd brought into his own home. "You returned, hoping to overthrow me, your father. Just as I returned twenty years ago, to overthrow my own father. But you have been too reckless. Too... hnn... *muteppou*. Careless."

"Why?" I asked, keeping my gaze lowered, keeping my mind empty. "Why did you have to kill Cayenne?"

"It was never my intention to do so. Cayenne DeLeon was like a daughter to me. I gave her all I could."

"To shape her into a tool."

"*Ie*. Not a tool. A weapon. We must all be weapons, Shiyo, to fight against our own encroaching deaths. Humanity did not learn the first time it destroyed itself. So my new Legacy will safeguard humanity, teach it, and never let it forget.

"But," he went on, cupping his ghostly cyber claw under my chin, lifting my eyes to meet his. "*What is done is done. So says Macbeth in Shakespeare's tragedy.*"

As he spoke, his form shifted, the edges brightened and sharpened. He grew taller, wider. Gradually, I watched his face and his glowing eyes dissipate, falling into a background of emptiness, enclosed inside a samurai's *kabuto*. He became his armor. Inexorable. Immovable. Unyielding.

"Since the time I cast you into hell," the deep voice bellowed from inside the helmet, "I had hoped to find Cayenne, for I needed a body. Living flesh to merge with the mainframe while simultaneously plunging my spirit into the grid. Inside two worlds at once. I needed her body, Shiyo, but yours will have to suffice."

The empty samurai armor wobbled in my vision, melting into purple quicksilver, sinking upward and pooling itself into a mass that ran down its arm and against my face. I felt it pushing through my skin, running up into my eyes and nostrils, into my ears, coating my skull and spine.

Despite the horror of the very real, *very end* of all I ever was, I remained calm. I still knew something he did not know. I still held the real power. I could not speak, but I could think.

Lady, I said, within my own mind.

And I felt his response.

Nani?

It was Lady *Macbeth's line.*

With what remained of my own will, I called the black katana to my hands. My mother had waited patiently for me, for twenty years, to find her, so she hadn't minded waiting a little longer. She would always be there when I needed her. I cradled the katana in my lap. I did not need to draw the blade and strike. Its presence alone was all the weapon I needed.

The empty samurai felt the spirit stir inside the black blade, the very weapon its twin brother had used to cut it from this world, and it recoiled backward, extracting its liquid metal tendrils from my body.

Zenjiro.

A soft, tender voice sounded in *Yomi*, echoing across the emptiness.

You must let our daughter go.

Mizuko. It's really you. Why? Why didn't you answer me when I called for you? Why didn't you make yourself known when I searched for you? I searched and searched. I was alone. In the dark.

Because our daughter lived, and I gave her shelter. And she must live. On her own, without us.

But ... the Legacy.

I opened my eyes and came forward off the rock, kneeling before the tall, empty samurai. I raised the black katana with both hands and set it gently at its armored feet. I wanted my parents to be together, even if I had never had the chance to be with them.

She is the Legacy now.

The empty samurai, the manifested form of Zenjiro Shiromatsu's vengeful spirit, kneeled before the black katana and lowered a shaky, armored fist over it. But it could not bring itself to grasp it. A thin mist of pink rose from the weapon, it caressed the empty *kote* gauntlet.

Be with me, my mother's voice called. *We have found each other again, Zenjiro.*

The armor rattled. My father's spirit was afraid, quaking with so much fear.

Let go.

The invisible fingers reached, hesitated, then balled into a fist.

I cannot! It shrieked. *I WILL NOT!!*

It grasped my neck and rose, its form already re-melting, its metal piercing my body and worming through my throat, drowning my lungs, filling my heart.

I'd come so close. *We* had come so close, my mother and I. I had my doubts about my father, Zenjiro Shiromatsu, and I was sorry to feel her disappointment. We had tried, together, to bring him peace. And we had failed.

Beneath us, I felt the pink mist recede, draw back into the blade, and dissipate from this world forever. My mother's spirit knew I would be all right, and so she could be at rest. The black material of the sheath cracked, dried, fell apart like rotten wood upon a forest floor. The wrapping around its hilt withered, its threads snapping. The blade itself tarnished, rusted, ate holes in itself, and turned to dust.

And I laughed in my father's empty face—even as his spirit invaded every part of my being, taking over my body—because behind his shoulder, I saw the charred remains of Jonathan Smythe in the wreckage of the quadcopter. Then my eyes were on the ceiling, glowing purple, seeing through the physical barriers to the base of the reconstructed Shiromatsu family home, the ghostly Himeji Castle, and the twin mainframes he'd merged in its throne room. And in the living world, I saw the beautiful blonde woman with the scarred head sit up in the chair that hung in space within what used to be the ShiroKaz tower boardroom. I saw her extract the old-fashioned USB that enabled the data cube to talk with the monstrous machine. I saw all of this and I laughed until I couldn't laugh anymore.

Phase four was complete. I'd done my job well. The reverse-engineered patch was uploaded, erasing my father's life's work, the code that could house his spirit on the grid. The new Legacy was no more. And my father didn't even know it yet.

He could have me, if he still wanted me.

But he could not have Mizuko. She was gone from him.

And he would have eternity to think about all he had lost.

Goodbye, I thought. *Cayenne.*

"Nani?"

Hearing my thoughts, my father's voice spoke through me, through the metal-coated mouth of the body that had been mine. Now he knew all I knew, and I felt all he felt. Together, we panicked. We choked on the final traces of the purple spirit as it lodged itself in me, the ghost possessing the flesh.

Your code is gone, asshole. Sayonara!

"What?" The body that used to be mine spilled over onto the floor, writhing. Turning over and staring through the ceiling, watching the woman ascend the stairwell to the roof, to the borrowed getaway transport that awaited. All of the tinmen had been called away. All of the ghost army had been dismissed. All of the grand dragon's attention had been on me.

Your control. Your Legacy. It's all gone. Erased.

"What have you done?!"

Inside the body of Shinjiro Asai, Tatsuhiro found that I would not so easily step aside. I would not cower and let him have what he thought was his. Reality rippled around the thing's flesh, pushing and pulling parts of itself into and out of the underworld. Neither of us had the anchors. Neither of us had any power over the other. The unstoppable force had met the immovable object.

"NO!" the spirit shrieked again, over and over. "NO NO!!"

Goodbye, Cayenne.

Above us, the ghostly castle cracked. The will that had been holding it all together fractured irreparably. The foundation stones shook loose, falling away a few at a time, then faster and faster, tearing away bricks and beams and load-bearing structures. The spectral mainframe at its core split apart, all the thousand-thousand *kami* that had been trapped in its motherboards and magnetic drives freed, obeying the natural urge to be somewhere else, shooting like celestial light from a supernova. The giant castle sagged and fell inward upon us, crushing us with all of its weight, and we could do nothing to stop it from dragging us under, punching the body of Shinjiro Asai through the thin veil separating worlds, rocketing it to the farthest reaches of the widening, spiraling abyss below all things.

Sayonara.

EPILOGUE

ONG-RANGE AIR TRANSPORTS IN 2079 AREN'T MADE OF
metal.

The industry that manufactured the specialized radiation-re-
pelling, carbon-fiber material made its formula free to the
public, publishing it on the global grid within moments of
its conception.

She'd seen that it was done personally, overseeing the
young R&D technician as his fingertips punched in the message she dictated.

*To all the world, we gladly release this technology, fur-
thering our shared goal of a cleaned planet Earth and a
reconnected humanity.*

"Send it," she said.

"*Hai*, DeLeon-sama," he said.

And now, three months later, on the eve of the new
year, Cayenne DeLeon sat comfortably in the cabin of the
prototype high-speed aircraft her cluster of corporations
dreamed up, designed, tested, and built. The logo for the
recently formed Asai Corporation—a violet dawn sunrise,

a simple half circle over a line—was displayed proudly on the fuselage.

The company was of her own making. She had wasted no time in consolidating all of NeOsaka's disparate groups together, regardless of their cultural, ethnic, and national status, their age, their religion. Who their family had been in the world before didn't matter. Who they were now did. She had gathered together the rich heads of the so-called mega-corporations in the same room as poor community leaders, and there was even a representative from the city's criminal element, the Syndicate, all standing shoulder to shoulder in the massive, renovated open space of the board-room of what had at one time been Shiromatsu Kazama Corporate Tower. It was the first consultants' meeting in a long line of what would eventually shape the New Direction, a plan to reverse the poisoning of the atmosphere and the wasteland all over the world, and it would start in NeOsaka and spread outward. All information would be shared, all ideas would be considered, all the world's peoples would work together. Humanity would claw itself back from the brink of its own destruction. Its mistakes would be learned from, and its future survival ensured.

There were holdouts at first. Mostly from the remnants of NeOsaka's mega-corps. Cayenne expected this. She remembered that first meeting, how she'd asked Mr. Lim to stay behind so the two of them could chat privately. She'd shown him something that had helped him reframe his mindset. Something she alone could do that could take everything from him anyway if he refused to allow Asaicorp's takeover of Hachiman's assets. She brought him, for just a few heartbeats, to some place she alone could travel.

Today, Mr. Lim was part of the international delegation seated in the plane on its way to Madrid, Spain. He had insisted on safeguarding the physical assets, the briefcase full of physical data cubes that contained all of Asaicorp's body of knowledge. Since he was a military man, Cayenne let him enjoy this fantasy that violence could at some point be the answer.

She'd left her most trusted advisor, Gustav Fischer, behind in NeOsaka to run things in her stead, continuing the clean-up projects and construction of the next sub-orbital radiation shield that would within the next year be gifted to Japan's closest neighbor and recent ally, Singapore. Gustav had tried to name the city-sized platform after its function. "A scrubber," he called it, since what it really did was pull in irradiated particulates from the air and separate the good from the bad, recycling on the molecular level, and producing another clean energy source. But the word "scrubber" had always made Cayenne wince. "Shield will do," she told him. He'd just shrugged and smiled, then muttered curses in German.

The plane touched down, and the first day went well. A city-wide celebration had been planned well in advance of the scheduled forums and summits that would fill the following week. Cayenne had … bittersweet memories of this city, moments of unforgettable lessons learned and accomplishments alongside moments of indelible dread at the direction of her own future. But she smiled, and drank, and danced, and talked about *everyone's* future that first day. And it was not as bad as she'd thought it might be… without…

Exhausted, bittersweet phantoms followed her all the way back to her hotel room that night. Promises made, and promises lost. Not necessarily promises broken.

Cayenne soaked her tired bones in the bathtub, dried herself, and found beside her pajamas the object she'd kept tucked under her pillow every night for two years. She crawled into bed and dialed the lights to zero with a command of her neuromod. There, in the dark, she clung to hope.

Her breathing slowed, and she drifted off, crossing the veil between the world of the living and the realm of the dead. Dead, but not forgotten. Never forgotten. Leaving her physical body behind to rest, her spirit searched all night, every night, following the lights of the *kami* through the Spanish streets, and farther down, into the streets no living thing could see. She searched, even though she knew what she searched for was probably far, far out of her reach. Taken by a magnitude of power she would never understand.

Her living body was strong, healthy. And in the morning of her second day in Madrid, she was well rested, ready to face the first real day of healing this side of the world.

She felt the warm sun through the window, its light glowing through her closed eyelids. Her hand closed tightly around the *omamori* charm, its hollyhock seal, its silk ribbon, the scratched *kanji*. And she spoke the same word that she spoke every morning.

My name.

"Shin."

And she hoped beyond hope that I would answer her. For two years, she had not known what had really happened to me, but she knew enough to put the pieces together. Tatsuhiro and I were immortal, and we could never outdo each other. I had sacrificed myself to bring him to a place from which he could never rise again, and there we stayed. A darkened house at the very bottom of the underworld. I heard her calling every night, but I could not answer. If I left, then the dragon would be unleashed.

The dragon and I would talk. My father and I. The two of us in the blackest, emptiest pit, unable to see what monsters we'd believed ourselves had become in the dual, true death we shared. Unable to see that neither of us were monsters at all.

Until one day, a light found us. It was our family. And we saw ourselves as they saw us, loved, always, even if we were monsters. I saw my mother's hand slide into my father's, the two of them turning back to me and smiling. Together. Then they were gone, but not forgotten. But their light remained for me, and in it, I saw myself, truly. I was beautiful. And I was loved.

Cayenne said my name.

And I shifted beside her, closing my hand over her hand, pulling her close. I felt the warmth of her against me.

And she felt mine.

"I'm here," I whispered in her ear.

She smiled and kissed the back of my hand.

ACKNOWLEDGMENTS

ASIDE FROM THE USUAL PEOPLE—THE GREAT EDITING, development, marketing, and everything team at 4 Horsemen Publications, the artists Jaka Prawira and JohnnyD whom I met virtually at artstation where I hired them for some stellar concept art of this book, the wife, the kids, the fans who are always so, so patient with me when I meet them at cons and good-naturedly humor me when I say, "Part 2 is coming next year I swear!", our men and women in uniform serving overseas and within the confines of our shores who work tirelessly to keep us safe while the rest of us sleep, my students who I see, on a daily basis, five out of seven days of the week who always present me with something new to ponder that keeps my life interesting enough to live—you know, all those usual types of people...

I don't really have many others to thank here. Maybe that makes me a jerk, I don't know, but this particular book was a very personal and private project. No one else really knew what I was up to.

Well, in the end, I would like to acknowledge YOU for reading The White Shadow. Remember, forgiveness is always stronger.

BOOK CLUB QUESTIONS

1. What does a person need from others to feel a sense of belonging?

2. What do you/did you think of Shin's bravado in the earlier chapters of The White Shadow? Were her thoughts, words, and actions justifiable? Is she just as despicable as they felt?

3. Why do you think Shin, who had all of this power, didn't think to start helping people sooner? What were her reasons? Are these justified?

4. How much trust should people put in the rich and the elite of our society to forge humanity's path forward? Do corporations know better than governments? Do corporations operate better than governments? Why or why not?

5. What are the negative impacts of the exponential enhancements of the world's technologies for the past

century? On our current trajectory, what negative impacts will new technologies have on our future?

6. So what are the positive outcomes of all this technology? Is it all worth it? Why or why not?

7. Would you ever want to enhance your body with cybernetic implants? If so, what would you get, and why? How much would be too much? If not, why not?

8. At what point does a living thing become a machine?

9. At what point does a machine become a living thing?

10. In what ways was Tatushiro's end goal justified? What are the dangers of allowing just a single entity to be in charge of all the world's machinery and networks? What are the benefits?

AUTHOR BIO

J OSEPH ASPHAHANI IS AN AVID VIDEO GAMER, EFFECTIVE high school teacher, and enthusiastic candidate for whatever sort of cybernetic limb enhancement your mega-corp is planning for the inexorable dystopian future. When he's not getting hopelessly lost in simulated worlds, he's often dreaming up worlds of his own. He resides in Chicago with his wife and two children.

Discover more at
4HorsemenPublications.com

10% off using HORSEMEN10

www.ingramcontent.com/pod-product-compliance
Lightning Source LLC
Chambersburg PA
CBHW020335010826
48970CB00012B/833